EX LIBRIS

VINTAGE CLASSICS

THE COMPLETE PROSE TALES OF ALEXANDR SERGEYEVITCH PUSHKIN

Alexandr Sergeyevitch Pushkin was born on 26 May 1799 in Moscow. He studied at the Lyceum at Tsarkoye Selo and began writing poetry at a young age. His first major work, *Ruslan and Ludmilla*, was published in 1820, the same year he was expelled from St Petersburg for composing revolutionary epigrams. *Eugene Onegin*, his masterpiece, was published in 1823–31. Pushkin married Natalya Goncharova in 1832 and died in a duel defending her honour on 29 January 1837.

The Complete Prose Tales of Alexandr Sergeyevitch Pushkin

TRANSLATED FROM THE RUSSIAN BY

Gillon Aitken

VINTAGE BOOKS
London

Published by Vintage 2008

6 8 10 9 7 5

First published by Barrie & Rockliff (Barrie & Jenkins Ltd), 1966
New edition published by Michael Russell (Publishing) Ltd, 1978
First published by Vintage in 1993
This revised edition published by Vintage in 2008

Vintage
Random House, 20 Vauxhall Bridge Road,
London SW1V 2SA

www.vintage-classics.info

Addresses for companies within The Random House Group Limited
can be found at: www.randomhouse.co.uk/offices.htm

The Random House Group Limited Reg. No. 954009

A CIP catalogue record for this book
is available from the British Library

ISBN 9780099529477

The Random House Group Limited supports the Forest Stewardship
Council (FSC®), the leading international forest certification organisation.
Our books carrying the FSC label are printed on FSC® certified
paper. FSC is the only forest certification scheme endorsed by the
leading environmental organisations, including Greenpeace.
Our paper procurement policy can be found at
www.randomhouse.co.uk/environment

Typeset by Palimpsest Book Production Limited, Grangemouth,
Stirlingshire

Printed and bound by CPI Group (UK) Ltd, Croydon, CR0 4YY

CONTENTS

INTRODUCTION

Pushkin has always held the supreme position in Russian literature. It was his genius, in his prose as well as in his verse, which laid the foundations upon which a national literature could be built. Until his emergence, writing in Russia, excepting a handful of works, had been predominantly imitative, pursuing pseudo-classical principles and closely reflecting the trends of various Western European cultures – French in particular. The lyrical simplicity and precision of Pushkin's poetry and the natural, straightforward grace of his prose perfectly expressed the Russian mood; and in that expression Pushkin gave to Russia for the first time in her history a literature whose inspiration came from herself, and which succeeded in setting the tone for successive generations of Russian writers. But his achievements were more than national: his universality of vision, his ability to transmute what he saw and what he understood into language of the utmost purity and point have created for him a permanent place in the literature of the world.

Alexandr Sergeyevitch Pushkin was born in Moscow on May 26th, 1799. On his father's side, he was of ancient boyar stock; on his mother's, and as his physical appearance hinted at, he was descended from an Abyssinian Prince whose so was taken from his father as a hostage and later presented to the Emperor Peter the Great. Pushkin's pride in his unusual ancestry is reflected in the unfinished novel about his great-grandfather, *The Moor of Peter the Great*, which forms part of this collection.

Pushkin's early childhood was unremarkable. He was brought up in a literary household – both his father and his uncle wrote verse – but the influence of his parents was a remote one. Stronger, certainly, was that of his nurse, Arina Rodionovna, whose deep knowledge of Russian folklore instilled in him a love of the Russian language and engendered much material for his later and more popular compositions. As a counterweight to the effect of the widespread usage of the French language in Russia at that time, Arina Rodionovna's place in Pushkin's life is important: in educated circles, French was the language of the day; Pushkin received a primarily French education, and his early reading – by the age of ten, he was a voracious reader – was drawn from his father's excellent French library.

At the age of twelve, Pushkin was sent to the Lyceum at Tsarskoye Selo. He remained there for six years. Discipline was lax, and his poetic instinct was quick to show itself. He wrote first in French, then in Russian. By 1814, his poems had begun to be printed; by the time he left the Lyceum and went to St Petersburg in 1817, Pushkin had already been claimed as the new voice of Russian poetry. Derzhavin, Zhukovsky, Karamzin, eminent writers of an older generation, were among those swiftly to recognise in the ease and grace of Pushkin's early verse the careless quality of genius. Pushkin's first important work, *Ruslan and Ludmilla*, was published in 1820: a long poem in the romantic vein, it brought him to the attention of a wide public and firmly established his reputation.

By the time of its publication, Pushkin was serving as an

official in Southern Russia – exiled by the Tsar Alexander I for his part in a revolutionary movement against the government. His exile lasted over five years, spent mostly in the South – at Ekaterinoslav, at Kishinev and in Odessa. It was a period in which his poetic genius flowered and he grew to maturity. He became aware of the richness and diversity of his gifts, responding to new influences available to him in the Crimea and the Caucasus. With the leisure that exile entailed, he learned English and Italian – and 'discovered' Byron, who opened up another world to him and left a lasting impression.

Between 1820 and 1826, Pushkin's output was prodigious: he wrote two long poems in the Byronic manner, *The Prisoner of the Caucasus* and *The Bakhchisarai Fountain*, numerous lyrics and ballads, and a further long poem, *The Gypsies*, which had a considerable popular success; in addition, he completed *Boris Godunov*, his play based on the claim of 'false' Demetrius to be the son of Ivan the Terrible. He also began the masterpiece for which he is best known, *Eugene Onegin*, a vivid 'novel in verse' of great technical brilliance and virtuosity.

Pushkin completed the final canto of *Eugene Onegin* in 1831; at once a story of the emotions and a picture of contemporary Russian life, it is the work by which, if he had written nothing else, his reputation would be uniquely assured. Thereafter, prose was to concern him more than verse – although, before his death in 1837, he wrote a number of verse dramas and, in 1833, one of his finest poetic works, *The Bronze Horseman*.

In 1829, on his return from a second visit to the Caucasus, Pushkin became engaged to Natalya Goncharova, a young society beauty. His engagement marked a turning-point in his life: until that time he had been recklessly passionate and hot-headed, and his liberal political views had incurred the disapproval of both church and state. His work had been subjected to constant censorship – even the personal censorship of Tsar Nicholas I, who succeeded Tsar Alexander I a few months before the ill-fated Decembrists' Revolt in 1825, with which Pushkin had been incidentally involved. From the age of thirty, and particularly following his marriage in 1831, he began to conform: he had become more serious; the effects of censorship had been wearying. This turning-point coincided with the composition of his earlier prose writing.

In 1836, Pushkin received an anonymous letter suggesting that his wife was having a love affair with Baron Georges d'Anthès, an Alsatian nobleman in the Russian diplomatic service. He was persuaded to withdraw his challenge to d'Anthès to a pistol duel. However, fresh insinuations made a duel inevitable. It took place on January 27th, 1837. d'Anthès was slightly wounded; Pushkin received injuries which proved fatal, and he died on January 29th at the age of thirty-seven.

Written in 1827–28, *The Moor of Peter the Great*, which Pushkin intended as a novel but left unfinished after seven chapters, was the first of his prose tales; it aroused great interest, containing as it does some of Pushkin's finest prose. Less ornate in style, and closer to the mood of his verse – models of simplicity and precision – are *The Tales of the Late Ivan Petrovitch Belkin*, published in 1831 and, as their title suggests, attributed to the hand of a narrator. Although Pushkin attached great importance to these five tales, which were to him experimental in nature, he was nervous as to how they would be received and preferred to shelter behind the touchingly created figure of Belkin. *The History of the Village of Goryukhino*, ascribed also to Belkin, was written in 1830, but not published until 1857. *A Novel in Letters* and

Roslavlev, both intended as larger works, were written in 1829 and 1831 respectively.

In 1832, Pushkin completed the eighteen chapters that exist of *Dubrovsky*; he had worked out a detailed plan for the novel's conclusion but never returned to it. Written with great vividness, elaborately contrived, simple in style, *Dubrovsky* offers, as well as a thrilling story, a valuable impression of Russian country life at that time. *The Queen of Spades* and *Kirdjali* were both published in 1834: the former is Pushkin's most successful prose work of a short kind – and is surely one of the greatest short stories in world literature: scarcely more than 10,000 words in length, brilliantly compressed, it achieves an altogether unforgettable effect. *Kirdjali* is the stirring account of the life of a Moldavian brigand.

The Captain's Daughter, the longest of Pushkin's completed prose tales, was written between 1833 and 1836: based on true events which Pushkin wrote as history in his *The History of the Pugachev Rebellion*, it is a masterpiece of narrative and construction. *Egyptian Nights*, in which both prose and poetry have a place, is one of the more exotic of Pushkin's unfinished works. Written in 1835, it displays the extraordinary ease and vitality of Pushkin's style and his ability at once to bring a situation or a character brilliantly to life.

This volume comprises, in chronological order, all of Pushkin's prose tales. The present edition is a revision of the translation originally published in 1966, and the translator wishes again to register his appreciation of the help given to him by Mrs Bobby Ullstein in the final preparation of that text. He wishes, too, to thank Dr David Budgen for his scholarly assistance in the publication, by Angel Classics, of a separate edition of *The Tales of the Late Ivan Petrovitch Belkin* in 1983. As to the process of revision, it is the translator's hope that the modifications, almost entirely of nuance, he has brought to his earlier efforts will play some part, however small, in perpetuating a regard among English readers for Pushkin's extraordinary genius.

G. A., 2008

THE COMPLETE
PROSE TALES OF
ALEXANDR SERGEYEVITCH PUSHKIN

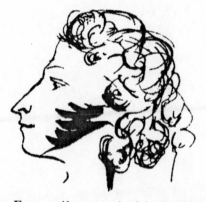

From a self-portrait sketch by Pushkin

The Moor of
Peter the Great

By the iron will of Peter
Was Russia transformed.

YAZYKOV

Chapter One

I am in Paris;
I have begun to live, not merely to breathe.

DMITRIEV

Among those young men sent abroad by Peter the Great for the acquisition of knowledge essential to a country in the process of reorganisation was his godson, the Moor Ibrahim. He was educated at the military academy in Paris, passed out as an Artillery Captain, distinguished himself in the Spanish War, and after being severely wounded he returned to Paris. In the midst of his vast labours, the Tsar never ceased to enquire after his favourite, and always received flattering reports of his progress and conduct. Peter was extremely pleased with him and more than once summoned him back to Russia; but Ibrahim was in no hurry. He used various pretexts to postpone his departure: now his wound, now a wish to improve his knowledge, now a shortage of money; and Peter indulgently acceded to his requests, besought him to take care of his health, thanked him for his enthusiasm in the quest for knowledge, and although extremely frugal in his own personal expenditure, he did not spare his exchequer where it concerned Ibrahim, adding fatherly advice and words of caution to the ducats which he sent him.

According to the evidence of all historical records, nothing could compare with the sheer giddiness, the folly and the luxury of the French at that time. The last years of the reign of Louis XIV, noted for the strict piety, the solemnity and the decorum of the Court, had left no traces behind them. The Duke of Orleans, combining many brilliant qualities with vices of every sort, unfortunately possessed not the slightest degree of hypocrisy. The orgies which took place at the Palais Royal were no secret to Paris; the example was contagious. It was at this time that Law appeared. Greed for money was united to a thirst for enjoyment and dissipation. Estates vanished; morals went by the board; Frenchmen laughed and calculated, and the state fell to pieces to the skittish music of the satirical vaudevilles.

At the same time, society presented a most diverting picture. Culture and the longing for amusement drew together all manner of men. Wealth, courtesy, fame, talent, eccentricity even – everything that provided food for curiosity or gave promise of entertainment was received with the same indulgence. Writers, scholars and philosophers abandoned the quiet of their studies and appeared in the circles of the *haut-monde,* to pay tribute to fashion and to lead it. Women reigned, but no longer demanded adoration. Superficial good manners took the place of profound respect. The exploits of the Duke of Richelieu, the Alcibiades of modern Athens, belong to history and give an indication of the morals of the period:

> *Temps fortuné, marqué par la license,*
> *Où la folie, agitant son grelot,*
> *D'un pied léger parcourt toute la France,*
> *Où nul mortel ne daigne être dévot,*
> *Où l'on fait tout excepté pénitence.*

The appearance of Ibrahim, his outward aspect, his culture and his native intelligence gave rise to general attention in Paris. All the ladies wanted to see *le nègre du Czar* at their houses, and they vied with one another to catch him. The Regent more than once invited him to his gay evening parties. He attended suppers enlivened by the youth of Arouet, the old age of Chaulieu, and the conversations of Montesquieu and Fontenelle. He did not miss a single ball, fête or first night, and gave himself over to the general whirl with all the ardour of his years and his nature. But the thought of exchanging these distractions, these brilliant amusements for the dry simplicity of the Petersburg Court was not the only thing that bound Ibrahim to Paris; he had other, more pressing ties. The young African was in love.

The Countess D**, no longer in the first bloom of her youth, was still renowned for her beauty. On leaving a convent at the age of seventeen, she had been married to a man with whom she had had no time to fall in love, and who had then not bothered to gain her love. Rumour attributed many lovers to her, but thanks to society's indulgent attitude, she enjoyed a good reputation, since it was impossible to reproach her with any ridiculous or scandalous adventure. Her house was the most fashionable in Paris, and the best Parisian society gathered there. Ibrahim was introduced to her by young Merville, who was generally reckoned to be her latest lover – which impression he tried with all his means to justify.

The Countess received Ibrahim politely, but without any particular attention; he felt flattered by this. People generally regarded the young Moor as a freak, and, surrounding him, overwhelmed him with compliments and questions; this curiosity, although concealed beneath an air of graciousness, offended his vanity. The delightful attention of women, almost the sole aim of man's exertions, not only gave him no pleasure, but even filled his heart with bitterness and indignation. He felt that for them he was a kind of rare beast, an exceptional and strange creation, accidentally transferred to their world, and possessing nothing in common with them.

He even envied those who remained unnoticed and considered them to be fortunate in their insignificance.

The thought that nature had not created him for the joys of a reciprocated passion rid him of all conceit and vain pretension, and this gave a rare charm to his behaviour with women. His conversation, which was simple and dignified, pleased the Countess D**, who had wearied of the endless jesting and pointed raillery of French wit. Ibrahim was often at her house. She gradually grew accustomed to the young Moor's appearance, and even began to find something rather pleasant about the curly head, so black amid the powdered wigs in her drawing-room. (Ibrahim had been wounded in the head and wore a bandage instead of a wig.) He was twenty-seven; he was tall and well-built, and more than one beauty gazed at him with feelings more flattering than mere curiosity; but the prejudiced Ibrahim either did not notice this, or looked upon it as mere coquetry. Yet when his glances met those of the Countess, his distrust vanished. Her eyes expressed such charming good nature, her manner towards him was so simple and natural that it was impossible to suspect her in the least of flirtatiousness or mockery.

The thought of love had not occurred to him – but to see the Countess every day had already become essential. He sought everywhere to meet her, and each meeting seemed to him as an unexpected favour from heaven. The Countess guessed at the nature of his feelings before he did himself. It cannot be denied that a love without hope and without demands touches a woman's heart more surely than all the ploys of the seducer. When Ibrahim was present, the Countess followed his every movement, listened to all that he said; without him, she grew pensive and lapsed into her usual state of absent-mindedness. Merville was the first to observe their mutual inclination and he congratulated Ibrahim. There is nothing that enflames love more than the encouraging observations of an outsider. Love is blind, and having no confidence in itself, it is quick to grasp at the least support. Merville's words aroused Ibrahim. The possibility of possessing the woman he loved had until then not entered his head; his soul was suddenly lit up with hope; he fell insanely in love. In vain did the Countess, alarmed by the frenzy of his passion, attempt to counter it with friendly admonitions and sensible advice; and she herself was beginning to falter. Indiscreet compliments followed one another with speed. Finally, carried away by the strength of the passion she inspired in him and succumbing to its influence, she gave herself to the rapturous Ibrahim.

Nothing is concealed from the eyes of an observant world. The Countess's new attachment soon became known to all. Some ladies were astonished at her choice; to many it seemed perfectly natural. Some laughed; others regarded her behaviour as unpardonably indiscreet. In the first intoxication of passion Ibrahim and the Countess noticed nothing, but soon the equivocal jokes of the men and the pointed comments of the women began to reach their ears. Ibrahim's solemn, cold manner had hitherto protected him from such attacks; he suffered them impatiently and did not know how to retaliate. The Countess, accustomed to the respect of society, was unable to see herself with equanimity as the object of sneers and gossip. At times she complained to Ibrahim in tears, at times reproached him bitterly and implored him not to defend her, lest by some useless bluster he should ruin her completely.

Her situation was made the more difficult by a new circumstance. The consequences of incautious love began to show themselves. Words of consolation and advice, proposals – all were exhausted, all rejected. The Countess foresaw inevitable ruin and awaited it with despair.

As soon as the Countess's condition became known, tongues began to wag with a new force. Sensitive women gasped with horror; the men laid bets among themselves as to whether the Countess would give birth to a white or a black child. Epigrams were freely exchanged at the expense of her husband, who alone in all Paris neither knew nor suspected anything.

The fateful moment drew near. The Countess's condition was appalling. Ibrahim visited her every day. He saw her mental and physical strength gradually ebbing. Her tears, her terror broke out anew at every moment. At last she felt the first labour pains. Measures were instantly taken. Means of removing the Count were found. The doctor arrived. Two days previously, a poor woman had been persuaded to give up her new-born infant into the hands of strangers; a trusted accomplice was sent to fetch it. Ibrahim waited in the study next to the very bedroom in which the unhappy Countess lay. Not daring to breathe, he listened to her muffled groans, to the whisperings of the maidservant, and to the orders of the doctor. She was in labour for a long time. Her every groan tore at his soul; each interval of silence filled his heart with terror. Suddenly he heard the weak cry of a child and, unable to contain his joy, he rushed into the Countess's room. A black baby lay on the bed at her feet. Ibrahim drew near to it. His heart beat violently. He blessed his son with trembling hands. The Countess smiled faintly and stretched out a weak hand to him. But the doctor, fearing that the shock might prove too much for the patient, drew Ibrahim away from the bed. The new-born child was placed in a covered basket and taken out of the house by a secret stairway. The other child was brought in and its cradle placed in the bedroom of the mother. Ibrahim left, somewhat relieved. The Count was expected. He returned late, learned of the safe delivery of his wife, and was most pleased. Thus the public, who had been expecting a considerable scandal, was deceived in its hope, and was forced to seek consolation in malignant gossip.

Everything resumed its normal course, but Ibrahim felt that his fate was certain to change, and that sooner or later his attachment to the Countess D** would reach her husband's ears. In that event, whatever happened, the Countess's ruin would be inevitable. He loved her passionately and was passionately loved; but the Countess was self-willed and frivolous. This was not the first time that she had loved. Repugnance and loathing could take the place of her heart's most tender feelings. Ibrahim already foresaw the moment when her love might cool; until then he had not known jealousy, but with horror he now had a presentiment of it; he felt that the anguish of separation would be less tormenting, and he therefore determined to sever the ill-fated association and return to Russia, whither Peter and an obscure feeling of duty had been summoning him for a long time.

Chapter Two

> *Beauty no longer affects me as it did;*
> *Joy has lost a part of its delight,*
> *My mind is not so free of care,*
> *I am less happy . . .*
> *I am tormented by the desire to do honour,*
> *I hear the sound of glory calling!*
>
> DERZHAVIN

Days, months passed, and the enamoured Ibrahim could not resolve to leave the woman he had seduced. The Countess grew more and more attached to him. Their son was being brought up in a distant province. Gossip was dying down, and the lovers began to enjoy a greater peace, silently remembering the storm of the past and trying not to think of the future.

Ibrahim was one day at the house of the Duke of Orleans when the Duke, walking past him, stopped and handed him a letter, telling him to read it at his leisure. The letter was from Peter. The Tsar, guessing at the cause of Ibrahim's absence, had written to the Duke to say that he had no intention of forcing his will upon Ibrahim, that he left it to him to decide whether or not to return to Russia, and that, in any event, he would never desert his former foster-son. This letter moved Ibrahim to the depths of his heart. From that moment his fate was decided. On the following morning he announced to the Regent his intention of setting out for Russia instantly.

'Think what you're doing,' the Duke said to him. 'Russia is not your native land. I don't suppose you'll ever see your torrid birthplace again, but your long stay in France has made you equally alien to the climate and the way of life in semi-savage Russia. You were not born a subject of Peter. Heed my advice: take advantage of his gracious permission. Stay in France, for whom you have already shed your blood, and rest assured that your services and qualities will not pass unrewarded here.'

Ibrahim thanked the Duke sincerely, but remained firm in his intention.

'I am sorry,' the Regent said to him, 'but perhaps you're right.'

He promised to release him from the army and wrote in detail about the matter to the Russian Tsar.

Ibrahim was soon ready for his journey. The day before his departure, he spent the evening, as usual, at the house of the Countess D**. She knew nothing of his plans; Ibrahim had not had the courage to reveal them to her. The Countess was calm and cheerful. On several occasions she beckoned him to her and joked about his pensiveness. The guests dispersed after supper. The Countess, her husband and Ibrahim remained in the drawing-room. The unhappy Ibrahim would have given everything in the world to have been alone with her; but Count D** seemed so peaceably installed before the fire that it was impossible to hope that he would leave the room. All three were silent.

'*Bonne nuit*,' said the Countess at last.

Ibrahim's heart missed a beat and he suddenly felt all the pain of separation. He stood motionless.

'*Bonne nuit, messieurs*,' the Countess repeated.

Still he did not move . . . Eventually his eyes grew dim, his head began to swim, and he could scarcely walk out of the room. Arriving home, scarcely conscious, he wrote the following letter:

> '*I am going away, dear Leonora; I am leaving you for ever. I am writing to you because I have not the courage to explain matters to you in any other way.*
>
> '*My happiness could not have lasted. I have enjoyed it in spite of fate and nature. You would have grown tired of me; your enchantment would have vanished. This thought has pursued me always – even in those moments when I have seemed to forget everything at your feet, intoxicated by your passionate self-denial, your infinite tenderness . . . The frivolous world mercilessly decries that very thing which, in theory, it permits: its cold scorn would sooner or later have defeated you, humbled your ardent spirit and eventually you would have grown ashamed of your passion . . . And what would have become of me? No! It is better to die, better to leave you before this appalling moment comes about . . .*

'Your tranquillity is more dear to me than anything: you could not enjoy it with the eyes of the world fixed upon you. Remember all that you have suffered, all the insults to your self-esteem, all the torments of fear; remember the terrible birth of our son. Consider: should I subject you further to such agitations and dangers as these? Why strive to unite the fate of so tender and beautiful a creature as yourself to the miserable lot of a negro, a pitiful creation scarcely worthy to be classed as human?

'Good-bye, Leonora, good-bye, my dear and only friend. I am leaving you – you, the first and last joy of my life. I have neither country nor relatives. I am going to sad Russia, where my total solitude will be a consolation to me. Serious affairs, to which from this moment I will dedicate myself, will, if not stifle, at least divert me from the torturous memories of days of ecstasy and bliss ... Good-bye, Leonora, I tear myself away from this letter as if from your embraces; good-bye, be happy ... And think sometimes of a poor negro, of your faithful Ibrahim'.

That same night he left for Russia.

The journey did not seem as terrible as he had expected. His imagination triumphed over reality; and the further he left Paris behind him, the more vivid and closer did the objects he was for ever leaving present themselves to him.

Without realising it, he reached the Russian frontier. Autumn had already set in, but in spite of the bad state of the roads he was driven with the speed of the wind, and on the morning of the seventeenth day of his journey he arrived at Krasnoye Selo, through which at that time the highway ran.

There were still another twenty-eight versts to Petersburg. While the horses were being changed Ibrahim went into the post-house. In a corner, a tall man wearing a green kaftan and with a clay pipe in his mouth was reading the Hamburg newspapers, leaning with his elbows on the table. Hearing somebody come in, he looked up.

'Ah, Ibrahim!' he cried, rising from the bench. 'How are you, my godson?'

Ibrahim, recognising Peter, rushed forward to him in delight, but respectfully stopped short. The Tsar drew near, embraced him and kissed him on the forehead.

'I was told you were coming,' said Peter, 'and came here to meet you. I've been waiting for you since yesterday.' Ibrahim could not find words to express his gratitude. 'Order your carriage to follow on behind,' the Tsar continued. 'You come and sit with me, and we'll go home.'

The Tsar's carriage was driven up; he and Ibrahim sat down and they set off at a gallop. After an hour and a half they reached Petersburg. Ibrahim stared with curiosity at the newly-born capital which was rising out of the marshes at the bidding of its master. Half-finished dams, canals without quays, wooden bridges everywhere testified to the recent victory of man's will over the hostile elements. The houses seemed to have been built in a hurry. In all the town only the Neva, as yet unadorned by its granite frame but already covered with war- and merchant-ships, was magnificent. The imperial carriage stopped at the palace of the so-called Tsaritsin Garden. Peter was met on the steps by an attractive woman of about thirty-five, dressed in the latest Parisian fashion. Peter kissed her on the lips and taking Ibrahim by the hand, he said:

'Do you recognise my godson, Katenka? I beg you to be kind and gracious to him as before.'

Catherine fixed him with her dark, penetrating eyes, and stretched out her hand to him affably. Two young beauties standing behind her, tall and slim and fresh as roses, approached Peter respectfully.

'Lisa,' he said to one of them, 'do you remember the little Moor who used to steal my apples for you at Oranienbaum? Here he is: I introduce him to you.'

The Grand Duchess laughed and grew red. They went into the dining-room, where the table had been laid in expectation of the Tsar. Inviting Ibrahim to join him, the Tsar sat down to dine with his family. The Tsar conversed with him on various topics during dinner and questioned him about the Spanish War, France's internal affairs and the Regent, whom he liked, while finding much in him to condemn. Ibrahim was endowed with a sharp and observant mind; Peter was very pleased with his replies; he recalled some incidents in Ibrahim's childhood, relating them with such good humour and merriment that nobody could have suspected this kind and hospitable host of being the hero of Poltava, of being the severe and powerful reformer of Russia.

After dinner the Tsar, in accordance with Russian custom, went off to rest. Ibrahim was left with the Empress and the Grand Duchesses. He tried to satisfy their curiosity with his descriptions of the Parisian way of life, of the festivities and the ever-changing fashions. Meanwhile, some of the persons who belonged to the inner circle of the Tsar had assembled at the palace. Ibrahim recognised the magnificent Prince Menshikov, who, on seeing a Moor in conversation with Catherine, looked proudly askance at him; Prince Yakov Dolgoruky, Peter's strict councillor; the learned Bruce, described by the people as the Russian 'Faust'; the young Raguzinsky, a former comrade of Ibrahim; and others who had come to the Tsar to make their reports and to receive orders.

The Tsar reappeared after a couple of hours. 'Let us see,' he said to Ibrahim, 'whether you have forgotten your old duties. Take a slate and follow me.'

Peter shut himself up in his workroom and occupied himself with the affairs of the state. In turn he worked with Bruce, with Prince Dolgoruky, with the chief of the police, General Devier, and dictated several decrees and decisions to Ibrahim. Ibrahim could not help but marvel at the alertness and strength of his intelligence, the power and flexibility of his attention and the variety of his activities. When their work had finished, Peter took out a pocket-book in order to assure himself that all that had been scheduled for that day had been carried out. Then, leaving his workroom, he said to Ibrahim:

'It's already late; I dare say you're tired; spend the night here as you used to in the old days. I'll wake you up tomorrow.'

Ibrahim, left alone, could scarcely come to his senses. He was in Petersburg, seeing again the great man near whom, while not yet appreciating his worth, he had spent his childhood. With a feeling almost of contrition, he confessed in his heart that, for the first time since his separation from the Countess D**, his thoughts had not dwelt exclusively upon her throughout the day. He saw that the new way of life that was awaiting him – the activity and constant work – could revive his soul, fatigued by passion, idleness and secret despondency. The thought of working together with a great man and, with him, of playing some part in the fate of a great nation, awoke in him for the first time the noble feeling of ambition. In this frame of mind he lay down on the campbed which had been prepared for him, and then the accustomed dream took him back to distant Paris, to the embraces of his dear Countess.

Chapter Three

Like clouds in the sky,
Our thoughts change at the slightest breeze,
And what we love today, we hate tomorrow.

KYUKHELBEKER

The next day Peter woke Ibrahim as he had promised, and congratulated him on his promotion to the rank of Lieutenant-Colonel in the Grenadier company of the Preobrazhensky regiment, of which he himself was the Colonel. The courtiers surrounded Ibrahim, each in his own way trying to flatter the new favourite. The haughty Prince Menshikov pressed his hand in a friendly way; Sheremetev enquired after his Parisian acquaintances. Golovin invited him to dinner; and others followed his example, so that Ibrahim received invitations for at least a month.

Ibrahim began to lead a monotonous but busy life and, in consequence, did not suffer from boredom. He grew daily more attached to the Tsar and became better able to appreciate his lofty mind. To follow the thoughts of a great man is a most rewarding study. Ibrahim saw Peter in the Senate, arguing with Buturlin and Dolgoruky; deciding important questions of legislation at the Admiralty Collegium, which was consolidating Russia's naval power; he saw him with Feofan, Gavriïl Buzhinsky and Kopievitch in his hours of leisure, inspecting translations of foreign publications or visiting some merchant's factory, a craftsman's workshop or a scholar's study. Russia presented herself to Ibrahim as one huge workshop, where only machines moved and where each workman, subject to a fixed plan, was occupied with his own job. He considered it his duty to work hard at his own bench also, and tried to regret the gaiety of Parisian life as little as possible. But it was more difficult to dispel from his thoughts that other, dear recollection: he often thought of the Countess D**, imagined her justifiable indignation, her tears and her grief . . . But at times a terrible thought oppressed his heart: the distractions of the *haut-monde*, a new attachment, another happy man – he shuddered; jealousy began to set his African blood boiling, and hot tears were ready to course down his dusky face.

He was sitting in his study one morning, surrounded by business papers, when all of a sudden he heard a loud greeting in French. Ibrahim turned quickly round, and the young Korsakov, whom he had left behind in Paris amid the whirl of society, embraced him with joyful exclamations.

'I have only just arrived,' said Korsakov, 'and have dashed straight here to you. All our Parisian friends send their best wishes, and regret your absence. The Countess D** ordered me to summon you back without fail, and here is a letter for you from her.'

Ibrahim seized it with trembling hand and looked at the familiar handwriting of the address, not daring to believe his eyes.

'How glad I am,' continued Korsakov, 'that you haven't yet died of boredom in this barbarous Petersburg! What do people do here? How do they occupy themselves? Who is your tailor? Have they at least opened an opera house?'

Ibrahim answered distractedly that the Tsar was probably working at that moment in the dockyard. Korsakov laughed.

'I can see you don't want me here just at the moment,' he said. 'We'll be able to talk to our hearts' content some other time. I'll go and present myself to the Tsar.'

With these words he turned on his heel and hastened out of the room.

Ibrahim, left alone, hastily unsealed the letter. The Countess tenderly upbraided him, charging him with dissimulation and distrustfulness. She wrote:

> *'You say that my tranquillity is more dear to you than anything in the world. Ibrahim, if this were true, could you have driven me to the condition to which the unexpected news of your departure reduced me? You were frightened that I would detain you; be assured that, in spite of my love, I would have known how to sacrifice it to your well-being and to what you consider to be your duty.'*

The Countess ended her letter with passionate assurances of her love, and besought him to write to her from time to time – even though there should be no hope of their seeing one another again.

Ibrahim read the letter twenty times through, kissing the precious lines with rapture. He was burning with impatience to hear about the Countess, and was on the point of setting out for the Admiralty in the hope of finding Korsakov still there, when the door opened and Korsakov himself appeared once more. He had already presented himself to the Tsar and, as usual, seemed to be highly pleased with himself.

'*Entre nous*,' he said to Ibrahim, 'the Tsar is an exceedingly strange man. Imagine, I found him in some sort of sackcloth vest, on the mast of a new ship, whither I was forced to clamber with my dispatches. I stood on a rope ladder, and without room enough to make a decent bow, I became utterly confused – a thing that has never happened to me before. However, the Tsar, having read my papers, looked me over from top to toe and was no doubt pleasantly struck by the taste and elegance of my clothes; at least he smiled, and invited me to this evening's Assembly. But I am a total stranger to Petersburg and during my six years' absence have completely forgotten the customs of the place. Pray be my mentor and call for me this evening and introduce me.'

Ibrahim agreed and hastened to turn the conversation to a subject more interesting to him.

'Well, and how is the Countess D**?'

'The Countess? At first she was naturally most upset at your departure; and then, of course, she gradually became more cheerful and took on a new lover – do you know whom? That long-legged Marquis R**. Why do you show the whites of your Moorish eyes like that? Does it seem strange to you? Surely you know that lasting grief is not an expression of human nature – particularly feminine nature. Think it over while I go and rest after my journey, and don't forget to call for me.'

What feelings filled Ibrahim's heart? Jealousy? Rage? Despair? No, but deep, oppressive grief. He kept on repeating to himself: 'I foresaw it; it had to happen.' Then he opened the Countess's letter, read it through once more, hung his head and wept bitterly. He wept for a long time. His tears relieved his heart. Looking at his watch, he saw that it was time to go. Ibrahim would have liked to excuse himself from attending the Assembly, but it was a matter of duty, and the Tsar was strict in his demand for the presence of those in his confidence. He dressed and went to call on Korsakov.

Korsakov was sitting in his dressing-gown, reading a French novel.

'So early?' he said on seeing Ibrahim.

'Heavens above,' replied the other, 'it's already half-past five. We shall be late. Get dressed as quickly as you can and we'll go.'

Flustered, Korsakov jumped up and began to ring the bell with all his might. Servants came running in, and he hurriedly began to dress. His French valet handed him a pair of scarlet-heeled slippers, blue velvet breeches and a pink coat embroidered with spangles; his wig was hastily powdered in the hall and brought in to him. Korsakov fitted it on his cropped head, demanded his sword and gloves, turned round about ten times before the looking-glass, and announced to Ibrahim that he was ready. The footmen handed each man his bearskin cloak, and they set off for the Winter Palace.

Korsakov overwhelmed Ibrahim with questions. Who was the most beautiful woman in Petersburg? Who was known as the best dancer? Which dance was at that time in fashion? Ibrahim satisfied his curiosity with extreme reluctance. In the meantime they reached the palace. A number of long sledges, old-fashioned carriages and gilded coaches already stood on the grass. Liveried coachmen with moustaches were crowded around the steps; as were fast-moving footmen, glittering with tinsel and plumes, and with maces in their hands; hussars, pages, ungainly footmen piled up with the fur cloaks and muffs of their masters – in all a retinue which was held by the noblemen of that time to be quite indispensable. At the sight of Ibrahim, a general murmur went up among them: 'The Moor, the Moor, the Tsar's Moor!' He hurriedly led Korsakov through this motley crowd. A palace lackey opened the door wide to them and they entered the hall. Korsakov was dumbfounded. In the great room, lit by tallow candles burning dimly amid the clouds of tobacco smoke, magnates with blue ribbons across their shoulders, ambassadors, foreign merchants, officers of the Guards in their green uniforms, shipmasters in jackets and striped trousers moved backwards and forwards in crowds to the uninterrupted sound of the music of wind instruments. The ladies were seated around the walls, the young ones glittering with all the splendour of fashion. Their dresses were brilliant with silver and gold; from exuberant farthingales their slender figures rose like flower-stems; diamonds sparkled in their ears, in their long curls and around their necks. They glanced gaily to right and left, waiting for their cavaliers and for the dancing to begin. The elderly ladies had slyly endeavoured to combine the new fashions of dress with the now banished style of the past, their bonnets resembling the small sable head-dress of the Tsaritsa Natalya Kirilovna and their gowns and mantillas somehow recalling the sarafan and the *dushegreika*. They seemed to attend these newly instituted entertainments more with astonishment than with pleasure and cast vexed glances at the wives and daughters of the Dutch skippers who, in dimity skirts and red jackets, sat knitting their stockings and laughing and conversing among themselves as if they were at home. Korsakov could not come to his senses.

Noticing the new arrivals, a servant approached them with beer and glasses on a tray.

'*Que diable est-ce que tout cela?*' Korsakov asked Ibrahim in a whisper.

Ibrahim could not help smiling. The Empress and the Grand Duchesses, resplendent in their beauty and their dress, strolled among the rows of guests, talking affably to them. The Tsar was in the adjoining room. Korsakov, wishing to present himself, could scarcely make his way through the ever-moving crowd. In this room were mainly foreigners, who sat solemnly smoking their clay pipes and downing the contents of their earthenware jugs. Bottles of beer and wine, leather pouches of tobacco, glasses of punch and chess-boards were disposed on the tables. At one of these Peter was playing draughts with a broad-shouldered English skipper. They were zealously saluting each other with volleys of tobacco smoke, and the Tsar was so puzzled by an unexpected move on the part of his opponent that he failed to notice Korsakov as he darted around them. At this moment a fat man with a large bouquet on his chest came bustling into the room and announced in a loud voice that the dancing had begun. He left again instantly, followed by a great number of the guests, Korsakov among them.

Korsakov was struck by an unexpected spectacle. Along the entire length of the ballroom, to the sound of the most melancholy music, ladies and gentlemen stood in two rows facing each other; the gentlemen bowed low; the ladies curtsied even lower, first to the front, then to the right, then to the left, to the front again, to the right again and so on. Korsakov stared wide-eyed at this fanciful way of passing the time and bit his lip. The bowing and curtsying continued for nearly half an hour; at last they stopped, and the fat gentleman with the bouquet proclaimed that the ceremonial dances were over and ordered the musicians to play a minuet. Korsakov was delighted and prepared to shine. Among the young guests present, there was one that particularly pleased him. She was about sixteen, dressed expensively but with taste, and was sitting next to an elderly gentleman of imposing and stern appearance. Korsakov flew up to her and asked her to do him the honour of dancing with him. The young beauty looked at him in confusion and seemed lost for an answer. The gentleman sitting beside her frowned severely. Korsakov was awaiting her decision when the gentleman with the bouquet came up to him, led him into the middle of the ballroom and said in a pompous voice:

'Sir, you have done wrong: in the first place, you approached this young lady without making the necessary three bows to her; in the second place, you took it upon yourself to choose her, when, in a minuet, it is the right of the lady and not the gentleman to choose. For this, you must be severely punished – that is, you must drain the Goblet of the Great Eagle.'

Korsakov grew more and more astonished. He was immediately surrounded by the other guests, who noisily demanded the immediate execution of the law. Peter, hearing the laughter and shouting, came through from the adjacent room; he was extremely keen on being personally present at such punishments. The crowd parted before him, and he entered the circle where stood the culprit and, before him, the marshal of the Assembly holding a huge goblet filled with malmsey wine. He was vainly trying to persuade the offender to comply willingly with the law.

'Aha!' said Peter, seeing Korsakov. 'So they've caught you, brother! Come on, *monsieur*, drink up and no wry faces!'

There was nothing for it. The unfortunate dandy, without pausing for breath, drained the entire contents of the goblet and handed it back to the marshal.

'Listen here, Korsakov,' Peter said to him. 'Your breeches are made of velvet, such as I myself don't wear, and I am far richer than you. That's extravagance; take care I don't quarrel with you.'

Hearing this reproof, Korsakov made to leave the circle, but he staggered and nearly fell, to the indescribable pleasure of the Tsar and the whole merry company. This episode did not in the least spoil the entertainment and smooth running of the main function, but enlivened it yet more. The gentlemen began to scrape their feet and bow and the ladies to curtsy and click their heels with great zeal, no longer paying the least attention to the rhythm of the music. Korsakov was unable to take part in the general gaiety. The young lady whom Korsakov had chosen, on the instruction of her father, Gavrila Afanassyevitch, went up to Ibrahim and, lowering her blue eyes, shyly offered him her hand. Ibrahim danced the minuet with her and then led her back to her place; afterwards, having sought out Korsakov, he conducted him out of the ballroom, sat him down in his carriage, and drove home. At the start of the journey, Korsakov kept muttering incoherently:

'Damned Assembly ...! Damned Goblet of the Great Eagle!'

But he soon fell into a heavy sleep, and was not aware of how he got home, or how he was undressed and put to bed. Waking with a headache on the following morning, he had but a dim recollection of the bowing and curtsying, the tobacco smoke, the gentleman with the bouquet and the Goblet of the Great Eagle.

Chapter Four

Unhurriedly our forebears ate,
Unhurriedly were passed around
The jugs and silver bowls
With steaming beer and wine.

RUSLAN AND LUDMILLA

I must now acquaint my benevolent reader with Gavrila Afanassyevitch Rzhevsky. He was descended from an ancient noble family, possessed huge estates, was hospitable, was a lover of falconry, and had a great number of household servants – in a word, he was a Russian nobleman through and through; as he himself put it, he could not endure 'the foreign spirit' and endeavoured to preserve in his house the ancient customs that were so dear to him.

His daughter was seventeen years old. She had lost her mother while still a child. She had been brought up in the old style – that is, surrounded by governesses, nurses, playfellows and maidservants; she was able to embroider in gold, but could neither read nor write. In spite of his aversion to everything foreign, her father could not oppose her wish to learn German dances from a captive Swedish officer living in the house. This estimable dancing master was about fifty. His right leg had been shot through at the battle of Narva, and he was not for that reason particularly accomplished at minuets and gallops; his left leg, however, executed the most difficult *pas* with amazing skill and agility. His pupil did credit to his efforts. Natalya Gavrilovna was known as the finest dancer at the Assemblies, and this fact added to Korsakov's offence. Korsakov himself had called the following day to apologise to Gavrila Afanassyevitch, but the jaunty elegance of the young dandy had not endeared itself to the proud nobleman, who wittily dubbed him 'The French monkey'.

It was a holiday. Gavrila Afanassyevitch was expecting some relatives and friends. The long table in the old-fashioned dining-hall was being laid. The guests were arriving with their wives and daughters, who had at last been emancipated by the edicts and personal example of the Tsar from the domestic enslavement they had previously suffered. Natalya Gavrilovna carried round a silver tray laden with gold cups to each of the guests, and as each man drained his cup he regretted that the kiss, formerly received on such occasions, was no longer the custom. They sat down at the table. In the place of honour, next to the host, sat his father-in-law, Prince Boris Alexeyevitch Lykov, an old nobleman of seventy; the other guests arranged themselves according to the antiquity of their families, thus recalling the happy times when such respect was generally paid – the men on one side of the table, the women on the other. Occupying their customary places at the end of the table, sat the house-keeper in old-fashioned costume and head-dress, a prim and wrinkled dwarf of thirty and the captive Swede in his faded blue uniform. A host of servants bustled around the table, which was laid with a great quantity of dishes; among them was the steward, made conspicuous by his severe expression, large paunch and lofty immobility. The first few minutes of dinner were devoted solely to the appreciation of our old-fashioned Russian cooking; the sound of plates and the clinking of spoons alone broke the general silence. At last, the host, seeing that the time had come to entertain his guests with some pleasant conversation, turned and asked:

'And where is Yekimovna? Call her here!'

Several servants rushed off in various directions, but at that moment an old woman, powdered and rouged, adorned with flowers and tinsel, and wearing a low-necked brocade gown, entered the room, singing and dancing. Her appearance excited general enthusiasm.

'Good day to you, Yekimovna,' Prince Lykov said to her. 'How are you?'

'Happy and well, friend: singing and dancing and looking for sweethearts.'

'Where have you been, fool?' asked the host.

'Arraying myself, friend, for our dear guests, for this holy day, by order of the Tsar, by command of my master, to be in foreign style a laughing-stock for all the world.'

A loud burst of laughter went up at these words, and the fool took her place behind the host's chair.

'The fool talks a great deal of nonsense, but on occasions her nonsense has some truth in it,' said Tatyana Afanassyevna, the host's eldest sister, whom he greatly respected. 'Indeed, our present-day fashions are the laughing-stock of the world. But since you gentlemen have shaved off your beards and put on short coats, there is of course no point in making a fuss about women's rags; but it really is a pity about the smock, the maiden's ribbons and the female head-dress! Just look at our modern beauties – it's as pitiable as it's laughable: their hair frizzed like tow, greased and covered with French chalk;

stomachs so tightly laced that they almost snap in two; farthin-gales so blown out with hoops that they have to enter a carriage sideways and stoop to get through a door. They can't stand, they can't sit, and they can't breathe – martyrs indeed, the poor things!'

'Ah, Tatyana Afanassyevna,' said Kirila Petrovitch T**, a former governor of Ryazan where, in somewhat question-able manner, he had acquired three thousand serfs and a young wife. 'As far as I am concerned, my wife can wear what she pleases – provided she doesn't go out and order new dresses every month and then discard the others while they're still practically new. In the old days, the grandmother's sarafan used to form part of her granddaughter's dowry, but now-adays the gown worn by the mistress today you'll see on the back of her servant tomorrow. What's to be done? Alas, it spells the ruin of the Russian nobility!'

With these words he sighed and looked across at his wife, Marya Ilyinitchna who, it seemed, was not in the least pleased with his praise of the past or his condemnation of the latest customs. The other ladies shared her displeasure, but they were silent, since modesty was deemed at that time to be an essential attribute in a young lady.

'And who is to blame?' said Gavrila Afanassyevitch, filling a bowl with some effervescing kvass. 'Aren't we ourselves? The young women play around, and we encourage them.'

'But what can we do when we're not free to do as we want?' retorted Kirila Petrovitch. 'Any husband would be only too glad to shut his wife up in her rooms but, to the sound of beating drums, she is summoned to the Assembly. The husband follows the whip, but the wife goes in search of clothes. Ah, these Assemblies! The Lord has sent them upon us as a punishment for our sins!'

Marya Ilyinitchna sat as if on needles, her tongue itching to speak. Finally, she could bear it no longer and, turning to her husband, she asked him with a sour smile what he found so wrong with the Assemblies.

'This is what I find wrong with them,' her husband replied heatedly: 'since their institution, husbands have no longer been able to control their wives; wives have forgotten the words of the Apostle: "Let the wife reverence her husband." No longer do they busy themselves with domestic affairs, but with new dresses. They do not think of ways in which to please their husbands, but of ways in which to attract the attention of frivolous officers. And is it becoming, madam, for a Russian nobleman or noblewoman to associate with tobacco-smoking Germans and their maidservants? Have you ever heard of such a thing as dancing and talking with young men far into the night? It would be all very well with relatives, but with strangers, with people one doesn't even know . . . !'

'I should like to say just a word, although perhaps I shouldn't,' said Gavrila Afanassyevitch, frowning: 'I confess – these Assemblies are not to my liking. Before you know where you are, you are knocking up against some drunkard, or being made drunk yourself to become a general laughing-stock. And then you've got to watch out that some rake doesn't start fooling around with your daughter – the young people of today couldn't be more spoiled. At the last Assembly, for instance, the son of Yevgraf Sergeyevitch Korsakov made such a fuss about Natasha that it brought the blood to my cheeks. The next day I see someone drive straight into my courtyard and I think, who in the name of heaven is this? Can it be Prince Alexandr Danilovitch? No such thing! It's young Ivan Yegrafovitch Korsakov! He could not stop at the gate and make his way up to the steps on foot – oh no! He flew in, bowing and chattering. The fool, Yekimovna, can do a marvellous imitation of him – here, fool, do your imitation of the foreign monkey.'

The fool, Yekimovna, seized a dish-cover and, putting it

under her arm as if it were a hat, began to twist about and bow and scrape in every direction, repeating:

'*Monsieur ... Mademoiselle ... Assemblée ... pardon ...*'

General and prolonged laughter again showed the guests' pleasure.

'Exactly like Korsakov,' said the old Prince Lykov, wiping away tears of laughter when calm had been gradually restored. 'But why conceal the truth of the matter? He is not the first, and nor will he be the last, to return to Holy Russia from abroad as a buffoon. What do our children learn abroad? To scrape and chatter in heaven knows what gibberish, to show disrespect to their elders and chase after other men's wives. Of all the young men educated abroad (the Lord forgive me!) the Tsar's Moor shows the most resemblance to a man.'

'Of course,' observed Gavrila Afanassyevitch, 'he is a level-headed and decent man, and not simply a weathercock ... But who's that who's driven through the gates into my court-yard? Not that foreign monkey again? What are you gaping for, you dolts?' he continued, turning to the servants. 'Run and stop him, and in future...'

'Are you raving, greybeard?' interrupted the fool, Yekimovna. 'Or are you blind? That's the imperial sledge – the Tsar has come.'

Gavrila Afanassyevitch hurriedly stood up from the table; everybody rushed over to the windows, and indeed they saw the Tsar, leaning on his orderly's shoulder, mounting the steps. There was a general confusion. The host rushed forward to meet Peter; the servants dashed hither and thither, as if demented; the guests took fright, and some even began to think of how to leave for home as soon as possible. Peter's thundering voice was suddenly heard in the hall. All fell silent, and the Tsar entered, accompanied by his host, over-come with joy.

'Good day, ladies and gentlemen,' said Peter cheerfully.

Everyone bowed low. The Tsar's sharp eyes sought out the host's young daughter in the crowd; he summoned her to him. Natalya Gavrilovna advanced boldly enough, even though she was blushing not only to her ears, but also down to her shoulders.

'You become more beautiful every day,' the Tsar said to her and, as was his habit, he kissed her on the forehead. Then, turning to the guests, he said:

'I have disturbed you? You were dining? Sit down again, I beg of you, and give me some aniseed-vodka, Gavrila Afanassyevitch.'

The host rushed over to his stately steward, snatched the tray from his hands, and himself filled a golden goblet and handed it to the Tsar with a bow. Peter drank the vodka, ate a biscuit and for the second time invited the guests to continue with their dinner. All resumed their former places with the exception of the dwarf and the housekeeper, who did not dare to remain at a table honoured by the presence of the Tsar. Peter sat down next to his host and asked for some soup. The imperial orderly handed him a wooden spoon mounted with ivory and a knife and fork with green bone handles, for Peter never used any cutlery other than his own. The dinner, which a moment before had been noisy with laughter and conversation, was continued in silence and constraint. The host, through respect and delight, ate nothing; the guests also stood on ceremony and listened with reverence as the Tsar conversed in German with the captive Swede about the campaign of 1701. The fool, Yekimovna, spoken to on one or two occasions by the Tsar, replied with a sort of shy *hauteur,* which, be it noted, was by no means a sign of natural stupidity on her part. The dinner finally came to an end. The Tsar stood up, and after him all the guests.

'Gavrila Afanassyevitch,' he said to his host, 'I'd like a word with you in private.'

And taking him by the arm, he led him into the drawing-room and shut the door behind him. The guests remained in the dining-room, whispering to each other about this unexpected visit and, for fear of being indiscreet, quickly dispersed one after another for home, without thanking their host for his hospitality. His father-in-law, daughter and sister conducted them quietly to the door and remained alone in the dining-room, waiting for the Tsar to come out.

Chapter Five

I will obtain for you a wife,
Or not a miller be.

ABLESIMOV

Half an hour later, the door opened and the Tsar came out of the drawing-room. With a solemn nod of the head he returned the triple bow of Prince Lykov, Tatyana Afanass-yevna and Natasha, and passed straight into the hall. The host handed him his red sheepskin coat, led him out to his sledge, and on the steps thanked him once more for the honour he had shown him. Peter drove off.

Returning to the dining-room, Gavrila Afanassyevitch seemed greatly preoccupied. He angrily ordered the servants to clear the table as quickly as possible, sent Natasha off to her room and, informing his sister and father-in-law that he wished to speak to them, he led them into the bedroom in which he was accustomed to rest after dinner. The old Prince lay down on the oak bed; Tatyana Afanassyevna sat herself down in the old-fashioned armchair and moved a foot-stool up for her feet; Gavrila Afanassyevitch locked all the doors, sat down on the bed at Prince Lykov's feet and in a low voice began:

'It was not for nothing that the Tsar visited me today. Guess what he wanted to talk to me about.'

'How can we know, my dear brother?' said Tatyana Afanassyevna.

'Has the Tsar appointed you to a governorship somewhere?' said his father-in-law. 'It's about time he did. Or have you been offered an embassy? Why not? Men of distinction and not mere secretaries are sent to foreign sovereigns.'

'No,' replied his son-in-law, frowning. 'I am a man of the old school, and nowadays our services are not required, although it may be that an orthodox Russian nobleman is worth as much as these modern upstarts, pancakemen and heathens – but that's quite another matter.'

'Then what was he talking about with you for so long, brother?' said Tatyana Afanassyevna. 'Can some misfortune have befallen you? The Lord save and defend us from that!'

'No, there's no misfortune, but I confess I was set thinking.'

'What is it, brother? What's it all about?'

'It concerns Natasha. The Tsar came to make a match for her.'

'God be thanked!' said Tatyana Afanassyevna, crossing herself. 'The girl is of marriageable age, and the match-maker reflects the suitor. God grant them His love and advice; it is a great honour. For whom does the Tsar ask her hand?'

'Hm!' grunted Gavrila Afanassyevitch. 'For whom? That's just it – for whom?'

'Well, for whom then?' repeated Prince Lykov, who was beginning to doze off.

'Guess,' said Gavrila Afanassyevitch.

'My dear brother,' the old lady replied, 'how can we guess! There are plenty of marriageable men at Court, each of whom would be glad to take your Natasha as his wife. Is it Dolgoruky?'

'No, not Dolgoruky.'

'Well, God be with him: he's far too supercilious. Sheïn? Troyekurov?'

'No, neither of them.'

'I don't take to them either: they're flighty and too full of the foreign spirit. Well, is it Miloslavsky?'

'No, not he.'

'God be with him: he's rich but stupid. Who then? Yeletsky? Lvov ? It can't be Raguzinsky? No, I can't guess. For whom, then, does the Tsar want Natasha?'

'For the Moor Ibrahim.'

The old lady cried out and clasped her hands. Prince Lykov raised his head from the pillow and repeated in astonishment:

'For the Moor Ibrahim!'

'My dear brother!' said the old lady in a tearful voice. 'Do not ruin your own dear child – do not deliver Natasha into the clutches of that black devil!'

'But how,' retorted Gavrila Afanassyevitch, 'how am I to refuse the Tsar, who in return promises to bestow his favour on us, on me and all our family?'

'What!' exclaimed the old Prince, who was by now wide awake. 'Natasha, my granddaughter, to be married to a bought negro!'

'He is not of humble birth,' said Gavrila Afanassyevitch; 'he is the son of a Moorish sultan. The pagans took him prisoner and sold him in Constantinople, and our local ambassador rescued him and presented him to the Tsar. His elder brother came to Russia with an appreciable ransom and . . .'

'My dear Gavrila Afanassyevitch!' the old lady interrupted. 'We all know the fairy-tale about Bova Korolevitch and

Yeruslan Lazarevitch! Tell us rather how you replied to the Tsar's proposal.'

'I told him that we were under his authority, and that it was our duty as his servants to obey him in all things.'

At that moment a noise was heard from behind the door. Gavrila Afanassyevitch went to open it, but felt some resistance from the other side. He pushed harder – the door opened, and they saw Natasha lying in a faint upon the blood-stained floor.

Her heart had sunk when the Tsar had shut himself up with her father. Some presentiment whispered to her that the matter concerned her, and when Gavrila Afanassyevitch sent her away, saying that he must speak with her aunt and grandfather, she had been unable to resist the impulse of feminine curiosity, had crept softly through the inner rooms to the bedroom door, and had not missed a single word of the whole terrible conversation. On hearing her father's last words, the unfortunate girl had fainted and, in falling, had injured her head against an iron chest in which her dowry was kept.

Servants hastened to the scene; they picked Natasha up, carried her to her room, and laid her down on her bed. After a while she regained consciousness and opened her eyes; but she recognised neither her father nor her aunt. A violent fever set in; in her delirium she raved about the Tsar's Moor and about the wedding, and then suddenly, in plaintive, piercing tones, she cried out:

'Valerian, dear Valerian, my life! Save me! There they are! There they are ... !'

Tatyana Afanassyevna glanced anxiously at her brother, who turned pale, bit his lip and silently left the room. He returned to the old Prince who, unable to climb the stairs, had remained below.

'How is Natasha?' he asked.

'Very bad,' replied the distressed father. 'Worse than I thought: she's delirious and raves about Valerian.'

'Who is this Valerian?' asked the alarmed old man. 'Surely not the orphan, the archer's son, who was brought up in your house?'

'The same, to my misfortune,' replied Gavrila Afanass-yevitch. 'His father saved my life at the time of the rebellion, and the devil put into my head the idea of taking the accursed young wolf into my house. When, at his own request, he was enrolled into the regiment two years ago, Natasha burst into tears as she said goodbye to him and he stood as if turned to stone. I was suspicious at the time and spoke to my sister about it. But since that day Natasha has never referred to him, nor has anything been heard about him. I imagined that she had forgotten him, but it seems that this is not the case. But it is decided: she shall marry the Moor.'

Prince Lykov did not protest; it would have been in vain. He returned home. Tatyana Afanassyevna remained at Natasha's bedside. Gavrila Afanassyevitch, having sent for the doctor, locked himself in his room. In his house all became sadly subdued.

The unexpected offer of the Tsar to make a match for him astonished Ibrahim quite as much as it had Gavrila Afanass-yevitch. This is how it happened. He and Peter were working together when the Tsar said:

'I observe, my friend, that you are downhearted. Tell me frankly: what it is that you want?'

Ibrahim assured the Tsar that he was quite content with his lot and wished for nothing better.

'Good!' said the Tsar. 'If there is no reason for your low spirits, I know then how to cheer you up.'

When they had finished their work, Peter asked Ibrahim:

'Did you like the girl you danced the minuet with at the last Assembly?'

'She is very charming, Sire, and seems to be a good-hearted and modest girl.'

'Then I shall make you better acquainted with her. Would you like to marry her?'

'I, Sire?'

'Listen, Ibrahim: you are on your own in this world, without birth or kindred, a stranger to all except myself. If I were to die today, what would become of you tomorrow? You must get settled while there's still time; find support in new ties, marry into the Russian nobility.'

'Sire, I am happy with your protection and favour. May God grant that I do not outlive my Tsar and benefactor – I wish for nothing more. But even if I did think about getting married, would the young lady and her relatives consent? My appearance . . .'

'Your appearance! What nonsense! A fellow like you? A young girl must obey her parents, and we'll see what old Gavrila Rzhevsky has to say when I myself am your matchmaker.'

With these words the Tsar ordered his sledge and left Ibrahim sunk deep in thought.

'Marry!' thought the African. 'Why not? Must I be fated to spend my life in solitude, without knowing the greatest rewards and most sacred duties of man, merely because I was born under a stronger sun? I cannot hope to be loved, but that is a childish objection! How can one believe in love? How can love exist in the frivolous heart of a woman? Such charming fallacies I have rejected for ever, and have chosen more practical attractions. The Tsar is right: I must consider my future. Marriage with the young Rzhevsky will unite me to the proud Russian nobility, and I shall no longer be a stranger in my new fatherland. I shall not demand love from my wife, but will be content with her fidelity; her friendship I shall acquire by unfailing tenderness, trust and devotion.'

Ibrahim attempted to get back to his work, but his imagination was too excited. He left his papers and went for a stroll along the banks of the Neva. Suddenly, he heard Peter's voice and, looking round, he saw the Tsar, having dismissed his sledge, walking after him with a bright expression on his face.

'It's all fixed, my friend!' Peter said, taking him by the arm. 'I have betrothed you. Go and call on your future father-in-law tomorrow, but see that you gratify his nobleman's pride. Leave your sledge at the gate and go through the courtyard on foot. Talk to him of his services and his noble family, and you'll make a lasting impression on him. And now,' he continued, shaking his cudgel, 'lead me to that scoundrel Danilytch; I must talk to him about his latest pranks.'

Thanking Peter heartily for his fatherly solicitude, Ibrahim accompanied him as far as Prince Menshikov's magnificent palace and then returned home.

Chapter Six

A sanctuary lamp burned dimly before the glass case in which glittered the gold and silver frames of the family icons. Its flickering light weakly lit up the curtained bed and the little table covered with labelled medicine-bottles. Near the stove a servant-maid sat at her spinning-wheel, and the faint noise of the spindle was the only sound to break the silence of the room.

'Who's there?' asked a weak voice.

The servant-maid instantly stood up, went over to the bed, and gently raised the curtain.

'Will it soon be daylight?' Natalya asked.

'It's already midday,' the servant-maid replied.

'Good heavens! Then why is it so dark?'

'The shutters are closed, miss.'

'Help me to get dressed then, quickly.'

'I must not, miss, the doctor has forbidden you to get up.'

'Am I ill then? How long have I been ill?'

'Two weeks now.'

'Really? And I feel as if I only went to bed yesterday.'

Natasha was silent; she tried to collect her confused thoughts. Something had happened to her, but what exactly it was she could not remember. The servant-maid stood before her, awaiting her orders. At that moment a dull noise was heard from below.

'What was that?' asked the sick girl.

'They've just finished eating,' the servant-maid replied, 'and are getting up from the table. Tatyana Afanassyevna will be here presently.'

Natasha seemed pleased by this; with a feeble hand she waved away the servant-maid, who drew the curtain and sat down again at her spinning-wheel.

A few minutes later, a head in a broad white bonnet with dark ribbons appeared round the door, and asked in a low voice:

'How is Natasha?'

'Hello, auntie,' the patient said quietly, and Tatyana Afanassyevna hastened across to her.

'The mistress has regained consciousness,' said the servant-maid, carefully drawing an armchair up to the bed.

With tears in her eyes the old lady kissed the pale, languid face of her niece and sat down beside her. A German doctor in a black coat and a scholarly looking wig, who had followed her into the room, felt Natasha's pulse and announced first in Latin and then in Russian that the danger had passed. Asking for some paper and ink, he wrote out a fresh prescription and left. The old lady got up, kissed Natalya once more and immediately hurried downstairs to Gavrila Afanass-yevitch with the good news.

In the drawing-room, in uniform, his sword at his side and with his hat in his hand, the Tsar's Moor sat respectfully talking to Gavrila Afanassyevitch. Korsakov, stretched out on a down sofa, was listening to them absent-mindedly and teasing an estimable Russian greyhound. Tiring of this occupation, he went across to the looking-glass, the habitual refuge of the idle, and in it he saw Tatyana Afanassyevna vainly beckoning to her brother from the doorway.

'You are wanted, Gavrila Afanassyevitch,' said Korsakov, turning to him and interrupting Ibrahim.

Gavrila Afanassyevitch immediately went out to his sister, closing the door behind him.

'I am amazed at your patience,' said Korsakov to Ibrahim. 'For a full hour you have been listening to all that rubbish about the antiquity of the Lykov and Rzhevsky families – and have even added your own moral observations! In your place *j'aurais planté là* the old trifler and all his tribe, including Natalya Gavrilovna, who's mincing about pretending to be ill – *une petite santé* ... Tell me honestly: are you really in love with that affected little thing? Listen to me, Ibrahim, and follow my advice for once; I am in fact far more sensible than I appear. Get this crazy notion out of your head. Don't marry. It doesn't look to me as though your betrothed has any especial liking for you. Anything can happen in this world. For instance: I am not really such an ugly fellow, and yet it has been my experience to deceive husbands who were, by the Lord, no worse than myself. And you yourself – remember our Parisian friend, the Countess D**? It's useless to hope for female fidelity; happy is he who can look upon it with indifference! But you! With your ardent, brooding and suspicious nature, with your flat nose, your thick lips and your rough, woolly head – for you to hurl yourself into the dangers of marriage!'

'I thank you for your friendly advice,' interrupted Ibrahim coldly, 'but you know the saying: "It's not one person's affair to rock another's children"...'

'Take care, Ibrahim,' replied Korsakov, laughing, 'that one day you're not called upon to prove the truth of that – in the literal sense.'

In the meantime, the conversation in the next room was becoming heated.

'You'll kill her,' the old lady was saying. 'She can't stand the sight of him.'

'Well, judge for yourself,' her obstinate brother retorted. 'He has been coming here as her betrothed for a fortnight already, and he hasn't yet seen his bride-to-be. He may eventually begin to think that her illness is a mere invention, and that we are seeking only to delay matters in order to get rid of him somehow or other. And what will the Tsar say? Three times already he has sent for news of Natalya's health. You can say what you like, but I don't propose to quarrel with him.'

'Dear Lord above!' said Tatyana Afanassyevna. 'What will become of the unfortunate girl? At least allow me to prepare her for such a visit.'

Gavrila Afanassyevitch consented to this and returned to the drawing-room.

'The danger has passed, thank God!' he said to Ibrahim. 'Natalya is much better. Were it not for having to leave our dear guest Ivan Yegrafovitch here alone, I would take you upstairs for a glimpse of your betrothed.'

Korsakov congratulated Gavrila Afanassyevitch on Natalya's recovery, asked him not to worry on his account, assured him that he had to leave, and hurried into the hall without allowing his host to show him out.

Meanwhile, Tatyana Afanassyevna hastened to prepare the sick girl for the appearance of the dreaded visitor. Entering the bedroom, she sat down breathless by the side of the bed and took Natasha's hand, but before she had time to utter a single word the door opened. Natasha asked who it was.

The old lady felt faint and her whole body grew numb. Gavrila Afanassyevitch drew back the curtain, looked coldly at the patient and asked her how she was. The patient tried to smile but could not. She was struck by her father's stern expression and was seized by a feeling of anxiety. At that moment, it seemed to her that someone else was standing by the end of the bed. With an effort she raised her head and of a sudden recognised the Tsar's Moor. And then she remembered everything, and all the horror of her future came to her. But her exhausted frame received no perceptible shock. Natasha lowered her head to the pillow and closed her eyes, her heart beating painfully. Tatyana Afanassyevna made a sign to her brother that the patient wished to sleep, and they all quietly left the room, except for the servant-maid, who again sat down at the spinning-wheel.

The unhappy young beauty opened her eyes; seeing that no one was by her bedside, she called the servant-maid and sent her off to fetch the dwarf. But at that very moment a little old figure, round as a ball, rolled up to the bed. Lastochka (for so was the dwarf called) had followed Gavrila Afanassyevitch and Ibrahim upstairs as fast as her short legs could carry her and, faithful to that curiosity innate in all members of the fair sex, had hidden behind the door. Seeing her, Natasha sent the servant-maid away, and the dwarf sat down on a stool by the bedside.

Never had so small a body contained within it so much mental activity. She meddled in everything, knew everything and concerned herself with everything. In a sly, insinuating manner, she had managed to acquire the affection of her masters and the loathing of the rest of the household, over which she ruled in the most despotic fashion. Gavrila Afanassyevitch listened to her tales, complaints and petty requests; Tatyana Afanassyevna constantly sought her opinion and was guided by her advice; and Natasha had boundless affection for her and confided to her all the thoughts and emotions of her sixteen-year-old heart.

'Do you know, Lastochka,' she said, 'that my father proposes to marry me to the Moor?'

The dwarf sighed deeply, and her wrinkled face became more wrinkled than ever.

'Is there no hope?' continued Natasha. 'Won't my father take pity on me?'

The dwarf shook her cap.

'Won't my grandfather or aunt intercede on my behalf?'

'No, miss. While you were ill, the Moor succeeded in casting a spell over everybody. The master is out of his mind about him, the Prince raves about no one else, and Tatyana Afanassyevna is for ever saying: "It's a pity he's a Moor as we couldn't wish for a better suitor."'

'Oh my God, oh my God!' moaned poor Natasha.

'Don't be sad, my beauty,' said the dwarf, kissing her feeble hand. 'Even if you do become the Moor's wife, you'll still be able to do as you like. It's not the same as it was in the old days: husbands no longer keep their wives under lock and key. I have heard that the Moor is rich: your house will have everything you want – you'll be living in clover . . .'

'Poor Valerian,' said Natasha, but so softly that the dwarf could only guess what she had said, being unable to hear the words.

'That's just it, miss,' she said, lowering her voice mysteriously. 'If you thought less about the archer's orphan, you wouldn't have raved about him in your delirium, and your father wouldn't be angry.'

'What?' said the alarmed Natasha. 'I raved about Valerian and my father heard? And he was angry?'

'That's just the trouble,' the dwarf replied. 'If you were to ask him now not to marry you to the Moor, he would think that Valerian was the cause. There's nothing for it: you must yield to your father's wishes, and what will be, will be.'

Natasha did not utter a word in reply. The thought that her heart's secret was known to her father affected her imagination deeply. One hope remained to her: to die before the fulfilment of the hateful marriage. This thought consoled her. Weak and sad at heart, she resigned herself to her fate.

Chapter Seven

In the house of Gavrila Afanassyevitch, to the right of the hall, there was a narrow room with one small window. In it stood a plain bed covered with a blanket; in front of the bed was a small deal table, on which a tallow candle was burning and where lay some open sheets of music. An old blue uniform and an equally old three-cornered hat hung on the wall below a cheap, popular print of Charles XII on horseback, which was fastened to the wall by three nails. The notes of a flute sounded from this humble abode. The captive dancing-master, its lonely occupant, in a nightcap and a nankeen dressing-gown, was relieving the boredom of a winter's evening by playing some old Swedish marches, thereby recalling the gay times of his youth. Having devoted two full hours to this exercise, the Swede unpieced his flute, put it in its box and began to undress.

At that moment the latch on his door was raised, and a tall, good-looking young man in uniform entered the room.

The surprised Swede stood up before his unexpected visitor.

'You don't recognise me, Gustav Adamytch,' said the young visitor, his voice full of emotion. 'You don't remember the boy whom you taught the Swedish articles of war, and with whom you nearly caused a fire in this very room by firing off a child's cannon.'

Gustav Adamytch looked at him intently.

'Aaah!' he exclaimed at last, embracing him. 'How are you? What are you doing here? Sit down, you young scamp, and let's have a talk....'

1827

(Pushkin never completed this story.)

A Novel in Letters

1. *Lisa to Sasha*

You were, of course, my dear Sashenka, surprised by my unexpected departure for the country. I hasten to explain everything to you frankly. My state of dependence has always been burdensome to me. It is true that Avdotya Andreyevna brought me up on equal footing with her niece; but I was always the foster-child in her house, and you cannot imagine how many petty grievances are bound up with this name. There was much I had to put up with, many ways in which I had to give in, many things pretend not to see, while my pride meticulously took note of the faintest slight. My very equality with the Princess was a burden to me. When we appeared at a ball, dressed alike, I used to be vexed at not seeing a string of pearls around her neck. I felt that she was not wearing them in order not to be different from me, and this thoughtfulness affronted me. Can they suspect in me, I thought, envy or some such childish mean-spiritedness? However courteous the behaviour of men towards me, my pride was continually being hurt; their coolness or their friendliness, everything seemed to me disrespectful. In short, I was a miserable creature, and my naturally tender heart was becoming embittered. Have you noticed that all girls in ward with distant relatives, *demoiselles de compagnie* and such like, are usually either inferior servants or unbearable cranks? I respect the latter and excuse them with all my heart.

Exactly three weeks ago I received a letter from my poor grandmother. She complained of her loneliness and summoned me to her in the country. I decided to take advantage of this opportunity. With difficulty I wheedled Avdotya

Andreyevna into letting me go and had to promise to return to Petersburg in the winter; but I have no intention of keeping my word. Grandmother was exceedingly pleased to see me; she had not really expected me to come. Her tears moved me more than I can say. I have come to love her deeply. At one time she moved in society and she has retained much of the politeness of that time.

I am now living *at home,* I am my own mistress, and you will not believe what a veritable delight that is to me. I became used to country life immediately, and the absence of luxury is not at all strange to me. Ours is a dear little village: an old house on the hill, a garden, a pond, pine woods around. In the autumn and winter it is all a little sad, but in the spring and summer it should seem like an earthly paradise. We have few neighbours, and I have not yet seen anyone. I really do love the solitude, as in the elegies of your Lamartine.

Write to me, my angel, your letters will be a great comfort to me. Tell me about the balls you have attended and of our mutual acquaintances. Even if I have become a hermit, I have not entirely renounced the bustle of the world – news of it will be entertaining for me.

Pavlovskoye Village

2. *Sasha's Reply*

Dear Lisa,

Imagine my surprise when I learned of your departure for the country. Seeing Princess Olga alone, I thought that you were unwell and could not believe her words. The next day I receive your letter. Congratulations, my angel, on your new way of life. I am delighted that you like it. Your complaints about your previous condition of life moved me to tears, but they did seem to me to be too bitter. How can you compare yourself with foster-children and *demoiselles de compagnie?* Everyone knows that Olga's father was wholly indebted to yours, and that their friendship was as sacred as the closest relationship. You seemed to be content with your fate. I never suspected you of such touchiness. Confess: is there not some other, secret reason for your hurried departure? I suspect ... but you are too modest with me, and I am afraid of angering you with my blind guesses.

What can I say to you about Petersburg? We are still in the country, but almost everybody has already left. The balls begin in about two weeks' time. The weather is excellent. I walk a great deal. The other day we had some guests to dinner – and one of them asked if I had any news of you. He said that your absence at the balls is as noticeable as a broken string in a piano, and I completely agree with him. I only hope that this attack of misanthropy will not last long. Return, my angel, or I shall have no one this winter with whom to share my innocent observations, no one to whom to transmit the epigrams of my heart. Forgive me, my dear – consider and change your mind.

Krestovsky Island

3. *Lisa to Sasha*

Your letter has comforted me greatly. So vividly did it remind me of Petersburg that I seemed to hear your voice. How amusing your everlasting assumptions are! You suspect me of some deep, mysterious feelings, some unhappy love affair – is that not so? Calm yourself, my dear: you are mistaken. I resemble a heroine only in so far as I live in the depths of the country and pour out tea, like Clarissa Harlowe.

You say that you will have no one this winter to whom to pass on your satirical observations – but what is our correspondence for? Write to me about everything you notice. I repeat to you that I have not at all renounced the world, that everything connected with it continues to interest me. As evidence of this, I beg you to write and tell me who it is who finds my absence so noticeable? Not our amiable chatter-box, Alexey R——? I am sure that I have guessed ... My ears were always at his disposal, which is only what he wanted.

I have become acquainted with the *** family. The father is cheerful and hospitable, the mother a fat, jolly woman with a great passion for whist; the daughter, a slim, melan-choly girl of about seventeen, brought up on novels and fresh air. She spends her whole day in the garden or in the fields with a book in her hands, surrounded by yard dogs, talks about the weather in a sing-song voice and enthusiastically treats one to jam. I found a whole book-case filled with old novels at their house. I intend to read my way right through it and have started on Richardson. One must live in the country in order to be able to read about the much-praised *Clarissa*. Blessedly, I began with the translator's preface and, having noted his assurance that although the first six parts are dull, the last six will in full measure reward the patience of the reader, I bravely set about the task. I read the first, the second, the third volumes ... at last reach the sixth – dull beyond endurance. Well, I thought, now I shall be rewarded for my labour. And what? I read about Clarissa's death, the death of Lovelace, and that is the end. Each volume consisted of two parts, and I did not notice the changeover from the six dull parts to the six interesting ones.

Reading Richardson gave me cause for meditation. What a dreadful difference there is between the ideals of grand-mothers and granddaughters! What do Lovelace and Adolphe have in common? The role of women does not change, however. Clarissa, apart from her ceremonial curtsies, still resembles the heroine of the latest novels. Is it because, in men, the ways of appealing depend on fashion and the opinion of the day . . . whereas, for women, these things are based on feeling and nature, which are eternal.

You see: as usual, I am talkative with you. Don't you be chary, either, of written conversation. Write to me as often and as much as you can: you cannot imagine what waiting for the post means in the country. Looking forward to a ball cannot compare with it.

4. *Sasha's Reply*

You are mistaken, dear Lisa. In order to humble your pride, I declare that R— does not notice your absence at all. He has attached himself to Lady Pelham, an Englishwoman who has arrived recently, and he never leaves her side. To his discourses she replies with a look of innocent amazement and the tiny exclamation: 'Oh!' . . . and he is in raptures. You should know that your devoted Vladimir ** asked me about you, and that he mourns for you with all his heart. Are you satisfied? I think you are, very satisfied; and, as is my wont, I take the liberty of supposing that you have already guessed as much yourself. Joking aside, ** is very taken with you. In your place, I should lead him on as far as possible. So what, he is an excellent suitor. Why not marry him? – you would live on the English Embankment, give Saturday evening parties, and every morning you would drop in on me. Stop making a fool of yourself, my angel, come back to us and marry **.

A few days ago, there was a ball at K**'s. There was a big crowd of people. We danced until five in the morning. K. V. was dressed very simply: a white crêpe dress, without even a garland, but on her head and around her neck diamonds worth half a million. That's all! As usual, Z. was dressed most amusingly. Where does she get her clothes from? On her dress were sewn, not flowers, but some kind of dried mushrooms. Did you send them to her, my angel, from the country? Vladimir ** did not dance. He is going on leave. The Ss were there (probably the first to arrive), sat up the whole night without dancing and were the last to leave. The older girl, it seems, was wearing rouge – high time . . . The ball was a great success. The men were dissatisfied with the supper, but they must always be dissatisfied with something. For me it was all very gay, even though I danced the cotillon with an unbearable diplomat, St —, who, to his natural stupidity, has added an absent-mindedness picked up in Madrid.

Thank you, my heart, for your report on Richardson. Now I have some understanding of him. With my impatience, I cannot hope to read him right through; even with Walter Scott, I find the number of pages excessive.

By the way: it seems that the romance between Yelena N. and Count L. is finishing – at least, he is in such low spirits, and she is giving herself such airs, that it is probable that the wedding has been fixed. Forgive me, my love, are you pleased with my chatter today?

5. *Lisa to Sasha*

No, my dear matchmaker, I do not think of leaving the country and returning to you for my own wedding. I confess frankly that I liked Vladimir **, but at no time did I consider marrying him. He is an aristocrat, and I a humble democrat. I hasten to explain, and observe with pride, that, like the true heroine of a novel, I belong by birth to the oldest Russian nobility, while my knight is the grandson of a bearded millionaire. But you know what our aristocracy means. However, whatever he is, ** is a man of the world; I could perhaps have pleased him, but he is not going to sacrifice for me a rich bride with useful relatives. If I ever do marry, I shall choose some forty-year-old landowner from here. He will occupy himself with his sugar-factory, I with the household – and I shall be quite happy not dancing at Count K's ball, and not giving Saturday evenings at home on the English Embankment.

With us, it is winter: in the country, *c'est un événement*. It altogether changes our way of life. Solitary walks cease, we hear the tinkling of little bells, hunters come out with their dogs; with the first snow everything becomes clearer and gayer. I in no way expected it. Winter in the country used to frighten me; but everything in the world has its bright side.

I have become better acquainted with Mashenka ***, and have grown fond of her; there is much that is good in her, much that is original. I learned to my surprise that ** is a near relative of the family. Mashenka has not seen him for seven years, but she is enchanted with him. He spent one summer with them, and Mashenka is constantly recounting to me all the details of his life at that time. Reading copies of her novels, I come across his faint, pencilled comments in the margins; it is clear that he was a child then. He was astonished by thoughts and feelings at which now, of course, he would laugh; at least, a pure and sensitive soul is discernible. I read a great deal. You cannot imagine how strange it is to read, in 1829, a novel written in 1775. It seems as if, suddenly from our drawing-room, we enter an ancient hall, upholstered with damask, seat ourselves on satin-covered, down armchairs, see around us strange dresses but familiar faces, and recognise in them our uncles and grandmothers, but grown younger. In the main, these novels have no other virtue. The action is interesting, the plot thoroughly complicated; but Belcourt's language is oblique, and Charlotte's answers are insincere. A clever man could have adopted a set plan and set characters, have amended the style and the absurdities, have filled out what was left unsaid – and an excellent and original novel would have emerged. Tell my ungrateful R— this from me. Stop him wasting his intelligence in conversations with Englishwomen! Get him to embroider new designs on the old canvas, and to give us, in a small frame, a picture of society and its members whom he knows so well.

Masha has a good knowledge of Russian literature – in general, people here are more concerned with letters than in Petersburg. Here they subscribe to magazines, take a lively interest in their wrangles, believing both sides in turn, and getting angry on behalf of their favourite writer if he is criticised. Now I understand why Vyazemsky and Pushkin like provincial girls so much. They are their true public. I have started looking at magazines, and am reading the reviews in the *Herald of Europe*, but their platitudes and servility have struck me as revolting: it is comic to see seminarists pompously reproaching, for immorality and indecency, works which all of us read – us, Petersburg's sensitives!

6. *Lisa to Sasha*

My dear, I cannot pretend any longer, I need the help and advice of a friend. **, the one I ran away from, of whom I am afraid as of misfortune, is here. What shall I do? My head is in a whirl, I am lost, for God's sake decide what I should do. I will tell you everything . . .

Did you notice how, last winter, he never left my side? He did not come to our house, but we met everywhere. In vain did I arm myself with coolness, even with an appearance of disdain, but I could not get rid of him. At balls, he always knew how to find the place next to mine; out walking, we were constantly meeting; at the theatre, his lorgnette was forever focused on our box.

At first my self-esteem was flattered. Perhaps I allowed him to observe this too clearly. At any rate, assuming new rights, he spoke to me at every moment about his feelings, now expressing his jealousy, now complaining. I thought with horror: whatever will this lead to ... and acknowledged with despair his power over my soul. I left Petersburg, thinking to put a stop to this evil at the very beginning. My resoluteness, the belief that I was fulfilling my duty, comforted my heart, and I began to think about him with more indifference and with less bitterness. Suddenly I see him.

I see him. It was ***'s name-day yesterday. I arrived for dinner, entered the drawing-room, crowded with guests. Men in Uhlan uniforms, ladies encircled me, and I kissed everyone all round. Unaware of anyone in particular, I sat down beside the hostess and looked around. ** was in front of me. I was stupefied. He said a few words to me with an expression of such tenderness, such sincere joy, that I had not the strength to conceal either my confusion or my pleasure.

We moved to the table. He sat opposite me; I did not dare to glance at him, but noticed that his eyes were all the time fixed on me. He was silent and distracted. At any other time, the general desire to attract the attention of a newly-arrived Guards officer would have entertained me greatly: the uneasiness of the young ladies, the awkwardness of the men and their guffaws at their own jokes, and all the while the polite coolness and total unconcern of the guest. After dinner he came up to me. Conscious of the necessity to say something, I asked him quite irrelevantly whether he had come our way on business. 'I have come for one business, on which depends the happiness of my life,' he replied in a low voice and left me at once. He sat down to play Boston with three old ladies (including my grandmother), and I went upstairs to Mashenka, where I lay down until evening under the pretext of a headache. In truth, I was worse than unwell. Mashenka did not leave me. She is in raptures with **. He will stay with them for a month or longer. She will be with him all day long. She is in love with him, for sure – and may God grant that he will fall in love with her. She is slim and strange – just what men need.

What shall I do, my dear? Here, it is impossible to escape his pursuit. Already, he has succeeded in enchanting my grandmother. He is coming to visit us and, again, there will be confessions, complaints, vows, *and to what end?* He will secure my love and my confession – and then reflect on the disadvantages of marriage and find some excuse for going away and leaving me ... What a terrible future! For God's sake, stretch out your hand to me: I am sinking.

7. Sasha's Reply

What it is to relieve one's heart with a full confession! You should have done so long ago, my angel! From where came your desire not to confess to me something I have known for a long time: ** and you are in love with one another—what is wrong with that? Good luck to you. You have a gift for looking at things from God knows what angle. You are asking for misfortune—be careful that you do not bring it upon yourself. Why should you not marry **? Where are the insuperable obstacles? He is rich, and you are poor? Nonsense! He is rich enough for two—what more do you want? He is an aristocrat; and you, by name and upbringing, are surely also an aristocrat?

Not long ago there was an argument on the subject of ladies in high society. I heard that R— once declared himself on the side of the aristocracy because they wear better shoes. So is it not clear that you are an aristocrat from head to feet?

Forgive me, my angel, but your pathetic letter has made me laugh. ** went to the country in order to see you. What a horror! You are perishing, you demand my advice. You really have become quite the provincial heroine! My advice is to marry as soon as possible in your wooden church, and to return to us in time to appear as Fornarina in the tableaux which are being devised at S**'s. Joking aside, the conduct of your knight has moved me. Of course, in the old days, a lover, in order to be regarded with favour, went off to the Holy Land to fight for three years; but, in these days, to travel five hundred versts from Petersburg for the sake of seeing the mistress of his heart – surely that signifies much? ** deserves to be rewarded.

8. *Vladimir ** to His Friend*

Do me a favour, spread the rumour that I am on my death-bed. I intend to extend my leave, but wish at all costs to observe the decencies. I have been living in the country for two weeks already, but how time has flown. I am taking a rest from Petersburg life, of which I was terribly tired. Not to love the country is forgivable in *une jeune fille* just released from her cell or in an eighteen-year-old cadet. Petersburg is an ante-room, Moscow the housemaids' quarters, and the country is our study. A decent man, of necessity, passes through the ante-room, rarely looks into the housemaids' quarters, but sits in his study. That is how I shall end up. I shall retire, marry, and go off to my village in the Saratov district. The profession of a landowner is not unlike that of the Service. To be concerned with the management of three thousand souls, whose well-being depends entirely upon us, is more important than commanding a platoon or transcribing a diplomatic dispatch.

The state of neglect in which we leave our peasants is unforgivable. The more rights we have over them, the greater must be our responsibility towards them. We leave them to the mercy of a dishonest steward, who oppresses them and robs us. We mortgage our future incomes and ruin ourselves, and old age catches us worrying and in want.

This is the cause of the swift decline of our nobility: the grandfather was rich, the son is needy, the grandson will go begging. Ancient families fall into decay; new ones arise and in the third generation go under again. Fortunes are merged, and not one family knows who its forebears were. To what will such political materialism lead? I do not know. But it is time to put a stop to it.

I was never able to see without regret the decline of our historic families. No-one among us, beginning with those who belong to them, thinks much of them. What pride in recollection can you expect from people at whose houses a monument may be inscribed: To Citizen Minin and Prince Pozharsky? Which Prince Pozharsky? What does it signify, Citizen Minin? There was a courtier, Prince Dmitri Mikhailovitch Pozharsky, and there was a Kozma Minitch Sukhoruky, a commoner elected by the whole state. But our Fatherland has forgotten even the real names of its saviours. The past does not exist for us. A miserable people!

A gentry stemming from meritorious bureaucrats cannot replace an hereditary aristocracy, whose family traditions ought to be part of our national heritage. But what sort of family traditions would one get from the children of a collegiate assessor?

Speaking on behalf of the aristocracy, I do not pose as an English lord, like the diplomat Severin, grandson of a tailor and a cook; my descent, although I am not ashamed of it, does not give me any such right. But I am in agreement with La Bruyère: *Affecter le mépris de la naissance est un ridicule dans le parvenu et une lâcheté dans le gentilhomme.*

All this I have thought out, living in a strange village and observing how the smallholding gentry manage their affairs. These gentlemen are not in the Service and are themselves concerned in the management of their estates, but I must say: may God let them ruin themselves as we did! What savagery! For them the times of Fonvizin have not yet passed. Prostakovs and Skotinins still flourish among them!

This, however, does not apply to the relative with whom I am staying. He is a very kind man, his wife is a very kind woman, his daughter is a very kind girl. You can see that I, too, have become very kind. Indeed, since I have been in the country, I have become most benevolent and forbearing – the result of my patriarchal life and the presence of Lisa ***. I was downright bored without her. I came to persuade her to return to Petersburg. Our first meeting was magnificent. It was my aunt's name-day. The whole neighbourhood was there; and Lisa appeared – she could hardly believe her eyes when she saw me. She was unable not to acknowledge to herself that it was solely on her account that I came here; at any rate, I endeavoured to make her feel that. In this my success surpassed my expectations (which means much). The old ladies are enchanted with me, and the women cling to me 'because they are patriots'. The men are extremely displeased by my *fatuité indolente*, which is still a novelty here. They rage the more because I behave with the utmost courtesy and decorousness, and they do not understand at all, although they feel me to be an impudent fellow, what exactly my impudence consists of. Good-bye. What are our lot doing? *Servitor di tutti quanti.* Write to me at the village of **.

9. *The Friend's Reply*

I have executed your commission. Yesterday I announced at the theatre that you had been taken ill with a nervous fever, and that you are probably no longer of this world – so enjoy life while you are still not risen from the dead.

Your moral meditations on the subject of estate management make me happy for you. This sums it up:

> *Un homme sans peur et sans reproche,*
> *Qui n'est ni roi, ni duc, ni comte aussi.*

The state of the Russian landowner, it seems to me, is most enviable.

The existence of ranks in Russia is essential, if only for posting-stations where, without them, horses would be unobtainable.

Having taken up these important deliberations, I quite forgot that you are now no longer concerned with them – you are occupied with your Lisa. Why do you play the part of Faublas, and for ever spend your time getting mixed up with women? It is not worthy of you. In this respect you have lagged behind the times, and act like a *ci-devant,* hoarse-voiced Guardee of 1807. So far this is a defect, but soon you will be funnier than General G**. Is it not wiser to accustom oneself in good time to the severity of mature years, and voluntarily withdraw from one's fading youth? I know that I preach in vain, but that is my mission.

All your friends send you greetings and very much regret your premature death – including, your former friend, who has returned from Rome in love with the Pope. How typical of her this is, and how it must excite you! Will you not return for the sake of rivalry *cum servo servorum Dei?* That would be just like you. I shall await you daily.

10. *Vladimir ** to His Friend*

Your admonishments are unjust. It is not I, but you who have lagged behind the times – by ten whole years. Your speculative and consequential judgements belong to the year 1818. At that time, strictness of principle and political economy were the fashion. We attended balls without removing our swords, it was considered indecent for us to dance, and we had no time for the ladies. I have the honour to report to you that all that has now changed. The French quadrille has replaced Adam Smith, we go through life and enjoy ourselves as best we can. I follow the spirit of the times; but you are static, you are *ci-devant, un homme stéréotype*. Why do you wish to lead a sedentary life alone on the Opposition benches? I hope that Z. will put you on the true road; I entrust you to her Vatican coquetry. As for me, I have entirely given myself over to the patriarchal way of life; I go to bed at ten o'clock in the evening, ride over the fresh snow with the local landowners, play Boston for penny stakes with the old ladies, and get angry when I lose. Lisa I see every day – and fall hourly more in love with her. There is much that is captivating about her. That calm, generous composure in the treatment of others – a charm of Petersburg high society; and, all the while, something lively, forbearing, well-born (as her grandmother puts it); nothing harsh or cruel in her opinions; she does not shrink before new experiences, like a child being given rhubarb. She listens and understands – a rare quality in our women. I was often amazed at the dull-wittedness or impurity of imagination of otherwise very agreeable ladies. Frequently they take for a coarse epigram or a trivial impropriety a subtle joke or a poetical greeting. In such a case, the look of coldness they assume is so destructively repelling that the most passionate love cannot stand up against it.

I experienced this with Yelena ***, with whom I was madly in love. I spoke some tenderness to her; she took it for coarseness, and complained about me to her friend. I was greatly disillusioned. Besides Lisa, I have Mashenka *** to amuse me. She is charming. These girls who have grown up under apple-trees and among hay-stacks, raised by nannies and by nature, are far nicer than our monotonous beauties who, until their wedding-day, follow the opinions of their mothers and, after it, those of their husbands.

Good-bye, my dear. What news is there in the world? Announce to everyone that I have at last taken up poetry. The other day I composed an inscription for Princess Olga's portrait (for which Lisa scolded me very charmingly): 'Stupid as truth, boring as perfection.' Or is 'Boring as truth, stupid as perfection' better?

They both indicate a thought. Ask V. to think up the first verse and from now on consider me a poet.

1829

(Pushkin never completed this story.)

The Tales of the Late Ivan Petrovitch Belkin

> Mme Prostakova: Indeed, 'tis so, sir, he's
> always been a one for
> tales, ever since he were a boy.
> Skotinin: Mitrofan takes after me.
>
> FONVIZIN

From the Editor

Having taken upon ourselves the task of publishing the tales of I. P. Belkin, herewith presented to the reader, we thought it desirable to preface them with a brief account of the life of the late author, and thereby satisfy in part the justifiable curiosity of those who treasure our native literature. It was to this end that we approached Marya Alexandrovna Trafilina, next of kin and heiress to Ivan Petrovitch Belkin. Unfortunately, she was unable to provide us with any information at all about the deceased, never having had the slightest acquaintance with him. However, she advised us in this regard to seek the assistance of a certain worthy gentleman, a former friend of Ivan Petrovitch. We followed this advice and, in answer to our letter, we received the following valuable reply. We print it without alteration or comment, as a precious monument to a noble understanding and a touching friendship, and at the same time as a perfectly adequate biographical record:

'My dear Sir,
    'I had the honour of receiving on the 23rd day of this month your esteemed letter of the 15th, in which you express your desire for detailed information concerning the birth and death, the service, the family circumstances, the occupations and disposition of the late Ivan Petrovitch Belkin, my erstwhile sincere friend and neighbour in the country. It is with the greatest pleasure that I undertake to fulfil your

wishes, and I am sending you, my dear Sir, all that I can remember of his conversation, and also some observations of my own.

'Ivan Petrovitch Belkin was born of honourable parentage in the year 1798 at the village of Goryukhino. His late father, Second-Major Pyotr Ivanovitch Belkin, married a young lady of the Trafilin family, Pelageya Gavrilovna. He was not a rich man, but he was prudent and he conducted the affairs of his estate with the utmost competence. His son received his early education at the hands of the village sexton, and it is to this worthy man that he seemed to owe his love of reading and his taste for Russian literature. In 1815, he joined a chasseur regiment (I do not recall the number), in which he remained throughout his service until the year 1823. The death of his parents within a short time of each other forced him to resign his commission and return to his hereditary estate at the village of Goryukhino.

'Taking over the management of his estate, Ivan Petrovitch, owing to his inexperience and soft-heartedness, soon let it fall into neglect, and allowed the strict discipline his late father had maintained to relax. Dismissing his efficient and conscientious village-elder, with whom the peasants (as is their wont) were dissatisfied, he handed over the management of his estate to his old housekeeper, who had gained his confidence through her skill in telling stories. This stupid old woman had never been able to tell the difference between a twenty-five-rouble note and a fifty-rouble note; the peasants, many of whom she knew intimately, stood in no fear of her at all. They chose a new village-elder, who connived with them to cheat their master, and indulged them to such an extent that Ivan Petrovitch was forced to abolish the system of *corvée,* and impose an extremely low quit-rent in its place; even so, the peasants took advantage of their master's weakness and managed to wheedle all sorts of artful exemptions out of him during the first year, and in the year following, more than two-thirds of their payments were made in kind – nuts, bilberries and the like, and even then there were arrears.

'As a friend of Ivan Petrovitch's late father, I saw it as my duty to offer my advice to his son, and on several occasions volunteered to re-establish the former order, which he had been unable to maintain by himself. It was with this in mind that I rode over to see him one day. I demanded the household accounts, sent for that rascal of a village-elder, and began to inspect them in the presence of Ivan Petrovitch. The young landowner at first followed my investigations with the greatest possible attention and care, but as soon as it appeared from the accounts that in the previous two years the number of peasants had increased while that of the poultry and cattle belonging to the estate had appreciably decreased, Ivan Petrovitch professed himself satisfied by these preliminary reckonings and would listen to me no further; and at the very moment I had thrown that rogue of an elder into the utmost confusion by my stern questioning and investigation and had reduced him to complete silence, I heard, to my considerable vexation, the sound of Ivan Petrovitch snoring loudly in his chair. Thereafter, I ceased to interfere in the affairs of his estate and left such matters (as he did himself) to the will of the Almighty.

'Our friendly relations, however, were by no means

impaired by all this, because, while deploring his weakness and that ruinous negligence which is so common nowadays among our young gentry, I had a sincere liking for Ivan Petrovitch. Indeed, it would have been impossible not to have liked so gentle and honest a young man. For his part, Ivan Petrovitch showed me the respect due to my years, and was warmly attached to me. Up to the time of his death, we met almost daily, and he valued my simple conversation, although, as regards habits, manner of thinking and disposition, we had very little in common.

'Ivan Petrovitch led a moderate life, and avoided all forms of excess; I never once saw him the slightest bit tipsy (a perfect miracle this, in our part of the world); he had a great inclination towards the opposite sex, but in fact was as bashful as a young girl.'

[Here follows an anecdote which we omit as superfluous; at the same time, however, we should like to assure the reader that it contains nothing injurious to the memory of Ivan Petrovitch Belkin. – *The Editor.*]

'Apart from the tales to which you refer in your letter, Ivan Petrovitch left behind a quantity of manuscripts, some of which I have in my possession, and some of which his former housekeeper has used for various domestic purposes. For example, last winter, all the windows in her wing of the house were pasted up with the first part of a novel, which he never completed. It seems that the above-mentioned tales were his first attempts at writing. Ivan Petrovitch himself stated that the greater part of them were true and related to him by various persons. The names of almost all the characters, however, were invented by Ivan Petrovitch himself; those of the hamlets and villages have been borrowed from this district, my own village being mentioned somewhere. This was not out of any evil intention, but merely want of imagination.'

[Indeed, each of the tales in Mr Belkin's manuscript bears the inscription, in the author's own handwriting: 'Related to me by So-and-So' (rank or title, and initials). For the curious among our readers, we quote the following: 'The Postmaster' was told to him by Titular Councillor A. G. N.; 'The Shot' by Lieut.-Colonel I. L. P.; 'The Undertaker' by a steward, B.V., and 'The Blizzard' and 'Peasant-Lady' by a young lady, K. I. T. – *The Editor*.]

'In the autumn of the year 1828, Ivan Petrovitch caught an extremely severe cold which developed into a fever, and he died, despite the indefatigable efforts of our local doctor, a man of great skill, particularly in the treatment of chronic diseases such as corns and the like. Ivan Petrovitch passed away in my arms in his thirtieth year, and he was buried next to his parents in the graveyard of the village of Goryukhino.

'Ivan Petrovitch was of medium height, and he had grey eyes, fair hair and a straight nose; his face was lean and of light complexion.

'And that, my dear Sir, is all I have been able to recall of the life, occupations, disposition and physical appearance of my late friend and neighbour. However, should you see fit to make use of any part of my letter, I would ask you with the utmost respect to refrain from mentioning my name, for although I greatly respect and admire men of letters, I have no wish to be counted among them; indeed, I think that would be indecorous in a man of my years.

'With sincere respect, etc., I remain . . .'

16th November, 1830
Village of Nenaradovo

Considering it our duty to respect the wishes of our late author's friend, we convey our deepest thanks to him for the information that he has provided, and trust that our readers will appreciate his sincerity and kindness.

A.P.

The Shot

I

And so we duelled.
BARATYNSKY

I swore to kill him — fairly, in a duel.
(It was my turn to shoot.)
Evening on Bivouac

We were stationed in the small town of ***. The life of an army officer is familiar to everyone. In the morning, drill and riding-school; dinner with the Commanding Officer or at some Jewish inn; punch and cards in the evening. There was not a single house open to us in *** – nor was there a single marriageable young lady. We used to meet in one another's rooms, where all we had to look at was each other's uniform.

There was only one man in our circle who was not a soldier. He was about thirty-five, which made us think of him as an old man. His experience made him very superior; and his habitual moroseness, his stern disposition and his withering tongue created a strong impression on our young minds. The facts of his life were somewhat mysterious; he seemed to be a Russian, and yet he had a foreign name. At one time or other he had served in the Hussars, with some success; nobody knew the reasons that had prompted him to resign his commission and settle down in that wretched little town, where he lived at the same time poorly and extravagantly, always going about on foot in a black threadbare frock-coat, and yet keeping open house for all the officers in our regiment. Admittedly, his dinners consisted only of two or three courses, and were prepared by an ex-soldier, but the champagne flowed like water. Nobody knew what his circumstances were, or what his income was, and nobody dared inquire. He possessed a number of books, mostly on military subjects or novels. He was always willing to lend these, and he never asked for them back; equally, he never returned a book that he had borrowed. His main occupation was pistol-shooting. The walls of his room were riddled with bullet-holes and resembled a honey-comb. His valuable collection of pistols was the only luxury in the wretched clay-walled cottage in which he lived. The skill which he had acquired with this weapon was incredible, and if he had proposed shooting a pear off somebody's cap, there was not a single man in our regiment who would have hesitated to offer his own head. Conversation among us frequently turned to duelling; Silvio (as I propose to call him) never took any part in it. When asked whether he had ever fought a duel, he replied curtly that he had but entered into no details, and it was evident that he found such questions disagreeable. We came to the conclusion that there lay on his conscience the memory of some unfortunate victim of his terrifying skill. It certainly never entered our heads to suspect him of anything like cowardice. There are some people whose very appearance forbids such suspicions. But then a chance event took place which astonished us all.

One day about ten of us officers were dining at Silvio's. We had drunk the usual amount – that is, a very great deal. After dinner we asked our host to keep bank for us. For a long time he refused, for he rarely played cards; at last, however, he ordered the cards to be brought, and after pouring about fifty golden ducats on to the table he sat down to deal. We gathered around him, and the game began. It was Silvio's custom to maintain absolute silence while he played, never entering into argument or explanation. If a player happened to make a miscalculation, Silvio either paid up the difference immediately or recorded the surplus. We were all aware of this and made no attempt to interfere with his way of playing. But among us was an officer only recently transferred to the regiment. While playing, this officer absent-mindedly doubled the stake. Silvio took up the chalk and, as was his habit, corrected the score. The officer, thinking that Silvio had made a mistake, began to argue. Silvio continued to deal in silence. The officer, losing patience, picked up the brush and corrected what he considered to be the mistake. Silvio took up the chalk and again righted the score. The officer, heated by the wine, the gambling and the laughter of his comrades, considered himself deeply insulted, and in his rage he seized a brass candlestick from the table and hurled it at Silvio, who only just managed to avoid being hit. We were acutely embarrassed. Silvio rose, white with anger and, his eyes flashing, said: 'Sir, be so good as to leave, and thank God that this happened in my house.'

None of us had the slightest doubt as to what would follow, and we already looked upon our new comrade as a dead man. The officer left Silvio's house, saying that he was ready to answer for the insult at the convenience of the gentleman in control of the bank. We continued to play for a few more minutes, but, sensing that our host was no longer in the mood, we withdrew one after another, and dispersed to our various quarters, talking of the vacancy that could shortly be expected in the regiment.

At riding-school the following day we were already asking

one another whether the unfortunate lieutenant was still alive when he suddenly appeared among us. We put the same question to him. He replied that as yet he had heard nothing from Silvio. This astonished us. We went to see Silvio and found him firing shot after shot at an ace pasted on the gate. He received us as usual, making no mention of the incident of the previous evening. Three days went by, and the lieutenant was still alive. Was it possible, we wondered in amazement, that Silvio was not proposing to fight? Silvio did not fight. He contented himself with a very brief explanation and made peace with the lieutenant.

This lowered him greatly in the eyes of us young men. Lack of courage is the last thing to be forgiven by the young, who as a rule regard valour as the foremost of human virtues, and as an excuse for every conceivable vice. However, little by little, the affair was forgotten and Silvio regained his former influence.

I alone could not feel the same about him. Endowed by nature with a romantic imagination, I had been more attached than the others to this man whose life was such a mystery, and whom I regarded as the hero of some strange tale. He liked me; at least with me alone he would drop his usual sharp tone and talk of various subjects simply and with unaccustomed charm. But after that unfortunate evening I never ceased to be conscious that his honour had been stained and that it remained so by his own choice. I could not treat him as before. I was ashamed to meet his eyes. Silvio was too intelligent and experienced not to notice this and to guess its cause. It seemed to pain him. At least, on one or two occasions I noticed that he wanted to explain matters to me; but I avoided such encounters and Silvio steered clear of me. Thenceforward I saw him only in the company of my comrades, and our former confidential talks ceased.

The distractions of the capital prevent its inhabitants from having any conception of many sensations that are only too familiar to the inhabitants of villages or small towns; such as, for example, that of waiting for the day on which the post arrives. On Tuesdays and Fridays our regimental office was always filled with officers, expecting money, letters or newspapers. Parcels and letters were usually unsealed on the spot and news exchanged, so that the office always presented a very lively scene. Silvio, whose letters were sent through the regiment, was usually also to be found there. One day he was handed a letter which he tore open with extraordinary impatience. His eyes gleamed as he read swiftly through the contents. The officers, each concerned with his own letters, noticed nothing.

'Gentlemen,' he said to them, 'circumstances demand my immediate departure; I must leave tonight. I trust you will not refuse to dine with me for the last time. I shall expect you too,' he continued, addressing me. 'Without fail!'

With these words he rushed out of the office. The rest of us, after agreeing to meet at Silvio's, went our separate ways.

I arrived at Silvio's house at the appointed time and found almost the entire regiment there. All his things were already packed; nothing remained but the bare, bullet-riddled walls. We sat down at the table; our host was in exceedingly good spirits, and his gaiety quickly spread to the rest of us. Corks popped without end, our glasses never ceased to foam and hiss, and with the utmost warmth we wished our departing host a good journey and every success. It was already late in the evening when we rose from the table. As we sorted out our caps, Silvio bade farewell to each of us; just as I was about to leave, he took me by the arm and stopped me.

'I must talk to you,' he said softly.

I stayed behind.

The guests had all gone. The two of us were alone; we sat down opposite each other and lit our pipes in silence. Silvio seemed preoccupied; all trace of his compulsive gaiety had vanished. The grim pallor of his face, his flashing eyes, and the thick smoke issuing from his mouth made him look like the Devil incarnate. Several minutes passed; at last, Silvio broke the silence.

'We shall probably never see each other again,' he said. 'However, before we part, I should like to talk to you. You may have noticed that I don't really care what other people think of me, but you I like, and it would pain me to leave you under a false impression.'

He stopped and began to refill his pipe; I said nothing, and averted my eyes.

'You thought it strange,' he continued, 'that I did not demand satisfaction from that drunken madcap R**. You will agree that with choice of weapons I held his life in my hands, and that my own was scarcely in danger at all. I could make you believe that my moderation was due to sheer magnanimity, but I will not lie to you. If I could have punished R** without endangering my own life in any way at all, I should never have pardoned him.'

I looked at Silvio in astonishment. Such a confession as this left me completely dumbfounded. Silvio continued:

'The truth is that I have no right to risk my life. Six years ago I received a slap in the face, and my enemy is still alive.'

My curiosity was strongly aroused.

'And you didn't fight him?' I asked. 'Perhaps circumstances separated you?'

'I did fight him,' answered Silvio, 'and I'll show you a souvenir of our duel.'

Silvio rose from his chair and took from a cardboard box a braided red cap with a gold tassel (what the French call a *bonnet de police*). He put it on; it could be seen that a bullet had penetrated it about two inches above the forehead.

'You know already,' continued Silvio, 'that I served in the

*** Hussar regiment. And you understand my temperament: I've always been used to taking first place in everything; it's been a kind of mania of mine ever since I was a boy. Wild behaviour was the fashion in our day, and in the army I was the biggest fire-eater of them all. We used to boast of our drunkenness, and I once outdrank the famous Burtsov, celebrated by Denis Davydov in his poems. Duels were constant occurrences in our regiment; in all of them I had to be either a second or an active participant. Commanding officers came and went, and I was looked upon as a necessary evil by all of them, but my comrades worshipped me.

'I was calmly (or not so calmly) enjoying my reputation when a young man from a rich and distinguished family (I won't mention the name) joined up with the regiment. Never in my life have I met anyone so brilliant or so blessed by fate. Just imagine – youth, intelligence, good looks, boundless gaiety, reckless courage, a great name, an inexhaustible supply of money – which he never kept track of and which never ran out – and then imagine the effect he was bound to have on us. My supremacy was shaken. Fascinated by my reputation, he began to seek my friendship, but I acted coldly towards him, and without thinking any the worse of me he avoided my company. I conceived a hatred for him. His successes in the regiment and in the society of ladies drove me to utter desperation. I tried to pick a quarrel with him; he could match my epigrams with epigrams of his own, which always struck me as wittier and more spontaneous than mine, and which, needless to say, were incomparably more amusing; he jested, while I seethed. Finally, however, at a ball given by a Polish landowner, seeing him as the object of all the ladies' attention, and in particular that of the hostess, with whom I was having an affair at the time, I went up to him and whispered something crass in his ear. He flared up and struck me in the face. Our hands flew to our swords; the ladies fainted; we were separated, and that very night we went out to fight a duel.

'Dawn was breaking. I stood at the appointed spot with my three seconds and awaited my opponent with indescribable impatience. It was spring and the sun was already beginning to make itself felt. I saw him in the distance. He was on foot, his uniform-coat draped over his sword, accompanied by one second. We went to meet him. He approached, carrying his cap which was full of cherries. The seconds measured out twelve paces. I was to shoot first, but I was so carried away by fury that I could not rely on the steadiness of my hand, and so, in order to give myself time to cool down, I yielded first shot to him; my opponent, however, would not agree to this. We decided to draw lots; the winning number fell to him, ever fortune's favourite. He took aim and his bullet went through my cap. It was my turn. At last I held his life in my hands. I gazed at him eagerly, trying to detect the faintest trace of uneasiness in him. He stood within pistol range, picking ripe cherries from his cap and spitting out the stones so that they almost fell at my feet. His indifference infuriated me.

'What's the use, I thought, of taking his life when he sets no store by it? A wicked thought flashed through my mind. I lowered my pistol.

'"You do not seem to be in the mood for death," I said to him. "Do please finish your breakfast; I should hate to disturb you."

'"You would not be disturbing me in the least,"he replied. "Be so good as to fire ... or if you'd prefer not, just as you please ... The next shot is yours; I shall always be at your service."

'I turned to my seconds, informed them that I did not wish to shoot at that moment, and with that the duel ended.

'I resigned my commission and retired to this small town.

Since that time, not a single day has passed without my thinking of revenge. And now my chance has come . . .'

Silvio took the letter that he had received that morning from his pocket and handed it to me to read. Someone, his business agent I believe, had written to him from Moscow with the news that a 'certain person' had announced his engagement to a beautiful young lady.

'You will guess who this "certain person" is,' said Silvio. 'I am going to Moscow. We shall see whether he faces death with the same indifference on the eve of his wedding as when he faced it eating a capful of cherries!'

With these words Silvio rose, flung his cap to the floor, and began to walk up and down the room like a caged tiger. I had listened to him with bated breath, strange, conflicting emotions stirring within me.

A servant entered and announced that the horses were ready. Silvio grasped my hand tightly; we embraced. He climbed on to the buggy, already loaded with his two trunks, one containing his pistols and the other his personal belongings. We bade each other farewell once more, and the horses galloped off.

II

Several years passed, and domestic circumstances forced me to settle in a poor little village in the district of N**. Busy as I was with the management of my estate, I never ceased to sigh for my former noisy and carefree life. The hardest thing of all was having to accustom myself to spending the spring and winter evenings in complete solitude. I managed somehow or other to while away the time until dinner, by conversing with the village-elder, driving around to see how the work was going, or visiting some new project on the estate; but as soon as dusk began to fall I hadn't the least idea what to do with myself. The contents of the small number of books I had unearthed from the cupboards and store-room I already knew by heart. All the stories that the housekeeper, Kirilovna, could remember had been related to me over and over again. The songs of the women-folk depressed me. I took to drinking unsweetened liqueurs, but they gave me a headache; moreover, I confess that I was afraid of becoming one of those who *drink to drown their sorrows* – of all types of drunkenness the most pitiable, and I have seen many examples of it in our district. The only near neighbours I had were two or three such wretches, whose conversation consisted for the most part of hiccoughs and sighs. Solitude was preferable to their company.

Four versts from my house was the wealthy estate of Countess B**, but, apart from the steward, nobody lived there. The Countess had visited her estate only once, during the first year of her marriage, and even then had not stayed much longer than a month. However, during the second spring of my seclusion, rumour had it that the Countess and her husband were coming to visit their estate in the summer. And indeed, they arrived at the beginning of June.

The arrival of a rich neighbour is an important event in the lives of country-dwellers. Landowners and servants talk about it for two months beforehand and three years afterwards. For my part, I confess that the news of the arrival of a young and beautiful neighbour had a powerful effect upon me; I burned with impatience to see her, and the first Sunday after her arrival I set off after dinner to the village of ***, in order to introduce myself to their Excellencies as their nearest neighbour and most humble servant.

The footman showed me into the Count's study and then went off to announce me. The spacious study was furnished with the greatest possible luxury; book-cases, each surmounted by a bronze bust, lined the walls; a large looking-glass hung above the marble fireplace; the floor was fitted with green cloth over which carpets were scattered. Unaccustomed to such luxury in my own modest quarters, and for so long shut away from the opulence of other people's lives, I began to feel nervous, and awaited the appearance of the Count in some trepidation, as a suppliant from the provinces might await the arrival of a minister. The doors were opened, and a very handsome man of about thirty-two entered the room. The Count approached me with an open and friendly air. I tried to recover my composure, and was on the point of introducing myself when he waved formalities aside. We sat down. His conversation, which was frank and agreeable, soon allayed my nervousness; I was just beginning to feel myself again when suddenly the Countess entered, and I became more embarrassed than ever. She was indeed beautiful. The Count introduced me; I wished to seem at my ease, but the more nonchalant I tried to appear, the more awkward I felt. In order to give me time to recover myself and to become accustomed to a new acquaintance, they began to talk to each other, treating me without ceremony, as a good neighbour might. Meanwhile, I began to walk up and down the room, looking at the books and pictures. I am no judge of pictures, but there was one which attracted my attention. It depicted a view in Switzerland, but it was not the painting that struck me so much as the fact that two bullets had been shot through it, very close together.

'That was a good shot,' I said, turning to the Count.

'Yes,' he replied, 'a very remarkable shot. Are you a good shot?' he continued.

'Fairly good,' I replied, glad that the conversation had at last touched on a subject that was close to my heart. 'I can hit a card at thirty paces – with a pistol I know, of course.'

'Really?' said the Countess, with a look of great interest. 'And you, my dear, could you hit a card at thirty paces?'

'We'll see … some other time,' replied the Count. 'In my day I used to be quite a good shot, but it's four years now since I picked up a pistol.'

'Oh,' I remarked, 'in that case I'll wager Your Excellency couldn't hit a card at twenty paces. Pistol-shooting requires daily practice; I know that from experience. I was reckoned one of the best shots in our regiment. But once it so happened that I didn't handle a pistol for a whole month, while mine were being repaired – and what do you think, Your Excellency? The first time I shot again after that, I missed a bottle four times running at twenty-five paces. Our captain – a witty and amusing fellow he was – happened to be standing by and said to me: "Your hand seems loth to slay a bottle, my friend!" No, Your Excellency, you must never neglect your practice, or you'll quickly lose your skill. The best shot I ever met used to practise at least three times a day. It was just as much a habit with him as a glass of vodka.'

The Count and Countess were pleased that I had begun to talk.

'And what sort of a shot was he?' the Count asked me.

'I'll tell you how good he was, Your Excellency. If he saw a fly settle on the wall – you're smiling, Countess, but I swear to God it's true – if he saw a fly, he'd shout: "Kuzka, my pistol!" Kuzka would fetch him a loaded pistol, and bang! – the fly would be driven into the wall.'

'Amazing!' exclaimed the Count. 'And what was his name?'

'Silvio, Your Excellency.'

'Silvio!' cried the Count, jumping up from his chair. 'You knew Silvio?'

'Indeed, Your Excellency, we were close friends; the whole regiment took to him like a brother. But it's five years now since I've heard anything of him. Your Excellency knew him as well then, I presume?'

'Yes, I knew him very well. Did he ever tell you ... no, he couldn't have – did he ever tell you of a very strange incident in his life?'

'Does Your Excellency refer to the occasion he was struck in the face by some madcap at a ball?'

'Did he ever tell you who that madcap was?'

'No, Your Excellency, he didn't ... Oh! Your Excellency,' I continued, as the truth dawned upon me, 'forgive me ... I didn't know ... could it have been you?'

'It was,' replied the Count, visibly disturbed, 'and that picture with the bullet-holes is a memento of our last meeting ...'

'Oh my dear,' said the Countess. 'Don't talk about it, for heaven's sake – I couldn't bear to listen.'

'No,' rejoined the Count, 'I will tell the whole story. He knows how I insulted his friend; he should know how Silvio avenged himself.'

The Count drew up a chair for me, and with the liveliest possible interest I listened to the following story.

'Five years ago I got married. We spent our honeymoon here, on this estate. To this house I owe the happiest moments of my life – and one of my most painful memories.

'One evening we were out riding together. My wife's horse grew restless for some reason, and, feeling nervous, she handed me the reins and went home on foot. I rode on ahead. I saw a travelling carriage in the courtyard, and was told a man was waiting for me in my study, and that he had refused to give his name, saying only that he had business with me.

I came into this room and in the twilight I saw a man, unshaven and covered in dust, standing just here by the fireplace. I went up to him, trying to see if I knew his features.

'"You don't recognise me, Count?" he asked in a shaking voice.

'"Silvio!" I cried, and I confess I felt as if my hair were standing on end.

'"Correct," he replied. "It is my shot. I have come for it. Are you ready?"

'A pistol protruded from his side pocket. I measured out twelve paces and stood in the corner over there, beseeching him to be quick and fire before my wife returned. He hesitated, and asked for a light. Candles were brought in. I closed the door, gave orders that nobody should enter the room, and again asked him to fire. He drew his pistol and took aim . . . I counted the seconds . . . I thought of her . . . a terrible minute passed. Silvio lowered his hand.

'"I'm sorry," he said, "that my pistol is not loaded with cherry-stones – bullets are so heavy. It seems to me that this is not a duel but murder; I am not accustomed to aiming at an unarmed man. Let us begin again, and cast lots to see who should fire first."

'My head began to spin . . . I think I made some objection . . . Eventually, we loaded another pistol; we screwed up two pieces of paper; he placed them in his cap – the same one that I had once shot through; I once again drew the lucky number.

'"You're devilish lucky, Count," he said with a grin that I shall never forget.

'I cannot understand what came over me, or how he forced me to do it . . . but I fired and hit that picture there.'

(The Count pointed at the picture with the bullet-holes. His face was burning like fire; the Countess was paler than her own handkerchief. I was unable to hold back an exclamation.)

'I fired,' the Count repeated, 'and thank God I missed. Then Silvio – he was terrible to behold at that moment – began to take aim at me. Suddenly the door opened, and Masha rushed in with a shriek and threw herself on my shoulder. Her presence restored my courage.

'"My dear," I said to her, "surely you can see we're joking? How frightened you look! Go and have a drink of water and then come back; I should like to introduce my old friend and comrade to you."

'But Masha didn't believe me.

'"Tell me, is my husband speaking the truth?" she asked, turning to the terrible Silvio. "Is it true that you're both only joking?"

'"He is always joking, Countess," replied Silvio; "he once struck me in the face for a joke, he shot through my cap for a joke, and just now he missed me for a joke. Now *I* feel in the mood for a joke . . ."

'With these words he made as if to take aim again – in front of *her*! Masha threw herself at his feet.

'"Get up, Masha, for shame!" I cried in a frenzy. "And you, sir, will you not cease to make fun of an unfortunate woman? Are you going to fire or not?"

'"No, I'm not going to fire," Silvio replied. "I am satisfied. I have witnessed your fear and panic; I forced you to shoot at me, and that is enough. You will remember me; I commit you to your conscience."

'Then he turned to go, but, stopping in the doorway, he glanced back at the picture through which my bullet had passed, shot at it almost without aiming, and vanished. My wife lay in a faint; the servants, not daring to stop him, stared at him in horror. He went out on to the porch, called to his coachman, and had disappeared before I had time to collect my senses.'

The Count was silent. And that is how I learned the end

of a story whose beginning had once impressed me so deeply. I never met its hero again. Rumour has it that Silvio commanded a detachment of Hetairists in Alexander Ypsilanti's uprising and was killed at the battle of Skulyani.

The Blizzard

> Through snowy wastes the carriage hies,
> The horses bravely plunge . . .
> And yonder now the eye descries
> A wayside church forlorn . . .
> And all at once a blizzard flings
> A myriad whirling flakes;
> Over the sledge, on whistling wings
> A sable raven flies,
> Its cry an augury of doom!
> The horses hasten on,
> Their senses pierce the distant gloom,
> Their manes bestride the air . . .
>
> ZHUKOVSKY

Towards the end of the year 1811, such a memorable period for us all, there lived on his estate at Nenaradovo the worthy Gavrila Gavrilovitch R**. He was well known throughout the district for his kindness and hospitality, and his neighbours were constantly visiting him – to eat or drink, or to play Boston at five kopecks a stake with his wife, Praskovya Petrovna, or some of them to look at his daughter, Marya Gavrilovna, a pale, slender young lady of seventeen. She was considered a good and profitable match, and many hoped to catch her for themselves or for their sons.

Marya Gavrilovna had been brought up on French novels and was by consequence in love. The object of her choice was a poor army subaltern, who was on leave of absence on his estate. It goes without saying that the young man returned her love with equal passion, and that the parents of his beloved, observing their mutual inclination, forbade their daughter even to think of him, and received him with greater hostility than if he were a retired district assessor.

Our lovers corresponded and met each other daily, either in the seclusion of a pine copse or by an old chapel. There they vowed eternal love, lamented their lot and made all kinds of plans. Corresponding and conversing in this way, they (very naturally) arrived at the following conclusion: since we cannot exist without each other, and the will of heartless parents is the only obstacle to our happiness, why not simply disregard it? It need hardly be mentioned that this happy thought originated in the mind of the young man, and that it greatly pleased the romantic fancy of Marya Gavrilovna.

Winter came and put a stop to their meetings; correspondence between them, however, became even more lively. In every letter he wrote, Vladimir Nikolayevitch besought her to give herself up to him, marry him in secret, and live in hiding with him for a while, after which they would throw themselves at the feet of her parents, who would surely be moved by the heroic constancy of their love and their unhappiness, and be bound to exclaim: 'Children, let us embrace you.'

Marya Gavrilovna vacillated for a long time; numerous plans for elopement were rejected. At last she consented: on the appointed day she was to excuse herself from supper and retire to her room under the pretext of a headache. Her maid was let into the plot. Marya and her maid were to go out by the back door into the garden, at the end of which they would find a sledge waiting for them; they were to seat themselves in this and drive the five versts from Nenaradovo to the village of Zhadrino, straight to the church, where Vladimir would be waiting for them.

On the eve of the decisive day, Marya Gavrilovna did not sleep all night; she packed and tied up some linen and clothes in a bundle, wrote a long letter to a sensitive young lady-friend of hers, and another to her parents. She bade them farewell in the most moving terms, ascribing her action to the invincible force of passion, and finished by declaring that she would consider the moment when she was permitted to throw herself at the feet of her beloved parents as the happiest of her life. Sealing both letters with a Tula seal, upon which were engraved two flaming hearts with an appropriate inscription, she threw herself on her bed just before dawn and fell into a light sleep. But every few minutes she was awoken by terrible dreams. Once she dreamed that at the very moment she took her seat in the sledge to drive to her wedding, her father stopped her, dragged her over the snow with agonising speed, and then threw her into a dark, bottom-less vault – into which she plunged headlong with an inde-scribable sinking of the heart. And then she saw Vladimir, pale and bloodstained, lying on the grass; expiring, he implored her in piercing tones to make haste and marry him . . . Other hideous and senseless visions swam before her one after another. At last she got up, even paler than usual, and with a genuine headache. Her father and mother noticed her restlessness; their tender solicitude and their endless inquiries – 'What's the matter with you, Masha? Are you ill, Masha?' – tore at her heart. She tried to put their minds at rest and appear cheerful, but she could not. Evening came. The thought that this was the last day she would spend among her family weighed heavily on her heart. She felt scarcely alive; in secret she bade farewell to all the persons and objects that surrounded her.

Supper was served; her heart beat violently. In a trembling voice she announced that she did not want any supper, and began to take leave of her father and mother. They kissed her and blessed her as usual; she could hardly keep the tears from her eyes. On reaching her room, she flung herself into an armchair and burst into tears. Her maid urged her to be calm and to take courage. Everything was prepared. In half an hour Masha was for ever to leave her parents' house, her own room, her quiet girlish life ... Outside, a blizzard raged; the wind howled and the shutters shook and rattled; everything seemed to her like a threat and a portent. Soon all was quiet in the house, and everyone asleep. Masha wrapped a shawl round her head, put on a warm cloak, took her box in her hand, and went out on to the back porch. Her maid followed her, carrying two bundles. They stepped down into the garden. The blizzard had not abated; the wind blew in their faces, as if striving to stop the young delinquent. They fought their way to the bottom of the garden. In the road a sledge was waiting for them. The horses, chilled to the marrow, would not keep still. Vladimir's coachman was pacing up and down in front of the shafts, trying to quiet the straining beasts. He helped the young lady and her maid to take their seats and stow their bundles and the little box in the sledge, took up the reins, and off the horses flew. Having entrusted the young lady to the care of fate and the skill of Teryoshka the coachman, let us now turn to our young lover.

Vladimir had been driving about all day. In the morning, he had visited the priest at Zhadrino and persuaded him after some difficulty to officiate at the wedding; he had then gone to seek out witnesses from among neighbouring landowners. The first he visited, a forty-year-old retired cornet by the name of Dravin, consented with pleasure. The adventure, he declared, reminded him of his younger days, of pranks in the Hussars. He persuaded Vladimir to stay and dine with him, assuring him that he would have no difficulty at all in finding two other witnesses. And indeed, immediately after dinner, moustachioed and with spurs on his boots, the surveyor Schmidt appeared with the son of the captain of the district police, a boy of about sixteen who had recently joined up with an Uhlan regiment. They not only accepted Vladimir's proposal but vowed that they were ready to lay down their lives for him. Vladimir embraced them with delight and returned home to make his preparations.

It had already been dark for some time. Giving detailed instructions, Vladimir dispatched the trustworthy Teryoshka to Nenaradovo with his troika, and then, ordering his small one-horse sledge to be harnessed, he set out alone for Zhadrino, where Marya Gavrilovna was due to arrive in about two hours' time. The road was familiar to him, and it was only a twenty-minute drive.

But scarcely had Vladimir left the village behind him and got out into open country than the wind blew up and such a blizzard developed that he was unable to see a thing. In no time at all the road was deep in snow. His surroundings disappeared in a murky yellow fog through which the white snowflakes swirled; the sky merged with the earth. Vladimir found himself in a field and tried in vain to regain the road; his horse pushed on at random, repeatedly charging into a snowdrift or stumbling into a ditch; and the sledge never ceased to overturn. All Vladimir's efforts were concentrated on not losing his way. But it seemed to him that more than half an hour had already passed, and he had not yet reached the copse at Zhadrino. A further ten minutes elapsed, and the copse was still not to be seen. Vladimir drove across a field full of deep ditches. The blizzard did not abate and the sky became no clearer. The horse began to tire, and the sweat rolled off him in great drops despite the fact, for most of the time, that he was up to his belly in snow.

At last Vladimir realised he had been travelling in the wrong direction. He stopped, began to think, recollect and reconsider, and became convinced that he should have turned to the right. He did so now. The horse could hardly move. The journey had already lasted for more than an hour. Zhadrino could not be far. But still Vladimir went on and on; the field seemed endless. Nothing but snowdrifts and ditches everywhere, the sledge constantly overturning, constantly having to be righted again. Time was passing. Vladimir began to get exceedingly anxious.

At last something dark appeared not far off. Vladimir turned the sledge in that direction. As he approached, he saw a copse. 'Thank God!' he thought. 'Nearly there.' He drove along the edge of the copse, hoping to get back on to the road he knew or, alternatively, to make a complete detour round the copse, for Zhadrino was situated just behind it. He soon found a road and drove into the dark wood, stripped bare by winter. The wind could not rage here; the road was smooth; the horse rallied and Vladimir felt calmer.

On and on he went, and there was still no sign of Zhadrino; the copse seemed endless. Vladimir realised with horror that he had entered an unfamiliar wood. He was overwhelmed by despair. He struck the horse; the poor beast broke into a trot but soon grew tired and, after a quarter of an hour, went on at walking pace despite all the exertions of the unfortunate Vladimir.

Gradually, the wood began to thin out, and at last Vladimir emerged from it; but still there was no sign of Zhadrino. It must now have been about midnight. The tears raced down his cheeks; he went on regardless. The blizzard subsided, the snowclouds dispersed, and before him lay a plain, covered by a white, undulating carpet of snow. The night was fairly clear. Not far off he saw a hamlet of four or five huts. He drove towards it. At the first hut he leapt out of his sledge, ran to the window, and began to knock. A few minutes later the wooden shutter was raised, and an old man thrust out his grey beard.

'What d'you want?'

'Is it far to Zhadrino?'

'Be it far to Zhadrino, you say?'

'Yes, yes, is it far?'

'Not far; 't be about ten versts.'

At this reply, Vladimir clutched at his hair and stood rooted to the spot, like a man who has been condemned to death.

'Where be you from?' continued the old man.

Vladimir had not the spirit to answer the question.

'Can you find horses to take me to Zhadrino, old man?' he asked.

'What sort of horses d'you think we'd have here?' replied the old man.

'Well then, can I get hold of a guide? I will pay whatever he asks.'

'Wait,' said the old man, lowering the shutter. 'I will send you my son; he'll guide you.'

Vladimir waited. Scarcely a minute had gone by before he began to knock again. The shutter was raised and the beard reappeared.

'What d'you want?'

'Where is your son?'

'He'll be out in a minute; he's putting his boots on. Are you cold? Come in and warm yourself.'

'No, thank you. Send your son out quickly.'

The door creaked; the lad came out with a thick staff in

his hand and walked on ahead, sometimes pointing out the road, sometimes searching for it under the snowdrifts.

'What's the time?' Vladimir asked him.

'Soon be light,' replied the young peasant.

Vladimir uttered not another word.

The cocks were crowing and it was already light when they reached Zhadrino. The church was locked. Vladimir paid the guide and went over to the priest's house. There was no sign of the troika. And what news awaited him!

But let us return to the worthy landowners of Nenaradovo, and see what is happening there.

Nothing.

The old couple awoke and went into the drawing-room, Gavrila Gavrilovitch in his nightcap and flannel jacket, Praskovya Petrovna in a quilted dressing-gown. The samovar was brought in and Gavrila Gavrilovitch sent a maidservant to find out how Marya Gavrilovna was and what sort of night she had had. The maidservant returned and reported that Marya Gavrilovna had not slept very well, but that she now felt better and would soon come down to the drawing-room. And indeed, presently, Marya Gavrilovna came in and greeted her father and mother.

'How is your head, Masha?' asked Gavrila Gavrilovitch.

'Better, Papa,' replied Masha.

'I expect it was the fumes from the stove yesterday,' said Praskovya Petrovna.

'I expect so, Mama,' Masha replied.

The day passed well enough, but that night Masha felt ill. A doctor was sent for from town. He arrived the following evening and found the sick girl delirious. A raging fever developed, and for two weeks she lay between life and death.

Nobody in the house knew about her proposed elopement. The letters written the previous night had been burned; and the maid, fearing her master's wrath, said nothing. The priest, the retired cornet, the moustachioed surveyor and the young dragoon were all discreet, and not without reason. As for Teryoshka the coachman, he never uttered a word too many, even when under the influence. And thus the secret was kept by more than half a dozen conspirators. But Marya Gavrilovna herself, during her long delirium, divulged her secret. However, her words made so little sense that her mother, who never left her bedside, was only able to gather that her daughter was madly in love with Vladimir Nikolayevitch, and that her love was probably the cause of her illness. She consulted her husband and some of her neighbours, and at last it was unanimously decided that such was evidently the fate of Marya Gavrilovna, that love laughs at locksmiths, that poverty is not a crime, that you marry a man and not his riches, and so on. Moral platitudes are wonderfully useful when we can find little to justify our actions by ourselves.

Meanwhile, the young lady began to recover. Vladimir had not been seen for a long time in the house of Gavrila Gavrilovitch. He must have been scared off, they thought, by the reception he usually received. It was decided to send for him and inform him of a piece of unexpected good news – consent to the marriage. Imagine the amazement of the landowners of Nenaradovo when, in reply to their invitation, they received a half-crazed letter from him. He announced that he would never set foot in their house again, and asked them to forget an unhappy wretch whose only hope was death. A few days later they discovered that Vladimir had rejoined his regiment. This was in the year 1812.

It was a long time before anyone dared speak of this to the convalescent Masha. She herself never referred to Vladimir. Some months afterwards, finding his name on the list of those who had distinguished themselves and had been severely wounded at the battle of Borodino, she fainted, and it was feared that she would have another attack of fever. However, thank heaven, her fainting fit had no serious consequences.

A further misfortune befell her: Gavrila Gavrilovitch died, leaving her as the heiress to all his property. But her inheritance was no consolation to her; she shared the grief of poor Praskovya Petrovna in all sincerity, and vowed never to be parted from her. They both left Nenaradovo, a place of sad memories for them, and went to live on their estate at ***.

Here, too, suitors crowded around the rich and charming young lady, but she never gave the slightest cause for hope to any of them. Her mother sometimes urged her to make her choice, but Marya Gavrilovna would always shake her head and become pensive. Vladimir was no longer alive; he had died in Moscow on the eve of the entry of the French. His memory seemed to be held sacred by Masha; at any rate, she kept everything that could remind her of him: the books that he had once read, his drawings, the melodies and verses that he had copied out for her. The neighbours, hearing of all these things, marvelled at her constancy and awaited with curiosity the hero who was destined to triumph at last over the melancholy fidelity of this virgin Artemisia.

Meanwhile, the war had come to a glorious end. Our regiments were returning from abroad, and the people ran out to meet them. The bands played the songs of the defeated enemy: 'Vive Henri Quatre', Tyrolean waltzes and airs from *Joconde*. Officers who had gone away to join the campaign as mere lads returned as grown men, matured by the air of the battlefield and with crosses on their tunics. Soldiers chatted gaily with one another, peppering their speech with French and German words. Unforgettable times! Glorious, delirious times! How strongly did the Russian heart beat at the word 'Fatherland'! How sweet the tears of reunion! How united we were in our national pride and our love for the Tsar! And for him – what a moment!

The women, the women of Russia, were beyond comparison in those times. Their usual coldness vanished. Their fervour was truly intoxicating when, welcoming the victors back:

'"Hurrah! Hurrah!" the women cried, And flung their bonnets in the air!'

What officer of that time will not confess that he is indebted to some Russian woman for his best and most precious reward ...?

During this brilliant period, Marya Gavrilovna lived with her mother in the district of *** and did not see how both capitals celebrated the return of the troops. But in the provincial towns and villages the general fervour was perhaps even greater. The very appearance of an officer in these places assured him of a veritable triumph, and the lover in a frock-coat did not stand much of a chance in his vicinity.

We have already stated that, in spite of her aloofness, Marya Gavrilovna was as before surrounded by suitors. But these were all forced to beat a retreat when the wounded Colonel Burmin of the Hussars made his appearance at her estate, with the cross of St George in his button-hole, and with what the local young ladies termed an 'interesting pallor'. He was about twenty-six. He was on leave of absence at his estate, which was in the same neighbourhood as that of Marya Gavrilovna. Marya Gavrilovna singled him out for very special attention. Her habitual pensiveness gave way to greater animation in his presence. It cannot be said that she flirted with him; but the poet, observing her behaviour, would have said:

'*Se amor non è, che dunche ...*'

Burmin was indeed a most charming young man. He had just the sort of mind that women like; he was well-mannered and observant, free of all pretension and light-heartedly satirical. His behaviour towards Marya Gavrilovna was simple and frank; but whatever she did or said, his eyes and his soul followed her. He seemed to be quiet and modest in character, although rumoured once to have been quite a young blade; however, this in no way discredited him in the eyes of Marya Gavrilovna, who (like all young ladies) was only too happy to excuse behaviour that indicated a bold or ardent nature.

But more than anything else – more than his tenderness, more than his pleasant conversation, more than his 'interesting pallor', more than his bandaged arm – it was the reserve of the young hussar that stimulated her curiosity and imagination. She could not but observe that he was greatly taken with her; and no doubt he too, with his shrewdness and experience, had already noticed that she showed a preference for him. How was it then that she had not yet seen him at her feet and heard a declaration of his love? What held him back? Was it timidity, which is inseparable from true love; was it pride; or was it the artfulness of a practised lover? It was a mystery to her. After a great deal of thought she decided that timidity was the sole cause of his restraint, and she determined to encourage him by greater attention and, should circumstances demand it, even by a show of tenderness. She made preparations for a *dénouement* which would take him completely by surprise, and impatiently awaited the moment of romantic explanation. A mystery, of whatever kind it be, always weighs heavily on the female heart. Her military tactics had the desired effect: at least Burmin fell into such a reverie, and his dark eyes rested on Marya Gavrilovna with such fire, that it seemed the decisive moment was at hand. The neighbours spoke of marriage as a foregone conclusion, and the good Praskovya Petrovna rejoiced that her daughter had at last found a suitor worthy of her.

One day the old lady was seated in the drawing-room,

laying out the cards for a game of *grande patience,* when Burmin entered the room and immediately inquired as to the whereabouts of Marya Gavrilovna.

'She's in the garden,' the old lady replied; 'go to her, and I'll wait for you here.'

Burmin went out, and the old lady crossed herself and thought: 'Perhaps things will be settled this very day!'

Burmin found Marya Gavrilovna beneath a willow-tree by the pond, with a book in her hand and wearing a white dress, the very picture of the heroine of a novel. After the usual observations and inquiries, Marya Gavrilovna deliberately ceased to keep up the conservation, thus intensifying their mutual embarrassment, which could be dispelled only by a sudden and decisive declaration of love. And that is what occurred: sensing his predicament, Burmin declared that he had long sought an opportunity to reveal his heart to her, and requested a moment of her attention. Marya Gavrilovna closed her book and dropped her eyes as a sign of her consent.

'I love you,' Burmin said, 'I love you passionately . . .' (Marya Gavrilovna blushed and lowered her head still further.) 'I have behaved imprudently in abandoning myself to what is a highly agreeable habit for me – the habit of seeing and hearing you daily . . .' (Marya Gavrilovna recalled Saint-Preux's first letter.) 'But it is now too late to resist my fate; the memory of you, your charming and incomparable image, will henceforward be the torment and the joy of my life; but I have yet to fulfil a certain painful obligation, and that is to reveal to you a terrible secret which places an insuperable barrier between us . . .'

'It has always existed,' Marya Gavrilovna broke in with animation; 'I could never have been your wife . . .'

'I know,' he replied softly, 'I know that you once loved another, but death and three years of mourning . . . Dear, kind Marya Gavrilovna, do not seek to deprive me of my last consolation! The thought that you would have agreed to make me happy if . . . don't speak, for God's sake, don't speak. You torture me. Yes, I know, I feel you would have been mine, but – I am the most wretched creature on this earth – I am already married!'

Marya Gavrilovna looked at him in astonishment.

'I am already married,' continued Burmin; 'I have been married for four years, and I do not know who my wife is, where she is, or whether we shall ever see one another again!'

'What are you saying?' exclaimed Marya Gavrilovna. 'How strange this is! Continue; I will tell you my story afterwards . . . but continue, I entreat you.'

'At the beginning of the year 1812,' Burmin said, 'I was hastening to Vilna, where our regiment was stationed. I had arrived late one evening at a posting-station, and ordered horses to be harnessed as soon as possible, when suddenly a terrible blizzard sprang up, and the postmaster and the drivers advised me to wait. I took their advice, but was filled with an inexplicable anxiety; it seemed as though someone were urging me on. Meanwhile, the blizzard did not abate; I grew impatient, again gave orders for the horses to be harnessed, and set out into the teeth of the storm. The driver took it into his head to drive by the river and thus shorten the journey by three versts. The banks of the river were covered with snow; the driver drove past the place where we should have turned on to the road, and we found ourselves in strange country. The storm had still not abated. I saw a light and ordered the driver to make for it. We arrived at a village; in the wooden church there was a light. The church was open, and several sledges stood behind the fence. People were walking about inside the porch.

'"This way! This way!" voices cried.

'I ordered the driver to proceed in that direction.

'"Where in the name of heaven have you been loitering?" someone asked me. "The bride has fainted; the priest does not know what to do, and we were all about to go home. Come as quickly as you can."

'Without uttering a word I leapt from my sledge and went into the church, which was dimly lit by two or three candles. A girl was seated on a bench in a dark corner of the church; another girl was rubbing her temples.

'"Thank God!" said the latter. "You've arrived in the nick of time; you've nearly killed my young mistress."

'An old priest approached me with the question: "All right to begin?"

'"Begin, Father, begin," I replied absently.

'They lifted the young lady to her feet. I thought she was rather pretty . . . I was seized by an incomprehensible, unpardonable light-headedness; I placed myself at her side in front of the lectern . . . The priest was in a hurry; three men and a maidservant supported the bride and paid attention only to her. We were married. "Kiss," we were told. My wife turned her pale face towards me. I was on the point of kissing her when she cried out: "No! Oh, no! He is not the one! He is not the one!" and fell senseless. The witnesses stared at me in alarm. I turned, ran out of the church without anyone trying to stop me, threw myself into the sledge, and cried "Away!"'

'My God!' cried Marya Gavrilovna. 'And do you know what has become of your poor wife?'

'I have no idea,' answered Burmin. 'I neither know the name of the village in which I was married, nor can I remember the name of the posting-station I had come from. At the time I attached so little importance to my wicked prank that when I left the church I fell asleep and didn't wake up until the third posting-station. The servant I had at the time died on campaign, and so I now have no hope of discovering who it was I played so cruel a joke upon, and who is now so cruelly avenged.'

'My God! My God!' said Marya Gavrilovna, seizing his hand. 'So it was you! Don't you recognise me?'

Burmin turned pale ... and threw himself at her feet ...

The Undertaker

And do we not coffins every day behold,
The grey hairs of our ageing universe?

DERZHAVIN

The last of the effects of the undertaker, Adrian Prokhorov, were loaded up on the hearse, and for the fourth time a couple of scrawny nags trudged their way from Basmannaya Street to Nikitskaya, where the undertaker had moved with his entire household. Locking up the shop, he nailed a poster to the gate announcing that the house was to be let or sold, and then set out on foot for his new dwelling. Approaching the little yellow house which had for so long captured his imagination, and which at last he had managed to buy for a considerable sum, the old undertaker was surprised to find that his heart did not rejoice. When he crossed the unfamiliar threshold and found his new home in turmoil, he sighed for his old tumbledown hovel, where for the past eighteen years the strictest order had prevailed. He began to scold his two daughters and the maidservant for their slowness, and then set about helping them himself. Soon order was established: the icon-case, the china cupboard, the table, the sofa and the bed were all installed in their appropriate corners in the back room; in the kitchen and drawing-room were stacked the various tools of the master's trade – coffins of every size and colour, cupboards full of mourning hats, cloaks and torches. Over the gate was hung a sign depicting a plump Cupid holding a torch upside down in his hand and bearing the inscription: 'Plain and painted coffins sold and upholstered; coffins hired and repaired.' His daughters withdrew to their own room and Adrian, after inspecting his new house, sat down by the window and called for the samovar to be heated.

The enlightened reader will know that both Shakespeare and Walter Scott portrayed their grave-diggers as merry and waggish fellows, the more to stir our imagination through contrast. Out of respect for the truth, however, we cannot follow their example and are forced to confess that the character of this undertaker was in perfect accord with his gloomy profession. Adrian Prokhorov was by habit both mournful and grave. On the rare occasions on which he opened his mouth, it was either to scold his daughters, when he came across them gazing idly out of the window at the passers-by, or to demand an exorbitant price for his wares from those who had the misfortune (or sometimes the good fortune) to need them. Thus it was that Adrian, seated at the window and drinking his seventh cup of tea, was as usual lost in dismal reflection. He was recalling the downpour that had overtaken the funeral procession of the retired brigadier at the town gate the previous week. Many of his cloaks had shrunk as a result of it, many hats had lost their shape. He foresaw unavoidable expenditure, for his ancient stock of funeral dress was in pitiable condition. He had been hoping to compensate for his losses from the funeral of old Tryukhina, the merchant's wife, who had had one foot in the grave for over a year. But Tryukhina now lay dying at Razgulyay, and Prokhorov feared that her heirs, in spite of their promises, would not bother to send so far for him, but would make an arrangement with the nearest contractor.

These reflections were suddenly interrupted by three Masonic knocks at the door.

'Who's there?' cried the undertaker.

The door opened and a man, instantly recognisable as a German craftsman, entered the room and approached the undertaker with a cheerful air.

'Forgive me, dear neighbour,' he said in that type of Russian accent which to this day we cannot hear without laughing, 'forgive me for intruding, but I wanted to make your acquaintance as soon as possible. I am a shoemaker, my name is Gottlieb Schultz, and I live across the street from you, in that little house you can see from your windows. I am celebrating my silver wedding tomorrow, and I have come to ask you and your daughters to have dinner with me.'

The invitation was graciously accepted. The undertaker asked the shoemaker to sit down and have a cup of tea and, thanks to the open-hearted nature of Gottlieb Schultz, they were soon chattering away together most affably.

'How's business with you then, good sir?' Adrian inquired.

'Oh my, oh my,' replied Schultz. 'Mustn't complain. Of course my trade isn't like yours. The living can do without shoes, but the dead can't get by without coffins.'

'Very true,' observed Adrian, 'but if a living person has no money to buy shoes (no offence), he goes barefoot; a dead beggar, however, gets his coffin for nothing.'

The conversation continued in this vein for some time. At last the shoemaker got up and, renewing his invitation, took leave of the undertaker.

The next day, at exactly twelve o'clock, the undertaker and his daughters passed through the gateway of their newly bought house, and set off to visit their neighbour. I will not stop to describe Adrian Prokhorov's Russian kaftan or the European attire of Akulina and Darya, deviating in this respect from the normal practice of modern novelists. I deem it not superfluous, however, to observe that both daughters were wearing the yellow hats and red shoes they reserved for special occasions.

The shoemaker's small room was filled with guests, for the most part German craftsmen with their wives and apprentices. There was only one Russian official present, police constable Yurko, a Finn who, in spite of his humble calling, enjoyed the particular favour of the host. Like Pogorelsky's postman, he had discharged his duties 'justly and honestly' for the past twenty-five years. The fire of 1812 which destroyed the ancient capital had also destroyed his yellow sentry-box. But as soon as the enemy had been driven away, a new one appeared in its place, painted grey and with white Doric columns, and Yurko, 'with axe in hand and clad in tunic of serge', again began his pacings up and down before it. He was known to most of the Germans living near the Nikitsky Gate, and some of them had even been obliged to spend Sunday night in his care. Adrian hastened to make his acquaintance, seeing him as a person whom, sooner or later, he might have need of, and when the guests sat down at the table, Adrian and Yurko sat together. Herr and Frau Schultz and their seventeen-year-old daughter Lottchen, while dining with their guests, helped the cook to serve and pass round the food. Beer flowed like water. Yurko ate for four. Adrian was eager not to be outdone, and his daughters behaved themselves correctly. The conversation, which was conducted in German, became louder and louder every minute. Suddenly, the host demanded the attention of his guests and, uncorking a tar-sealed bottle, declared in a loud voice in Russian:

'To the health of my good Luise!'

The sekt foamed. The host tenderly kissed the fresh face of his forty-year-old helpmate, and the guests noisily drank to the health of the good Luise.

'To the health of my dear guests,' proclaimed the host, uncorking another bottle. Thanking him, the guests drained their glasses once more.

Then followed a succession of toasts. They drank to the health of each individual guest, to the health of Moscow and of at least a dozen small German towns, to the health of all trades in general and each one in particular, and to the health of all craftsmen and apprentices. Adrian drank with zeal and became so merry that he even proposed some humorous toast himself. Suddenly one of the guests, a fat baker, raised his glass and exclaimed: 'To the health of those for whom we work – *unserer Kundleute!*'

This proposal, like all the others, was taken up joyfully and unanimously. The guests began to bow to one another – the tailor to the shoemaker, the shoemaker to the tailor, the baker to both of them, and then everybody to the baker, and so on. Yurko, amid mutual salutations, turned to his neighbour and cried out:

'Come on, then, my good sir, drink to the health of your dead!'

Everybody hooted with laughter, but the undertaker considered himself insulted and frowned. Nobody noticed this, and the guests continued to drink. The bells for vespers had already started to ring when they rose from the table.

It was late when the guests dispersed, and most of them were tipsy. The fat baker and the bookbinder, whose face seemed bound in red morocco, took hold of Yurko by the arms and led him to his sentry-box, observing as they did so the Russian proverb: 'One good turn deserves another.'

The undertaker arrived home drunk and angry. 'Why should my trade,' he asked himself aloud, 'be judged less

honourable than others? Is an undertaker brother to a
hangman? Why did those heathens laugh at me? Is an undertaker a clown at a Christmas fair? I wanted to ask them to
a housewarming, and give them all a princely feast, but I'm
damned if I will now! No, I'll invite those for whom I work:
the Orthodox dead.'

'Hush, sir,' cried the maidservant, who was helping him
off with his boots. 'What nonsense are you jabbering? Cross
yourself this minute! Invite the dead to a housewarming!
Whatever next!'

'By God!' continued Adrian, 'I will invite them – and
tomorrow, too! Do me the favour, noble benefactors all, of
feasting with me tomorrow evening. Let God be our
provider!'

With these words the undertaker went off to bed and was
soon snoring away.

It was still dark outside when Adrian was roused.
Tryukhina, the merchant's wife, had died during the night,
and a messenger sent by her bailiff had ridden over post-
haste to Adrian with the news. The undertaker gave him a
ten-kopeck tip for vodka, hurriedly got dressed, took a cab
and drove to Razgulyay. The police had already stationed
themselves at the door of the dead woman's house, and
tradesmen were strutting up and down outside like ravens
scenting a dead body. The dead woman was laid out on a
table, her face as yellow as wax, but not yet deformed by
decay. Relations, neighbours and members of her household
were crowded around her. All the windows were open;
candles were burning; priests were reading the prayers for
the dead. Adrian went up to Tryukhina's nephew, a young
merchant wearing a fashionable frock-coat, and informed
him that the coffin, candles, pall and other funeral acces-
sories would be supplied by him immediately and in good
condition. The heir thanked him abstractedly, saying that he

would not bargain about the price, but would put complete faith in the undertaker's conscience. The undertaker, as was his custom, vowed that he would not charge a single kopeck too much, and, after exchanging significant glances with the bailiff, he went home to set about his various preparations. The whole day was spent in to-ing and fro-ing between Razgulyay and the Nikitsky Gate. By the evening everything had been arranged and, dismissing the cab, Adrian went home on foot. It was a moonlit night. The undertaker reached the Nikitsky Gate safely. Outside the Church of the Ascension, our friend Yurko hailed him and, recognising the undertaker, wished him good night. It was late. The undertaker was approaching his house when suddenly it seemed to him that somebody went up to his gate, opened it and disappeared inside.

'What can this mean?' thought Adrian. 'Who could be wanting me again? Is it a thief come to rob me? Or do lovers visit my foolish daughters by night? That would be the last straw!'

The undertaker thought of calling upon the aid of his friend Yurko. At that moment, however, somebody else approached the gate and was about to go in, but, seeing the master of the house hastening towards him, stopped and raised a three-cornered hat. His face seemed familiar to Adrian, but in his haste he was unable to examine it very closely.

'You've come to visit me,' said Adrian, out of breath. 'Go in, I beseech you.'

'Don't stand on ceremony, my friend,' the other replied in a hollow voice. 'You go first and show your guests the way!'

And indeed, Adrian had no time to stand on ceremony. The gate was open and he went up the steps, followed by the other. It seemed to Adrian that there were people walking about his rooms.

'What the devil's happening?' he thought, and hurriedly entered the room, and ... his legs gave way beneath him.

The room was full of corpses. The moon, shining through the window, lit up their blue and yellow faces, sunken mouths, dull, half-closed eyes, and protruding noses. With horror, Adrian recognised in them people whom he had helped to bury, and in the guest who had come in with him, the brigadier who had gone to his grave in pouring rain. All of them, men and women, surrounded the undertaker, bowing to him and greeting him, with the exception of one poor fellow, recently buried free of charge, who was so ashamed of his tattered clothes that he did not gather round with the others but stood meekly in the corner. All the others were decently dressed: the women in bonnets and ribbons, the officials in their uniforms, albeit unshaven, and the merchants in their Sunday clothes.

'You see, Prokhorov,' said the brigadier, speaking for the whole honourable company, 'we have all risen to your invitation. Only those who were incapable, who have fallen completely to pieces, and who are now nothing but fleshless bone, have stayed at home. One of them, however, could not resist coming, so eager was he to visit you ...'

At this moment a small skeleton pushed its way through the crowd and made for Adrian. Its skull smiled affectionately at the undertaker. Shreds of light-green and red rag and mouldering linen hung from it here and there as from a pole, and the bones of its legs rattled in high jackboots, like pestles in mortars.

'You don't recognise me, Prokhorov,' said the skeleton. 'Don't you remember the retired sergeant of the Guards, Pyotr Petrovitch Kurilkin, the very same to whom you sold your first coffin in 1799 – a deal one, although you said it was oak?'

With these words the skeleton stretched out its arms in

bony embrace, but Adrian, mustering up all his strength, shrieked and pushed it away. Pyotr Petrovitch reeled back, fell and crumbled to pieces. A murmur of indignation arose from among the corpses; all stood up for the honour of their comrade, and they heaped such threats and curses upon Adrian that the poor host, deafened by their cries and almost crushed to death between them, lost his presence of mind, himself fell on the bones of the retired sergeant of the Guards, and lost consciousness.

The sun had long been shining on the bed on which the undertaker lay. At last he opened his eyes and saw before him the maidservant heating up the samovar. With horror he recalled the events of the previous day. Tryukhina, the brigadier, and Sergeant Kurilkin appeared dimly before his mind. He waited in silence for the maid to begin the conversation and inform him of the outcome of his nocturnal adventure.

'How you have slept, Adrian Prokhorovitch!' said Axinya, handing him his dressing-gown. 'Your neighbour, the tailor, came to see you, and the police constable dropped by to say that it was the district police inspector's name-day today, but you were still in your dreams and we didn't like to wake you.'

'But has anyone from the late Tryukhina's come to see me?'

'The late Tryukhina? Is she dead then?'

'Fool! Didn't you help me prepare for the funeral yesterday?'

'Have you taken leave of your senses, sir, or are you still under the influence? What sort of funeral did we have yesterday? You spent the whole day carousing with the German, came home drunk, fell into your bed, and didn't wake up till now – till the bells stopped pealing for mass.'

'I don't believe you!' exclaimed the undertaker, rejoicing.

'It's as I said,' replied the housemaid.

'Well, if that's so, make the tea quickly and call my daughters.'

The Postmaster

The low collegiate registrar
A posting-station turns to tsar.
PRINCE VYAZEMSKY

Who has neither cursed nor quarrelled with the master of a posting-station? Who, in a moment of rage, has not demanded the fatal book in which to enter unavailing complaints of ill-treatment, churlishness and inefficiency? Who does not regard postmasters as outcasts of mankind, the equal, in their artfulness and dishonesty, to those clerks of the old Muscovite administration, or at least to the brigands of Murom? Let us be fair, however, and try to place ourselves in their position, and we shall then perhaps begin to show much greater indulgence in our judgement of them. What is a postmaster? Why, he is a veritable martyr among petty officials, protected from blows only by his rank – and then not always (here I appeal to the conscience of my readers). What are the duties of this dictator, as Prince Vyazemsky has jokingly called him? Is not his work true slave-labour? He rests neither by day nor by night. It is upon the postmaster that the traveller vents all the accumulated irritations of a tiresome journey. If the weather is intolerable, the road appalling, the driver obstinate, or the horses idle, it is the postmaster who is to blame. The traveller who enters his poor dwelling regards him as an enemy; and the postmaster is fortunate if he succeeds in getting rid of his uninvited guest quickly. But if there should happen to be no horses ... ? Heavens, what curses, what threats are poured down upon his head! In rain and mud, he is obliged to run from house to house; in storm and January frost, he has to go out on to the porch to take momentary respite from the shouting and jostling of the exasperated traveller. A general arrives: the trembling postmaster gives him his last two troikas – including the one he had set aside for the government courier. The general departs without a word of thanks. Five minutes later, the tinkling of bells again – and the government courier flings his order for fresh horses on the table.

If only we were to take all this into careful consideration, indignation would give way to sincere compassion in our hearts. I will add this: over a period of twenty years I have travelled the length and breadth of Russia; almost all the post-roads are known to me; I am acquainted with several generations of drivers; there are few postmasters whom I do not know by sight, few with whom I have not had dealings; quite soon I hope to publish a collection of interesting observations picked up during my travels; for the moment, I will only say that postmasters as a whole have been presented to the general public in an extremely false light. These much maligned postmasters are as a rule peaceful people, obliging by nature, sociably inclined, free from exaggerated pretensions about themselves, and not especially fond of money. From their conversation (foolishly disdained by so many travellers) one can glean much that is interesting and instructive. For my own part, I confess that I prefer their conversation to that of many a senior official travelling on government business.

It will come as no surprise to the reader that I number

postmasters among my friends. Indeed, the memory of one is particularly dear to me. Circumstances once brought us together, and it is of him that I now intend to tell my obliging readers.

In the month of May, 1816, I happened to be travelling through the province of ***, on a road now no longer in existence. I was of low rank, and my travel allowance was enough for two horses only. This caused postmasters to treat me with little ceremony, and I would frequently have to take by force what I considered mine by right. Being young and hot-headed, I was indignant at the baseness and faint-heartedness of the postmaster who harnessed to the carriage of some senior official the horses which had already been prepared for my troika. It took me as long to accustom myself to this kind of treatment as to being passed over by some discriminating waiter at a Governor's dinner. Nowadays, both these instances seem to me to be in the order of things. Indeed, what would become of us if instead of the generally accepted rule of 'Let rank yield to rank', we were to apply some other, such as 'Let mind yield to mind'? What arguments there would be! Whom would the servants serve first? But to return to my tale.

It was a hot day. Three versts from the posting-station at ***, a light drizzle began; a minute later, it had changed into driving rain and I was soaked to the skin. On arrival at the station, my first concern was to change my clothes as quickly as possible, my second to ask for some tea.

'Hey, Dunya!' cried the postmaster. 'Get the samovar ready and go out and fetch some cream.'

At these words a young girl of about fourteen emerged from behind a partition and ran out into the porch. I was struck by her beauty.

'Is that your daughter?' I asked the postmaster.

'Indeed it is, sir,' he replied with a look of contented pride;

'and she is so bright and quick – just like her mother, God rest her soul.'

While the postmaster set about copying out my order for fresh horses, I occupied myself by examining the pictures that adorned his humble but neat abode. They depicted the story of the Prodigal Son. In the first, a venerable old man, in night-cap and dressing-gown, was to be seen taking leave of a young man, obviously restless and hastily accepting his father's blessing and a bag of money. The next vividly portrayed the dissipated life of the young man, seated at a table and surrounded by false friends and shameless women. Further on, the ruined youth, a three-cornered hat on his head and dressed in rags, was tending swine and sharing in their repast; on his face was a look of profound sorrow and repentance. The last picture portrayed his return to his father: the good old man, in the same night-cap and dressing-gown, was running out to meet him; the Prodigal Son was on his knees; in the distance, the cook could be seen killing the fatted calf, and the elder brother asking the cause of such re-joicings. Beneath each picture I read some appropriate German verses. All this I have retained in my memory to this day, along with the pots of balsam, the bed with the brightly coloured curtain drawn across it, and the other objects of the household. I can still see, as if it were today, the master of the house himself, a man of about fifty, fresh-faced and cheerful, in a long green frock-coat to which were pinned three medals on faded ribbons.

Scarcely had I finished settling accounts with my old driver than Dunya returned with the samovar. The little minx was quick to observe the impression she had made on me, and coyly lowered her big blue eyes. I began to talk to her; she answered without the slightest timidity, like a girl who has been out in the world. I offered her father a glass of punch. To Dunya I handed a cup of tea, and the three of us began to chat away as if we had known one another for years.

The horses had long been ready, but I was reluctant to part from the postmaster and his daughter. At last I took leave of them; the father wished me a good journey, and the daughter led me to my carriage. In the porch I stopped and asked her to allow me to kiss her. Dunya consented . . . Many a kiss can I count 'since first I did indulge', but not one has left me with a memory so sweet and so lasting.

A few years passed, and circumstances again led me along the same road, and through the same places. I remembered the postmaster's daughter and rejoiced at the thought that I might see her again. 'But perhaps the old postmaster has been replaced,' I thought. 'And Dunya will be married by now.' The thought also occurred to me that one or other of them might have died, and I approached the posting-station of *** with sad forebodings.

My horses drew up before the postmaster's little house. Entering the room, I immediately recognised the pictures depicting the story of the Prodigal Son. The table and the bed stood in the same place as before, but there were no longer any flowers in the window, and everything in the room pointed to decay and neglect. The postmaster lay sleeping under a sheepskin coat. My arrival awoke him and he got up . . . It was certainly Samson Vyrin, but how he had aged! While he copied out my order for fresh horses, I looked at his grey hair, his deeply lined and unshaven face, his bent back – and I was astonished that three or four years could have changed so healthy and cheerful a person into a feeble old man.

'Don't you recognise me?' I asked him. 'We're old friends.'

'Could be,' he replied morosely. 'This is a main road; many a traveller passes through here.'

'And how is your Dunya?' I continued.

The old man frowned.

'Heaven knows!' he replied.

'I suppose she's married?' I asked.

The old man pretended not to hear me and went on reading through my order in a whisper. I ceased my questioning and ordered some tea. I began to grow more and more curious, and I hoped that punch would loosen the tongue of my old friend.

I was not mistaken; the old man did not refuse the proffered glass. I noticed that rum dispelled his moroseness. With the second glass he became talkative; he remembered, or at least pretended to remember, who I was, and I heard from him a story which at the time both absorbed and moved me deeply.

'So you knew my Dunya?' he began. 'Who did not know her? Ah, Dunya, Dunya! What a lass she was! Everyone who came here praised her; nobody had an unkind word for her. The ladies were always giving her presents – one would give her a kerchief, another a little pair of earrings. The gentlemen who were travelling through used to stop longer, to dine or have supper, so they'd say, but really only to take a longer look at her. However angry a gentleman might be, at the sight of her he'd quieten down and start treating me civilly. Believe it or not, sir, but government couriers and messengers used to stay talking to her for half-an-hour at a time. It was she that kept the house together; she did the cleaning, the cooking, and looked after everything. She was the apple of my eye, sir. I used to dote on her like an old fool. Didn't she get enough love? Didn't I cherish my child? Didn't she have a good life here with me? But no, there's no escaping misfortune; Fate is master unto itself.'

And he proceeded to tell me his sad story in detail.

Three years before, one winter's evening as the postmaster

was ruling lines in a new ledger, and his daughter was sewing a dress behind the partition, a troika had driven up, and a traveller in a Circassian cap and a greatcoat and muffler entered the room, demanding horses. There were no horses available. At this piece of news, the traveller was just about to start shouting and brandishing his whip when Dunya, accustomed to such scenes, ran out from behind the partition and sweetly inquired of the traveller whether he would like anything to eat. Dunya's appearance had its usual effect. The traveller's rage subsided; he agreed to wait for the horses and ordered supper for himself. After removing his wet shaggy cap, unwinding his muffler and pulling off his greatcoat, the traveller was seen to be a handsome young hussar with a trim black moustache. He made himself comfortable, and began merrily chatting away with the postmaster and his daughter. Supper was served. Meanwhile, the horses had arrived, and the postmaster ordered that they should be immediately harnessed to the traveller's sledge, without even being fed; but, on returning to the house, he found the young man lying almost unconscious on the bench – he felt faint, his head ached, he was unfit to travel any further . . . What was to be done? The postmaster gave up his bed to him, and it was decided, if the sick man were no better in the morning, that they would send for the doctor at S**.

The following day the hussar was worse. His batman rode into town for the doctor. Dunya wrapped his head in a kerchief soaked in vinegar and sat at his bedside with her sewing. In the presence of the postmaster, the sick man moaned and uttered scarcely a single word, though he did drink two cups of coffee and, between groans, managed an order for dinner. Dunya never left his side. He was constantly asking for something to drink, and each time he asked, Dunya would hand him a tankard of the lemonade she had herself prepared. The sick man moistened his lips, and as he returned the tankard, he would weakly squeeze Dunya's hand in gratitude. The doctor arrived before dinner. He felt the sick man's pulse and, after speaking to him in German, announced in Russian that the patient only needed rest and would be quite fit to renew his journey in a couple of days or so. Handing him twenty-five roubles for his visit, the hussar invited the doctor to dinner; the doctor accepted; they both ate with a hearty appetite, drank a bottle of wine between them and parted the best of friends.

Another day went by, and the hussar had completely recovered. He was exceedingly cheerful, joking all the time, sometimes with Dunya, sometimes with the postmaster, whistling tunes, chatting with the travellers, entering up their orders in the ledger; and the good postmaster became so fond of him that he was sad at the prospect of parting with his amiable lodger on the morning of the next day. It was a Sunday; Dunya was getting ready to go to mass. The hussar's sledge was brought round. He said goodbye to the postmaster, rewarding him lavishly for his board and lodging; and he took leave of Dunya, offering, as he did so, to drive her as far as the church, which was at the other end of the village. Dunya stood in perplexity.

'What are you frightened of?' her father asked her. 'His Honour is not a wolf; he won't eat you: ride with him as far as the church.'

Dunya got into the sledge and sat down beside the hussar, the servant leapt up on to the coachman's seat, the driver whistled, and the horses galloped off.

The unfortunate postmaster could never understand how he could have allowed his Dunya to go off with the hussar, how he could have been so blind, what he could have been thinking of. Not half an hour had gone by before he started to chafe and fret, and he was seized with such anxiety that he could bear it no longer, and went to the church himself to seek her out. As he approached, he saw that the people were already coming out, but Dunya was to be seen neither in the churchyard nor in the porch. He hurried into the church; the priest had left the altar; the sexton was extinguishing the candles, and in one corner two old women were still praying; yet there was no sign of Dunya. Her wretched father could scarcely bring himself to ask the sexton whether she had been at mass. The sexton replied that she had not been in the church. More dead than alive, the postmaster made his way home. He had but one hope left: perhaps Dunya, in the rashness of her youth, had taken it into her head to drive on as far as the next posting-station, where her godmother lived. In acute agitation he awaited the return of the troika in which he had let her go. But there was no sign of the driver. Eventually, towards evening, the driver returned alone and drunk, and the bearer of the most appalling news: Dunya had gone on from the next posting-station with the hussar.

This was too much for the old man and he immediately took to his bed – that same bed on which the young impostor had lain the previous day. Putting two and two together, the postmaster now guessed that the young man's illness had been faked. The poor old man contracted a violent fever and was taken to S**, another postmaster being temporarily appointed in his place. He was treated by the same doctor who had visited the hussar, and who now confirmed that the young man had been perfectly well, that he had guessed his evil intentions at the time, but, fearing the hussar's whip, had kept silent. Whether the German spoke the truth or whether he merely wished to boast of his shrewdness, his disclosures did nothing to console his unfortunate patient. Scarcely had the postmaster recovered from his illness than he asked the chief postmaster at S** for two months' leave of absence and, without saying a word of his intentions to anyone, set out on foot to look for his daughter. From his order for fresh horses, he learned that Captain Minsky had been travelling from Smolensk to Petersburg. The driver who had taken him said that Dunya had spent the whole journey in tears, although it appeared that she had gone of her own free will.

'Perhaps I shall be able to bring my lost lamb home,' thought the postmaster.

Impelled by this thought, he arrived in Petersburg. After putting up for the night at the barracks of the Izmaylov Regiment, in the house of a retired non-commissioned officer who was an old comrade of his, he began his search. He soon discovered that Captain Minsky was in Petersburg, living at the Hotel Demutov. The postmaster resolved to call on him.

Early next morning he arrived at Minsky's rooms, and requested that His Honour might be informed that an old soldier wished to see him. The batman, busy cleaning a boot on a boot-tree, announced that his master was still asleep and that he did not receive anyone before eleven o'clock. The postmaster went away and returned at the appointed hour. Minsky himself came out to him, in a dressing-gown and a red skull-cap.

'Well, my friend, what do you want?' he asked.

The old man's blood boiled, tears welled up in his eyes, and he was only able to answer in a trembling voice: 'Your Honour ... for the love of God, I beg you ... !'

Minsky darted a glance at him, flushed crimson, took him by the hand, led him into his study and locked the door.

'Your Honour!' continued the old man. 'I've not come to cry over spilt milk, but at least give me back my poor Dunya. You've had your fun with her; don't ruin her for nothing, I beg you.'

'What's done cannot be undone,' said the young man in the utmost confusion. 'I am guilty before you and I am only too ready to beg your forgiveness, but do not imagine that I could forsake Dunya. I give you my word of honour that she shall be happy. What do you want with her? She loves me; she has grown used to a new way of life. Neither you nor she would be able to forget what has happened.'

Then, thrusting something up the old man's sleeve, he opened the door, and the postmaster, without realising how he got there, found himself in the street.

He stood motionless for a long time. At last, he saw that there was a roll of paper inside the cuff of his sleeve; he drew it out and unfolded several crumpled five- and ten-rouble notes. Tears again welled up in his eyes – but this time they were tears of indignation. He screwed up the notes into a ball, flung them to the ground, trampled them underfoot, and walked away. Having gone a few paces, he stopped and thought . . . and retraced his steps . . . but the notes had disappeared. A well-dressed young man, seeing him, ran up to a cab, clambered in and shouted: 'Drive on!' The postmaster did not pursue him. He made up his mind to return home to his posting-station, but first he wanted to see his poor Dunya once more. Two days later he returned to Minsky's rooms for this purpose; but the batman told him sternly that his master was receiving nobody, barged him out of the entrance-hall and slammed the door in his face. The postmaster stood outside for some time and then went away.

That same evening he was walking along Lityeynaya Street after attending a service at the church of Our Lady of Sorrows. Suddenly an elegant droshky dashed by in front of him, and the postmaster recognised Minsky. The droshky drew up at the entrance of a three-storeyed house, and the hussar ran up the steps. A happy thought flashed through the postmaster's mind. He turned back and, coming alongside the coachman, asked:

'Whose horse is that, my friend? Not Minsky's, is it?'

'Yes, it is,' replied the coachman. 'Why do you ask?'

'Well, the trouble is your master ordered me to deliver a

note to his Dunya, but I've gone and forgotten where this Dunya of his lives.'

'She lives here – on the second floor. But you are too late with your note, my friend; the master's already up there with her now.'

'No matter,' replied the postmaster, his heart filled with indescribable emotion. 'Thank you for telling me, but I'd better do my duty all the same.'

And with these words he went up the stairs.

The doors were locked; he rang, and after a few seconds of painful suspense, a key rattled in the lock and the door was opened.

'Does Avdotya Samsonovna live here?' he asked.

'Yes,' replied a young servant. 'What do you want with her?'

The postmaster walked into the hall without replying.

'You can't come in! You can't come in!' the servant cried after him. 'Avdotya Samsonovna has visitors.'

The postmaster went on regardless. The first two rooms were in darkness, but there was a light in the third. He went up to the open door and stopped. Inside the room, which was beautifully furnished, Minsky sat deep in thought. Dunya, dressed in the height of fashion, was seated on the arm of his chair, like an Englishwoman riding side-saddle. She was gazing tenderly at Minsky and winding his black curls around her sparkling fingers. The poor postmaster! Never had his daughter seemed to him so beautiful; he could not help admiring her.

'Who's there?' she asked, without raising her head.

The postmaster was silent. Receiving no reply, Dunya raised her head ... and with a shriek fell upon the carpet. Alarmed, Minsky rushed to pick her up, but, suddenly catching sight of the old postmaster in the doorway, he left Dunya and went up to him, trembling with rage.

'What do you want?' he asked him, grinding his teeth. 'Why do you steal after me everywhere like a brigand? Are you out to murder me? Get out!'

And seizing the old man by the scruff of his neck with a powerful hand, he pushed him out on to the stairs.

The old man returned to his lodging. His friend advised him to put in an official complaint; but the postmaster thought it over and, with a resigned shrug, decided to let matters rest. Two days later he left Petersburg and returned to his station, where he took up his duties once again.

'It is now almost three years,' he concluded, 'since I've been without Dunya. I've heard no news of her at all; God only knows whether she is alive or dead. All manner of things come to pass in this world of ours. She is not the first, nor will she be the last, to be seduced by some passing young scapegrace, kept for a while, and then discarded. There are many young fools like her in Petersburg – one day they're decked out in satin and velvet, and the next they're sweeping the streets with their skirts along with the common riffraff. When you think sometimes – that Dunya might end up like that, you can't help wishing her in the grave, God forgive me . . .'

Such was the story of my friend the old postmaster, a story that was more than once interrupted by tears, which, like the fervid Terentyitch in that beautiful ballad of Dmitriev's, he wiped away picturesquely with the skirt of his coat. These tears were caused partly by the punch, of which he drank five glasses during the course of his story; nevertheless, they moved me deeply. After I had bidden him farewell, it was a long time before I could get the thought of the old postmaster out of my head, and long did I reflect on poor Dunya . . .

Passing through the village of *** not long ago, I remembered my friend the postmaster once again. I learned that the posting-station of which he had been in charge was no longer in existence. To my enquiry whether the old postmaster was still alive, nobody was able to offer a satisfactory reply. I therefore resolved to find out for myself and, hiring some privately-owned horses, I set off for the village of N**.

It was autumn. Grey clouds covered the sky, and a cold wind was blowing across the bare fields, snatching the red and yellow leaves from the trees through which it passed. I arrived in the village at sunset and drew up outside the postmaster's little house. A fat peasantwoman came out on to the porch (where once poor Dunya had kissed me), and in reply to my questions told me that the old postmaster had been dead for a year or so, that his house had been taken over by a brewer, and that she was the brewer's wife. I regretted my useless journey and the seven roubles that I had spent in vain.

'What did he die of?' I asked the brewer's wife.

'Drank himself to death, sir,' she replied.

'And where is he buried?'

'On the outskirts of the village, next to his good wife.'

'Could someone show me the grave?'

'Why not? Hey, Vanka, you've played around with that cat for long enough. Take the gentleman to the cemetery and show him the postmaster's grave.'

At these words a ragged little boy with red hair and blind in one eye ran up and led me to the outskirts of the village.

'Did you know the postmaster?' I asked him on the way.

'I should think I did! He taught me how to carve whistles. He used to come out of the inn (God rest his soul!) and we used to call to him, "Grandpa, grandpa, give us some nuts!", and he would give us all nuts. He'd spend all his time with us.'

'And do the travellers remember him?'

'There aren't many travellers nowadays; the assessor passes through sometimes, but he doesn't have anything to do with the dead. A lady came to the village last summer though, and she asked about the old postmaster, and then went and visited his grave.'

'What sort of a lady?' I asked with curiosity.

'A fine lady she were,' the boy replied; 'she was travelling in a carriage drawn by six horses, and she had three little boys with her, and a nurse, and a black pug-dog. When she heard that the old postmaster was dead, she burst out crying, she did, and said to the children: "You stay here quietly, while I go to the graveyard." I offered to show her the way, but the lady replied: "I know the way myself." And she gave me a five-kopeck silver piece – such a nice lady . . . !'

We arrived at the graveyard, a bleak spot with not even a fence, dotted with wooden crosses and with not a single tree to give it shade. Never in my life have I seen such a cheerless graveyard.

'This is the old postmaster's grave,' the boy said to me, jumping upon a mound of sand, in which had been stuck a black cross with a copper icon on it.

'And the lady came here?' I asked.

'Yes,' answered Vanka. 'I watched her from a distance. She lay just here, and for a long time too. And then she went back to the village, called the priest, gave him some money and then drove away . . . She gave me a five-kopeck silver piece – a really fine lady she was!'

And I too gave the small boy a five-kopeck piece, and no longer did I regret the journey or the seven roubles that I had spent on it.

Peasant-Lady

Sweet Dushenka in any guise,
A sight she is to please men's eyes.

BOGDANOVITCH

Situated in one of our most distant provinces was the estate of Ivan Petrovitch Berestov. In his youth he had served in the Guards, but, resigning his commission at the beginning of 1797, he had gone to live on his estate, and since that time had never left it. He married a poor gentlewoman, who died in childbirth while her husband was away on a hunting expedition. The administration of his property soon consoled him in his loss. He designed and built his own house, established a cloth factory on his estate, contrived to treble his income, and quickly came to consider himself the wisest man in the whole district; in which opinion he was not gainsaid by his neighbours, who came to visit him with their families and dogs. On week-days he went about in a corduroy jacket, and on Sundays and holidays he would put on a frock-coat of homespun cloth. He kept all the household acounts himself and read nothing except the *Senate Gazette*. In general he was liked, although he was considered proud. There was only one person who did not get on with him, Grigory Ivanovitch Muromsky, his nearest neighbour, and a Russian nobleman of the old school. Having squandered the greater part of his fortune in Moscow, and having become a widower at this time, Muromsky had retired to his sole remaining estate and there continued to waste his money in a novel way. He laid out an English garden, on which he expended almost all his remaining capital. His stable-boys were dressed like English jockeys. His daughter had an English governess. He cultivated his land according to English principles. 'But Russian corn thrives not on alien methods,' and in spite of considerable reduction in expenditure, Grigory Ivanovitch's income showed no increase. Even in the country he discovered means of accumulating fresh debts; for all this, however, he was considered no fool, and was in fact the first landowner in his province to hit on the idea of mortgaging his estate with the Board of Guardianship – a transaction held at the time to be extraordinarily complicated and daring. Of all those who censured him, Berestov, whose chief characteristic was a loathing of innovations, was the most severe. Berestov could not speak dispassionately of his neighbour's anglomania, and was perpetually seeking an opportunity to criticise him. When showing a guest over his estate, he would reply to his visitor's praise of his management with sly irony: 'Ah, yes, we are not like our neighbour Grigory Ivanovitch here – we are not the sort to ruin ourselves in the English fashion. We're happy enough to keep ourselves fed in Russian style.' Thanks to the zeal of neighbours, these and similar quips were brought to the ears of Grigory Ivanovitch in greatly embellished form. The anglomaniac bore criticism no less impatiently than do our journalists; he was enraged and dubbed his critic a bear and a provincial.

Such were the relations that existed between these two landowners when Berestov's son returned home to his father's estate. Educated at the university of ***, he proposed to go into the army, but his father would not agree to this. The young man felt himself entirely unsuited to the civil service. Neither would yield to the other, and in the meantime Alexey lived the life of a nobleman, cultivating his moustache in preparation for the army, should he win his way.

Alexey was a fine young man indeed. It would, for sure, be a pity if his handsome figure were never to be shown off by a military uniform, and if, instead of cutting a dash on horseback, he were to spend his youth poring over official papers. The neighbours, noticing how he always rode at the head of the hunt, regardless of obstacles, were unanimous in their opinion that he would never make a successful departmental chief. The young ladies looked him over – some more than once; but Alexey paid little heed to them, and they attributed his coldness to a love affair. Indeed, a piece of paper bearing the address to which he had sent one of his letters was passed around among them:

'To Akulina Petrovna Kurochkina, in Moscow, opposite the Alexeyevsky Monastery, at the house of the coppersmith Savelyev, with the humble request that this letter be delivered to A. N. R.'

Those of my readers who have never lived in the country cannot imagine how charming these provincial young ladies are! Brought up in the open air, in the shade of the apple-trees in their gardens, they obtain all their knowledge of life and of the world from books. Solitude, freedom and reading develop in them, very early on, feelings and passions unknown to our frivolous townswomen. For these young ladies the jingle of harness-bells is in itself an adventure, a trip to the nearest town a major event in their lives, and the visit of a guest leaves behind long, sometimes life-long memories. Of course, anybody is at liberty to laugh at some of their peculiarities, but the jokes of a superficial observer cannot destroy their essential qualities, of which the chief is that singularity of character, that *individualité*, without which, in the opinion of Jean-Paul, there can be no human greatness. In towns and capital cities women perhaps receive a better education, but their characters are quickly levelled out by the ways of the world, and their souls rendered as uniform as their headdress. This is said neither in judgement nor in censure; even so, *nota nostra manet,* to use the words of an ancient scribe.

It is not difficult to imagine the sort of impression Alexey would be bound to make on young ladies such as these. He was the first gloomy, disenchanted person they had met, the first to speak of spent pleasures and a faded youth; moreover, on his finger he wore a black ring engraved with a death's head. This was all extraordinarily novel to the province. The young ladies went out of their minds about him.

But none was so preoccupied with him as the daughter of our anglomaniac, Lisa (or Betsy, as her father, Grigory Ivanovitch, called her). Since the fathers of these two young people never visited each other's houses, Lisa had not yet seen Alexey, although among the other young ladies of the neighbourhood he had become the sole topic of conversation. Lisa was seventeen years old. Her attractive, dark-skinned face was lit up by dark eyes. She was an only child and consequently very spoilt. Her high spirits and incessant pranks were the delight of her father and the despair of her governess, Miss Jackson, a strait-laced spinster of forty, who powdered her face, dyed her eyebrows and read all the way through *Pamela* twice a year – for all of which she received two thousand roubles a year and almost died of boredom in this *barbarous Russia* of ours.

Lisa was looked after by her maid Nastya, who, although older than her mistress, was quite as high-spirited. Lisa was very attached to her, shared all her secrets and planned all her tricks with her. In short, Nastya was a much more significant figure in the village of Priluchino than any *confidante* in a French tragedy.

'May I go out on a visit today?' Nastya asked one day, as she was dressing her mistress.

'Of course. Where to?'

'To Tugilovo, to the Berestovs'. It's the name-day of their cook's wife, and she came over yesterday to invite us to dinner.'

'Really!' said Lisa. 'The masters are at daggers drawn, and yet the servants entertain each other.'

'What do we care about the masters?' retorted Nastya. 'Besides, I belong to you, not to your father. You haven't yet quarrelled with young Berestov; let the older people fight it out among themselves if it gives them any pleasure.'

'Try to get a glimpse of Alexey Berestov, Nastya, and tell me exactly what he looks like and what sort of a person he is.'

Nastya promised that she would do so, and Lisa waited impatiently throughout the day for her return. Nastya came back in the evening.

'Well, Lisaveta Grigoryevna,' she said as she entered the room, 'I have seen the young Berestov. I had plenty of opportunity to take a good look at him; he was with us all day.'

'What! Tell me everything, tell me everything in order.'

'Certainly. We set out from here, I, Anisya Yegorovna, Nenila, Dunka ...'

'Yes, yes, I know about that. And then?'

'But let me tell you everything in order. We got there just before dinner. The room was full of people – people from Kolbino, Zakharyevo, the steward's wife and daughters, people from Khlupino ...'

'But what about Berestov?'

'Wait a minute. We sat down at the table: the steward's wife sat on the right of the hostess, I sat next to her ... The daughters sulked, but I don't give a rap for them ...'

'Oh, Nastya, how tedious you are with your endless detail!'

'Aren't you impatient? Well, we got up from the table ...
we had been sitting there for about three whole hours, and
the dinner was excellent; for dessert there was blancmange –
blue, red and candy-striped. So we got up from the table and
went out into the garden to play tag, when the young master
joined us.'

'Well, and is it true that he is so good-looking?'

'Amazingly good-looking, a real Adonis, you might say.
Tall, handsome, rosy-cheeked ...'

'Really? And I always thought he'd have a pale face. Well?
How did he seem to you – sad and thoughtful?'

'By no means! I've never seen such a madcap in all
my life. He took it into his head to join in the game with
us.'

'Join in the game with you! Impossible!'

'Not at all impossible! And what's more, whenever he
caught anybody, he gave her a kiss.'

'Come, Nastya, you're making it all up.'

'No, I'm not. It was as much as I could do to keep out of
his way. He was with us all day.'

'But I heard he was in love and never looked at anyone.'

'I don't know anything about that, but he certainly looked
at me a good deal too much, and at Tanya, the steward's
daughter – and at that Pasha from Kolbino: I have to say, he
didn't leave any of us out, the scamp!'

'How extraordinary! And what do they say about him in
the house?'

'An excellent master, so they say: so kind and cheerful.
Only one thing wrong with him: he's so fond of running after
the girls. But that's no fault to my mind; he'll quieten down
as he gets older.'

'How I should love to see him,' said Lisa with a sigh.

'Well, that's not so difficult, is it? Tugilovo isn't far from
here – only three versts. Set out for a walk or a ride in that

direction, and you'll be sure to meet him. He goes out early every morning with his gun.'

'No, that wouldn't be right, he might think I was running after him. And anyway, our fathers get on so badly that I can't possibly ever get to know him ... Ah, Nastya! I'll tell you what! I'll dress up as a peasant-girl!'

'Yes, that's it! Put on a coarse shirt and smock and then walk boldly across to Tugilovo. I can guarantee that Berestov will not pass you by if he meets you.'

'And I can talk just like the local peasants. Oh, Nastya, dear Nastya! What a splendid idea!'

And Lisa went to bed resolved to carry out her sprightly plan without delay. The next day she set about putting it into action. She sent to the market for some coarse cloth, some blue nankeen and some brass buttons and, with Nastya's aid, cut out a shirt and a smock for herself. She then set all the maidservants to work on the sewing, and by the evening everything was ready. Lisa tried on her new outfit and, inspecting herself before the looking-glass, she had to confess that she had never looked so pretty. She rehearsed her part, bowing low as she walked, tossing her head several times like one of those china dolls whose heads move about, spoke in peasant accents, giggled behind her shirt sleeve – and earned Nastya's full approval. Only one thing troubled her: when she tried walking about the yard barefoot, the turf pricked at her tender feet, and she found that she could not bear the sand and the gravel. Here too Nastya came to her aid: she measured Lisa's feet, ran into the fields to find the shepherd Trofim, and from him ordered a pair of bast shoes to fit her.

Lisa awoke the next morning at the crack of dawn. The rest of the house was still asleep. Nastya was at the gate, waiting for the shepherd. The horn was sounded and the village flock moved slowly past the landowner's house. As

Trofim walked by, he handed Nastya a pair of small, gaily-coloured bast shoes and received fifty kopecks in payment from her. Lisa quietly put on her peasant dress, whispered instructions concerning Miss Jackson in Nastya's ear, went out by the back door, and ran through the kitchen-garden into the fields beyond.

In the east the dawn was radiant, and the golden ranks of clouds seemed to be awaiting the sun like courtiers their sovereign. The clear sky, the morning freshness, the dew, the slight breeze and the singing of the birds filled Lisa's heart with childlike joy. Fearful of meeting someone she knew, she seemed not to walk but to fly. As she approached the copse which formed the boundary to her father's estate, Lisa walked more slowly. It was here that she was to wait for Alexey. She did not know why but her heart beat wildly: it is the fear that accompanies our youthful pranks which constitutes their principal charm. Lisa entered the twilight copse. She was greeted by its deep, echoing voice, and gradually her gaiety gave way to a mood of blissful contemplation. She thought . . . but who can say exactly what a girl of seventeen thinks about in a copse, alone on a spring morning between the hours of five and six? And thus she walked on, lost in thought, shaded by tall trees on either side of her, when suddenly a fine pointer ran barking up to her. Lisa cried out in alarm. But at that moment a voice called out: '*Tout beau, Sbogar . . . ici*', and a young hunter emerged from behind a clump of bushes.

'Don't be afraid, my dear,' he said to Lisa, 'my dog doesn't bite.'

Lisa, already recovered from her alarm, was quick to take advantage of the situation.

'But, sir,' she said, assuming a half-frightened, half-bashful expression, 'I am frightened – he looks so fierce; I'm afraid he'll come at me again.'

Alexey (the reader will have recognised him) had been gazing intently at the young peasant girl.

'If you're afraid, I'll accompany you,' he said. 'Will you allow me to walk beside you?'

'Who's to stop you?' Lisa replied. 'You may do as you please; anyone is free to use the road.'

'Where do you come from?'

'From Priluchino: I am the daughter of Vasily the blacksmith. I was going to pick some mushrooms.' (Lisa was carrying a small bark basket by a piece of string.) 'And you, sir? From Tugilovo?'

'Yes,' replied Alexey. 'I'm the young master's valet.'

Alexey wanted to be on an equal footing with her. But Lisa looked at him and laughed.

'You never are,' she said. 'I'm not the fool you take me for. I can see that you are the young master himself.'

'What makes you think so?'

'Why, everything about you.'

'But . . .'

'As if I couldn't tell the difference between master and servant. You're dressed different, you talk different, and you call your dog different.'

Alexey was finding Lisa more and more attractive with each minute that passed. Accustomed as he was to treating pretty village-girls with little ceremony, he attempted to put his arms round her; but Lisa sprang back from him and suddenly assumed an expression of such coldness and severity that Alexey, amused as he was, attempted no further advances.

'If you wish us to remain friends,' she said gravely, 'be good enough not to forget yourself.'

'Who taught you such airs and graces?' asked Alexey, bursting into laughter. 'Could it be my friend Nastenka, your young mistress's maid? I see now how enlightenment spreads.'

Lisa felt that she had been speaking out of character and instantly reverted to her role of peasant-girl.

'Do you think I've never been in the master's house?' she said. 'I use my ears and eyes, I do. However,' she continued, 'I won't find many mushrooms if I stand here chattering with you much longer. You go your way, sir, and I'll go mine. Fare you well . . .'

Lisa made as if to go, but Alexey seized her by the hand.

'What is your name, my dear?'

'Akulina,' replied Lisa, trying to free her fingers from Alexey's grasp. 'But let me go, sir. It's time I went home.'

'Well, Akulina, my friend, I shall certainly be paying a visit to your father, Vasily the blacksmith.'

'What!' exclaimed Lisa quickly. 'For God's sake, don't do that. If they were to find out at home that I had been chattering alone with a gentleman in a copse, I'd really catch it. My father Vasily the blacksmith, he would beat me to death, he would.'

'But I must see you again.'

'I'll be back here for mushrooms.'

'But when?'

'Happen tomorrow.'

'Dear Akulina, I would kiss you if I dared. Tomorrow, at the same time, then?'

'Yes, yes.'

'And you'll not deceive me?'

'I'll not deceive you.'

'Do you swear it?'

'I swear by Holy Friday that I'll come.'

The young couple parted. Lisa left the wood, crossed the fields, crept into the garden and rushed headlong into the farm building where Nastya was waiting for her. There she changed her clothes, replying abstractedly to the impatient questioning of her *confidante*, and made her appearance in the drawing-room. The table was laid, breakfast was ready and Miss Jackson, already powdered and laced into the shape of a wine-glass, was cutting thin slices of bread and butter.

Lisa's father praised his daughter for her early morning walk. 'There is nothing so healthy,' he said, 'as getting up at dawn.'

And he quoted several examples of human longevity drawn from English journals and observed that anybody who lived to be more than a hundred abstained from vodka and rose at dawn in both winter and summer. But Lisa paid him no attention. In her mind she was going over all the circumstances of the morning's meeting, the entire conversation between Akulina and the young hunter, and her conscience was beginning to worry her. In vain she told herself that their conversation had not overstepped the bounds of decorum, that her escapade could have no serious consequences – but conscience spoke louder than reason. The promise she had given for the following day troubled her more than anything, and she came near to deciding to go back on her solemn vow. But Alexey, after waiting for her in vain, might go into the village to look for the daughter of Vasily the blacksmith, the real Akulina, a fat pock-marked peasant-girl, and thus guess the trick that Lisa had so thoughtlessly played on him. This thought horrified her, and she decided that she would go to the copse the following morning, again disguised as Akulina.

For his part Alexey was in an ecstasy of delight, and thought of nothing but his new acquaintance all day. And in his dreams at night, the vision of the beautiful, dark-skinned Akulina appeared before him. Dawn had scarcely broken before he was up and dressed. Without even giving himself time to load his gun, he went out into the fields with his faithful Sbogar and hastened to the place of the promised rendezvous. A half-hour of unbearable waiting passed; at last he caught sight of a blue smock flashing among the bushes, and he rushed forward to meet the charming Akulina. She smiled at the rapture of his gratitude; but Alexey immediately noticed signs of unease and despondency on her face. He wanted to know their cause. Lisa confessed that she considered her behaviour to be frivolous, that she was sorry for it, that on this occasion she had not wished to go back on her word, but that this meeting must be the last, and she asked him to break off an acquaintance which could do neither of them any good. All this was of course spoken in a peasant accent; but such thoughts and feelings, rare in a simple peasant-girl, astonished Alexey. He used all his eloquence in his attempt to dissuade Akulina from her intentions; he assured her of the innocence of his feelings, promised never to give her cause for repentance, to obey her in all things, and implored her not to deprive him of the joy of seeing her alone – if only every other day or twice a week. He spoke the language of true love and indeed, as he spoke, he felt himself to be completely in love. Lisa listened to him in silence.

'Give me your word,' she said finally, 'that you will never go into the village in search of me, nor make any inquiries about me. Give me your word that you will not seek to meet me at any other time than I say.'

Alexey was about to swear by Holy Friday but she stopped him with a smile.

'I don't demand vows,' she said. 'Your promise is enough.'

After this they conversed in a friendly way, strolling side by side through the wood until Lisa said to him: 'It's time for me to go home now.'

They parted and, left alone, Alexey fell to wondering how a simple peasant-girl had managed to gain such a powerful influence over him in two meetings. His relations with Akulina held the charm of novelty for him, and although the strange peasant-girl's demands seemed to him severe, the thought of going back on his word never even entered his head. The fact was that Alexey, in spite of his sinister black ring, his mysterious correspondence, and his air of gloomy disenchantment, was a cheerful, ardent young man with a good heart, capable of appreciating innocent pleasures.

Were I to follow my own inclinations, I would here begin a minute and detailed description of the two young people's meetings, of their increasing mutual liking and trust, their occupations, their talks; but I realise that the great majority of my readers would not share my pleasure in this. Such details generally appear false and affected, and I shall therefore omit them, merely observing that before two months had passed, Alexey was hopelessly in love and Lisa, although less demonstrative about her feelings, was by no means indifferent. They were both happy in the present and thought little of the future.

The thought of nuptial ties had quite frequently crossed their minds, but they never spoke to each other on the subject. The reason for this was obvious: Alexey, attached as he was to his dear Akulina, was always aware of the distance that separated him from the poor peasant-girl; and Lisa, knowing of the hatred that existed between their respective fathers, dared not hope for a reconciliation between them. Moreover, her vanity was secretly tickled by the vague, romantic hope of seeing the heir of Tugilovo at the feet of the daughter of the Priluchino blacksmith. And then suddenly there occurred an event which threatened to change their mutual relations.

One fine, cold morning (one of those in which our Russian autumn so abounds), Ivan Petrovitch Berestov went out riding, taking with him, in case of any sport, five or six greyhounds, his whipper-in and a few stable-boys with rattles. At the same time, Grigory Ivanovitch Muromsky, tempted by the fine weather, ordered his bob-tailed filly to be saddled, and himself set out for a gentle trot around his English-style estate. As he rode up to the wood he caught sight of his neighbour, proudly seated in his saddle, wearing a Cossack jacket lined with fox-fur, and awaiting the appearance of a hare which his stable-boys, with loud cries and shakings of rattles, were harrying out of a clump of bushes. If Grigory Ivanovitch could have foreseen this encounter, he would have undoubtedly turned in another direction; as it was, however, he came upon Berestov quite unexpectedly and suddenly found himself not more than a pistol shot away from him. There was no help for it. Muromsky, the civilised European, rode up to his enemy and greeted him courteously. Berestov returned his salute with the reluctant obedience of a chained bear. Just then the hare leapt out of the wood and ran for the open fields. Berestov and his whipper-in both yelled at the tops of their voices, unleashed the dogs, and galloped off in hot pursuit. Muromsky's mare, which had never hunted, took fright and bolted. Muromsky, who proclaimed himself a fine horseman, let her have her head, inwardly rather pleased at the incident, which had relieved him of unwelcome company. But the horse, galloping up to the edge of a ditch she had failed to notice, suddenly shied and threw Muromsky. Falling rather heavily on the frosty ground, he lay there cursing his bob-tailed mare, which, as if suddenly coming to her senses, halted as soon as she felt herself to be riderless. Ivan Petrovitch galloped up to Muromsky and inquired whether he had hurt himself. Meanwhile, the whipper-in managed to catch hold of the guilty horse and stood holding her by the bridle. He helped Muromsky back into the saddle, and Berestov invited the latter back to his house. Muromsky felt obliged to accept the invitation; and thus Berestov returned home in triumph, having caught a hare and bringing back his enemy, wounded and almost a prisoner of war.

The two neighbours conversed in perfectly friendly fashion

over breakfast. Muromsky, confessing that his fall had made him unfit to return home on horseback, asked Berestov to lend him a carriage. Berestov accompanied him down the steps, and Muromsky would not take his leave before he had extracted Berestov's word of honour that he (together with Alexey Ivanovitch) would drive over to dine with him at Priluchino the following day. And so, as a result of the timidity of a bob-tailed mare, the long-standing and deep-rooted enmity that existed between the two men showed signs of coming to an end.

Lisa ran out to meet Grigory Ivanovitch.

'What's happened, Papa?' she cried in astonishment. 'Why are you limping? Where's your horse? Whose carriage is that?'

'You'll never guess, *my dear*,' Grigory Ivanovitch replied, and he related all that had happened.

Lisa could not believe her ears. Grigory Ivanovitch, without giving her time to recover, announced that both the Berestovs would be dining with him on the following day.

'What are you saying?' she cried, turning pale. 'The Berestovs – father and son! To dine with us tomorrow! No, Papa, you may do as you wish, but I certainly won't show myself.'

'Have you taken leave of your senses?' demanded her father. 'Since when have you become so shy? Or do you nurse a hereditary hatred for the Berestovs like some romantic heroine? Enough of this nonsense . . .'

'No, Papa, not for the world or anything in it will I appear before the Berestovs.'

Grigory Ivanovitch shrugged his shoulders and gave up the argument, knowing that there was nothing to be gained by opposing her, and he went to rest for a while after his memorable ride.

Lisaveta Grigoryevna went up to her room and summoned

Nastya. Together they held a long conference on the subject of the morrow's visit. What would Alexey think when he recognised, in the well-bred young lady, his Akulina? What would his opinion be of her conduct, her morals, her discretion? On the other hand, Lisa very much wanted to see what sort of impression so unexpected a meeting would have on him ... An idea suddenly flashed through her mind. She immediately told it to Nastya; they were both delighted with it and determined at all costs to put it into practice.

At breakfast the following morning Grigory Ivanovitch asked his daughter if she still proposed to hide from the Berestovs.

'Papa,' replied Lisa, 'I'll receive them if that's what you want, but only on condition that however I appear before them and whatever I do, you will not scold me or give any sign of surprise or displeasure.'

'Up to your old tricks again!' Grigory Ivanovitch said with a laugh. 'All right, all right, I agree. Do what you like, my black-eyed madcap.'

With these words he kissed her on the forehead, and Lisa ran off to make her preparations.

At exactly two o'clock, a home-built carriage drawn by six horses entered the drive and rounded the bright green circle of the lawn. The older Berestov, aided by two of Muromsky's liveried footmen, mounted the steps. Behind him came his son, who had arrived on horseback, and together they entered the dining-room where the table had already been laid. It would have been impossible for Muromsky to have received his neighbours with greater cordiality; he invited them to take a look at his garden and menagerie before dinner and led them along the carefully kept gravel paths. The older Berestov inwardly deplored the time and labour wasted on such useless whims, but from courtesy kept silent. His son shared neither the disapproval of his father, the thrifty landowner, nor the enthusiasm of his host, the vain anglo-maniac; he was impatiently awaiting the appearance of the host's daughter, of whom he had heard so much, and although his heart, as is known to us, was already taken, a beautiful young woman always held claim to his imagination.

Returning to the drawing-room, the three of them sat down. The older men reminisced about the old days and exchanged tales of their service in the army, while Alexey reflected on the role he would play in the presence of Lisa. He decided that an air of cold indifference would best suit the circumstances and he prepared himself accordingly. The door opened and he turned his head with such indifference, with such haughty nonchalance, that it might have made the heart of even the most hardened coquette shudder. Unfortunately, it was not Lisa but old Miss Jackson, powdered, corseted, with eyes downcast, who entered the room with a small curtsy; Alexey's magnificent tactical manoeuvre was therefore wasted. Hardly had he time to gather his strength anew when the door again opened and this time Lisa entered. They all stood up. Her father was about to introduce her to his guests, when suddenly he stopped short and hastily bit his lip ... Lisa, dark-skinned Lisa, was powdered up to the ears and even more made-up than Miss Jackson herself: false curls, much fairer than her own hair, were fluffed up like the wig of Louis XIV; sleeves *à l'imbécile* stuck out like the hooped petticoats of Madame de Pompadour; her waist was so tightly laced that her figure resembled the letter *X,* and all her mother's jewels which had not yet been pawned sparkled upon her fingers, neck and ears. Alexey could not possibly have recognised his Akulina in this ludicrously brilliant young lady. Berestov kissed her hand and Alexey unwillingly followed suit. As his lips touched her small white fingers, he fancied he felt a tremor run through them. At the same time, he caught sight of a little foot, intentionally put forward to show off an extremely coquettish shoe. This reconciled him somewhat to the rest of her dress. As for the paint and the powder, it must be admitted that, in the simplicity of his heart, Alexey did not at first notice these; neither, later, did he suspect them. Grigory Ivanovitch remembered his promise and tried not to show his surprise; but his daughter's prank struck him as so amusing that he had difficulty in restraining his laughter. The prim Englishwoman, however, found nothing to be amused at. She suspected that the paint and the powder had been purloined from her dressing-table, and a crimson flush of rage showed through the artificial pallor of her cheeks. She threw furious glances at the young offender who, postponing explanations to some future date, pretended not to notice them.

They sat down at the table. Alexey continued in his role of preoccupied distraction. Lisa spoke only in French, and in an affected sing-song voice. Her father kept looking at her, unable to understand the purpose of her behaviour and yet finding it extremely amusing. The English governess sat in a state of mute fury. Ivan Petrovitch alone seemed to feel completely at home; he ate for two, drank his normal fill, laughed at his own jokes and conversed with ever-increasing friendliness and gaiety.

They finally rose from table. The guests departed and Grigory Ivanovitch gave vent to laughter and questions.

'What on earth put it into your head to fool them like that?' he asked Lisa. 'And do you know something? Powder suits you excellently. I do not begin to understand the secrets of a lady's toilet but, if I were you, I should begin using powder – not too much, of course, just a little.'

Lisa was enchanted at the success of her plan. She threw her arms around her father's neck, promised to think about the advice he had given her, and then ran off to pacify the irate Miss Jackson, who was loth to open her door and listen to Lisa's excuses. Lisa explained that she had felt ashamed to appear before strangers with so dark a complexion, but that she had not dared to ask ... She was sure that good, kind Miss Jackson would forgive her, and so on and so forth. Miss Jackson, once satisfied that Lisa had not intended to make a laughing-stock of her, calmed down, kissed Lisa and, in token of reconciliation, gave her a small jar of English powder, which Lisa accepted with every indication of sincere gratitude.

The reader will guess that Lisa lost no time in keeping her rendezvous in the copse on the morning of the following day.

'You were at my master's house last night, sir?' she said as soon as they met. 'What did you think of the young mistress?'

Alexey replied that he had not noticed her.

''Tis a pity!' exclaimed Lisa.

'Why?' asked Alexey.

''Cause I wanted to ask whether what they say is . . .'

'What do they say?'

'. . . is true – that I be like her.'

'What rubbish! She's a positive monster compared to you.'

'Oh, sir, you shouldn't speak like that of our young mistress. She is so fair and so elegant-like. Who could speak of me and her in the same breath?'

Alexey vowed to her that she was more beautiful than any of the fairest young ladies in the world and, in order to assure her completely, he began to describe her mistress in such amusing terms that Lisa split her sides with laughing.

'Still,' she said with a sigh, 'the young mistress may be comical, but beside her I am nothing but a poor ignorant fool.'

'What a thing to worry about,' said Alexey. 'If you like, I'll start giving you lessons in reading and writing at once.'

'Can you mean it!' exclaimed Lisa. 'All right then. After all, what's the harm in trying?'

'None at all, my dear. Why don't we begin straight away?'

They sat down. Alexey took a pencil and a note-book from his pocket, and in no time at all Akulina had learned the alphabet. Alexey was speechless at her ability to pick it up so quickly. The next morning she wanted to try writing. At first the pencil would not obey her, but within a few minutes she was able to trace the letters quite accurately.

'It's a miracle,' said Alexey. 'We're having quicker results than the Lancaster system.'

And indeed, by the third lesson, Akulina was already able to pick her way through *Natalya, the Boyar's Daughter.* She astounded Alexey by the observations she made while reading, and then by covering a whole sheet of paper with aphorisms drawn from the story.

A week passed and they were exchanging letters. Their post-box was the hollow of an old oak-tree, and Nastya secretly performed the duties of postman. There Alexey would bring his letters, written in a bold, round hand, and there, on ordinary blue writing-paper, he would find the scribblings of his beloved. Akulina's literary style was visibly improving and her mind began to develop with noticeable speed.

In the meantime, the acquaintanceship which had so recently sprung up between Ivan Petrovitch Berestov and Grigory Ivanovitch Muromsky was growing steadily stronger, and it soon developed into a friendship as a result of the following circumstances. Muromsky frequently reflected that, when Ivan Petrovitch died, his estate would pass into the hands of Alexey Ivanovitch; in which case Alexey Ivanovitch would become one of the richest landowners in the province. He reflected further that there were no reasons why Alexey should not marry Lisa. Old Berestov, for his part, while admitting certain eccentricities in his neighbour (or, as he termed them, 'certain English follies'), did not however deny that he had many excellent qualities – for example, an unusual resourcefulness. Grigory Ivanovitch was a close relation of Count Pronsky, a man of great power and distinction; the Count could be very useful to Alexey, and Muromsky (so thought Ivan Petrovitch) would probably be glad of an opportunity to marry off his daughter to such advantage. Having kept their reflections to themselves for some time, the old men at last revealed the nature of their thoughts to each other, embraced, and promised to go into the matter with the utmost thoroughness. Each began to consider his own side of the affair. Muromsky foresaw the difficulty of persuading his Betsy to become closer acquainted with Alexey, whom she had not seen since that memorable dinner. It had seemed then that they had no particular liking for each other; at any rate, Alexey had not returned to Priluchino and on each occasion that Ivan Petrovitch honoured them with a visit, Lisa retired to her room. But, thought Grigory Ivanovitch, if Alexey were to come here every day, then surely Betsy would not be able to prevent herself from falling in love with him. That was the natural order of things. Time would settle everything.

Ivan Petrovitch felt less concern as to the success of his intentions. That very evening he summoned his son to his study, lit his pipe and said after a short pause: 'Well, Alyosha, how is it you have not spoken of a military career for quite some time now? Aren't you attracted by a Hussar's uniform any more?'

'No, father,' replied Alexey respectfully. 'I realise that you don't want me to go into the Hussars; my duty is to obey you.'

'Good,' replied Ivan Petrovitch, 'I see that you are an obedient son. I am greatly relieved; I don't wish to force you to do things against your will. I will not compel you – at least, not for the present – to enter the civil service. On the other hand, however, I intend to get you married.'

'To whom, father?' asked the astonished Alexey.

'To Lisaveta Grigoryevna Muromsky,' replied Ivan Petrovitch. 'An excellent match, eh?'

'But sir, I am not thinking of getting married just yet.'

'You're not thinking, so I have thought for you, and my mind is made up.'

'That's as may be – I don't even like Lisa Muromsky.'

'You will, with time. Habit makes the heart grow fonder.'

'I don't feel capable of making her happy.'

'Don't you worry yourself about making her happy. Well? Is this your idea of fatherly respect? I see!'

'Whatever *you* wish, *I* do not wish to marry and I will *not* marry.'

'You *will* marry her or, as God is my witness, I'll curse you and sell up this whole estate and squander the money so that you won't get a single kopeck. I'll give you three days to think it over – and in the meantime keep out of my sight!'

Alexey knew that once his father got an idea into his head, nothing would drive it out – not even a nail, as Taras Skotinin once said. But Alexey took after his father, and it was just as difficult to persuade him to change his mind. He went to his room and began to ponder on the limits of parental authority, on Lisaveta Grigoryevna, his father's solemn promise to cut him off without a kopeck and, finally, Akulina. For the first time he saw clearly that he was passionately in love with her. The romantic idea of marrying a peasant-girl and living by his own labours crossed his mind, and the more he thought about this decisive step, the more reasonable it seemed. The meetings in the copse had been interrupted for some time by the rainy weather. In his most legible handwriting and in a highly frenzied style he wrote a letter to Akulina, informing her of the doom that threatened them both, and offered her his hand forthwith. He at once took the letter to the post-box in the hollow of the old oak-tree, and then went to bed, extremely pleased with himself.

The next day, Alexey, firm in his resolve, rode off early in the morning to see Muromsky in order to put his case before him frankly. He hoped to stir the other's magnanimity and win him over to his side.

'Is Grigory Ivanovitch at home?' he asked, leaving his horse by the steps of the house at Priluchino.

'No, sir,' replied the servant. 'Grigory Ivanovitch went out early this morning.'

'What a nuisance!' thought Alexey. 'Well, perhaps Lisaveta Grigoryevna is at home, then?'

'Yes, sir, she is.'

And Alexey jumped off his horse, handed over the reins to the footman, and entered the house unannounced.

'All will be settled,' he thought as he approached the drawing-room. 'I will explain everything to the lady herself.'

He went in . . . to be thunderstruck! Lisa . . . no, Akulina, his dear, dark-skinned Akulina, not in a smock, but in a white morning-gown, was seated before the window, reading his letter; she was so preoccupied that she did not hear him enter. Alexey could not restrain an exclamation of joy. Lisa started, raised her head, uttered a cry and tried to run away. Alexey rushed forward to stop her.

'Akulina! Akulina!'

Lisa tried to free herself from him.

'*Mais laissez-moi donc, monsieur – mais êtes-vous fou?*' she repeated as she struggled.

'Akulina, my dear! My dear Akulina!' he repeated, kissing her hands.

Miss Jackson, a witness to this scene, did not know what

to make of it. At that moment the door opened and Grigory Ivanovitch entered the room.

'Aha!' said Muromsky. 'You seem to have sorted things out by yourselves . . .'

The reader will spare me the unnecessary task of describing the *dénouement*.

The History of the
Village of Goryukhino

Should God grant me readers, they will perhaps be curious to know how it came about that I decided to write the history of the village of Goryukhino. To satisfy that curiosity, I must enter into a few preliminary details.

I was born of upstanding and honourable parents on 1st April, 1801, in the village of Goryukhino and I received my elementary education from the sexton of our parish church. It is to this estimable man that I owe what was later to develop into my taste for reading and literary study in general. My progress was slow, but it was solid, for almost everything that I knew at the age of ten has remained in my memory, which is weak by nature and which I was not permitted, on account of my poor state of health, to overburden.

The calling of a man of letters has always seemed to me to be the most enviable of all. My parents, respectable but simple folk, educated in accordance with the old ways, used never to read anything and, apart from an alphabet bought for me, some almanacs and Kurganov's *Latest Handbook of Sample Letters*, there were no books to be found in all the house. The reading of the *Handbook* was for a long time my favourite exercise. I knew it by heart and yet daily found in it new treasures hitherto unnoticed. Next to General Plemyannikov, to whom my father had at one time been aide-de-camp, Kurganov seemed to me the world's greatest man. I enquired about him from everybody, but unfortunately no-one was able to satisfy my curiosity. He was known to nobody personally, and to all my questions the only reply that came was that Kurganov was the author of the *Latest Handbook of Sample Letters*, which I knew perfectly well already. Like some ancient demi-god, his being was lost in the shadow of obscurity; I sometimes even doubted that he genuinely existed. It struck me that his name was an invention, and the legend surrounding him a hollow myth awaiting the investigations of some latter-day Niebuhr. Even so, Kurganov continued to haunt my imagination and, in trying to give some shape to his mysterious figure, I eventually decided that he must resemble a certain member of the district court by the name of Koryuchkin, a little old man with a red nose and flashing eyes.

In 1812 I was taken to Moscow and placed in the boarding-school of Karl Ivanovitch Meyer, where I spent no longer than three months, for we were sent home before the invasion of the enemy, and I returned to the country. When the heathen Twelve Nations had been driven off, my parents wanted to take me back to Moscow to see whether Karl Ivanovitch had returned to his former residence and, if not, to send me to another school, but I implored my mother to let me stay in the country, arguing that my poor health did not permit me to get up at seven o'clock in the morning, the usual time of rising in boarding-schools. And thus, by the time I reached the age of sixteen, my education remained at an elementary level, and I was still playing ball-games with my companions in the village – the only science in which I had gained reasonable proficiency at boarding-school.

I then enlisted as a cadet in the *** Infantry Regiment, in which I remained until last year, 18**. My time with the regiment left me with few pleasant impressions beyond obtaining my commission and winning 245 roubles when I had only one rouble sixty kopecks in my pocket. The death of my beloved parents forced me to resign my commission and return to the estate I had inherited.

This period of my life is of such importance to me that I intend to expand upon it, begging in advance the forgiveness of my benevolent reader if I trespass on his indulgent attention.

It was a cloudy autumn day. Arriving at the posting station at which I had to turn off for Goryukhino, I hired some fresh horses and took the country road. Although I am of a placid temperament, I was so impatient to see again the places where I had passed my happiest years that I continually urged the driver on, now promising him rewards and now threatening him with blows, and since it was easier for me to poke him in the back than to take out and untie my purse, I own that on two or three occasions I did strike him, something I had never done before, having, I don't know why, a particular liking for drivers as a class. In turn the driver urged on his troika, but it appeared to me that, in the way of drivers, while he exhorted the horses and waved his whip, he also tightened the reins at the same time. At last I caught sight of the copse at Goryukhino, and ten minutes later we drove into the courtyard of the manor house. My heart beat violently. I looked around me with indescribable emotion. It was eight years since I had seen Goryukhino. The birch saplings I had watched being planted by the fence had grown into tall, spreading trees. The courtyard, which had at one time been graced by three neat flower-beds, separated by wide gravel paths, was now an unmown meadow in which a brown cow grazed. My britchka stopped at the front door. My servant went to open the door but it was boarded up, even though the shutters were open and the house seemed to be inhabited. A woman came out of one of the peasants' cottages and asked me what I wanted. On learning that her master had arrived she ran back into her cottage, and I was soon surrounded by household servants. Seeing their faces, familiar and unfamiliar, I was moved to the depths of my heart, and I embraced them all in friendly fashion. My boyhood companions were now men, and the girls who used to sit about on the floor waiting for errands to run were now married women. The men wept. To the women I remarked without ceremony how they had grown older and received the spirited reply: 'And how you've lost your looks, master.' I was taken round to the back steps where, like the long-suffering Odysseus, I was greeted by my old wet-nurse with a tearful, sobbing embrace. The bath was hastily heated. The cook who, having nothing else to do, had grown himself a beard, offered to prepare dinner for me – or rather supper, since it had by now grown dark. The rooms previously occupied by my wet-nurse and my late mother's maidservants were immediately cleaned up for me. And thus I found myself in the humble home of my parents and went to sleep in the same room in which I had been born twenty-three years before.

Some three weeks passed in business of every kind – I spent a great deal of time with land-assessors, departmental chiefs and every imaginable form of provincial official. I finally took over my inheritance and assumed possession of my patrimony. I was content; but soon the boredom of having nothing to do began to torment me. I was not yet acquainted with my worthy and respected neighbour ***. I was a complete stranger to domestic tasks. The conversation of my wet-nurse, whom I promoted to the rank of housekeeper and major-domo, consisted of fifteen family anecdotes, all of great interest to me, but since she always related them in exactly the same way, she became for me another *Handbook of Sample Letters,* in which I knew where I should find each line on each page. That venerable handbook itself I found in the store-room among rubbish of every sort and in sorry condition. I brought it out into the light and began to read, but Kurganov had lost his charm for me; I read him through once and never opened the book again.

In this extremity it occurred to me to attempt some form of composition myself. The benevolent reader already knows that my beggarly education never went beyond the elementary stage and that I had had no occasion to make up for its neglect, playing as I did until my sixteenth year with servants' boys, and then moving from province to province, from quarters to quarters, spending my time with Jews and camp-hawkers, playing strip billiards and marching through mud.

Moreover, the calling of a writer seemed to me to be so sophisticated and, for the uninitiated, so unattainable that the idea of taking up the pen at first frightened me. Could I dare to aspire to become a writer when my ardent wish to meet even one of their number had never been fulfilled? But this reminds me of an incident which I propose to recount as evidence of my undying passion for our native literature.

In the year 1820, while still a cadet, I happened to be on Government orders in Petersburg. I stayed there a week and despite the fact that I knew not a single soul, I spent an exceedingly jolly time; each day I would trip along to the theatre to take a seat in the gallery of the fourth circle. I learned the names of all the actors, and fell passionately in love with *** who, one Sunday, played with great skill the role of Amalia in the drama *Hatred and Repentance*. Returning from headquarters in the mornings, I formed the habit of calling in at a small coffee-house and reading the literary journals over a cup of chocolate. One day I was sitting there, absorbed in a critical review in *Good Intentions,* when someone in a pea-green overcoat came up to my table and gently took from beneath my journal a copy of the *Hamburg Gazette.* I was so intent on the article that I did not even look up. The stranger ordered a beefsteak and sat down opposite me; I went on reading without paying him any attention. In the meantime, the stranger ate his luncheon, angrily scolded the waiter for some carelessness, drank half a bottle of wine and left. Two young men were also having luncheon.

'Do you know who that was?' one of them asked the other.

'Yes, B**, the writer.'

'The writer!' I could not help exclaiming, and leaving the journal unfinished and the chocolate undrunk, hastened to pay my bill and, without waiting for the change, ran out into the street. Looking all about me, I saw in the distance the pea-green overcoat and, almost at a trot, set out after it along the Nevsky Prospect. I had not gone a few paces before I suddenly felt myself being stopped – I looked round and saw a guards officer, who observed that I should not have knocked him off the pavement, but rather stopped and stood to attention. I became more careful after this reprimand; but unluckily for me I seemed every minute to meet an officer and every minute be forced to stop, and so the writer got further and further ahead of me. Never before had my army greatcoat weighed me down so heavily, and never before had I so envied those who wore epaulettes. At last, at the Anichkin Bridge, I caught up with the green overcoat.

'May I inquire,' I said, saluting, 'whether you are Mr B**, whose excellent articles I have had the good fortune to read in *Amateur of Enlightenment*?'

'No, I am not, sir,' he replied, 'I am not a writer but an advocate. However, I know B** very well; I met him at the Politseysky Bridge only a quarter of an hour ago.'

And thus my respect for Russian literature cost me thirty kopecks in lost change, a service reprimand, almost an arrest – and all for nothing.

Despite all the objections of my reason, the daring thought of becoming a writer continually haunted me. At last, no longer able to oppose my natural inclination, I sewed together a thick exercise book with the firm intention of filling it. I considered and weighed the merits of all types of poetry (for I had not as yet entertained the idea of humble prose), and I decided that it had to be an epic poem drawn from the History of our Nation. It did not take me long to find a hero. I chose Rurik – and set to work.

I had acquired a certain aptitude for verses by copying out the notebooks that went the rounds of us officers, namely *The Dangerous Neighbour*, *Lines on a Moscow Boulevard*, *Presnensky Ponds* and so on. In spite of this my poem progressed slowly and I gave it up half-way through the third verse. I felt that the epic style was not for me, and began a tragedy on Rurik. But I just couldn't get the tragedy started ... I tried to turn it into a ballad – but somehow or other I couldn't master that form either. At last, inspiration dawned upon me and I began and succeeded in finishing an epigraph to accompany the portrait of Rurik.

Although my epigraph was not at all unworthy of attention, especially as the first composition of a young versifier, I yet felt that I was not a born poet and was content to go no further than this first attempt. But my creative efforts had so inclined me to literary occupation that I could no longer refrain from the exercise book and the ink-pot. I felt the desire to descend to prose. To begin with, not wishing to get involved in preliminary study, the formation of a plan, details of construction and so on, I resolved to record my separate thoughts, without any connection or order, just as they occurred to me. Unfortunately, the thoughts would not flow and in the course of two whole days the only observation that came to my mind was the following:

'He who disobeys the laws of reason and yields to the habit of following the promptings of his passions frequently strays from the path and undergoes a tardy repentance.'

This thought is true enough, of course, but by no means original. Discarding aphorisms, I turned my hand to writing tales, but lacking the skill to set out a clear fictional sequence of events, I selected such remarkable anecdotes as I had heard at various times from various people and tried to embellish the truth of them by a lively narrative and, some-times, with the fruits of my own imagination. In composing these tales, I gradually formed my style and learned to express myself correctly, pleasingly and freely. But soon my store of anecdotes ran dry and once again I began to search for a subject suitable for my literary activity.

The thought of abandoning these trivial and questionable anecdotes for the narration of true and great events had long excited my imagination. To be the judge, the observer and prophet of the course of history and of entire peoples seemed to me to be the supreme attainment for a writer. But about what historical event could I, with my pitiful education, possibly write which had not already been dealt with by highly erudite and meticulous scholars? What aspect of history had not already been exhausted by them? Should I write a world history? But did there not already exist the work of the immortal Abbé Millot? Should I settle for a national history? What could I say after Tatishchev, Bolitin and Golikov? And was I the sort of person to burrow among chronicles and penetrate the occult meaning of a dead language – I who had never been able to teach myself the Slavonic numerals? I considered a history on a smaller scale, for instance a history of our provincial capital – but even here, what insuperable obstacles I foresaw! A journey to the capital, a visit to the Governor and the Bishop, a request for admission to the archives, the monastery storerooms, and so on. A history of our local town would have been easier, but it could have no interest either for the scholar or for the layman and it would present little opportunity for fine writing. *** had been renamed in the year 17**, and the only event of note preserved in the chronicles of the town was the terrible fire which had occurred ten years before, destroying the bazaar and the administrative offices.

An unexpected incident resolved my doubts. An elderly

servant, while hanging up linen in the attic, came across an old basket full of chippings, litter and books. The whole household knew of my passion for reading. I was poring over my exercise book, nibbling at my quill and thinking of turning my hand to rural sermons, when my housekeeper triumphantly entered the room, dragging the basket with her and exclaiming joyfully: 'Books! Books!' 'Books!' I repeated ecstatically and threw myself on the basket. Indeed, I saw a whole pile of books, with green and blue paper covers. They turned out to be a collection of old almanacs. This discovery cooled my enthusiasm, but I was still pleased at the unexpected find, which was of books after all, and I generously rewarded my washerwoman's zeal with a silver half-rouble.

Left alone, I began to inspect the almanacs and soon became fascinated by them. They formed an unbroken series from 1744 to 1799 – i.e. exactly fifty-five years. The almanacs also contained sheets of blue paper, usually bound into them, which were covered in old-fashioned handwriting. Glancing through these pages, I saw with surprise that they contained not only observations about the weather and the household accounts, but also brief historical items concerning the village of Goryukhino. I lost no time at all in sorting through these invaluable records and soon found that they presented a complete history of my native village for almost a full century, in the strictest chronological order. They constituted an inexhaustible store of economical, statistical, meteorological and other erudite observations. From then on, the study of these records occupied me to the exclusion of all else, for I recognised the possibility of extracting from them a well-balanced, interesting and instructive narrative. Once I had become sufficiently familiar with these precious documents, I began to search for new sources of information for a history of the village of Goryukhino. The abundance of such sources soon astonished me. Having devoted six whole months to a preliminary study of them, the long-awaited moment came when I sat down to work – and with the help of God I completed the said work on 3rd November, 1827.

Now, like a certain fellow-historian whose name I forget, having finished my arduous task, I lay down my pen and sorrowfully go into my garden to reflect upon that which I have accomplished. It seems to me that, with the *History of Goryukhino* finished, there is no further need for me in this world, that my duty has been fulfilled, and that it is time for me to meet my Maker!

I append hereto a list of sources which were of service to me in the composition of my *History of Goryukhino*:

I. A selection of old almanacs in fifty-four parts. The first twenty parts are covered with writing in old-fashioned abbreviated script. This record was composed by my great-grandfather, Andrey Stepanovitch Belkin. It is remarkable for its clarity and brevity of style, for example: '*May 4th*. Snow. Trishka beaten for insolence. *6th*. Brown cow dead. Senka beaten for drunkenness. *8th*. Fine weather. *9th*. Rain and snow. Trishka beaten on account of the bad weather. *11th*. Fine weather. Fresh fall of snow. Hunted three hares . . .' And so on, without the least comment. The remaining thirty-five parts were written in a variety of hands, for the most part in the so-called 'shopkeeper's hand', with and without abbreviations, generally at some length, in a disconnected fashion and with no regard for spelling. In some places a female hand is noticeable. In this section notes may be found by my grandfather Ivan Andreyevitch Belkin and my grandmother Yevpraxiya Alexeyevna, as well as the steward Garbovitsky.

II. The record of the church sexton at Goryukhino. This curious manuscript was found at the house of my priest, who married the daughter of the chronicler. The first sheets had been torn out and used by the priest's children for makeshift kites. One of these kites fell in the middle of the courtyard. I picked it up and was about to return it to the children when I noticed some writing on it. From the first lines I saw that the kite was part of a record, and I fortunately succeeded in saving the rest of it. This record, acquired by me for a quarter of oats, is distinguished for its profound thought and its outstanding eloquence.

III. Oral legends. Whilst no source of information escaped my notice, I am particularly indebted to Agrafena Trifonova, the mother of Avdey the village-elder and reputedly former mistress of the steward Garbovitsky.

IV. Census capitation registers, with comments by former village-elders concerning the morals and condition of the peasants.

The region of Goryukhino, thus named after its capital, occupies an area of more than 580 hectares. The number of its inhabitants extends to sixty-three souls. To the north it is bounded by the villages of Deriukhovo and Perkukhovo, whose inhabitants are poor, of meagre build and undersized, and whose proud owners are devoted to the warlike exercises of the hare-hunt. To the south the River Sivka separates the village from the possessions of the free husbandmen of Karachevo, restless neighbours known for the violent cruelty of their nature. Circling it to the west are the prosperous fields of Zakharino, which thrives under the authority of wise and enlightened landowners. To the east the village adjoins wild uninhabited country, an impassable bog where only the bogberry grows, where only the monotonous croaking of frogs is heard and where, according to superstitious legend, some mysterious demon has his dwelling.

[N.B. This bog is called *Devil's Land*. It is said that a simple-minded shepherdess used to watch over a herd of pigs not far from this isolated spot. She became pregnant and was unable to find a satisfactory explanation for her condition. The voice of the people blamed the demon of the bog; but this tale is unworthy of the attention of a historian and, after Niebuhr, it would be unpardonable to believe it.]

From time immemorial Goryukhino has been famous for the fertility of its soil and its excellent growing climate. Rye, oats, barley and buckwheat flourish in its fields. A birch copse and a fir wood furnish the inhabitants with timber for the construction and fallen branches for the heating of their dwellings. There is no shortage of nuts, cranberries, bilberries and whortleberries. Mushrooms grow in unusual quantity, and, when fried in sour cream, make for pleasant although unwholesome nourishment. The village pond is full of carp, and pike and turbot are to be found in the River Sivka.

The inhabitants of Goryukhino are for the most part of medium height and of strong and manly build; their eyes are grey and their hair is blond or red. The women are remarkable for their snub-noses, their prominent cheek-bones and ample proportions.

[N.B. *Robust countrywoman*: this expression is met with frequently in the comments of the village-elder in the census capitation registers.]

The men are of sober morals, hard-working (especially on their own land), brave and of warlike disposition: many of them have fought single-handed with bears, and they have a reputation in the district for fist-fighting. In general, they are all partial to the sensual delights of drunkenness. In addition to domestic work, the women share a large part of their husbands' work; and they do not yield to them in courage, few of them having much fear of the village-elder. They make up a powerful public guard, keeping a tireless vigil in the court-yard of the manor house, and they are known as *spearwomen* (from the Slavonic word *spear*). The principal duty of these 'spearwomen' consists in beating a cast-iron plate with a stone, in this way intimidating anyone of evil design. They are as chaste as they are beautiful and respond sharply and spiritedly to the advances of any man bold enough to make them.

The inhabitants of Goryukhino have for long carried out a rich trade in bast, bast-baskets and bast-shoes. They are assisted in this by the River Sivka, which in the spring they punt across like the ancient Scandinavians, and which for the rest of the year they ford, taking the precaution before they do so of rolling up their trousers to the knees.

The language spoken in Goryukhino is quite definitely of Slavonic origin, although it differs from Slav as much as the Russian language does. It is full of abbreviations and trun-cations and some letters are either omitted altogether or else replaced by others. However, a Great Russian has little diffi-culty in understanding a native of Goryukhino, and vice versa.

As a rule, the men married in their thirteenth year and the women in their twentieth. For four or five years wives would beat their husbands. After that, the husbands would in turn beat their wives. Thus both sexes had their time of power and a balance was achieved.

The burial ceremony proceeded in the following way: on the day of death, the dead man was taken straight to the cemetery so that his corpse should not take up unnecessary space in his hut. An occasional result of this practice was that the corpse, to the indescribable delight of his relatives, would sneeze or yawn at the very moment of being conveyed in its coffin to the outskirts of the village. Wives would bewail their husbands, howling and repeating: 'Light of my life, my brave heart, to whom have you abandoned me? How shall I honour your memory?' On the return from the cemetery a wake would begin in honour of the dead man, and relatives and friends would be drunk for two or three days, or even a whole week, depending on their zeal and the extent of their attachment to his memory. These ancient ceremonies have been preserved to the present day.

The dress of the inhabitants of Goryukhino consisted of long shirts worn over breeches – a distinguishing mark of their Slav origins. In winter they wore sheepskin coats, but more for appearance than out of any need, for they usually only wore the sheepskin slung over one shoulder and discarded it on taking up even the slightest work that required movement.

From time immemorial, science, the arts and poetry have been in a more or less flourishing condition in Goryukhino. In addition to the priest and the church officials, there have always been literate people in the village. Records refer to the village-clerk Terenty, who lived around 1767 and who was able to write not only with his right hand but also with his left. This extraordinary man became famous throughout the district for his ability to compose letters and documents of every sort – petitions, civil passports and so on. After his skill, his obligingness and the part he played in various remarkable events had landed him in trouble more than once, he died in old age at a time when he was learning to write with his right foot, the script of both his hands having become too well-known. He plays, as the reader will see below, an important part in the history of Goryukhino.

Music was always the favourite art form of the educated inhabitants of Goryukhino, the balalaika and bagpipe giving delight to sensitive hearts; and they can still be heard now in the dwellings of the people, and especially in the ancient public house, adorned with branches of spruce-firs and the insignia of the double eagle.

Poetry at one time flourished in old Goryukhino. To this very day the verses of Arkhip the Bald are still remembered by posterity. In tenderness they can rival the eclogues of the celebrated Virgil, and they far surpass the idylls of Mr Sumarokov as far as beauty of imagery is concerned. And although the style is not as intricate as that to be found in the latest compositions of our muses, they are equal to them in invention and wit.

Let me quote the following satirical verse as an example:

'Towards the boyar's mansion
Repairs the Elder, Anton,
In his bosom carries
The boyar's monthly tallies;
My lord doth stare distraught,
He understandeth naught.
O Anton, you have been
And fleeced the boyars clean,
The village hungry goes —
Your wife in finest clothes'.

Having now familiarised my reader with the ethnographical and statistical situation of Goryukhino and with the character and customs of its inhabitants, I shall proceed with the narrative itself.

LEGENDARY TIMES
The Village-Elder Trifon

The system of government in Goryukhino has changed several times. The village was first under the authority of elders chosen by the community, then of stewards appointed by the landowners, and finally under the direct authority of the landowners themselves. The advantages and disadvantages of these different systems of government will be examined in the course of my narrative.

Details concerning the founding of Goryukhino and its original population are veiled in the mists of ignorance. Vague legends relate that Goryukhino was at one time a large, rich village, that all its inhabitants were well-off, and that the tithes were collected once a year and taken off, in several cart-loads, to an unknown recipient. At that time everything was bought cheaply and sold expensively. There existed no stewards and the village-elders treated the people fairly. The inhabitants did little work and lived in clover; even the shepherds kept guard over their flocks in boots. We should not be seduced, however, by this charming picture. The concept of a golden age is natural to all nations and proves only that people are never satisfied with the present and, having from experience little hope in the future, they embellish the irrecoverable past with all the colours of their imagination.

What is beyond doubt, however, is that the village of Goryukhino belonged from time immemorial to the distinguished Belkin family. But these ancestors of mine owned many other estates and did not turn their attention to this remote village. Goryukhino paid little in the way of taxes and was administered by elders chosen by the people at a village assembly called the Peasants' Council.

But in the course of time the ancestral properties of the Belkins were split up and fell into decay. The impoverished grandchildren of the wealthy grandfather were unable to give up their lavish ways and continued to demand from an estate which had shrunk to one tenth of its size the full income of former times. One threatening injunction followed another. The village-elder read them out at assembly; the other elders harangued, the people became agitated, and their masters, instead of double tithes, received cunning excuses and humble complaints, written on greasy paper and sealed with a half-kopeck piece.

A sombre cloud hung over Goryukhino, but nobody took notice of it. In the final year of Trifon's term – he was the last village-elder to be chosen by the people – on the day of the church festival, when all the people either crowded noisily around the place of entertainment (called the 'pot-house' in popular parlance) or wandered through the streets embracing each other and loudly intoning the songs of Arkhip the Bald, there drove into the village a covered wicker britchka drawn by a pair of broken-down nags, scarcely alive. On the box sat a Jew of ragged appearance, and from the carriage a head with a peaked cap on it leaned out and looked, it seemed with curiosity, at the merry-making crowd. The inhabitants greeted the carriage with laughter and coarse jokes.

[N.B. 'With the lapels of their coats turned up, the "madmen" jeered at the Jewish driver and chanted mockingly: "Jew, Jew, chew a pig's ear!"' – *From the records of the church sexton of Goryukhino*.]

But how great was their astonishment when the carriage stopped in the middle of the village and the traveller, jumping from it, called for the village-elder Trifon in an authoritative voice. This dignitary was in the 'house of entertainment' whence two elders led him deferentially forward, supporting him under the arms. The stranger looked at him sternly, handed him a piece of paper and ordered him to read it at once. The elders of Goryukhino were not in the habit of reading for themselves. The village-elder was illiterate. Avdey the village-clerk was sent for. He was found not far away, asleep under the fence in a side-street, and was brought before the stranger. But either through sudden fright or on account of some fateful premonition, he found that the words of the letter – which were written clearly enough – were blurred, and he was thus unable to make them out. The stranger, having sent the village-elder Trifon and the village-clerk Avdey off to bed with terrible curses, postponed the reading of the letter until the following day and went into the steward's hut, the Jew carrying his small trunk after him.

The inhabitants of Goryukhino looked on in dumb amazement at this unusual incident, but soon the carriage, the Jew and the stranger were forgotten. The day ended noisily and merrily and Goryukhino fell asleep unsuspecting of what lay in store for it.

At sunrise the inhabitants were awakened by knocking on their windows and a summons to the Peasants' Council. One by one the citizens appeared in the yard of the steward's hut which served as the Council's meeting-place. Their eyes were glazed and red, their faces swollen; yawning and scratching themselves, they looked at the man in the peaked cap, now wearing an old blue kaftan as he stood solemnly on the steps of the steward's hut, and tried to identify his features which they seemed somewhere to have seen before. The village-elder Trifon and the village-clerk Avdey stood beside him, hatless, and each wearing an expression of servility and deep distress.

'Is everyone here?' asked the stranger.

'Is everyone here?' repeated the village-elder.

'Every one of us,' replied the citizens.

Then the village-elder announced that an instruction had been received from their master, and he ordered the village-clerk to read it out so that the whole assembly should hear. Avdey stepped forward and read as follows in a loud voice:

'*Trifon Ivanov!*

'*The bearer of this letter, my agent ***, is proceeding to my patrimony, the village of Goryukhino, in order to take over the management of same. Immediately he arrives, assemble the peasants and inform them of my, their master's, wishes: namely, that the peasants are to obey the orders of my agent *** as they would my own, and that they are to fulfil without argument all which he demands of them; in the event of their not doing so, *** has the power to deal with them with the utmost severity. I have been forced to act in this way by their shameless disobedience and, Trifon Ivanov, by your criminal indulgence.*'

(signed) N.N.

[N.B. The chronicler writes: 'This fearsome communication I copied out at the house of Trifon the village-elder, where it is preserved in his icon-case along with other souvenirs of his authority over Goryukhino.' I did not succeed in finding the original of this document.]

Then ***, his legs spread out like the letter *X* and his arms akimbo like the letter *Phi,* made the following short, pithy speech:

'Take care you're not too smart with me – I know you're a spoilt lot; but I'll beat any nonsense out of your heads, don't you worry, quicker than it'll take you to get over yesterday's hangover.'

By now everyone's hangover had vanished. Thunderstruck, the people of Goryukhino hung their heads and dispersed in fear to their houses.

THE RULE OF THE STEWARD ***

*** took over the reins of government and began to put into practice a political system which deserves particular attention.

Principally, this system was founded on the axiom: the richer the peasant, the more spoiled he is, the poorer the peasant, the humbler he is. With this in mind, *** strove for humility, the principal Christian virtue, on the estate. He demanded a list of peasants and divided them into rich and poor. He then (1) reallocated the arrears among the well-to-do peasants and exacted them with the utmost severity; (2) immediately set to the plough those who were without means or idle revellers, and if their work did not measure up to his standards, he hired them out as labourers to other peasants, who paid him a voluntary tax. Those given into serfdom in this way had a full right to buy themselves out by paying, on top of any arrears due from them, a double annual tithe. The expense of all public services fell on the well-off peasants. The imposition of the army recruitment system was the crowning glory of this extortionate ruler, for what happened was that all the rich peasants bought themselves out of it one by one until only the ne'er-do-wells or those who had been ruined were left.

> [N.B. The accursed steward placed Anton Timofeyev in irons, but old Timofey bought his son out for one hundred roubles. The steward then put the irons on Petrushka Yeremeyev, whose father bought him out for sixty-eight roubles. The accursed fellow was about to put the irons on Lekha Tarasov when he ran away into the woods – and the steward,

exceedingly grieved at this, cursed and raged, and then sent Vanka the drunkard into the town and offered him as a recruit. *From a deposition by the peasants of Goryukhino.*]

Peasants' Councils were done away with. The steward would collect the tithes piecemeal the whole year through. On top of that, he imposed unexpected levies. The peasants, it seems, did not pay excessively more than before, but they were unable either to earn or to save enough money. Within three years Goryukhino was completely beggared. Goryukhino wasted away; the market place was empty, the songs of Arkhip the Bald unsung. The children went begging. Half the peasants were set to plough the master's land, while the other half were hired out. The day of the church festival became, according to the chronicler, not a day of joy and exultation, but one of annual grief and woeful commemoration.

1830

(Pushkin never completed this story.)

Roslavlev

While reading *Roslavlev,* I realised with amazement that the plot is based on a true happening extremely well-known to me. At one time, I was a friend of the unfortunate woman chosen by Mr Zagoskin as the heroine of his story. He brought anew to the public's attention an incident that had been forgotten, awakening feelings of indignation lulled to sleep by the passage of time, and disturbing the peace of the grave. I shall be the protectress of that shadow – and the reader, having respect for the sincerity of my motives, will forgive the inadequacy of my pen. I shall be compelled to speak much about myself, because my destiny was for a long time tied up with that of my poor friend.

I was brought out in society in the winter of 1811. I shall not describe my first impressions. It is easy to imagine for oneself what a sixteen-year-old girl, having exchanged a life bound by the school-room and teachers for one of continual balls, must feel. I gave myself over to the whirl of gaiety with all the vivacity of my years, and gave no thought to anything ... This was a pity: the times were worth observing.

Of the girls who came out with me, Princess ** was different from the others. (Mr Zagoskin called her Polina, and I shall leave her with that name.) We soon became friends, and here is how.

My brother, a young man of twenty-two, was one of the dandies of that period; he was a member of the Foreign Circle and lived in Moscow, leading a life of dancing and wild behaviour. He fell in love with Polina, and begged me to bring our families closer together. My brother was the idol of our entire family, and he could get what he wanted from me.

Having made friends with Polina in order to gratify my

brother's wish, I soon became sincerely attached to her. There was much that was strange in her character, still more that was attractive. Before I really understood her, I loved her. Unconsciously, I began to see with her eyes and think with her thoughts.

Polina's father was an estimable man, which is to say that he drove in a coach-and-six, wore a key and a star, and was nevertheless carefree and unpretentious. Her mother, on the other hand, was a sedate woman, notable for her pompousness and good sense.

Polina was to be seen everywhere, surrounded by admirers who paid court to her – but she was bored, and boredom gave her a proud, cold appearance. This suited her Grecian profile and dark brows excellently. I felt triumph when my satirical observations brought a smile to those regular and bored features.

Polina was a great reader of every kind of book. She had the key to her father's library. This consisted mainly of works of eighteenth-century writers. She was well acquainted with French literature, from Montesquieu to the novels of Crébillon. Rousseau she knew by heart. There was not a single Russian book in the library, with the exception of the works of Sumarokov, and these Polina never opened. She told me that she read Russian print with difficulty, and she probably read nothing in Russian, not even the verses dedicated to her by the Moscow versifiers.

At this point I shall allow myself a slight digression. Thanks to the will of God, it is about thirty years now since we, wretched people, were cursed with the inability to read Russian and, it would seem, to express ourselves in our native tongue. (N.B. It is reprehensible of the author of *Yury Miloslavsky* to go on repeating his vulgar accusations. We have all read his book, and I should have thought he owed something to one of us for the translation of his novel into French.)

The fact is that we would be delighted to read Russian; but it seems that our literature is no older than Lomonosov, and still extremely limited. It offers us, of course, several excellent poets, but one cannot ask of every reader an exclusive passion for verse. As for prose, we have only Karamzin's *History*. The first two or three novels appeared only two or three years ago, while in France, England and Germany books follow one after the other, each more remarkable than the last. We do not even see translations; but if we were to do so, to tell the truth, I should still prefer to read them in the original language. Our journals are of interest only to literary men. We are forced to cull everything, news and ideas, from foreign books; and so we think in a foreign language (at least those do who do think and follow the thoughts of the human race). This is what our most celebrated men of letters have confessed to me. The endless complaints of our writers about our neglect of Russian books resemble the complaints of Russian merchants, indignant that we should buy our hats at Sikhler's and not be content with the creations of the milliners of Kostroma. I return to my subject.

Recollections of fashionable life, in times of historical importance, are usually hazy and without significance. However, the appearance in Moscow of a certain traveller left on me a deep impression. The traveller was Madame de Staël. She arrived in the summer, at a time when most of the inhabitants of Moscow had dispersed to the country. Russian hospitality began to fuss; they went out of their way to entertain the celebrated foreigner. Of course, dinner parties were given for her. Men and women gathered just to look at her, and they were for the most part displeased by her. They saw in her a fat, fifty-year-old woman, not dressed according to her years. They did not like her tone; her speeches seemed excessively long, and her sleeves excessively short. Polina's father, who had known Madame de Staël in Paris, gave a dinner party for her, to which he invited all our Moscow wits. It was here that I met the authoress of *Corinne*. She sat in the place of honour, her elbows on the table, furling and unfurling a roll of paper with her beautiful fingers. She seemed to be out of spirits; several times she started to talk, but she could not keep the conversation going. Our wits ate and drank to their fill and, it seemed, were far more pleased with the Prince's fish soup than with the talk of Madame de Staël. The ladies conducted themselves formally. These wits and ladies only rarely broke the silence, convinced of the insignificance of their thoughts and feeling intimidated by the presence of the European celebrity. Throughout the entire dinner Polina sat as if on pins and needles. The attention of the guests was divided between the sturgeon and Madame de Staël. At every moment they awaited a *bon mot* from her; at last, an equivocal, and even somewhat bold comment escaped from her lips. Everyone snatched it up, exploded into laughter, and a whisper of amazement went round the table; the Prince was beside himself with delight. I glanced at Polina. Her face was burning, and tears showed in her eyes. The guests rose from the table, completely reconciled to Madame de Staël: she had made a pun, which they raced to spread about the town.

'What's the matter, *ma chère*?' I asked Polina. 'How could a harmless little joke upset you so much?'

'Oh, my dear,' Polina replied, 'I am in despair! How worthless our great society must seem to that unusual woman! She is accustomed to being surrounded by people who understand her, on whom a brilliant remark, a strong beat of the heart, an inspired word is never lost; she has been used to absorbing and highly cultured conversation. And here . . . my God! Not a single thought, not a single remarkable word in the course of three hours! Dull faces, dull pomposity – that's all! How bored she was! How tired she seemed! She realised what they wanted, what those apes of enlightenment could understand, and she threw them a pun. And they threw themselves at it! I burned with shame and was on the verge of tears ... But let – ' Polina continued warmly – 'let her take away an opinion of our society rabble such as they deserve. At least she has seen our kind and simple people, and understands them. You heard what she said to that unbearable old buffoon who, in order to gratify a foreigner, took it into his head to jeer at our Russian beards: "People who stood up for their beards a hundred years ago will in these days stand up for their heads". How amiable she is! How I love her! How I hate her persecutor!'

I was not the only one to notice Polina's confusion. Another pair of piercing eyes had rested on her at the same moment: the black eyes of Madame de Staël herself! I do not know what she thought, but after dinner she came over to my friend and began to talk to her. A few days later, Madame de Staël wrote to her the following note:

> 'Ma chère enfant, je suis toute malade. Il serait bien aimable à vous de venir me ranimer. Tâchez de l'obtenir de M-me votre mère et veuillez lui présenter les respects de votre amie. de S .'

I have this note in my keeping. Polina never explained to me the nature of her relationship with Madame de Staël, in spite of my great curiosity. She worshipped the famous woman, who was as good-natured as she was highly gifted.

What the passion for malicious gossip brings forth! Not long ago I recounted this story in certain very respectable company.

'Perhaps,' they remarked, 'Madame de Staël was none other than a spy of Napoleon, and Princess ** was passing secret information on to her.'

'For pity's sake,' I said, 'what would Madame de Staël, persecuted by Napoleon for ten years; kind, noble Madame de Staël, having escaped with difficulty to the protection of the Russian Emperor; Madame de Staël, friend of Chateaubriand and Byron – what would she be doing as a spy of Napoleon?'

'Perfectly possible,' retorted the sharp-nosed Countess B. 'Napoleon was such a devil, and Madame de Staël is an artful creature!'

Everyone was talking about the coming war, and, so far as I can remember, quite lightheartedly. It was fashionable to imitate the French tone of the time of Louis XV. Love of one's fatherland seemed pedantic. The intellectuals of the period exalted Napoleon with fanatical servility and joked about our misfortunes. Unhappily, the people who spoke up in defence of their country were a little simple-minded; they were derided – quite amusingly – and had no influence. Their patriotism was limited to a cruel censure of the use of the French language in society and the introduction of foreign words, and to threatening pranks opposite the Kuznetsky Bridge and such like. Young people spoke with contempt and indifference about everything Russian, and jokingly predicted for Russia the fate of the Rhenish Confederation. In brief, society was pretty rotten.

Suddenly, we were surprised by the news of the invasion and the Tsar's appeal. Moscow became agitated. Count Rastopchin's leaflets for the masses made their appearance; the people steeled themselves. The cynics grew quiet; the ladies were anxious. The persecutors of the French language and the Kuznetsky Bridge took a decisive lead in society, and the drawing-rooms became filled with patriots: those who had emptied their pockets of French tobacco and begun to take Russian; those who had burned French pamphlets by the dozen; those who had renounced Lafitte and started drinking kvass. Everyone gave up speaking French; everyone shouted about Pozharsky and Minin and began to preach about the people's war, preparing all the while to set out for their villages in the Saratov district.

Polina could not hide her contempt, just as previously she had been unable to hide her indignation. Such a quick change of attitude and such cowardice made her lose patience. On the boulevard, and at the Presnensky Ponds, she deliberately spoke French; at table, in the presence of servants, she deliberately impugned patriotic boasting; she deliberately spoke of the might of Napoleon's forces, of his military genius. Those present grew pale, afraid of being denounced, and hastened to reproach her for her partisanship of her country's enemy. Polina would smile contemptuously.

'May God grant,' she would say, 'that all Russian people should love their country as I do.'

She astonished me. I always knew Polina to be modest and of few words, and I did not understand from where she had acquired such audacity.

'Have mercy!' I said to her one day. 'Why do you want to interfere in matters which have nothing to do with you. Let the men fight and shout about politics; women do not go to war, and Bonaparte is of no concern to them.'

Her eyes began to shine. 'You should be ashamed of yourself,' she said. 'Do not women have a fatherland? Do they not have fathers, brothers and husbands? Is Russian blood alien to us? Or do you suppose that we are born only in order to whirl around at balls, and sit at home embroidering little dogs on canvas? No, I know the sort of influence women can have on the opinion of society, or even on the heart of a single man. I do not acknowledge the disparagement to which we are condemned. Look at Madame de Staël. Napoleon fought her as he fights the enemy forces . . . And my uncle still dares to ridicule her timidity at the approach of the French army!

"Be calm, dear lady: Napoleon is fighting Russia, not you . . ."
Yes, if my uncle were captured by the French, at least he
would be allowed to promenade in the Palais-Royal; but
Madame de Staël in such a case would have died in a state
prison. And Charlotte Corday? And our own Marfa
Posadnitsa? And Princess Dashkova? Am I a lesser person
than they? Certainly not in audacity of spirit and resolution.'

I listened to Polina with amazement. I had never suspected
her of such ardour, such ambition. Alas, to what has she
brought her unusual qualities of spirit, her manly loftiness
of mind? My favourite writer spoke the truth when he wrote:
Il n'est de bonheur que dans les voies communes.

The arrival of the Tsar aggravated the general excitement.
The ecstasy of patriotism at last took possession of high society.
Drawing-rooms turned into debating chambers. Everywhere
there was talk of patriotic sacrifice. The immortal words of
the young Count Mamonov, who contributed his entire estate,
were continually being repeated. Some mothers observed,
after that, that the Count was no longer such a desirable
match, but we were all in raptures about him.

Polina raved about him. 'What are you going to
contribute?' she once asked my brother.

'I have not yet taken possession of my estate,' the rake
replied. 'All in all, I have debts of 30,000 roubles: I will sacrifice those on the altar of my country.'

Polina became angry. 'For some people,' she said, 'honour
and the fatherland are trifles. Their brothers die on the field
of battle while they play the fool in a drawing-room. I do
not know if there exists a woman so low as to allow such a
buffoon to profess his love to her.'

My brother flushed. 'You are too exacting, Princess,' he
retorted. 'You demand that everyone should identify you with
Madame de Staël and declaim to you with tirades from
Corinne. Know that although a man may jest with a woman,

he may not jest about his country or its enemies.' With these words he turned away.

I thought that they had quarrelled irreconcilably, but I was mistaken: my brother's insolence appealed to Polina, and she forgave him for his uncalled-for joke and his bold outburst of indignation; and, learning a week later that he had entered Mamonov's regiment, she begged me to make it up between them. My brother was overjoyed. He proposed to her at once. She accepted, but put off the wedding until the end of the war. On the following day my brother set off for his regiment.

Napoleon marched on Moscow, our army retreating before him. Moscow became alarmed. One after another, the inhabitants left. The Prince and Princess, Polina's parents, persuaded my mother to go with them to their village at ***.

We arrived at ***, a large village twenty versts from the provincial capital. We had many neighbours, mostly people who had come from Moscow. Every day we gathered together; our country life resembled that of the town. Letters from the army arrived almost daily, and the old ladies searched on the map for the places where the troops were encamped and grew angry when they could not find them. Polina occupied herself solely with politics, read nothing but the newspapers and Rastopchin's proclamations, and did not open a single book. Surrounded by people of limited understanding, continually hearing nonsensical judgements and news without foundation, she fell into a deep depression; languor took possession of her soul. She despaired of the salvation of her country; it seemed to her that Russia was swiftly approaching her doom, and with each fresh report her hopelessness became more acute. The police announcements of Count Rastopchin caused her to lose all patience. Their facetious style struck her as the height of indecency, and the measures taken by Rastopchin as intolerably barbaric. She could not grasp the spirit – so

great in its horror – of those times, a spirit whose bold achieve-
ment saved Russia and freed Europe. She spent hours, her
elbows on a map of Russia, calculating distances, following
the rapid movements of the armies. Strange ideas came into
her head. Once she announced to me her decision to leave
the country, appear in the French camp, reach Napoleon and
then kill him with her own hands. It was not difficult for
me to persuade her of the madness of such a scheme. But the
thought of Charlotte Corday never left her mind for long.

Her father, as you know, was a reasonably carefree man;
he thought only of how to live in the country in a style as
similar as possible to that of Moscow. He gave dinner parties,
organised a *théâtre de société*, where French *proverbes* were
performed, and tried his hardest to vary our pleasures. Several
prisoner-of-war officers arrived in the town. The Prince was
delighted to have new faces around him and sought the
Governor's permission to have them billeted on us.

There were four of them – three quite insignificant men,
fanatically devoted to Napoleon, intolerable braggarts who
had paid for their boasts, it is true, with honourable wounds.
But the fourth was an extremely remarkable man.

He was then twenty-six years old. He came from a good
family. His face was pleasing, his manners excellent. We
noticed at once that he was different. He accepted our kind-
nesses with generous modesty. He spoke little, but his
discourses were sound. Polina liked him because he was the
first person she had met who was able clearly to interpret the
military operations and the movements of the troops. Having
himself been a witness of the retreat of the Russian forces,
he reassured her that it was not a senseless rout, and that it
disturbed the French quite as much as it embittered the
Russians.

'But are you not convinced,' Polina asked him, 'of the invin-
cibility of your Emperor?'

Sénicourt (I will call him by the name given to him by Zagoskin) – Sénicourt , remaining silent for a short while, replied that in his position it would be difficult to be frank. Polina insisted on an answer. Sénicourt admitted that the French army's march into the heart of Russia could become dangerous for them, that the advance of 1812 appeared to have come to an end, but that that did not signify anything decisive.

'Come to an end!' Polina exclaimed. 'But Napoleon all the time moves forward, and we all the time retreat!'

'The worse for us,' Sénicourt replied, and changed the subject.

Polina, who was tired of the cowardly predictions and foolish boasting of our neighbours, listened eagerly to such informed and impartial judgements. It was impossible to make any sense out of the letters I received from my brother. They were filled with jokes, both good and bad, questions about Polina, trivial assurances of love, etc. Reading them, Polina became annoyed and shrugged her shoulders.

'Confess,' she said, 'that your Alexey is an empty-headed man. Even with conditions as they are at the moment, he is capable of writing meaningless letters from the battlefield. What sort of conversation will he have for me in the course of a quiet family life?'

She was mistaken. The futility of my brother's letters proceeded not from his own worthlessness, but from a prejudice that was most offensive to us; for he supposed that it was necessary to use with women a language that suited their limited understanding, and that serious matters did not concern us. Such a view would be uncivil anywhere, but in our country it is also foolish. There is no doubt that Russian women are better educated, read more and think more than their menfolk, engaged in God knows what.

News spread of the battle of Borodino. Everyone talked

about it; everyone had his own accurate information, and everyone had a list of the killed and wounded. My brother did not write to us. We were extremely anxious. At last, one of the conveyors of news of every kind arrived to inform us that he had been taken prisoner, meanwhile announcing to Polina in a whisper that he was dead. Polina was deeply upset. She was not in love with my brother and was often irritated by him, but at that moment she saw him as a martyr and a hero, and she would weep secretly, away from my presence. On several occasions I caught her with tears in her eyes. This did not surprise me. I knew what painful unhappiness she felt at the fate of our suffering country. I had no suspicion of the cause of her grief.

I was strolling in the garden one morning; Sénicourt walked beside me; we were talking about Polina. I noticed that he felt her unusual qualities deeply, and that her beauty had made a powerful impression on him. I laughingly observed that his situation was most romantic – wounded knight, taken prisoner by the enemy, falls in love with noble chatelaine, touches her heart and at last receives her hand.

'No,' Sénicourt said to me, 'the Princess sees in me an enemy of Russia and will never agree to leave her country.'

At that moment Polina appeared at the end of the path, and we went to meet her. She approached with quick steps. I was struck by her pallor.

'Moscow has been taken,' she said to me, without replying to Sénicourt 's greeting. My heart sank, the tears began to flow. Sénicourt was silent, his eyes downcast. 'The noble, enlightened French,' she continued in a voice trembling with indignation, 'have fittingly marked the occasion of their triumph. They have set fire to Moscow. Moscow has been burning for two days already.'

'What are you saying?' shouted Sénicourt . 'It is impossible.'

'Wait for the night,' she replied drily, 'and perhaps you will see the glow.'

'My God! He has been destroyed,' said Sénicourt . 'Do you not realise that the burning of Moscow is the ruin of the entire French army, that there will be nowhere, anywhere, for Napoleon to hold out, that he will be forced to retreat as fast as he can through the ruined and empty countryside – at the approach of winter, with disaffected and disorganised troops? How could you think that the French have dug this hell for themselves! No, no, it is the Russians, the Russians who have set fire to Moscow. What terrible, barbaric magnanimity! Everything is now resolved: your country is out of danger; but what will happen to us, what will happen to our Emperor?. . .'

He left us. Polina and I could not collect ourselves. 'Is it possible,' she said, 'that Sénicourt is right, and that the burning of Moscow is the work of our own hands? If so . . . oh, how proud I am to have the name of a Russian woman! The world will marvel at our great sacrifice. Now, even our defeat does not frighten me, our honour is saved; never again will Europe dare to fight with a people who chop off their own hands and burn their capital.'

Her eyes shone, and her voice rang. I embraced her. Our tears of noble exaltation mingled with our ardent prayers for our country.

'You do not know?' Polina said to me with a look of inspiration. 'Your brother . . . he is happy, he is not a prisoner; rejoice, he died for the salvation of Russia.'

I screamed and fell unconscious into her arms . . .

1831

(Pushkin never completed this story.)

Dubrovsky

PART ONE

Chapter One

A few years ago, there lived on one of his estates a Russian gentleman of the old school, Kirila Petrovitch Troyekurov. His wealth, his distinguished birth and his connections made him a person of considerable importance in the provinces in which his property lay. His neighbours were ready to satisfy his slightest whim; local government officials trembled at the very sound of his name. Kirila Petrovitch accepted these signs of servility as his rightful due; his house was always full of guests, ready to amuse him in his hours of lordly idleness and to share in his noisy and sometimes wild entertainments. Nobody dared to refuse an invitation from him or, on certain days, to omit to pay his respects to him at the village of Pokrovskoye. In his domestic life, Kirila Petrovitch showed all the defects of a man to whom culture means nothing. Utterly spoiled by his surroundings, he was accustomed to giving way to every impulse of his passionate nature, to every fancy of his limited mind. Despite an unusually strong constitution, about twice a week he suffered from the effects of over-eating, and he got tipsy every night. In one of the wings of his house, there lived sixteen maidservants, engaged in work appropriate to their sex – that is, needlework. The windows of this wing were barricaded with wooden bars; the doors were kept locked, and the keys held by Kirila Petrovitch. At fixed hours of the day, the young captives were allowed out into the garden for a stroll, under the surveillance of two old women. From time to time Kirila Petrovitch found husbands for some of them, and new girls took their place. His treatment of his peasants and household servants was severe and arbitrary; but they were proud of their master's wealth and reputation, and in their turn took numerous liberties with their neighbours, putting their trust in Kirila Petrovitch's powerful protection.

Troyekurov's usual occupations consisted of riding over his extensive estates, prolonged feasting, and of the daily playing of practical jokes, which were usually at the expense of some new acquaintance, although even his oldest friends did not always escape such attentions – that is, however, with the single exception of Andrey Gavrilovitch Dubrovsky. This Dubrovsky, a retired lieutenant of the Guards, was his closest neighbour and the owner of seventy serfs. Troyekurov, haughty in his relations with people of the highest rank, respected Dubrovsky in spite of his humble standing. At one time they had been comrades-in-arms, and Troyekurov knew from experience his friend's impulsive and resolute nature. Circumstances had kept them apart for a long time. Dubrovsky, his affairs in disorder, had been obliged to resign his commission and settle down in his last remaining village. Kirila Petrovitch, hearing of this, offered him his protection, but Dubrovsky, while thanking him, chose to remain poor but independent. Some years later, Troyekurov, a retired *général-en-chef,* returned to his estate; they met and were delighted to see each other again. From that time, not a day passed without their meeting, and Kirila Petrovitch, who had never paid a single call on anyone in his life, used often to drop in at the little house of his old comrade. Being of the same age, of the same social class, and brought up in the same way, their natures and tastes were in part alike. In certain ways, too, their destinies were similar: both had married for love, both had soon been widowed, and both had been left with an only child. Dubrovsky's son was being educated in Petersburg, while the daughter of Kirila Petrovitch grew up under the eyes of her father, who often said to Dubrovsky:

'Listen, my dear Andrey Gavrilovitch: if that Volodya of yours makes good, I'll give Masha to him in marriage, even though he's as poor as a church mouse.'

Andrey Gavrilovitch would shake his head and make his customary reply:

'No, Kirila Petrovitch: my Volodya is no match for Marya Kirilovna. A nobleman of scant means, such as he, would do better to marry a girl of the same station and be head of his house, rather than become steward to some spoiled young lady.'

Everybody envied the harmony that existed between the haughty Troyekurov and his poor neighbour, and marvelled at the latter's boldness, when, at Kirila Petrovitch's table, he came straight out with his own opinion, regardless of whether it opposed that of his host or not. There were some who attempted to follow suit in this way and overstep the bounds of dutiful obedience, but Kirila Petrovitch attacked them with such venom that they quickly lost their taste for such attempts, and Dubrovsky remained the only one to whom the accepted law did not apply. An unexpected incident, however, altered all this.

One day in the beginning of autumn, Kirila Petrovitch made plans to go out hunting. On the eve of the expedition, the order was given to the grooms and huntsmen to be ready by five o'clock the next morning. A tent and field-kitchen had already been sent on to the place where Kirila Petrovitch was to dine. The host and his guests went to the kennels where more than five hundred harriers and greyhounds were housed in comfort and warmth, giving canine voice to their appreciation of Kirila Petrovitch's generosity. There was a hospital for sick dogs, supervised by staff-surgeon Timoshka, and a section where well-pedigreed bitches delivered and suckled their puppies. Kirila Petrovitch was proud of this superb establishment, and never let slip an opportunity to boast of it before his guests, all of whom had inspected it at least twenty times already. He strolled about the kennels, surrounded by his guests and accompanied by Timoshka and the chief grooms; before certain kennels he paused to enquire after the health of a sick dog, to pass some sharp, but usually justified comment, or to call a favourite dog to him and speak affectionately to it. The guests considered it their duty to pay rapturous tribute to Kirila Petrovitch's kennels. Dubrovsky alone was silent and frowning. He was an ardent huntsman. But his position only allowed him to keep two harriers and one pack of greyhounds; he could not restrain a certain feeling of envy at the sight of this magnificent establishment.

'Why are you frowning, my friend?' Kirila Petrovitch asked him. 'Don't you like my kennels?'

'Oh, the kennels are marvellous,' he replied drily, 'but I don't imagine your servants live as well as your dogs.'

One of the grooms took offence at this remark.

'Thanks to God and our master, we have no complaints about how we live,' he said, 'but it's only true to say that some noblemen wouldn't do badly by exchanging their estate for any one of our kennels here. He would be warmer and better fed.'

Kirila Petrovitch laughed loudly at his serf's insolent remark and his guests followed suit, even though they felt that the groom's joke could well apply to themselves. Dubrovsky turned pale and said not a word. At this moment some newly-born puppies were brought to Kirila Petrovitch in a basket; he busied himself over them, selecting two and ordering the remainder to be drowned. In the meantime Andrey Gavrilovitch vanished, nobody noticing him as he went.

Returning with his guests from the kennels, Kirila Petrovitch sat down to supper and, only then becoming aware of Dubrovsky's absence, enquired after him. The servants replied that Dubrovsky had gone home. Troyekurov instantly gave orders that he be overtaken and made to return without fail. Never in his life had he been out hunting without Dubrovsky, who was a fine and experienced judge of a dog's merits, and an infallible referee in all possible disputes connected with the sport. The servant who had galloped after him returned while they were still at table, and reported to his master that Andrey Gavrilovitch had refused to listen to him and had said that he had no wish to return. Kirila Petrovitch, as usual heated by drink, became enraged and sent the same servant for a second time with orders to tell Andrey Gavrilovitch that if he did not return at once to spend the night at Pokrovskoye, he, Troyekurov, would break off relations with him for all time. The servant galloped off again, and Kirila Petrovitch, rising from the table, dismissed his guests and went to bed.

The next day his first question was:

'Is Andrey Gavrilovitch here?'

In place of a reply, he was given a letter, folded into a triangle. Kirila Petrovitch ordered his clerk to read it aloud, and this is what he heard:

'Most Gracious Sir,
'I have no intention of going to Pokrovskoye until you send your groom Paramoshka to me with an apology; and

it will be up to me to decide whether to punish or pardon him. I cannot tolerate jokes from your serfs – or from you, for that matter; I am not a clown, but a nobleman of ancient family.

'Your obedient servant,
'Andrey Dubrovsky.'

According to present-day notions of etiquette, such a letter would be extremely discourteous; but Kirila Petrovitch was not so much angered by the letter's unusual style and mood as by its actual contents.

'What!' he thundered, leaping bare-footed from his bed. 'Send my people to him with an apology! Up to him to decide whether to punish or pardon! What does he think he's doing? Does he know with whom he's dealing? I'll teach him! He'll be sorry for this . . . He'll discover what it means to oppose Troyekurov!'

Kirila Petrovitch dressed and set out for the field with his usual pomp, but the hunt was not a success. Only one hare was seen throughout the entire day and that got away. Dinner in the field under a tent was also a failure, or at least was not to the liking of Kirila Petrovitch, who struck the cook, insulted his guests and, on the return journey, deliberately rode with the entire hunt across Dubrovsky's fields.

Several days passed and the enmity between the two neighbours did not subside. Andrey Gavrilovitch did not return to Pokrovskoye and Kirila Petrovitch, bored without him, gave loud vent to his irritation in the most insulting terms, which, thanks to the zeal of the local noblemen, reached Dubrovsky's ears in altered and embellished form. A fresh incident destroyed the last hope of a reconciliation.

Dubrovsky was one day driving about his small estate. Approaching a birch copse, he heard the sound of axe-blows and, a minute later, the crash of a falling tree. He hastened into the copse and came across some Pokrovskoye peasants calmly stealing his wood. On seeing him, they took to their heels. Dubrovsky and his coachmen caught two of them and led them back, tightly bound, to the courtyard of his house. Three enemy horses were also among the spoils of the victor. Dubrovsky was exceedingly angry: never before had Troyekurov's men, brigands as everyone knew, dared to play their pranks within the boundaries of his property, knowing of his friendly relations with their master. Dubrovsky realised that they were now taking advantage of the rift that had occurred between Troyekurov and himself, and he decided, against all the rules of war, to teach his captives a lesson with the same rods they had felled in his copse, and to attach the horses to his own stock and set them to work.

News of these events reached the ears of Kirila Petrovitch the same day. He was furious, and in the first flush of rage he was ready to lead his servants in an attack on Kistenevka (as was the name of his neighbour's estate), raze it to the ground, and to detain its owner as a prisoner in his own house. Such exploits did not seem to him to be unusual in any way. But his thoughts soon took another direction.

Striding up and down the hall with heavy steps, he happened to glance out of the window, and he saw a troika about to stop at the gate. A small man in a leather cap and a frieze overcoat stepped out of the carriage and walked towards the wing of the house occupied by the steward. Troyekurov recognised Shabashkin, the assessor, and sent for him. A minute later Shabashkin was standing before Kirila Petrovitch, bowing repeatedly and respectfully awaiting the other's orders.

'Good day to you – what's your name,' Troyekurov said to him. 'What have you come here for?'

'I was going to the town, your Excellency,' Shabashkin replied, 'and called in at Ivan Demyanov's to see whether there were any orders from your Excellency.'

'You've come at exactly the right time – what's your name. I need you. Have a glass of vodka and listen to what I have to say.'

So cordial a reception was a pleasant surprise to the assessor. He refused the vodka and began to listen to Kirila Petrovitch with the utmost attention.

'I have a neighbour,' said Troyekurov, 'an insolent fellow with a paltry estate. I want his property. What do you say?'

'If there are any documents, your Excellency . . .'

'Come, come, man, what sort of documents do you want? What are orders for? The whole point is to seize his estate without legal claim. One moment, however. At one time this estate belonged to us – it was bought from a certain Spitsyn, and then sold to Dubrovsky's father. Couldn't you make something out of that?'

'Scarcely, your Excellency, the sale was probably quite legal.'

'Think, man, and do your best to find a way.'

'If, for example, your Excellency could somehow obtain from your neighbour the title-deeds of his estate, authorising his possession of the land, then of course . . .'

'I know, that's just the trouble – all his papers were burned in a fire.'

'What, your Excellency, his papers were burned! What could be better? In that case, let us proceed in the name of the law, and there's no doubt that you will receive complete satisfaction.'

'You think so? Well, I leave it to you. I rely upon your enthusiasm, and you may be sure of my gratitude.'

Shabashkin, bowing almost to the ground, took his departure and at once began to busy himself with the devised scheme; and, thanks to his adroitness and speed, exactly a fortnight later Dubrovsky received from the town a request for immediate and acceptable evidence of his right to hold possession of the village of Kistenevka.

Andrey Gavrilovitch, astonished by this unexpected enquiry, wrote that very same day a somewhat rude reply, in which he explained that the village of Kistenevka had become his at the death of his late father, that he held it by right of inheritance, that Troyekurov had nothing whatsoever to do with the affair, and that any outside claims to his property were slanderous and fraudulent.

This letter produced an extremely favourable impression on the mind of Shabashkin, the assessor. From it he realised firstly that Dubrovsky was no businessman, and secondly that so hot-headed and incautious a man could easily be placed in a position of disadvantage. Andrey Gavrilovitch, having studied the assessor's enquiries in a calmer frame of mind, realised the necessity of a more thorough reply. He wrote a fairly businesslike letter, which later proved, however, to be inadequate.

The affair dragged on. Convinced of his rights, Andrey Gavrilovitch worried little about it. He had neither the means nor the inclination to scatter money about him, and although he had always been the first to jeer at the corrupt conscience of the clerkly tribe, the thought that he might become the victim of a cruel slander never entered his head. For his part, Troyekurov thought little of the affair he had set in motion. Shabashkin was seeing to it, acting in his name, bribing and intimidating judges and interpreting every conceivable aspect of the law to suit his own convenience.

And so, on February 9th, 18**, Dubrovsky received an invitation through the municipal police to appear before the district magistrate and hear his decision regarding the property disputed between himself – Lieutenant Dubrovsky, that is – and *Général-en-chef* Troyekurov, and to give his signature to a statement of satisfaction or dissatisfaction. That same day, Dubrovsky set out for the town; he was overtaken on the road by Troyekurov. They glanced at each other haughtily, and Dubrovsky observed a malicious smile on the face of his adversary.

Chapter Two

Having arrived in the town, Andrey Gavrilovitch spent the night with a merchant friend of his and, the next morning, appeared before the district court. Nobody paid any attention to him. Kirila Petrovitch arrived shortly after him. The clerks rose and put their pens behind their ears. The members of the court received him with expressions of profound servility, and an armchair was brought up for him out of respect for his rank, years and corpulence; he sat down by the open door. Andrey Gavrilovitch stood leaning against the wall. A deep silence ensued and the secretary began to read the findings of the court in a sonorous voice.

We are quoting these in full, assuming that everybody will be pleased to see one of the means whereby we in Russia can lose an estate to which we have an inalienable right.

'On the 27th day of October in the year 18**, the district court of ** considered the matter of the unlawful possession, by Lieutenant of the Guards Andrey son of Gavril Dubrovsky, of the estate belonging to *Général-en-chef* Kirila son of Pyotr Troyekurov and comprising, with ** souls of the male sex, land with meadows and appendages to the extent of ** measures in the hamlet of Kistenevka in the province of **. In connection with which suit it is evident that: on the 9th day of June in the year 18** past, the aforementioned *Général-en-chef* Troyekurov did file with this court a petition that his late father, Pyotr son of Yefim Troyekurov, Collegiate Assessor and Knight, did, on the 14th day of August in the year 17**, while serving as Provincial Secretary in the government administration of **, from a nobleman, the clerk in chancery Fadei son of Igor Spitsyn, purchase the estate comprising, in the aforementioned hamlet of Kistenevka (which village was then, according to the ** census, called the 'Kistenevka settlements') in the district of **, all that is listed in the fourth census: ** souls of the male sex, with all their goods and chattels, the farmstead, with tilled and untilled land, woods, hayfields, fishing in the stream called Kistenevka, and all appendages belonging to that estate, and the manor house built of wood – in short, all, without exception, that, by right of inheritance, fell to him at the death of his father, the nobleman, the Sergeant Igor, son of Terenty Spitsyn, and that was in his possession – of the people excluding not a single soul, of the land not a single measure, for the price of 2,500 roubles; and that, on the same day, in the ** chamber of the court of justice, the deed of title was completed, and his, Troyekurov's, father was then, on the 26th day of August, by the district court of **, installed in possession, and a seisin issued.

'That, finally, on the 6th day of September in the year 17**, his, Troyekurov's, father, by the will of God, died; meanwhile, he, the petitioner, *Général-en-chef* Troyekurov, from the year 17**, almost from infancy, had been on military service, for the most part campaigning abroad – for which reason he was unable to receive information of the death of his father, likewise of the property which had been left to him. Now, on retiring completely from that service, and on returning to the estates of his father, comprising, in diverse settlements, ** and ** in the provinces of ** and in the districts of ** and **, and souls up to 3,000 in all, he finds that one of such estates, with souls aforementioned and listed in the ** census (of which souls there are ** in that village according to the present census), with land and with all appendages, is in the possession, without any deeds of settlement, of the aforementioned Lieutenant of the Guards Andrey Dubrovsky. And, therefore, in connection with the petition aforementioned, showing evidence of that authentic deed of title given to his father by the vendor Spitsyn, he seeks, the aforementioned estate having been removed from the unlawful possession of Dubrovsky, for a decree to be issued as to his, Troyekurov's, appurtenance of it in full; and, for its wrongful appropriation, from which he has had the advantage of revenues received, having obtained the necessary information thereof, for the due exactions to be imposed on him, Dubrovsky, in accordance with the law obtaining in such matters, and wherewith for satisfaction to be granted to him, Troyekurov.

'In respect of the investigations carried out by the provincial court of ** concerning this petition, it is disclosed: that the aforementioned Lieutenant of the Guards Dubrovsky, at present in possession of the disputed estate, gave to the official Assessor the verbal explanation that the estate now in his possession, comprising, in the aforementioned village of Kistenevka, ** souls and land and appendages, fell to him, by right of inheritance, at the death of his father, Second Lieutenant of Artillery Gavril son of Yevgraf Dubrovsky, the estate having passed to him by purchase from the father of this petitioner, former Provincial Secretary and, later, Collegiate Assessor Troyekurov, according to a warrant of attorney issued by him on the 30th day of August in the year 17**, and witnessed in the district court of **, to Titular Councillor Grigory son of Vasily Sobolev; according to which warrant the deed of title to this estate was to pass from him, Troyekurov, to him, Dubrovsky, because, in that warrant, it was expressly stated that he, Troyekurov, did sell to his, Dubrovsky's, father all of the estate, with ** souls and with land, that had passed to him by deed of title from the clerk in chancery Spitsyn; and that he, Troyekurov, did receive the monies due to him under this agreement, that is 3,200 roubles, paid in full – and not returnable – by his, Dubrovsky's, father; and that he, Troyekurov, did ask the aforementioned trustee Sobolev to give to his, Dubrovsky's, father the official deed of purchase. And, in the meantime, it was decreed in the same warrant that his, Dubrovsky's, father should, on the occasion of the payment of all monies, take possession of that estate purchased from Troyekurov; and that, until the completion of the aforementioned deed of purchase, he should administer the estate as its lawful owner, and that neither he, the vendor Troyekurov, nor anyone else besides, should interfere with that estate. But precisely when and in what official place such a deed of title was given to his, Dubrovsky's, father by the trustee Sobolev is to him, Andrey Dubrovsky, unknown, for at that time he was in complete infancy, and, after the death of his father, he was unable to find such a deed; and he supposes that it was consumed by flames, along with other papers and property, at the time of the fire that occurred in their house in the year 17**, and which is well-known to the inhabitants of that settlement; and he contends that, from the day of the sale by the Troyekurovs, or of the handing over of the warrant of attorney to Sobolev, that is from the year 17**, and that from the death of his father, from the year 17** until the present day, they, the Dubrovskys, have been in undisputed possession of the aforementioned estate, which fact is attested to by local inhabitants, 52 men in all, who, on examination under oath, swore that, indeed, so far as they could recollect, the aforementioned Dubrovskys began to be in possession of the aforementioned, disputed estate 70 years before the present date, without contest from anybody – but in accordance with precisely what act or deed of purchase is unknown to them. They have no recollection of the aforementioned in this matter, previous purchaser of this estate, former Provincial Secretary Pyotr Troyekurov, being in possession of the estate. Thirty years before the present date, the house of the Dubrovskys was consumed by flames during the fire which occurred in their village during the night; while disinterested persons have admitted that the aforementioned, disputed estate was able to bear revenues, such revenues being reckoned, since that time, to be, annually, on an average, not less than 2,000 roubles.

'Against this, *Général-en-chef* Kirila son of Pyotr Troyekurov, on the 3rd day of January of this year, did file with this court the petition that, although the aforementioned Lieutenant of the Guards Andrey Dubrovsky had introduced to the investigation, instigated in connection with this suit, the warrant of attorney issued by his late father to Titular Councillor Sobolev for the estate sold to him, Gavril Dubrovsky, he had not only failed to present an authentic deed of title, but also had not at any time introduced any clear proof of the completion of such a deed, in accordance with Section 19 of the General Regulations, and of the ukaze issued on the 29th day of November in the year 1752. Hence, now, according to the ukaze issued on the ** day of May in the year 1818, that very warrant, in view of the death of him who had given it, his father, completely ceases to exist. Moreover, it is ordered that the reversion of disputed estates shall be, in the case of serfed estates, decided according to deeds of title; in the case of unserfed estates, according to inquiry.

'Presented by him, Troyekurov, then, in proof of his claim, is the Serfs' Act, whereby the estate concerned, which belonged to his father, having been removed from the unlawful possession of the aforementioned Dubrovsky, shall be, on the basis of the aforementioned decrees, restored to him, Troyekurov, by right of inheritance; and whereby, since the aforementioned landowners, the Dubrovskys, in possession, without any deeds of settlement, of an estate not belonging to them, have unlawfully had the advantage of revenues accruing therefrom and not belonging to them, whatsoever is, according to calculation, due shall be exacted from the landowner Dubrovsky, and wherewith satisfaction shall be granted to him, Troyekurov.

'Concerning the investigation of which matter, and according to the practice thereof and of the law, it is determined as follows in the district court of **:

'It is evident in this suit that: *Général-en-chef* Kirila son of Pyotr Troyekurov, concerning the aforementioned, disputed estate, at present in the possession of Lieutenant of the Guards Andrey son of Gavril Dubrovsky, and comprising, according to the present census, ** souls in all of the male sex and land and appendages in the village of Kistenevka, has presented an authentic deed of title for the sale, in the year 17**, of the said estate, by the nobleman, the clerk in chancery Fadei Spitsyn, to his late father, Provincial Secretary, later Collegiate Assessor, Troyekurov; and that, in addition, as is apparent from the inscription made to that deed of title, the purchaser, Troyekurov, was, in the same year, installed in possession of that estate by the district court of **, and a seisin issued; and that, against this, Lieutenant of the Guards Andrey Dubrovsky has presented the warrant of attorney, given to Titular Councillor Sobolev by the now departed purchaser, Troyekurov, for the completion of the deed of purchase in the name of his father, Dubrovsky . . . but, in such transactions, it is forbidden not only to affirm permanent title of serfed estates, but even, according to the ukaze issued on **, to allow temporary possession, since the warrant of attorney itself completely ceases to exist with the death of him who gives it. But, that, furthermore, Dubrovsky has not presented, from the beginning of these proceedings, that is from the year 18**, until the present time, any clear evidence in the matter of where and when the warrant for the deed of purchase of the aforementioned, disputed estate was indeed completed.

'And so this court is disposed, concerning the aforementioned estate, with ** souls and with land and appendages, in its present situation, to find in favour of *Général-en-chef* Troyekurov, in accordance with the deed of title presented therefor; and to enjoin the district court of ** to dispossess Lieutenant of the Guards Dubrovsky thereof, and to install *Général-en-chef* Troyekurov in possession of the estate which passed to him by right of inheritance, and to issue a seisin.

'Moreover, *Général-en-chef* Troyekurov, on account of the unlawful possession of his hereditary estate, petitions for the exaction, from Lieutenant of the Guards Dubrovsky, of revenues therefrom of which he has had the advantage. But that estate, according to the testimony of old inhabitants, was for several years in indisputed possession of the Dubrovskys, and it is not evident in this suit that there were, until the present time, any petitions, on the part of *Général-en-chef* Troyekurov, concerning such unlawful possession of that estate by the Dubrovskys. According to the law in this connection, it is ordered that he who, on respectful inquiry as to unlawful possession, is discovered to have sown land not his own or, by fencing, to have appropriated a farmstead not his own, shall restore that land, with sown corn, and that which has been fenced off, and any building thereon, to its rightful owner. Hence, this court is disposed to reject *Général-en-chef* Troyekurov's claim against Lieutenant of the Guards Dubrovsky, since the estate belonging to him is being restored to him, of it excluding not a thing. And if, when *Général-en-chef* Troyekurov takes possession of the estate, it should prove otherwise, then *Général-en-chef* Troyekurov is given leave, should he have any clear and lawful proof for such a claim, to petition as applicable.

'Which decision heretofore is, on the basis of the law and in a legal manner, announced equally to the petitioner as to the respondent, who have been summoned to this court for a hearing of this decision, and to subscribe to it their satisfaction or dissatisfaction.

'Which decision is undersigned by all present in this court.'

The secretary fell silent, and the assessor stood up, turned with a low bow to Troyekurov, and invited him to sign the proffered paper. Taking the pen, the triumphant Troyekurov signed his name beneath the decision of the court as a mark of his full satisfaction.

It was Dubrovsky's turn. The secretary carried the paper over to him. But Dubrovsky, his head bowed, stood motionless.

The secretary repeated his invitation: to subscribe his full and complete satisfaction or his manifest dissatisfaction, if, contrary to expectations, he truly felt that his own case was just, and in this event, to declare whether he intended to appeal to the appropriate authorities within that period of time prescribed by the law.

Dubrovsky remained silent . . . Suddenly he raised his head, his eyes flashed, he stamped his foot, and pushed the secretary back with such force that the other fell and, seizing the ink-well, he flung it at the assessor. Everybody was horrified.

'What! You don't respect the Church of God! Away with you, you vile breed!'

Then, turning to Kirila Petrovitch, he continued:

'Has such a thing ever been heard of, your Excellency? Grooms bringing dogs into the Church of God! Dogs running about in the church! I'll teach you a lesson!'

The guards, aroused by the noise, rushed in and with difficulty overpowered him. He was led out and seated in his sledge. Troyekurov left immediately after him, accompanied by the entire court. Dubrovsky's sudden fit of insanity had had a powerful effect on his imagination, and had soured his triumph.

The judges, who had been hoping for signs of his gratitude, were not honoured by a single pleasant word from him. He set out for Pokrovskoye that same day. Meanwhile, Dubrovsky lay in bed; the district surgeon, luckily not a complete ignoramus, bled him and treated him with leeches and Spanish flies. By the evening, the sick man's condition had improved and he had regained his senses. The next day he was taken back to Kistenevka, which hardly belonged to him any more.

Chapter Three

Some time passed, and the unfortunate Dubrovsky's health showed no improvement. True, the fits of insanity did not recur, but his powers grew visibly less. He forgot his former occupations, rarely left his room, and remained lost in meditation for whole days at a time. Yegorovna, a kind-hearted old woman who had once looked after his son, now became his nurse. She looked after him as if he were a child, reminding him of when it was time to eat and sleep, feeding him, and putting him to bed. Andrey Gavrilovitch meekly obeyed her, and had no dealings with anyone else. He was in no condition to think about his affairs or the running of his estate, and Yegorovna saw the necessity of informing young Dubrovsky, who was then serving with an infantry Guards regiment stationed in Petersburg, of all that had happened. And so, tearing a sheet of paper from the accounts-book, she dictated a letter to the cook, Khariton, the only person in Kistenevka who could read or write, and sent it off that same day to the post-office in the town.

But it is time the reader became acquainted with the real hero of our story.

Vladimir Dubrovsky had been educated in the Cadet Corps and, on graduating, had entered the Guards as a cornet. His father spared nothing to give his son a decent allowance, and the young man received more money from home than he was entitled to expect. Extravagant and ambitious, he indulged the most luxurious whims, gambled and fell into debt without the slightest regard for the future, foreseeing for himself, sooner or later, a rich bride – the dream of impoverished youth.

One evening, when several officers were in his quarters, lounging about on sofas and smoking through amber pipe-stems, Grisha, his valet handed him a letter, the inscription of which immediately caused the young man to start. He hastily unsealed it and read the following:

> 'Our master, Vladimir Andreyevitch!
>
> 'I, your old nurse, have decided to inform you of the health of your Papa. He is very poorly, sometimes raves, and sits like a stupid child all day long – but life and death are in God's hands. Come to us, my bright falcon; we will send horses to Pesochnoye for you. We hear that the district court is going to put us under the authority of Kirila Petrovitch Troyekurov, because they say we belong to him; but we have been your servants from time immemorial, and have never before heard anything like this. Living in Petersburg, you could inform the Tsar of this – he would not allow us to be wronged.
>
> 'I remain your faithful servant and nurse, Orina Yegorovna Buzyreva.
>
> 'I send my maternal blessing to Grisha – does he serve you well? It has been raining here for over a week, and the shepherd Rodya died just before Michaelmas Day.'

Vladimir Dubrovsky re-read these somewhat incoherent lines several times with unusual agitation. He had lost his mother in childhood and, scarcely knowing his father, had been sent to Petersburg at the age of eight. He had, nevertheless, a romantic affection for his father and enjoyed family life all the more for having so little experience of its quiet joys.

The thought of losing his father caused him acute distress, and the condition of the poor patient, which he divined from his nurse's letter, appalled him. He pictured his father, left on his own in a remote village, in the hands of a foolish old woman and a collection of servants, threatened by some calamity and dying helplessly, in bodily and spiritual torture. Vladimir reproached himself with criminal negligence. He had not received a letter from his father for a long time and had not thought to enquire after him, supposing him to have undertaken a journey or to be wrapped up in the cares of his estate.

He resolved to go to him and, should the condition of his sick father demand his presence, to resign his commission. His comrades, noting his anxiety, took their leave. Vladimir, left alone, wrote out a request for leave of absence, lit his pipe and became immersed in deep thought.

He put in his application for leave that same day, and three days later was on the high road.

Vladimir Andreyevitch drew near to the posting-station at which he was to turn off for Kistenevka. His heart was full of sad forebodings; he feared that his father would no longer be alive, and imagined the melancholy life that would be awaiting him in the village: remoteness, solitude, poverty and the cares of his estate – cares of which he knew nothing. Arriving at the posting-station, he went up to the postmaster and asked for fresh horses. The postmaster enquired where he was going, and announced that the horses sent from Kistenevka had already been awaiting him for four days. Soon, Anton, the old coachman who at one time used to take

Vladimir Andreyevitch over the stables, and to look after his pony, presented himself. Anton shed a few tears at the sight of him, bowed to the ground, told him that his old master was still alive and ran off to harness the horses. Vladimir Andreyevitch refused the luncheon that was offered to him, and hastened to set off. Anton drove him along the country lanes and they began to talk.

'Tell me please, Anton: what's this business between my father and Troyekurov?'

'Heaven knows, Vladimir Andreyevitch, my dear . . . They say the master had a quarrel with Kirila Petrovitch, and that the latter took him to court, although he's a law unto himself. It's not for us serfs to question the wills of our masters, but it was useless for your father to fight Kirila Petrovitch: a whip can't stand up to an axe.'

'It seems, then, that this Kirila Petrovitch does what he likes around here?'

'Indeed he does, master: they say he doesn't give a rap for the assessor, and the chief of police runs errands for him. The landowners assemble at his house to pay their respects – as they say, "Where there's a trough, there'll be swine."'

'Is it true that he's taking away our estate?'

'Oh, master, that's what we've heard. Some days ago the sexton from Pokrovskoye said at the christening at our elder's house: "The fun's over now; Kirila Petrovitch'll take you in hand." Mikita, the blacksmith, said to him: "Come now, Savelyitch, don't sadden your friend and distress the guests. Kiril Petrovitch is his own master, Andrey Gavrilovitch is his own master, and we all belong to God and the Tsar." But one can't stop people from talking.'

'So you don't want to come under the authority of Troyekurov?'

'Come under the authority of Troyekurov! The Lord save and preserve us from that! His own people have a raw enough deal at times, but strangers – he'd tear the flesh as well as the skin off them. No, may God restore Andrey Gavrilovitch to health and grant him life, and if God should take him, we would want nobody else but you, our benefactor. Don't abandon us and we'll stand by you.'

With these words Anton cracked his whip, shook the reins, and the horses broke into a sharp trot.

Touched by the devotion of the old coachman, Dubrovsky fell silent, and once more gave himself up to thought. More than an hour had passed when Grisha suddenly roused him with the exclamation:

'There's Pokrovskoye!'

Dubrovsky raised his head. They were driving by the bank of a wide lake, from which flowed a small river, winding its way into the distance among the hills; on one of these hills, above the dense foliage of a copse, there rose the green roof and belvedere of a huge stone-built house; on another, a church with five domes and an ancient belfry; scattered about were peasants' cottages with their kitchen-gardens and wells. Dubrovsky recognised these places; he remembered playing on that same hill with little Masha Troyekurov, who was two years younger than he and who, even then, gave promise of unusual beauty. He wanted to ask Anton about her, but a certain shyness held him back.

On approaching the big house, he caught sight of a white dress fluttering among the trees in the garden. At that moment Anton, driven by that vanity common to both town and country coachmen, struck the horses and sent them galloping at full pace over the bridge and through the village. Leaving the village behind them, they drove to the top of the hill, from where Vladimir could see a birch copse, and in an open piece of country on the left, a small grey house with a red roof; his heart began to beat violently. Before him he saw Kistenevka, and the humble dwelling of his father.

Ten minutes later he was driving into the courtyard of the house. He looked around him with indescribable emotion. It was twelve years since he had seen his birth-place. The birch saplings which had been planted by the fence at that time had grown into tall, branchy trees. The courtyard, formerly ornamented by three rectangular flower-beds, separated by wide, well-kept paths, was now an unmown meadow, in which a lame horse grazed. The dogs began to bark loudly but, on recognising Anton, they fell silent and wagged their shaggy tails. The servants came rushing out of their peasants' cottages and surrounded their young master with noisy exclamations of joy. With difficulty he made his way through the eager throng and ran up the crumbling steps. In the porch he was met by Yegorovna, who tearfully embraced her former charge.

'How are you, nurse, how are you?' he repeated, pressing the good old woman to his heart. 'And my father? Where is he? How is he?'

At that moment a tall, pale and gaunt old man, in a dressing-gown and night-cap, shuffled with difficulty into the hall.

'Hello, Volodka!' he said in a weak voice, and Vladimir warmly embraced his father.

The joy of meeting his son turned out to be too much for the old man. He grew weak, his legs gave way beneath him, and had his son not held him up, he would have fallen.

'Why did you get out of bed?' Yegorovna asked him. 'You can't stand properly and yet you want to do what everyone else does.'

The old man was carried back to his bedroom. He attempted to speak to his son, but his thoughts grew confused and his words became incoherent. He fell silent and began to doze. Vladimir was shocked at his condition. He installed himself in the bedroom and asked to be left alone with his father. The household servants obeyed him; then, turning to Grisha, they led him away to their own quarters, where they treated him country-fashion, welcoming his return with the utmost joy, and tiring him out with questions and compliments.

Chapter Four

> *On the table once laden there*
> *now stands a coffin.*
>
> DERZHAVIN

A few days after his arrival, young Dubrovsky decided to look into the affairs of the estate, but his father was in no condition to give him the necessary explanations; and there was no lawyer to whom he could go, because Andrey Gavrilovitch had not called upon the services of one. Looking through his father's papers, he could only find the assessor's first letter and a draft of his father's reply; from these, he was unable to form a very clear picture of the law-suit as it stood, and he resolved to await further developments, confident in the justice of the cause.

In the meantime, Andrey Gavrilovitch's health grew hourly worse. Vladimir foresaw that his father's end was in sight, and he never left the old man, who had fallen into complete dotage.

The time limit for an appeal had meanwhile expired. Kistenevka belonged to Troyekurov. Shabashkin appeared before him with bows and congratulations and asked him to appoint the date on which it would please his Excellency to assume possession of his newly-acquired property – either in person, or by designating someone to whom he could entrust this task. Kirila Petrovitch felt troubled. He was not by nature an avaricious person, but his desire for revenge had carried him too far and his conscience was disturbed. He knew what the condition of his adversary, the old comrade of his youth, was, and his victory brought no joy to his heart. He glared menacingly at Shabashkin, seeking to find some reason to upbraid him, but finding none, he exclaimed angrily:

'Go away! I've got no time for you.'

Shabashkin, seeing that he was out of sorts, bowed and made haste to depart. Kirila Petrovitch, left alone, began to pace up and down the room, whistling *Beat, Drums of Victory!*, a sure sign that his thoughts were unusually perturbed.

At last he gave orders for his racing sulky to be harnessed; he wrapped himself up in a warm coat (it was already the end of September), and drove himself out of the courtyard.

He soon caught sight of the little house of Andrey Gavrilovitch, and his heart was filled with conflicting emotions. Satisfied vengeance and the love of power to a certain extent smothered his more noble sentiments, but these latter eventually triumphed. He resolved to make it up with his old neighbour and to destroy all signs of their quarrel by returning him his property. Kirila Petrovitch, his heart relieved by this good intention, set off at a fast trot for his neighbour's estate, and drove straight into the courtyard.

The sick man was sitting at his bedroom window at the time. He recognised Kirila Petrovitch, and his face assumed an expression of terrible confusion: a crimson flush drove the habitual pallor from his cheeks, his eyes flashed, and he uttered a few inarticulate sounds. His son, who was sitting in the room doing the household accounts, raised his head and was struck by his father's condition. The sick man was pointing at the courtyard with an expression of horror and anger. He hastily began to gather up the folds of his dressing-gown, preparing to lift himself from his chair; he raised himself a little ... and then suddenly fell. His son rushed over to him; the old man lay senseless and without breathing – he had had a stroke.

'Quick! Quick! Send into the town for a doctor!' Vladimir cried.

'Kirila Petrovitch asks to see you,' a servant said, entering the room.

Vladimir threw him a wild glance.

'Tell Kirila Petrovitch to remove himself with all speed before I have him thrown out – go!'

The servant gladly hastened from the room to fulfil his master's orders. Yegorovna threw up her arms.

'Master!' she cried in a shrill voice. 'You'll lose your head! Kirila Petrovitch will destroy us all.'

'Silence, nurse,' Vladimir said angrily. 'Send Anton at once to the town for a doctor.'

Yegorovna left the room. There was nobody in the hall since all the servants had run out into the courtyard to look at Kirila Petrovitch. She went out on to the steps and heard the servant delivering his young master's reply. Kirila Petrovitch received it, seated in his sulky. His face became darker than the night; he smiled with disdain, threw a threatening glance at the servants, and then drove slowly out of the courtyard. He glanced at the window, where, a moment before, Andrey Gavrilovitch had been sitting, but he was no longer there. Forgetful of her young master's orders, the nurse stood on the steps. The servants chatted noisily about what had happened. Vladimir suddenly appeared among them, and said abruptly:

'There's no need for the doctor; my father is dead.'

There was a general confusion. The servants rushed into

their old master's room. He was lying in the armchair in which Vladimir had laid him; his right arm hung down to the ground, his head was resting on his chest, and there was no sign of life in his still warm body, already distorted in death. Yegorovna set up a wail; the servants surrounded the corpse, which had been left to their care, washed it and clothed it in a uniform tailored in 1797, and laid it out on that same table at which they had served their master for so many years.

Chapter Five

The funeral was held three days later. The body of the poor old man lay on the table, which was covered with a shroud and surrounded by candles. The dining-room was filled with servants, ready to carry out the body. The coffin was raised by Vladimir and three of the servants. The priest went ahead, followed by the sexton singing funeral prayers. The owner of Kistenevka crossed the threshold of his house for the last time. The coffin was carried through the copse. The church lay just behind it. It was a bright, cold day. Autumn leaves were falling from the trees.

Emerging from the copse, they saw the wooden church of Kistenevka and the cemetery shaded by ancient lime-trees. It was there that the body of Vladimir's mother had been laid to rest; and there, beside her tomb, a fresh grave had been dug the previous evening.

The church was filled with peasants from Kistenevka, who had come to pay final homage to their master. The young Dubrovsky stood by the choir; he neither wept nor prayed, but his face looked ravaged. The sad ceremony was completed.

Vladimir was the first to take leave of the body, and he was followed by all the servants. The lid was brought up and the coffin sealed. The women wailed loudly, and from time to time the men wiped away their tears with the backs of their hands. Vladimir and the same three servants carried the coffin to the cemetery, accompanied by the entire village. The coffin was lowered into the grave, and all present threw in a handful of earth, helped to fill in the pit, bowed, and then dispersed. Vladimir hurriedly departed and, getting ahead of the others, disappeared into the Kistenevka copse.

In the name of her master, Yegorovna invited the priest and all the clergy to a funeral dinner, announcing at the same time that her young master did not propose to attend it. And so, Father Anton, his wife Fedotovna and the sexton set out on foot for the main house, conversing with Yegorovna on the virtues of the dead man, and on what seemed to lie in store for his heir. Troyekurov's visit and the reception he had received were already known to the entire neighbourhood, and local politicians foresaw grave consequences.

'What will be, will be,' said the priest's wife. 'But it'll be a pity if Vladimir Andreyevitch does not become our master. He is a fine young man, and no mistake.'

'But who else will become our master, if not he?' interrupted Yegorovna. 'Kirila Petrovitch need not get so excited. My bright falcon is no coward – he can stand up for himself and, with God's help, he won't lack supporters. Kirila Petrovitch is proud all right, but he certainly went away with his tail between his legs when my Grisha shouted to him: "Go on, you old cur! Get out of here!"'

'Oh, Yegorovna!' said the sexton. 'However did that Grisha manage to say it? I would sooner agree to bark at a bishop than look askance at Kirila Petrovitch. Even to look at him fills one with fear and makes one sweat, and one's spine seems to bend forward of itself . . .'

'Vanity of vanities!' said the priest. 'A funeral service will be sung for Kirila Petrovitch in the same way as one has just been sung for Andrey Gavrilovitch. The funeral will be grander perhaps, and there'll be more guests invited, but in the eyes of God all men are equal!'

'Oh, Father, we too wanted to invite the whole neighbourhood, but Vladimir Andreyevitch wouldn't have it. We've got quite enough food with which to entertain, never fear – but what would you have us do? Anyway, with so few people, at least we can do you proud, dear guests.'

These kind promises and the hope of finding a succulent pie awaiting them caused their steps to quicken, and they soon reached the main house, where the table was already laid and the vodka served.

In the meantime, Vladimir advanced further into the thick of the trees, endeavouring by motion and fatigue to stifle the affliction of his heart. He walked on without heeding the road. The branches repeatedly caught at and tore him, and his feet continually sank into the swampy ground, but he noticed nothing. At last he reached a small hollow, surrounded on all sides by the wood. A little stream ran silently among the trees, half of whose leaves had been blown off by the autumn winds. Vladimir stopped and sat down on the cold turf, and thoughts, each more gloomy than the last, oppressed his mind . . . He felt an acute sense of his loneliness. For him the future seemed overcast with menacing clouds. His enmity with Troyekurov presaged new disasters. His meagre property was likely to pass into strange hands – in which case beggary awaited him. For a long time he sat motionless in the same place, watching the gentle flow of the stream as it carried away a few withered leaves, keenly struck by its similarity to life – a comparison which has become commonplace. At last he noticed that it had started to grow dark; he got up and began to look for the road home, but he wandered about for some time in the unfamiliar wood before he came across the path which led straight to the gates of his house.

On his way back Dubrovsky met the priest and his clergy. He was struck by the thought that this boded ill for him. Involuntarily, he turned aside and hid behind a tree. They did not notice him and continued to talk eagerly among themselves as they went by.

'Get away from evil and do good,' the priest was saying to his wife. 'There's nothing to keep us here. Whatever happens here, it is no concern of ours.'

The priest's wife made some reply, but Vladimir could not make it out.

Approaching the house, he saw a large gathering of people: peasants and household servants were crowding the courtyard. Vladimir could hear an unusually loud noise and the sound of voices in the distance. Two troikas stood by the coach-house, and on the steps were several unknown men in uniform, apparently discussing something.

'What does this mean?' he asked Anton angrily, who ran forward to meet him. 'Who are these people, and what do they want?'

'Oh, Vladimir Andreyevitch, master,' the old man answered, out of breath. 'They're from the court. They're handing us over to Troyekurov, and taking us away from your Honour!'

Vladimir hung his head, and the servants surrounded their unhappy master.

'You are our master,' they cried, kissing his hands. 'We don't want any other master but you. Give us the order and we'll soon settle with these men from the court. We'd rather die than betray you.'

Vladimir looked at them, and he was troubled by strange thoughts.

'Stay here quietly,' he said to them, 'and I'll go and talk to these officials.'

'Yes, talk to them, master,' voices cried from the crowd. 'Put the wretches to shame!'

Vladimir went up to the officials. Shabashkin was standing with his cap on his head and his arms akimbo, looking arrogantly around him. The chief of police, a tall, fat man of about fifty with a red face and moustache, grunted as he saw Dubrovsky approach.

'And so I repeat to you what I have already said,' he said in a hoarse voice: 'in accordance with the decision of the district court, you now belong to Kirila Petrovitch Troyekurov, represented here by Mr Shabashkin. Obey him in all that he orders you; and you women had better love and respect him, for he has a great fancy for you.'

At this witty joke the chief of police roared with laughter. Shabashkin and the other officials followed suit.

Vladimir seethed with indignation. 'Will you kindly tell me what this means?' he asked the jovial chief of police in tones of forced calm.

'It means,' replied the scheming official, 'that we've come to install Kirila Petrovitch Troyekurov as the owner of this property, and to ask certain other people to remove themselves for good and all!'

'But you could have approached me, as the present master of the estate, and informed me of my dispossession before going to my peasants . . .'

'And who may you be?' Shabashkin asked with an arrogant stare. 'The former landowner, Andrey Gavrilovitch Dubrovsky is, by the will of God, dead, and we neither know you, nor wish to know you.'

'Vladimir Andreyevitch is our young master,' a voice rose from the crowd.

'Who dared to open his mouth?' the chief of police said

threateningly. 'What master? What Vladimir Andreyevitch? Your master is Kirila Petrovitch Troyekurov. Do you hear me, you blockheads?'

'No, he's not,' said the same voice.

'This is a revolt!' shouted the chief of police. 'Village-elder, come here!' The village-elder stepped forward. 'Find out this minute who dared to answer me back. I'll show him!'

The village-elder turned towards the crowd and asked who had spoken. All remained silent. Soon a murmur rose from the back ranks of the crowd; it grew louder, and in a minute had swollen to a tumultuous roar. The chief of police lowered his voice and tried the effects of persuasion.

'Come on, men, what are we waiting for?' the servants shouted. 'Down with them!'

The whole crowd moved forward. Shabashkin and the other officials beat a hasty retreat into the hall of the house and locked the door behind them.

'Let's tie them up, men!' shouted the same voice, and the crowd pressed forward.

'Stop!' yelled Dubrovsky. 'Fools! What do you think you're doing? Do you want to ruin both yourselves and me? Go back to your own houses and leave me in peace. Don't be afraid – the Tsar is merciful. I will send a petition to him. He will protect us. We are all his children. But how will he be able to help you if you become rebellious and behave like outlaws.'

Young Dubrovsky's speech, his ringing voice and impressive appearance had the desired effect. The crowd quietened down and dispersed. The courtyard became empty. The officials were seated in the hall. At last Shabashkin timidly unlocked the door, came out into the porch and, bowing humbly, began to thank Dubrovsky for his generous protection. Vladimir listened to him with disdain, but offered no reply.

'We have decided,' continued the assessor, 'with your permission to spend the night here. It's already dark, and your men might attack us on our way back. Be kind enough to give orders for some hay to be laid down on the drawing-room floor. We'll go home as soon as the dawn breaks.'

'Do as you like,' Dubrovsky replied drily. 'I am no longer the master here.'

With these words he went into his father's room and locked the door behind him.

Chapter Six

'So it's all over!' he said to himself. 'Only this morning I had a place to rest and a crust of bread to eat. Tomorrow I must abandon the house where I was born, and where my father died, to the man who brought about his death and my beggary!'

His eyes fixed themselves upon the portrait of his mother. The painter had depicted her with her elbow on a balustrade, wearing a white morning-gown and with a damask rose in her hair.

'And this portrait will become the property of my family's enemy,' thought Vladimir. 'Together with broken chairs, he'll have it thrown into the lumber-room, or he'll hang it in the hall as the object of his grooms' sneers and ridicule. And in her bedroom, the room where my father died, he'll establish his bailiff, or his harem. No, no! I'll not give him possession of this melancholy house from which he is driving me.'

Vladimir clenched his teeth – frightening thoughts were

turning over in his mind. The voices of the officials reached his ears – they were ordering the household about, demanding this, demanding that, breaking disagreeably into the midst of his mournful reflections. At last all was quiet.

Vladimir opened the chests of drawers and cupboards and began to go carefully through the papers of his dead father. For the most part they consisted of household accounts and correspondence on various matters. Vladimir tore them up without reading them. Among them he found a packet with the inscription: 'Letters from my wife'. Profoundly moved, Vladimir began to look through them. They were written at the time of the Turkish campaign and were addressed to the army from Kistenevka. She described to him her hermit's existence, her household occupations, and imploring him to return home to the arms of his loving wife, she tenderly bemoaned their separation. In one of them she expressed her anxiety concerning the health of the young Vladimir; in another, she rejoiced over his early intelligence and foresaw for him a happy and brilliant future. Vladimir, absorbed in his reading and completely wrapped up in the world of family happiness, forgot all else and did not notice how the time slipped by. The clock on the wall struck eleven. He put the letters into his pocket and, taking up a candle, he left the room. The officials were asleep on the floor of the drawing-room. Empty glasses stood on the table and a strong smell of rum pervaded the entire room. Vladimir passed them with revulsion on his way to the porch, the door to which he found to be locked. Unable to see the key anywhere, he returned to the drawing-room and found it lying on the table. Vladimir unlocked the door and stumbled over a man huddled up in the corner, an axe glittering in his hands. Turning towards him with the candle, Vladimir recognised the blacksmith Arkhip.

'What are you doing here?' he asked.

'Ah, Vladimir Andreyevitch, it's you!' answered Arkhip in a whisper. 'May the Lord save and preserve you! It's a good thing you were carrying a candle.'

Vladimir looked at him in amazement.

'What are you hiding here for?' he asked the blacksmith.

'I wanted ... I came ... I came to see if everything was all right in the house,' Arkhip stammered softly.

'But why did you bring an axe with you? '

'Why bring an axe? One can't go around without an axe at a time like this. These officials are such rascals, you know ...'

'You're drunk. Throw the axe down, and go and sleep it off.'

'Me drunk? Vladimir Andreyevitch, master, as God is my witness, I haven't touched a drop all evening, nor has it entered my head to do so. Whoever heard of clerks imagining that they can take us over, that they can drive our masters out of their house? How they snore, the wretches! If we bumped them off now, no one would be any the wiser.'

Dubrovsky frowned.

'Listen, Arkhip,' he said after a slight pause. 'Get the idea out of your head. It's not the fault of the officials. Light a lantern and follow me.'

Arkhip took the candle from his master's hands, discovered a lantern behind the stove, lit it, and they both walked quietly down the steps and out into the courtyard. The night-watchman began to beat upon the iron plate, and the dogs to bark.

'Who's on watch?' asked Dubrovsky.

'We are, master,' answered a thin voice. 'Vassilissa and Lukerya.'

'Go back to your homes,' Dubrovsky said to them. 'You're not needed any more.'

'You can leave off now," added Arkhip.

'Thank you, master,' replied the women, and immediately set out for their homes.

Dubrovsky went on. Two men approached him. They called out, and Dubrovsky recognised the voices of Anton and Grisha.

'Why aren't you asleep?' he asked them.

'This is no time for sleep,' replied Anton. 'To think that things have come to this . . .'

'Sssh!' interrupted Dubrovsky. 'Where's Yegorovna?'

'In her room at the house,' answered Grisha.

'Go and fetch her here and get all our people out of the house, so that there's nobody left there but the officials. And you, Anton, go and harness the carriage.'

Grisha went off and returned a minute later with his mother. The old woman had not undressed that night. With the exception of the officials, nobody in the house had closed an eye.

'Is everyone here?' asked Dubrovsky. 'There's no one left in the house?'

'No one but the officials,' answered Grisha.

'Fetch me some hay or straw,' said Dubrovsky.

The men ran off into the stables and returned with armfuls of hay.

'Put it under the steps. That's right. Now, my men, a light.'

Arkhip opened the lantern and Dubrovsky lit a splinter of wood from it.

'Wait a moment,' he said to Arkhip. 'In my haste I think I locked the door into the drawing-room. Run and unlock it.'

Arkhip ran up to the porch and tried the door to the drawing-room – the door was unlocked. Arkhip turned the key in the lock, muttering under his breath:

'Unlock it – not likely!'

He then returned to Dubrovsky.

Dubrovsky applied the lighted splinter to the hay, which burst into flames. The fire leaped into the air, lighting up the whole courtyard.

'Aieeee, Vladimir Andreyevitch, what are you doing?' Yegorovna yelled plaintively.

'Keep quiet!' said Dubrovsky. 'Well, my children, good-bye, I go where God takes me. Be happy with your new master.'

'Master, our benefactor,' the people replied, 'we would die rather than leave you – we'll come with you.'

The horses were brought round. Dubrovsky sat down in the carriage next to Grisha, and appointed a rendezvous for them all in the Kistenevka copse. Anton struck the horses, and they drove out of the courtyard.

A wind blew up. Within a minute the flames had spread to the whole house. A red smoke billowed up from the roof. Glass cracked and was scattered about, blazing beams began to fall, and piteous cries and screams were heard.

'Help, help, we're burning!'

'So you are,' said Arkhip, as he gazed at the fire with a wicked smile on his face.

'Arkhip, my dear,' Yegorovna said to him, 'save them, the poor wretches – God will reward you.'

'Oh no,' answered the blacksmith.

At that moment the officials appeared at the window and could be seen trying to break through the double frames. But the roof fell in with a crash, and their cries were no longer heard.

Soon all the servants had poured out into the courtyard. Screaming, the women rushed to save their ramshackle furniture. Children jumped up and down, gazing at the fire with glee. There was a blizzard of sparks and the nearby cottages caught fire.

'It's going well now,' said Arkhip. 'Just see how it burns, eh? It must look splendid from Pokrovskoye.'

At that moment something else attracted his attention. A cat was running along the roof of the blazing coach-house, at a loss to know where to jump off, since it was surrounded on all sides by flames. With piteous mewings, the poor creature was appealing for help, and several young boys were holding their sides with laughter at the sight of its desperate plight.

'What are you laughing at, you little devils?' the blacksmith asked them angrily. 'Have you no fear of God? You see one of God's creatures dying and yet you jump for joy?'

And positioning a ladder against the burning roof, he climbed up it to reach the cat. The cat understood his intention and, with a look of flustered gratitude, clutched at the blacksmith's sleeve. Half-burned, the blacksmith climbed down to the ground with his prize.

'Well, good-bye, lads,' he said to the confused servants. 'There's nothing more for me to do here. Good luck, and think well of me whatever I've done.'

The blacksmith went his way. The fire raged on for some time, and at last died down. Heaps of embers glowed brightly in the darkness of the night and the burned-out inhabitants of Kistenevka wandered around them.

Chapter Seven

The next day the news of the fire spread through the entire district. It was discussed by everybody and various guesses as to its cause were hazarded. Some affirmed that Dubrovsky's men, having got drunk at the funeral, set fire to the house through carelessness. Others blamed the officials, who, they maintained, had also become drunk while lodging at the house. Many believed that the house had caught fire accidentally and that the district court and every member of the household had been burned to death. Some guessed at the truth and declared that Dubrovsky himself, driven by bitterness and despair, had been the cause of the appalling disaster. On the following day, Troyekurov visited the scene of the fire and himself carried out an investigation. It was learned that the chief of police, the court assessor, the lawyer and the clerk, as well as Vladimir Dubrovsky, the nurse Yegorovna, the manservant Grisha, the coachman Anton and the blacksmith Arkhip had disappeared – no one knew where. All the servants testified that the officials had been burned to death when the roof fell in; and their charred bones were later discovered. The women, Vassilissa and Lukerya, said that they had seen Dubrovsky and Arkhip the blacksmith some minutes before the fire. According to general testimony, Arkhip the blacksmith was still alive and was probably the principal, if not the sole, instigator of the fire. Strong suspicion fell on Dubrovsky. Kirila Petrovitch sent a detailed description of the whole incident to the Governor, and a fresh law-suit was opened.

Soon other news gave fresh food for curiosity and gossip. Brigands had shown up in *** and had spread terror throughout the surrounding district. Measures taken against them by the authorities had proved inadequate. Robberies, each more remarkable than the last, followed one after another. There was no safety either on the roads or in the villages. Several troikas, filled with brigands, roamed the whole province in broad daylight, holding up travellers and mail-coaches, driving down into the villages and robbing and setting fire to the houses of the landowners. The band's chief gained a reputation for intelligence and daring, and also a certain magnanimity. Wonders were told of him. The name of Dubrovsky was on everyone's lips, and all were certain that he, and no other, stood at the head of this fearless band of miscreants. One factor caused all-round astonishment; Troyekurov's estates were spared. Not a single shed of his had been looted by the brigands, not a single farm-cart held up. With characteristic arrogance, Troyekurov ascribed this exclusion to the fear he had managed to instil throughout the entire province, as well as to the excellent police force he had established in his villages. At first the neighbours laughed among themselves at Troyekurov's conceit, and each day expected to hear that uninvited guests had visited Pokrovskoye, where the brigands could be expected to make a good haul. They were eventually forced, however, to agree with him and to admit that the brigands showed him inexplicable respect. Troyekurov triumphed and at the news of each fresh robbery on the part of Dubrovsky, he indulged himself in jokes at the expense of the Governor, the chiefs of police and the company commanders from whom Dubrovsky always escaped unharmed.

In the meantime, October 1st arrived – the day of the church festival in Troyekurov's village. But before proceeding to a description of these celebrations and the events following them, we must acquaint our reader with certain personages as yet unknown to him, or to whom we made slight reference at the beginning of our story.

Chapter Eight

The reader has probably already guessed that the daughter of Kirila Petrovitch, of whom we have as yet said only a few words, is the heroine of our story. At the time we are describing she was seventeen years old and her beauty was in full flower. Her father loved her to distraction, but treated her with his usual wilfulness – at one moment trying to gratify her slightest whim, at another terrifying her with his strict and, on occasions, cruel treatment. Certain of her affection, he had never been able to win her confidence. She was accustomed to keeping her thoughts and feelings from him, never being sure as to how they would be received. She had no companions and grew up in solitude. The neighbours' wives and daughters rarely came to see Kirila Petrovitch, whose customary conversation and amusements demanded the company of men and not the presence of ladies. It was not often that the young beauty appeared among the guests who feasted with Kirila Petrovitch. A vast library, for the most part consisting of books by eighteenth-entury French writers, was at her disposal. Her father, who never read anything except *The Complete Cookery Book*, was incapable of guiding her in her choice of books and Masha, after dipping into works of every sort, naturally enough settled on novels. In this way she completed her education, formerly begun under the guidance of Mademoiselle Mimi, to whom Kirila Petroyitch had shown the greatest favour and confidence, and whom he was eventually forced to send quietly away to another estate, when the consequences of this friendship became too apparent.

Mademoiselle Mimi had left pleasant enough memories behind her. She was a good-natured girl and had never misused the influence she had undoubtedly held over Kirila Petrovitch, in this respect differing from other favourites, whose reigns had been short. It seemed that Kirila Petrovitch himself had liked her more than the others, and the mischievous black-eyed boy of nine, whose features recalled those southern ones of Mademoiselle Mimi, was brought up under his care and recognised as his son, despite the fact that numerous bare-footed lads, as like to Kirila Petrovitch as one drop of water to another, ran about in front of the windows and were considered mere peasant-boys. For his little Sasha, Kirila Petrovitch had engaged in Moscow a French tutor, who arrived at Pokrovskoye at the time of the events just described.

Kirila Petrovitch was impressed by the tutor's pleasant appearance and simple manners. The tutor presented Kirila Petrovitch with his credentials and a letter from one of Troyekurov's relatives, in whose house he had lived as a tutor for four years. Kirila Petrovitch examined all these with satisfaction. The only thing that made him at all uneasy was the Frenchman's youth – not because he felt this charming deficiency to be incompatible with patience and experience, qualities both so essential in the unfortunate calling of a teacher, but because he had doubts, the nature of which he immediately resolved to make clear. For this purpose he summoned Masha (Kirila Petrovitch did not speak French, and she used to act as his interpreter).

'Come here, Masha. Tell this "Monsoo" that it's all right and that I'll take him on – but only on condition that he doesn't fool around with my girls. If he does, the son of a dog, I'll . . . Translate that to him, Masha.'

Masha blushed and, turning to the tutor, told him in French that her father relied upon his discretion and good behaviour.

The Frenchman bowed to her and replied that he hoped to win respect even though favour might be denied him.

Word for word, Masha translated his reply.

'Good, good,' Kirila Petrovitch said, 'but tell him not to concern himself with respect or favour. His job is to look after Sasha and teach him grammar and geography – translate that to him.'

Masha softened the coarse expressions of her father in translation, and Kirila Petrovitch dismissed the Frenchman to the wing of the house where a room had been appointed to him.

Masha paid no particular attention to the young Frenchman. Brought up with aristocratic prejudices, a tutor in her eyes was a kind of servant or artisan, and servants and artisans she did not regard as real men. She did not notice the impression she had made on Monsieur Deforge – his confusion, his trepidation, his altered tone of voice. For several days running after this she kept meeting him, but she did not honour him with her attention. In an unexpected way, however, her ideas about him underwent a complete change.

There were usually a few bear-cubs being reared on Kirila Petrovitch's estate, and these provided the owner of Pokrovskoye with one of his chief amusements. While still very young, the bear-cubs would be brought daily into the drawing-room where, for hours on end, Kirila Petrovitch would amuse himself with them, setting them to fight against the cats and puppies. When they were older, they would be chained up in readiness for serious baiting. From time to time a bear would be led out in front of the windows of the main house and an empty wine barrel, spiked with nails, rolled up. The bear would sniff at it, then touch it gently with its paw, which of course would be pricked; angered, it would push the barrel harder and thereby suffer greater pain. This would drive it into a complete frenzy, and with a growl it would hurl itself against the barrel, until the object of its fruitless rage was removed from the poor beast. On occasions, a couple of bears would be harnessed to a carriage and, whether they liked it or not, guests would be seated in it, whereupon the two beasts would be allowed to bound about at will. But Kirila Petrovitch's favourite joke deserves a fuller description.

A starving bear would be locked in an empty room and tied by a rope to a ring in the wall. The rope would almost reach across the room but not quite, so that the only corner free from the attack of the terrible beast would be that opposite the ring in the wall. Someone, usually a novice, would be led to the door of the room and then unexpectedly pushed in to join the bear. The door would then be locked and the unfortunate victim left alone with the shaggy hermit. The wretched guest, his coat ripped and bleeding from scratches, would quickly seek the safe corner, where he was sometimes forced to spend three whole hours pressed against the wall, watching the enraged beast, standing on its hind-legs two paces away from him, growling, jumping, and tearing and struggling to reach him. Such were the noble amusements of this Russian gentleman!

A few days after the arrival of the tutor, Troyekurov remembered his existence and decided to give him a taste of the bear-room. For this purpose he summoned him one morning and led him along a series of dark corridors. A door on one side was suddenly opened, and two servants pushed the Frenchman into the room and locked the door after him. Coming to his senses, the tutor caught sight of the chained bear. The beast began to sniff and snort at its visitor from a distance, and suddenly rising up on its hind-legs, it began to advance towards him. The Frenchman remained completely unperturbed, did not retreat but awaited the bear's attack. The bear drew close, and Deforge drew a small pistol from his pocket, placed it against the ear of the hungry beast and fired. The bear collapsed. Everyone came running up; the door was unlocked and Kirila Petrovitch entered the room, astonished at the outcome of his joke.

He demanded an immediate explanation of the whole affair: who had warned Deforge of the joke that had been prepared for him, and why had he got a loaded pistol in his pocket? He sent for Masha. Masha hastened to the spot and translated her father's questions to the Frenchman.

'I had not heard about the bear,' Deforge replied, 'but I always carry a pistol, for I do not propose to tolerate an insult for which, by my calling, I am unable to demand satisfaction.'

Masha looked at him in astonishment and translated his words to Kirila Petrovitch. Kirila Petrovitch made no reply, but ordered the bear to be taken away and skinned. Then, turning to his servants, he said:

'A fine young man! He's no coward – by God, he's no coward!'

From that moment he took a positive liking to Deforge and did not think to prove him again.

But this incident made a still greater impression on Marya Kirilovna. Her imagination was fired at the sight of Deforge, the dead bear at his feet, calmly talking to her. She saw that bravery, pride and self-respect were not the exclusive attributes of one class of society, and from that time onwards, she began to show the young tutor a respect which grew daily more pronounced. Definite relations were established between them. Masha had a beautiful voice and much musical ability. Deforge offered to give her lessons. After that, it will not be difficult for the reader to guess that Masha fell in love with him, even if she did not acknowledge it to herself.

PART TWO

Chapter Nine

The guests began to arrive on the eve of the church festival. Some stayed in the main house and its wings, some with the steward, some with the priest, and others in the houses of the more well-to-do peasants. The stables were filled with carriage-horses, the courtyards and coach-houses crowded out with a variety of vehicles. At nine o'clock in the morning the bells for mass were sounded, and everyone made their way to the new stone church, built by Kirila Petrovitch and annually adorned by his offerings. There were so many distinguished worshippers that the simple peasants could find no room within the church and stood in the porch and inside the church enclosure. The service had not yet begun – they were awaiting Kirila Petrovitch. He arrived at last in a coach drawn by six horses and walked triumphantly to his place, accompanied by Marya Kirilovna. The eyes of all, both men and women, turned towards her – the former in admiration of her beauty, the latter in careful examination of her dress. The mass began. The household choir sang in their stalls and

Kirila Petrovitch himself joined in the singing. He prayed, looking neither to the right nor to the left, and bowed with proud humility when the deacon made loud reference to 'the founder of this church'.

The service ended. Kirila Petrovitch was the first to approach the cross. All the others followed suit; and then, afterwards, the neighbours moved forward to pay their respects to him. The ladies surrounded Masha. As he left the church, Kirila Petrovitch invited everyone to dine with him and then, seating himself in his coach, he drove home. The guests followed him.

The rooms were filled with guests. New faces appeared at every moment, and the host could scarcely be approached for the crowd. The ladies sat in a sedate semi-circle, dressed in outmoded, faded, but expensive clothes, all wearing diamonds and pearls. The men crowded around the caviar and vodka, conversing among themselves in noisy differ-ence of opinion. The table in the dining-hall was set for eighty people. The servants were bustling about, placing bottles and decanters on the table and smoothing out the table-cloths. At last the steward announced that dinner was served, and Kirila Petrovitch was the first to set himself down at the table. He was followed by the ladies who, observing some form of seniority, solemnly took their seats. The young ladies, pressing round each other like a timid herd of kids, sat down next to one another. The men took their seats opposite. Seated next to young Sasha at the end of the table was the tutor.

The servants served the guests in order of rank, being guided in doubtful cases by Lavater's system and almost always correctly. The clatter of plates and spoons mingled with the noisy conversation of the guests. Kirila Petrovitch cheerfully surveyed his table, feeling to the full the happy satisfaction of a host.

At that moment a coach drawn by six horses was heard to enter the courtyard.

'Who's that?' the host asked.

'Anton Pafnutyitch,' replied several voices.

The doors opened and Anton Pafnutyitch Spitsyn, a fat man of about fifty with a round, pock-marked face, adorned by a treble chin, tumbled into the dining-hall, bowing and smiling and already preparing to make his excuses.

'Another place here,' called Kirila Petrovitch. 'Pray sit down, Anton Pafnutyitch, and tell me what you mean by missing my service and arriving late for dinner. It's most unlike you, who are so pious and also so fond of your food.'

'Forgive me,' Anton Pafnutyitch answered, tucking his napkin into the button hole of his pea-green kaftan, 'forgive me, Kirila Petrovitch – I started out early enough, but I hadn't gone ten versts before the tread of one of my front wheels broke in two. What was I to do? Fortunately, we were fairly near the village, but by the time we'd got there and found the blacksmith, and waited for everything to be repaired, exactly three hours had gone by – it was quite unavoidable. I didn't dare take the short cut through the Kistenevka wood, so I took the roundabout way . . .'

'What!' Kirila Petrovitch broke in. 'Well, you're certainly no hero. What are you afraid of?'

'What else, Kirila Petrovitch, but Dubrovsky? I was afraid I might fall into his clutches. He's not someone to be trifled with, no one slips through his hands, and he'd have flayed me alive twice if he had caught me.'

'Why such a distinction?'

'Why, Kirila Petrovitch? For the law-suit against the late Andrey Gavrilovitch Dubrovsky. Did I not, to please you – that is, I mean, in accordance with the voice of my conscience and the dictates of justice – show that the Dubrovskys were in unlawful possession of Kistenevka, and that their presence there was solely attributable to your bounty. The dead man (God rest his soul!) promised to get his own back on me, and surely his son will want to keep his father's word. So far the Lord has spared me. Until now, they've only plundered one of my barns, but I fear he'll get up to the house one of these days.'

'And there'll be plenty for him in the house,' Kirila Petrovitch observed. 'I'll wager that casket of yours is filled to the brim . . .'

'Indeed not, Kirila Petrovitch. Once it was full, but now it's quite empty.'

'None of that now, Anton Pafnutyitch. We know you. Where do you spend your money? You live like a pig at home, you never receive any guests, and you fleece your men. You spend all your time hoarding.'

'You're only joking, Kirila Petrovitch,' Anton Pafnutyitch muttered with a smile. 'As God is my witness, we're ruined.'

And Anton Pafnutyitch swallowed his host's gibe with a greasy mouthful of fish-pie.

Kirila Petrovitch left him to his fish-pie and turned to the new chief of police, who had never been a guest in his house before, and who was seated next to the tutor at the other end of the table.

'Well, Mr Chief of police, and are you going to catch Dubrovsky?'

The chief of police quailed, bowed, smiled and at last stammered:

'We will try, your Excellency.'

'Hm! We will try. People have been trying for a long time, and as yet to no avail. But then, why should you catch him? Dubrovsky's brigandage is a great blessing to chiefs of police, what with journeys here and there, investigations, horses and the money you put in your pockets. Why put an end to such a benefactor? Isn't that true, Mr Chief of police?'

'It's true indeed, your Excellency,' replied the chief of police, thoroughly confused.

The guests roared with laughter.

'I like the young man for his frankness,' said Kirila Petrovitch, 'but it's a pity about our late chief of police, Taras Alexeyevitch. If they hadn't burned him to death, things would be a lot quieter in the district. And what's the news of Dubrovsky? Where was he last seen?'

'At my house, Kirila Petrovitch,' said a woman's voice. 'He dined with me last Tuesday.'

All eyes turned towards Anna Savishna Globova, a simple-hearted widow, beloved by all for her kind and cheerful temperament. Everyone awaited her story with curiosity.

'You should first of all know that three weeks ago I sent my steward to the post-office with money for my Vanyusha. I don't spoil my son – indeed, I am not in the position to do so, even if I wanted to – but you know how it is: an officer of the Guards must put up a decent showing, and I share my small income with Vanyusha as best I can. Well, I was sending him two thousand roubles, and although the thought of Dubrovsky did enter my head once or twice, I considered that the town was near, only seven versts away, and that perhaps God would show his protection. However, in the evening, my steward returned, pale, in rags and on foot—

'"What's wrong? What's happened to you?" I gasped.

'"Mother Anna Savishna," he said to me, "I've been robbed by brigands. They almost killed me. Dubrovsky himself was among them and might have hanged me if he hadn't taken pity on me and let me go. But I've been robbed of everything, and they've taken away the horse and cart!"

'I was stunned. Heavenly Father, what'll become of my Vanyusha? There was nothing to be done. I wrote my son a letter, told him all that had happened, and sent him my blessing without a single farthing.

'One week passed, and then another. Suddenly, one day, a carriage drives into my courtyard. Some general or other asks to see me. "With pleasure," I say, and a swarthy man of about thirty-five, with black hair, a moustache and a beard, the living image of Kulnyev, enters the room. He introduces himself as the friend and former comrade-in-arms of my late husband, Ivan Andreyevitch. He said he was passing and, knowing that I lived there, could not resist calling in on his old friend's widow. I entertained him as best I could, and we talked about this and that until at last the subject of Dubrovsky arose. I told him of my misfortune. The general frowned.

'"That's strange", he said, "I have always heard that Dubrovsky doesn't simply attack anybody, but only those who are known to be rich, and that even then he only takes his share, so as not to leave them destitute. And he's never been accused of murder. There's some roguery going on here. Order your steward to be brought in."

'The steward was sent for and appeared before us. He became stupefied as soon as he saw the general.

'"Tell me, my man, how Dubrovsky robbed you, and how he wanted to hang you."

'"My steward began to tremble and fell at the general's feet.

'"Forgive me, master . . . I was overcome by temptation . . . I lied."

'"If that's the case," answered the general, "have the goodness to tell your mistress all that in fact happened, and I'll listen."

'The steward could not come to his senses.

'"Well,' continued the general, 'tell us where you met Dubrovsky."

'"By the two pine-trees, master, by the two pine-trees."

'"What did he say to you?"

'"He asked me whose servant I was, where I was going and why."

'"And then?"

'"And then he demanded the letter and the money."

'"Well?"

'" I gave him the letter and the money."

'"And he ... what did he do?"

'"Master, forgive me ... I am guilty."

'"What did he do?"

'"He gave me back the letter and the money and said: 'God be with you; go on to the post-office.'"

'"And what did you do?"

'"Forgive me, master, forgive me."

'"I'll deal with you later, my little pigeon," the general said sternly. "And you, madam, give orders for this ruffian's chest to be searched and then hand him over to me, and I'll teach him a lesson. Know that Dubrovsky himself was once an officer of the Guards, and that he would not harm a comrade."

'I guessed who his Excellency was, but did not say anything. His coachmen tied my steward to the box of his carriage. The money was found. The general finished dining with me and then left immediately afterwards, taking my steward with him. The steward was found in the wood the next day, tied to an oak-tree and flayed.'

Everybody listened to Anna Savishna's story in silence, especially the young ladies. Many of them cherished a secret respect for Dubrovsky, seeing him as a sort of romantic hero – in particular Marya Kirilovna, an ardent day-dreamer, brought up on the mysterious horrors of Mrs Radcliffe.

'And you assume that Dubrovsky himself was at your house, Anna Savishna?' Kirila Petrovitch asked. 'You are very much mistaken. I don't know who your visitor was, but I do know that it wasn't Dubrovsky.'

'Not Dubrovsky? Who else but he drives about on the high road, holding up and searching travellers?'

'I don't know, but I can assure you that you didn't see Dubrovsky. I remember him as a child. I don't know whether his hair has darkened, but at that time he was a fair, curly-haired boy. But what I do know for certain is that Dubrovsky is five years older than my Masha, and is therefore not thirty-five but round about twenty-three.'

'That is so, your Excellency,' proclaimed the chief of police. 'I have a description of Vladimir Dubrovsky in my pocket. It quite clearly states that he's twenty-three.'

'Ah!' said Kirila Petrovitch. 'In that case read out the description and we'll listen. It's just as well we know what he looks like, so that if we do come across him, we can make sure he doesn't get away.'

The chief of police took a rather soiled piece of paper from his pocket, unfolded it with an air of importance and began to read in a sing-song voice:

'Characteristics of Vladimir Dubrovsky, made up from the testimonies of his former servants. Age: twenty-three years. Height: medium. Complexion: fresh. Cleanshaven. Eyes: brown. Hair: fair. Nose: straight. Special characteristics: none.'

'Is that all?' asked Kirila Petrovitch.

'That is all,' replied the chief of police, folding up the piece of paper.

'I congratulate you, Mr Chief of police. What a document! It'll be easy to trace Dubrovsky from such a description! Who is not of medium height? Who has not got fair hair – or a straight nose, or brown eyes? From that report, I'm afraid you could talk to Dubrovsky for three hours on end and yet not recognise him. I must say, these officials are clever fellows!'

The chief of police meekly returned the piece of paper to his pocket, and silently devoted his attention to his goose and cabbage. In the meantime, the servants had already been round to the guests several times, filling each glass as they did so. Several bottles of Caucasian wine had been opened with a loud popping of corks, and had been gratefully accepted as champagne. Faces began to flush, and the conversation became louder, more incoherent and more lively.

'No,' continued Kirila Petrovitch, 'we'll never see another chief of police like the late Taras Alexeyevitch! He was no blunderer, no simpleton! It's a pity they burned the young fellow, as not a man among this gang of brigands would have got away from him. He would have caught every one of them, and Dubrovsky himself would not have escaped, nor been able to buy himself out. Taras Alexeyevitch would have taken his money but not let him go; that was the way of the fellow. It seems there's nothing for it but for me to take a hand in this affair, and go after the brigands with my own people. To begin with, I'll arm twenty men and have the copse freed of brigands. My people aren't cowards. Any one of them would take on a bear single-handed, and they certainly won't flinch before a gang of brigands.'

'And how is that your bear of yours, Kirila Petrovitch?' asked Anton Pafnutyich, reminded of the other's shaggy acquaintance and of the practical jokes he had himself suffered.

'Misha is no more,' replied Kirila Petrovitch. 'He met a glorious end at the hands of the enemy. There is his victor' – Kirila Petrovitch pointed at Deforge – 'in his normal guise as my Frenchman. He has avenged your ... if I may say so ... do you remember?'

'Do I remember?' replied Anton Pafnutyich, scratching his head. 'I remember it very clearly. So Misha is dead. I'm sorry about that, I really am! He was such an amusing beast, and so clever! You'll never find another bear like him. But why did "Monsoo" kill him?'

Kirila Petrovitch began to relate the exploit of his Frenchman with the greatest delight, for he had the enviable capacity of being able to draw personal credit for all that surrounded him. The guests listened to the tale of Misha's death with great attention, and looked in astonishment at Deforge, who, unaware that his valour was the subject of conversation, was sitting quietly at his place, occasionally correcting his lively charge.

The dinner, which had gone on for nearly three hours, came to an end. The host placed his napkin on the table, and everyone stood up and went into the drawing-room, where coffee, cards and a continuation of the drinking, so admirably begun in the dining-hall, awaited them.

Chapter Ten

At about seven o'clock in the evening, some of the guests made as if to leave, but the host, made merry by the punch, ordered the gates to be locked, and declared that nobody should leave the house until the following morning. Music was soon struck up, the doors to the ball-room were opened, and dancing began. The host and some of his closer friends sat in a corner, draining glass after glass and enjoying the gaiety of the younger people. The older women played cards. As in all places where there is no Uhlan or other brigade stationed, there were fewer men than women, even though all suitable men had been rounded up. The tutor distinguished himself above all others. He danced more than anyone else, being chosen by all the young ladies as partner, since they found that with him they could waltz most gracefully. He circled the room several times with Marya Kirilovna, followed by the ironic glances of the other young ladies.

Finally, at midnight, the tired host stopped the dancing, ordered supper to be served and himself retired to bed.

The departure of Kirila Petrovitch gave greater freedom to the company, which became more lively. The gentlemen ventured to take their seats beside the ladies. The girls laughed and whispered to their neighbours, while the older ladies talked to each other loudly across the table. The men drank, argued and laughed boisterously. In short, the supper was extremely vivacious and left behind it many agreeable memories.

One man alone was unable to join in the general merriment. Anton Pafnutyitch sat frowning and silent at his place, ate distractedly and seemed to be extremely worried. The conversation about the brigands had disturbed him. We will soon see that he had ample reason for apprehension.

Anton Pafnutyitch, in invoking God as a witness to the fact that his red coffer was empty, had neither lied nor transgressed: the coffer was indeed completely empty, and the money at one time kept in it had been transferred to a leather pouch which he wore next to his skin, beneath his shirt. It was only by means of this precaution that he was able to subdue his perpetual fears and his distrust of all. Being compelled to spend the night in a strange house, he was frightened that he might be shown to a bedroom in some remote corner of the house where thieves could easily break in. He searched the room with his eyes for some reliable companion and finally chose Deforge. His appearance of physical strength, and still more the bravery he had shown in his encounter with the bear, about whom poor Anton Pafnutyitch could not think without a shudder, decided him in his choice. When the guests got up from the table, Anton Pafnutyitch began to hover around the young Frenchman, grunting and clearing his throat, until finally he turned towards the latter and said:

'Hm, hm, would it be possible for me to spend the night in your room, "Monsoo", because you see . . . ?'

'*Que désire monsieur?*' Deforge asked with a courteous bow.

'It's a pity, "Monsoo," that you haven't yet learned to speak Russian. *Je veux, moi, chez vous coucher* – do you understand?'

'*Monsieur, très volontiers,*' replied Deforge. '*Veuillez donner des ordres en conséquence.*'

Anton Pafnutyitch, extremely pleased with his knowledge of the French language, went off at once to make the necessary arrangements.

The guests began to bid each other good-night, and each retired to the room which had been appointed to him. Anton Pafnutyitch accompanied the tutor to his wing of the house. It was a dark night. Deforge lit the way with a lantern, and Anton Pafnutyitch followed him quite cheerfully, from time to time pressing the hidden pouch against his chest to ensure that his money was still with him.

On arriving at the wing, the tutor lit a candle and they both began to undress. While doing so, Anton Pafnutyitch walked about the room, examining the locks and the windows, and shaking his head when he found that this inspection brought him no comfort. The door was locked by a single bolt, and the windows had not had their double frames put in yet. He attempted to complain of this to Deforge, but his knowledge of the French language did not run to so complicated an explanation. The Frenchman did not understand, and Anton Pafnutyitch was forced to swallow his complaints. Their beds stood opposite one another. Both lay down, and the tutor extinguished the candle.

'*Pourquoi vous toush-ez vous, pourquoi vous toush-ez vous?*' cried Anton Pafnutyitch, conjugating the Russian verb for 'to extinguish' after the French manner with the greatest difficulty. 'I cannot *dormir* in the dark.'

Deforge could not understand his exclamations and wished him good-night.

'Damned heathen!' Anton Pafnutyitch Spitsyn grumbled, pulling up the blanket around him. 'Why did he have to blow out the candle? So much the worse for him! I can't sleep without a light. "Monsoo", "monsoo",' he continued, *je veux avec vous parler.*'

But the Frenchman offered no reply and was soon snoring.

'Snoring – the beastly Frenchman!' thought Anton Pafnutyitch. 'And I can't even think about sleep. Thieves might get in through the unlocked door or climb through the window, and you couldn't wake him with a cannon-shot, the beast.

'"Monsoo", "monsoo" – oh, the devil take you!'

Anton Pafnutyitch fell silent. Fatigue and the effects of drink gradually overcame his fear. He began to doze and soon fell into a heavy sleep.

A strange awakening lay in store for him. In his sleep he felt that somebody was gently tugging at his shirt-collar. Anton Pafnutyitch opened his eyes, and in the pale light of the autumn morning, he saw Deforge standing before him. The Frenchman held a pocket pistol in one hand, while the other unfastened the sacred leather pouch. Anton Pafnutyitch was stunned.

'*Qu'est-ce que c'est, "monsoo", qu'est-ce que c'est?*' he uttered in a terrified voice.

'Quiet! Hold your tongue!' the tutor answered in perfect Russian. 'Be quiet, or you're lost! I am Dubrovsky!'

Chapter Eleven

We now ask leave of the reader to explain the latest events of our story in the light of preceding circumstances, hitherto untold.

At the posting-station of ***, in the house of the post-master already mentioned by us, there sat a traveller in one corner of the room. He wore a look of humble resignation – a characteristic which marked him out as being either a man without rank or a foreigner, and thence a person of no importance in the eyes of the postmaster. His britchka stood in the courtyard, waiting to be greased. Within it lay a small portmanteau, meagre testimony to the lightness of its owner's purse. The traveller asked for neither tea nor coffee, but merely looked out of the window and whistled, to the considerable displeasure of the postmaster's wife, who was seated behind the partition.

'The Lord has sent us a whistler!' she said in a low voice. 'He's whistling fit to burst, the accursed heathen!'

'What's wrong with it?' the postmaster asked. 'Let him whistle.'

'What's wrong?' his wife retorted angrily. 'Don't you know the saying?'

'What saying? That whistling whistles away your money? But, Pakhomovna, whistling or no whistling, we never have any money anyway.'

'Send him away, Sidorytch. You don't want to keep him. Give him his horses and let him go to the devil!'

'He can wait, Pakhomovna. I've only got three troikas in the stable; the fourth is resting. Anyway, some more import-ant travellers may arrive in a moment. I don't want to risk my neck for a Frenchman. There! See what I said! Here comes someone galloping up now. What a speed! D'you think it's a general?'

A carriage drew up at the steps of the posting-station. A servant jumped down from the box, opened the doors of the carriage and, a minute or so later, a young man, wearing a military great-coat and a white forage-cap, entered the posting-station. His servant followed him in with a small box which he put down on the window-sill.

'Horses!' demanded the officer imperiously.

'This instant!' the postmaster replied. 'Your order, please.'

'I have no order. I'm turning off the high road ... Don't you recognise me?'

The postmaster looked flustered for a moment and then rushed off to hurry up his drivers. The young man began to stroll up and down the room, and then went behind the partition and quietly asked the postmaster's wife who the other traveller was.

'God knows!' she answered. 'Some Frenchman or other. He's been waiting for horses for five hours, and he's never stopped whistling once in all that time. I'm sick of him, the wretch!'

The young man addressed the traveller in French. 'Where are you going?' he asked.

'To the next town,' the Frenchman replied, 'and from there to the estate of a landowner who has engaged me as a tutor without ever having set eyes on me. I had hoped to be there to-day, but the postmaster evidently thinks otherwise. It's difficult to obtain horses in this country, *monsieur l'officier.*'

'To which of the local landowners are you bound?' the officer asked.

'To *Monsieur* Troyekurov,' the Frenchman replied.

'To Troyekurov? Who is this Troyekurov?'

'*Ma foi, mon officier* ... I've heard nothing but bad about him. They say he's a proud and wilful gentleman, so harsh in his treatment of his domestics that none of them can live in harmony with him, that everyone trembles at the sound of his name, and that he stands on no ceremony with his tutors (*avec les outchitels*), two of whom he has already whipped to death.'

'Good Gracious! And you're resolved to work for such a monster?'

'What else can I do, *monsieur l'officier*? He's offered me a good salary – three thousand roubles a year, all found. Perhaps I'll get on better than the others. I have an aged mother, to whom I will send half my salary to cover her needs. From the rest of the money, I can save in five years a small capital, which would be sufficient to secure independence for me in the future. And then, *bonsoir*, I'll go back to Paris and invest the money in some commercial proposition.'

'Does anybody at Troyekurov's know you?' he asked.

'Nobody,' replied the tutor. 'He sent for me through a friend of his in Moscow, whose cook, a compatriot of mine, gave me a recommendation. You must know that I was not trained as a tutor, but as a confectioner, but I was told that the profession of a tutor was far more profitable in your country ...'

The officer was looking pensive. 'Listen,' he interrupted the Frenchman. 'What if I offered you ten thousand roubles in ready money to abandon this project and return to Paris at once?'

The Frenchman looked at the officer in amazement, smiled and shook his head.

'The horses are ready,' the postmaster said, entering the room.

The servant repeated the postmaster's words.

'In a minute,' replied the officer. 'Leave us for a moment.'

The postmaster and the servant withdrew.

'I'm not joking,' the officer continued in French. 'I can give you ten thousand roubles, and all I want is your absence and your papers.'

With these words, he unlocked his small box and drew several bundles of notes from it.

The Frenchman opened his eyes wide. He did not know what to make of it.

'My absence ... my papers,' he repeated in amazement. 'Here are my papers ... but you must be joking. Why my papers?'

'That's nothing to do with you. I ask you now – do you consent or not?'

The Frenchman, still unable to believe his ears, held out his papers to the young officer, who inspected them quickly.

'Your passport – good! Letter of recommendation, birth certificate – excellent! Well, here's your money, so now get back to Paris. Good-bye.'

The Frenchman stood as if turned to stone.

The officer returned.

'I'd forgotten the most important thing. Give me your word of honour that this'll remain a secret between us – your word of honour.'

'I give you my word of honour,' the Frenchman replied. 'But my papers – what shall I do without them?'

'At the first town you reach, announce that you've been robbed by Dubrovsky. They'll believe you and make out fresh documents for you. Good-bye. May God speed your journey back to Paris, and may you find your mother in good health.'

Dubrovsky left the room, took his seat in the carriage and galloped off.

The postmaster looked through the window, and when

the carriage had disappeared from sight, he turned to his wife and exclaimed:

'Pakhomovna, d'you know who that was? It was Dubrovsky!'

His wife rushed headlong to the window, but she was too late – Dubrovsky was already far away. She began to scold her husband.

'You have no fear of God, Sidorytch. Why didn't you tell me before? I'd have inspected him more closely, but now I'll have to wait until he comes back here again – if he ever does. Shameless – that's what you are, shameless.'

The Frenchman still stood as if petrified. His agreement with the officer, the money – it all seemed like a dream to him. But the bundle of notes was there in his pocket, eloquent testimony to the reality of this marvellous happening.

He decided to hire horses to take him as far as the next town. The driver went at walking-pace, and it was night when he reached the town.

Before reaching the town gates, where stood a ruined sentry-box but no sentry, the Frenchman ordered the driver to stop the carriage. He climbed down from it to continue his journey on foot, explaining by signs to the driver that he was giving him the carriage and the portmanteau by way of a tip. The driver was as stupefied by this act of generosity as the Frenchman himself had been at Dubrovsky's proposal. However, imagining that the foreigner had completely taken leave of his senses, the driver thanked him with a zealous bow and, not wishing to go into the town, set out for a house of entertainment well-known to him and with whose owner he was on the best of terms. There he spent the entire night and, the following morning he started out for home with his troika, minus both the carriage and the portmanteau, and with a swollen face and red eyes.

Dubrovsky, having taken possession of the Frenchman's

papers, boldly appeared, as we have already seen, before Troyekurov and established himself in his house. Whatever his secret intentions were (we shall learn about them later), there was nothing reprehensible in his behaviour. It is true, he concerned himself little with the education of young Sasha, to whom he gave full licence to sow his wild oats, and that he paid anything but strict attention to his lessons, which he gave only for the sake of appearances. He followed the musical progress of his other pupil with great assiduity, however, often spending whole hours at a time by her side at the piano. Everybody liked the young tutor: Kirila Petrovitch for his daring agility in the hunting-field; Marya Kirilovna for his untiring enthusiasm and shy attentiveness; Sasha for his indulgence towards his pranks; the household servants for his kindness and a generosity which seemed incompatible with his position. Dubrovsky himself appeared to be attached to the entire household and to be regarding himself as a member of it.

About a month had passed from the time of his introduction to the calling of tutor to the memorable day of the festival, and nobody had suspected that in this modest young Frenchman there lay hidden a ferocious brigand, whose name struck terror into the hearts of all the neighbouring landowners. Dubrovsky had never once left Pokrovskoye during this time, but rumours of his exploits of brigandage had not abated, thanks to the inventive imagination of the village-dwellers. It is possible, too, that his band had continued their activities in the absence of their leader.

Spending the night in the same room as a man whom he could regard as his personal enemy and one of the principal authors of his misfortunes, Dubrovsky had been unable to resist temptation. He knew of the existence of the pouch and he resolved to get hold of it. We have seen how he astonished poor Anton Pafnutyitch by his transformation from tutor to brigand.

At nine o'clock in the morning, the guests who had spent the night at Pokrovskoye gathered one by one in the drawing-room, where Marya Kirilovna, in her morning-gown, sat by the steaming samovar. Kirila Petrovitch, in a frieze coat and slippers, was drinking his tea from a large cup which resembled a slop-basin. The last to appear was Anton Pafnutyitch; he was so pale and seemed so distraught that everyone was struck by his appearance, and Kirila Petrovitch enquired after his health. Anton Pafnutyitch Spitsyn replied with a few meaningless phrases, all the time looking with horror at the tutor who sat there as though nothing had happened. A few minutes later a servant entered and announced to Spitsyn that his carriage was ready. Anton Pafnutyitch, despite the exhortations of his host, hastily took his leave of the company and, hurrying from the room, departed instantly. Nobody could understand what had happened to him, and Kirila Petrovitch decided that he had overeaten. After tea and a farewell breakfast, the remaining guests began to depart, and soon Pokrovskoye was empty of visitors, and everything resumed its normal course.

Chapter Twelve

Several days passed and nothing noteworthy occurred. The life of the inhabitants of Pokrovskoye was monotonous. Kirila Petrovitch daily went out hunting. Marya Kirilovna occupied her time with reading, walks and music lessons – particularly the lessons. She was beginning to understand her own heart and, with involuntary vexation, to confess to herself that she was by no means indifferent to the qualities of the young Frenchman. He, for his own part, never overstepped the bounds of respect and strict propriety, thus soothing her pride and allaying her timid doubts. With more and more confidence she gave herself over to the absorbing habit of his company. She was bored without Deforge, and when with him showed him constant attention, wishing to know his opinion on matters of every sort and always agreeing with him. Perhaps she was not yet in love, but at the first chance obstacle or sudden change of fate the flame of passion was ready to blaze up in her heart.

One day, on entering the drawing-room where the tutor awaited her, Marya Kirilovna was surprised to notice traces of embarrassment on his pale face. She opened the lid of the piano and sang a few notes, but Dubrovsky, excusing himself under the pretext of a headache, broke off the lesson, closed the book of songs, and surreptitiously slipped her a note. Marya Kirilovna had taken it before she had had time to reflect, and she instantly repented of her action. But Dubrovsky was no longer in the room. Marya Kirilovna went up to her own room, unfolded the note and read the following:

'Meet me in the arbour by the stream at seven o'clock tonight. It is essential that I talk to you.'

Her curiosity was strongly aroused. She had long been expecting a declaration of his love, both desiring and fearing it. It would have been pleasant to listen to a confirmation of that which she already guessed at, but she felt that it would be unbecoming for her to hear such a declaration from a man who, by his position, could never hope to receive her hand. She made up her mind to go to the *rendezvous*. On one point, however, she was hesitant: how should she receive the tutor's declaration? With aristocratic indignation, with friendly admonishment, with cheerful badinage, or with silent concern? In the meantime, she looked constantly at the clock. It grew dark. Candles were brought in, and Kirila Petrovitch sat down to play Boston with some neighbours who had just arrived. The clock in the dining-room struck a quarter to seven, and Marya Kirilovna slipped quietly out on to the steps, looked all around her, and ran into the garden.

The night was dark, the sky covered with clouds, and she found it impossible to see more than two paces ahead of her. But Marya Kirilovna went through the darkness along the paths she knew so well and, after a minute or so, found herself in the arbour. There she paused in order to regain her breath and so appear before Deforge with a semblance of calm indifference. But Deforge already stood before her.

'Thank you,' he said in a quiet, sad voice, 'for not denying me in my request. I'd have been desperate if you had not consented to come.'

Marya Kirilovna answered with a previously prepared expression:

'I hope you'll give me no cause to repent of my indulgence.'

He was silent and seemed to be plucking up his courage.

'Circumstances demand ... I must leave you,' he said at last. 'You will soon hear perhaps ... But before parting, I must explain something to you ...'

Marya Kirilovna offered no reply. In these words she saw the prelude to the expected avowal of love.

'I am not whom you suppose,' he continued, lowering his head. 'I am not the Frenchman, Deforge; I am Dubrovsky.'

Marya Kirilovna cried out.

'For God's sake don't be frightened. You mustn't be alarmed at my name. Yes, I am that unhappy wretch whom your father deprived of his last piece of bread, whom your father drove from his paternal home on to the highways as a robber. But you have no need to be frightened – neither for yourself, nor for him. All is over. I have forgiven him.

You have saved him. It was upon him that I was going to carry out my first bloody crime. I was circling the house, deciding upon the place where the fire should break out, and where I should enter his bedroom, so as to seal off all means of his escape, when you passed by me, like a heavenly vision, and my heart softened. I realised that the house where you lived was sacred, that not a single being tied to you by bonds of blood could fall beneath my curse. I renounced all thoughts of revenge, dismissed them as madness. I wandered through the gardens of Pokrovskoye for whole days, in the hope of catching sight of your white dress in the distance. In your carefree walks I followed you, creeping from bush to bush, happy in the thought that I was protecting you, that there was no danger in store for you in my secret presence. At last an opportunity presented itself. I established myself in your house. These last few weeks have been days of happiness for me. The memory of them will be the joy of my sad life . . . Today I received news which forbids me to stay here any longer. I must take leave of you today . . . now . . . But before doing this, I wanted to open my heart to you, so that you should not despise me, nor curse me. Think sometimes of Dubrovsky, and know that he was born for another fate, that his heart knew how to love you, that never . . .'

At that moment a soft whistle was heard, and Dubrovsky stopped talking. He seized her hand and pressed it to his burning lips. The whistle was heard for a second time.

'Good-bye,' said Dubrovsky. 'I'm being called – a moment's delay can destroy me.'

He went. Marya Kirilovna stood motionless. Dubrovsky returned suddenly and once more held her hand.

'If, at any time,' he said to her in a tender and moving voice, – 'if at any time unhappiness should overtake you, and you find yourself with nobody to look to for help and protection, will you promise to turn to me, and demand of me anything that might lead to your salvation? Will you promise not to reject my devotion?'

Marya Kirilovna wept silently. The whistle was heard for a third time.

'You will destroy me!' cried Dubrovsky. 'I will not leave you until you have given me an answer. Do you promise or not?'

'I promise,' the poor girl whispered.

Greatly agitated by her meeting with Dubrovsky, Marya Kirilovna returned from the garden. As she drew near to the house, it seemed to her that everyone was running about, that the house was full of movement, and that there was a crowd of people in the courtyard. A troika stood before the steps and, hearing the voice of Kirila Petrovitch in the distance, she quickly entered the house, fearing that her absence had been noticed. Kirila Petrovitch met her in the hall. Our friend, the chief of police, was surrounded by visitors who were showering him with questions. The chief of police, who was dressed for travelling and armed from head to foot, answered them with an air of mystery and bustle.

'Where have you been, Masha?' Kirila Petrovitch asked. 'Have you seen Monsieur Deforge?'

With the greatest difficulty Masha brought herself to say 'No.'

'Imagine!' continued Kirila Petrovitch. 'The chief of police has come to arrest him. He assures me that he is Dubrovsky himself.'

'He's got all the characteristics, your Excellency!' the chief of police replied respectfully.

'Eh, man!' Kirila Petrovitch broke in. 'You can go you know where with your characteristics! I'll not give up my Frenchman until I've been into this whole business myself. How can you believe the word of Anton Pafnutyitch, who is a coward and a liar? He must have dreamed that the tutor wanted to rob him. Why didn't he say anything to me about it the following morning?'

'The Frenchman intimidated him, your Excellency,' the chief of police replied, 'and extracted an oath of secrecy from him . . .'

'Rubbish!' decided Kirila Petrovitch. 'I'll get to the bottom of this affair this instant. Where's the tutor?' he asked the servant who entered the room.

'He cannot be found anywhere,' the servant replied.

'Then look for him,' cried Troyekurov, beginning to have his doubts. 'Show me your precious characteristics,' he said to the chief of police, who handed him the paper instantly. 'H'm, h'm, twenty-three years old . . . That's all right, but it doesn't prove a thing. What about the tutor?'

'He can't be found,' was the same reply.

Kirila Petrovitch began to feel uneasy. Marya Kirilovna felt more dead than alive.

'You are pale, Masha,' her father observed. 'Have they frightened you?'

'No, Papa,' Masha replied. 'I've got a headache.'

'Go to your room, Masha, and don't worry.'

Masha kissed her father's hand and went as quickly as possible to her room. Once there, she threw herself upon her bed and fell into a fit of hysterical sobbing. The maidservants came running up, undressed her, and with difficulty succeeded in calming her down with the aid of cold water and every conceivable form of smelling-salts. They laid her on her bed and she fell into a light sleep.

Meanwhile, the Frenchman was not to be found. Kirila Petrovitch paced up and down the hall, ominously whistling *Beat, Drums of Victory!* The visitors whispered among themselves and the chief of police looked foolish. The Frenchman still could not be found. He had doubtless been warned and had managed to make his escape. But how and by whom? It remained a mystery.

Eleven o'clock struck but nobody thought of sleep. At last Kirila Petrovitch said angrily to the chief of police:

'Well, you can't stay here all night. My house isn't a tavern. It won't be as the result of your sharpness that Dubrovsky – if he really is Dubrovsky – will be caught. Go home, and next time be a little quicker off the mark. It's time you all went home,' he continued, turning to his guests. 'Order your carriages. I want to get some sleep.'

Thus ungraciously did Troyekurov take leave of his guests.

Chapter Thirteen

Again some time passed without any incident worthy of note. But at the beginning of the following summer many changes took place in the domestic life of Kirila Petrovitch.

About thirty versts from Pokrovskoye lay the rich estate of Prince Vereisky. The Prince had been abroad for a long time, and the management of his entire estate had been in the hands of a retired major. There had been no dealings between Pokrovskoye and Arbatovo. But, at the end of May, the Prince returned from abroad and went to live in the village he had never in his life seen. Accustomed to a life full of distractions, he could not endure loneliness, and on the third day after his arrival he set out to dine with Troyekurov, with whom he had at one time been acquainted.

The Prince was about fifty but he looked a great deal older. Excesses of every sort had overtaxed his health and had left their indelible stamp. In spite of this, he had a striking and pleasant appearance and, being accustomed to move in polite society, he had acquired a certain charm of manner, especially with women. He had a constant need of amusement and fell an easy prey to boredom.

Kirila Petrovitch was extremely pleased with his visit, taking it as a sign of respect from a man who knew the world. As was his custom, he entertained his guest by taking him on a tour of inspection of his whole estate, and by showing him his kennels. But the Prince was almost suffocated by the smell of the dogs and, pressing a scent-sprinkled handkerchief to his nose, he hastened to leave the kennels. The old-fashioned garden with its clipped limes, its square pond and straight paths did not please him. He liked English and so-called landscape gardens. Nevertheless, he praised and admired all that he saw. A servant came to announce that dinner was served, and they went inside. The Prince, limping with exhaustion from his tour, already began to regret his visit.

But in the drawing-room they were met by Marya Kirilovna, and the old ladies' man was struck by her beauty. Troyekurov placed his guest next to her at the table. The Prince seemed refreshed by her presence, became quite vivacious, and on several occasions managed to attract her attention by his entertaining tales. After dinner Kirila Petrovitch proposed a ride, but the Prince excused himself, pointing at his velvet boots and joking about his gout. He suggested a carriage drive so as not to be separated from his charming neighbour. The carriage was harnessed. The two old men and the beautiful young girl took their seats and together they drove off. The conversation never flagged. Marya Kirilovna listened with pleasure to the witty and flattering compliments of a man of the world. Of a sudden, Vereisky turned to Kirila Petrovitch and asked:

'What's that burnt-out building we're passing? Who does it belong to?'

Kirila Petrovitch frowned. The memories that were stirred at the sight of the charred building were by no means agreeable to him. He replied that the land now belonged to him, but that it had formerly been the property of Dubrovsky.

'Dubrovsky?' Vereisky repeated. 'What! To the famous brigand?'

'To his father,' answered Troyekurov, 'who was a regular brigand himself.'

'What's become of our Rinaldo? Have they caught him? Is he still alive?'

'He is alive and at large, and so long as our chiefs of police cooperate with robbers, he will never be caught. By the way, Prince, Dubrovsky paid a call at Arbatovo, didn't he?'

'Yes, it seems that he burned or plundered something last year ... But don't you feel, Marya Kirilovna, that it would be interesting, in a curious way, to become better acquainted with this romantic hero?'

'Interesting, indeed!' said Troyekurov. 'She knows him already. He taught her music for three whole weeks but, thank God, took nothing for his lessons.'

Here Kirila Petrovitch began to relate the story of the French tutor. Marya Kirilovna sat as if on tenterhooks. Vereisky listened with profound interest, confessed to finding it all extremely strange, and then changed the subject. On his return, he ordered his carriage to be brought round and, despite Kirila Petrovitch's urgent entreaties that he should spend the night at Pokrovskoye, he left immediately after drinking some tea. But before driving off, he invited Kirila Petrovitch to pay him a visit, and to bring Marya Kirilovna with him. The proud Troyekurov promised that he would do this. The other's princely status, his two stars, and his three thousand serfs led him to consider Vereisky in some degree as his equal.

Two days after this occasion, Kirila Petrovitch set out with his daughter to return Prince Vereisky's visit. Approaching Arbatovo, he could not but admire the clean, cheerful-looking peasants' cottages and the big stone house, built along the lines of an English castle. Before the house lay a bright green meadow, in which grazed Swiss cattle with bells tinkling on their necks. An extensive park stretched all round the house. The host met his guests on the steps and gave his hand to the beautiful Marya Kirlovna. They entered a magnificent room, where the table had been laid for three. The Prince drew his guests to the window, and a delightful view unfolded itself before them. The Volga flowed past the windows, carrying laden barges under full sail and small fishing-vessels expressively referred to as 'soul-destroyers'. Beyond the river hills and fields spread out into the distance and a few scattered villages gave life to the landscape.

They then went to inspect the galleries of pictures bought by the Prince abroad. The Prince explained their various subjects to Marya Kirilovna, gave a brief life-history of the artists concerned, and pointed out their qualities and defects. He spoke about the pictures not in the conventional language of the pedantic connoisseur, but with feeling and imagination. Marya Kirilovna listened to him with pleasure. They sat down at the table. Troyekurov did full justice to the wines of his Amphitryon, and to the skill of his host's cook. Marya Kirilovna experienced not the least confusion or restraint in talking to a man whom she had only met once. After dinner the host suggested that they went out into the garden. They drank their coffee in an arbour by the banks of a wide lake, which was dotted with small islands. Suddenly the music of wind instruments was heard, and a six-oared boat drew up at the arbour. They boarded it and rowed over the lake, floating among the islands, some of which they visited. On one they came across a marble statue, on another could be seen a solitary cavern; on a third, a monument bearing a mysterious inscription awoke in Marya Kirilovna a girlish curiosity which was not altogether satisfied by the civil and equivocal answers of the Prince. Time slipped by imperceptibly, and dusk began to fall. The Prince, under the pretext of the cold air and the dew, hastened to return home, where the samovar awaited them. The Prince asked Marya Kirilovna to act as hostess in his old bachelor's home. She poured out the tea and listened to the inexhaustible flow of stories that poured from the lips of the courteous and loquacious Prince. Suddenly, an explosion was heard and a rocket lit up the sky. Prince Vereisky handed Marya Kirilovna a shawl and invited her and Troyekurov out on to the balcony. Before the house, in the darkness, different-coloured lights blazed, whirled about, ascended into the night air like sheaves of corn, like palms, like fountains. They poured down like rain, like showers of bright stars, went out and then burst forth into light again. Marya Kirilovna's delight was childlike. The Prince was enchanted by her exclamations of joy, and Troyekurov himself was extremely pleased, accepting *tous les frais* of the Prince as a sign of respect and a desire to please him.

Supper was of the same excellence as dinner had been. The guests went to the rooms which had been made ready for them, and the following morning took leave of their courteous host, after exchanging promises with him that they would see each other again soon.

Chapter Fourteen

Marya Kirilovna sat before the open window of her room, embroidering at her frame. Unlike Konrad's mistress, who stitched a rose with green silk in the midst of her amorous reflections, she did not confuse her threads. Beneath her needle the canvas faultlessly took on the design of the original pattern, despite the fact that her thoughts were not on her work, but far away.

Suddenly, a hand was stretched silently through the window. Someone placed a letter on the frame and vanished before Marya Kirilovna had had time to recover from her astonishment. At the same moment, a servant entered the room and told her that Kirila Petrovitch wanted to see her. She tremblingly concealed the letter behind her neckerchief and hastened to her father's study.

Kirila Petrovitch was not alone. Prince Vereisky sat with him. At the appearance of Marya Kirilovna, the Prince stood up and bowed silently and with an embarrassment unusual for him.

'Come here, Masha,' said Kirila Petrovitch. 'I have news for you, which I hope will give you joy. Here is a suitor for you – Prince Vereisky offers you his hand in marriage.'

Masha was dumbfounded, and a deathly pallor spread across her face. She was silent. The Prince went up to her, took her hand and with apparent emotion asked if she would consent to make him happy. Masha remained silent.

'Consent? Of course she consents,' said Kirila Petrovitch. 'But you know, Prince, how difficult young girls find it to say that word. Now, my children, kiss and be happy.'

Masha stood motionless. The old Prince kissed her hand. Suddenly tears began to run down her pale face. The Prince frowned lightly.

'Go on, off with you!' said Kirila Petrovitch. 'Go and dry your tears and come back your usual merry self. They always cry when they become betrothed,' he continued, turning to Vereisky – 'it seems to be the custom. Now, Prince, let's get down to business – that is, the dowry.'

Marya Kirilovna eagerly took advantage of the permission

to withdraw. She ran back to her room, locked herself in and gave full vent to her tears, as she imagined herself as the wife of the old Prince. All of a sudden he seemed hateful and repellent to her. The thought of the marriage terrified her – in the same way as the block or the grave might have done.

'No, no,' she repeated in despair. 'I'd rather die, I'd rather go into a convent – or marry Dubrovsky.'

At this point she remembered the letter and began to read it avidly, having a premonition that it was from him. Indeed it was written in his hand, and consisted only of the following words:

'This evening at ten o'clock in the same place.'

Chapter Fifteen

The moon shone. It was a still July night. A little breeze sprang up from time to time, and a soft rustling ran through the entire garden.

As light as a shadow, the beautiful young girl drew near to the appointed meeting-place. Nobody was yet in sight. Suddenly Dubrovsky, coming out from behind the arbour, appeared before her.

'I know all,' he said in a soft, sad voice. 'Remember your promise.'

'You offer me your protection,' replied Masha. 'Don't be angry when I say that this alarms me. How can you help me?'

'I could deliver you from the man you hate.'

'For God's sake don't touch him – don't dare to touch

him if you love me. I don't wish to be the cause of any disaster . . .'

'I won't touch him – as far as I am concerned, your wish is sacred. He owes his life to you. No crime will ever be committed in your name. You must remain unsullied by my misdeeds. But how can I save you from your cruel father?'

'There is still hope – I hope to move him by my tears and my despair. He is stubborn but he loves me dearly.'

'Vain hope! In those tears he will see only the customary timidity and revulsion which all young girls show when they marry for convenience and not for love. What if he should take it into his head to marry you off in spite of your feelings? What if he should have you led to the altar by force and have your destiny placed for ever in the hands of an old husband?'

'Then, then . . . there would be nothing else . . . Come for me, and I would be your wife.'

Dubrovsky trembled. A crimson flush spread across his pale face which, in the next moment, became even paler than before. His head bent, he was silent for a long time.

'Muster the full force of your being, implore your father, throw yourself at his feet, make him see all the horrors of a future in which your youth will wither at the side of an enfeebled and lecherous old man. Resolve to tell him the bitter truth – tell him that if he remains adamant, you'll find a protection that will horrify him. Tell him that riches will not give you a moment's happiness, that only poverty can be soothed by luxury – and then only until the novelty has worn off. Don't leave him alone, don't be frightened by his anger or his threats. While even a shadow of hope remains, for God's sake don't give up. If there is absolutely no alternative . . .'

Here Dubrovsky hid his face in his hands. He seemed to be choking. Masha wept . . .

'Oh, my wretched, wretched fate!' he said with a sigh of bitterness. 'I would give my life for you. To see you from afar, to touch your hand was ecstasy for me. And now, when it has become possible for me to press you to my beating heart and say: "My angel, let us always be together!", I, wretched man, must refuse such bliss, must reject it with all my strength. I do not dare to fall at your feet and thank heaven for an incomprehensible, undeserved reward. Oh, how I ought to hate him . . . but I feel no place in my heart for hatred now.'

He placed his hands softly around her slender waist and drew her gently to his heart. She leaned her head trustingly on the young brigand's shoulder. Both were silent.

Time flew.

'I must go,' Masha said at last.

Dubrovsky seemed as though he were coming out of a trance. He took her hand and placed a ring upon her finger.

'If you ever decide to have recourse to me,' he said, 'bring this ring here, and leave it in the hollow of this oak-tree. I will know what to do.'

Dubrovsky kissed her hand and vanished among the trees.

Chapter Sixteen

The courtship of Prince Vereisky was no longer a secret among the neighbours. Kirila Petrovitch received congratulations, and preparations were made for the wedding. Masha postponed from day to day the decisive explanation of her feelings. In the meantime she treated her elderly suitor with chilly constraint. The Prince did not worry about this. He was not concerned with her love – her silent consent was enough for him.

But time passed. Masha finally decided to act, and wrote a letter to Prince Vereisky. She attempted to awaken feelings of magnanimity within his heart, openly confessing that she felt not the slightest attachment to him. She implored him to abandon his suit, and to protect her from the authority of her father. She surreptitiously handed the letter to Prince Vereisky, who read it when he was alone. He was not in the least moved by his fiancée's frankness. On the contrary, he realised the necessity of speeding up the wedding, and for this purpose saw fit to show the letter to his future father-in-law.

Kirila Petrovitch was furious, and the Prince had difficulty in dissuading him from showing Masha that he knew about the letter. Kirila Petrovitch agreed not to speak of it to her, but resolved to waste no time and fixed the wedding for the following day. The Prince found this arrangement extremely satisfactory. He went to his bride and told her that her letter had greatly saddened him, but that he hoped in time to win her affection, that the thought of losing her was too great a burden to bear, and that he could not bring himself to agree to his own death-sentence. He then kissed her hand respectfully and withdrew, without saying a word to her of her father's intentions.

But scarcely had he left the courtyard than her father entered the room and bluntly ordered her to be ready for the following day. Marya Kirilovna, already greatly disturbed by the words of Prince Vereisky, burst into tears and threw herself at her father's feet.

'Papa!' she cried in a plaintive voice. 'Papa! Do not destroy me! I don't love the Prince and I don't want to marry him . . .'

'What does this mean?' thundered Kirila Petrovitch. 'Until now you've kept silent and consented, but now, when everything is decided, you take it into your head to be capricious, and want to go back on your word. Don't fool around; you'll gain nothing from me by doing so.'

'Don't destroy me!' repeated the unfortunate Masha. 'Why are you driving me away from you and giving me to a man I don't love? Do I bore you? I only want to stay here with you as before. Papa, you'll be sad without me, and even sadder when you think that I'm unhappy. Papa, don't force me, I don't want to get married . . .'

Kirila Petrovitch was moved, but he concealed his emotion and, pushing her away from him, he said sternly:

'This is all nonsense, do you hear? I am better aware than you of what will make you happy. Tears will not help you. Your wedding will take place the day after tomorrow.'

'The day after to-morrow!' exclaimed Masha. 'Oh, my God! No, no, it's impossible, it can't be. Papa, listen to me – if you have already decided to destroy me, I'll have recourse to a protector you wouldn't have believed possible. You'll see, you'll be appalled to what limits you have driven me.'

'What's this? What's this?' said Troyekurov. 'Threats! Threats to me, you insolent girl! Don't you know that I can do things to you which you would never imagine? You dare to frighten me with a protector. Let's see who this protector is.'

'Vladimir Dubrovsky!' replied Masha in despair.

Kirila Petrovitch thought that she had gone out of her mind and gazed at her in astonishment.

'Right!' he said to her after a pause. 'You may wait for your deliverer – but meanwhile you'll stay in this room and you'll not stir from it until the wedding itself.'

With these words Kirila Petrovitch left the room and locked the door behind him.

For a long time the wretched girl wept, imagining all that lay in store for her. The stormy scene she had had with her father had been a relief to her, however, and she was able to reason out her fate and what she would have to do more calmly. The principal thing was to escape the hateful marriage. The lot of a brigand's wife seemed rapture to her in comparison with the fate that awaited her. She glanced at the ring given to her by Dubrovsky. She passionately wanted to see him alone once more before the decisive moment, in order to consult him. Premonition told her that she would find Dubrovsky by the arbour in the garden that evening; she resolved to go and await him there as soon as dusk began to fall.

It grew dark. Masha prepared to go, but the door of her room was locked. A maidservant from the other side of the door informed her that Kirila Petrovitch had forbidden her to leave the room. She was under arrest. Deeply offended, she sat down by the window and stayed there until the small hours of the morning, without undressing and staring motionlessly into the darkness of the night. Towards dawn she began to doze, but her light sleep was haunted by sad visions, and the rays of the rising sun soon awoke her.

Chapter Seventeen

She awoke, and all the horror of her situation returned to her with her first thought. She rang the bell. The maid entered, and in answer to her questions replied that Kirila Petrovitch had been to Arbatovo the previous evening and had returned late, and that he had given strict instructions that nobody should let her out of her room or talk to her.

The maid added, furthermore, that there were no indications of any special preparations for the wedding, except that the priest had been forbidden to leave the village under any circumstances. Having delivered this news, the maid left Marya Kirilovna and again locked the door.

The words of the maid hardened the young captive's heart. Her head burned, her blood boiled. She decided to let Dubrovsky know all, and began to think of a method of leaving the ring in the hollow of the cherished oak-tree. At that moment, a small stone struck against the window of her room, causing the glass to tinkle; looking out into the courtyard, Marya Kirilovna saw young Sasha beckoning to her with secret signs. She was delighted to see him, knowing of his attachment to her. She opened the window.

'Good morning, Sasha,' she said. 'Why do you call me?'

'I've come to see if there's anything you want, sister. Papa is very angry and has forbidden the entire household to obey you, but tell me to do anything you like, and I'll do it.'

'Please, my dear Sashenka, listen to me. You know the old hollow oak-tree by the arbour . . . ?'

'Yes, sister.'

'Well, if you love me, run there as quickly as you can and put this ring into the hollow. But be sure that nobody sees you.'

With these words she threw the ring to him and closed the window.

The boy picked up the ring and ran off at full speed. In three minutes he found himself by the cherished tree. Here he stopped to regain his breath, looked all around him, and placed the ring in the hollow. His mission safely completed, he was on the point of returning to Marya Kirilovna to inform her of its success, when suddenly a red-haired urchin, squinting and in ragged clothes, darted out from behind the arbour, ran up to the oak-tree and placed his hand inside the hollow. Quicker than a squirrel, Sasha was on him and grasped him with both hands.

'What are you doing here?' he said threateningly.

'What's that to do with you?' replied the boy, trying to free himself.

'Leave that ring alone, you red-faced hare,' cried Sasha, 'or I'll teach you a thing or two.'

Instead of a reply, Sasha received a blow in the face from the other's fist. But he did not let go his grasp and shouted at the top of his voice:

'Help, thief! Here!'

The red-haired lad used all his strength in an attempt to get away. He seemed to be about two years older than Sasha, and much stronger, but Sasha was the more agile of the two. They fought for several minutes, until finally the red-haired boy gained the upper hand. He threw Sasha to the ground and seized him by the throat.

But at that moment a strong hand gripped the shaggy red hair, and the gardener Stepan lifted the boy several inches off the ground.

'Ah, you red-haired devil,' said the gardener. 'How dare you set about the young master.'

Sasha had by now leaped to his feet and recovered himself.

'If you'd fought cleanly, you'd never have got me down,' he said. 'Now give me back the ring and get out of here.'

'Not on your life,' replied the red-haired boy, twisting suddenly so that he managed to free his hair from Stepan's hands. He began to run off but Sasha caught up with him and pushed him in the back, and the urchin fell flat on the ground. The gardener got hold of him again and bound him with his belt.

'Give me back the ring!' cried Sasha.

'Wait, master,' said Stepan. 'We'll take him to the steward and let him deal with him.'

The gardener led his prisoner into the courtyard of the big house, accompanied by Sasha, who cast anxious glances at his trousers, which were torn and grass-stained. All of a sudden the three of them found themselves in front of Kirila Petrovitch, who was on his way to inspect the stables.

'What's this?' he asked Stepan.

Stepan briefly described all that had occurred. Kirila Petrovitch listened to him attentively.

'Well, you scamp,' he said, turning to Sasha. 'How did you get mixed up with him?'

'He stole the ring from the hollow, Papa – order him to give back the ring.'

'What ring? What hollow?'

'The one that Marya Kirilovna ... the ring ...'

Sasha broke off in confusion. Kirila Petrovitch frowned and shaking his head he said:

'So Marya Kirilovna is also involved. Confess everything or I'll give you such a thrashing that you won't know yourself ...'

'Before God, Papa ... I, Papa, I ... Marya Kirilovna didn't tell me to do anything, Papa.'

'Stepan, go and cut me a good, fresh birch rod ...'

'Wait, Papa, I'll tell you everything. I was running about in the courtyard today, when sister Marya Kirilovna opened her window. I ran up to the window, and she accidentally dropped a ring, which I then hid in the hollow ... and ... this red-haired boy wanted to steal the ring ...'

'Dropped it accidentally and you wanted to hide it ... Stepan, fetch me a birch rod.'

'Wait, Papa, I'll tell you everything. Sister Marya Kirilovna told me to run to the oak-tree and put the ring in the hollow, so I ran and put it there, and this beastly boy ...'

Kirila Petrovitch turned to the 'beastly boy' and asked him sternly:

'Who do you belong to?'

'I am one of the house-servants of my master, Dubrovsky,' the red-haired boy replied.

Kirila Petrovitch's face darkened.

'It seems that you don't recognise me as your master,' he replied. 'Very well. What were you doing in my garden?'

'I was stealing raspberries,' the boy replied with great equanimity.

'Aha! Like master, like servant. Judge the flock by its priest. And do my raspberries grow on oak-trees?'

The boy made no reply.

'Papa, order him to give me back the ring,' said Sasha.

'Quiet, Alexandr,' replied Kirila Petrovitch, 'and don't forget that I'm going to deal with you later. Go to your room. Well, you don't seem to be a fool, you squint-eyed rascal. Give me the ring and go home.'

The boy unclenched his fist and showed that there was nothing in it.

'If you tell me everything, I won't flog you, and will even give you five kopecks for nuts. If you don't, I'll do something to you that you little expect. Well?'

The boy still made no reply, but stood with his head bent, assuming an expression of veritable idiocy.

'Right!' said Kirila Petrovitch. 'Lock him up somewhere, and see that he doesn't run away, or I'll have the whole household flayed alive.'

Stepan led the boy into the pigeon-loft, locked him up in there, and set Agafiya, the old poultry-woman, to keep watch over him.

'Now go straight into the town for the chief of police,' said Kirila Petrovitch, following the boy with his eyes, 'and as quickly as you can.'

'There can be no doubt about it. She's been keeping in touch with that accursed Dubrovsky. But can she really have summoned him to her aid?' thought Kirila Petrovitch, as he paced up and down the room, angrily whistling *Beat, Drums of Victory!* 'Perhaps I'm hot on his tracks at last, and he won't get away from us this time. We must take advantage of this opportunity. Ah, bells! Thank God, it's the chief of police!'

'Hey!' he said. 'Bring that boy we've just locked up here to me.'

In the meantime, a small carriage had driven into the yard and our friend the chief of police, covered with dust, entered the room.

'Wonderful news!' Kirila Petrovitch said to him. 'I've caught Dubrovsky.'

'Thank heaven, your Excellency!' said the chief of police joyfully. 'Where is he?'

'That is, not Dubrovsky himself, but one of his band. They're bringing him along now. He'll help us to catch his leader. Here he is.'

The chief of police, expecting some menacing brigand, was astonished to see a rather weak-looking thirteen-year-old boy. Incredulously, he turned to Kirila Petrovitch and awaited an explanation. Kirila Petrovitch then began to relate the events of the morning, making no mention, however, of Marya Kirilovna.

The chief of police listened to him attentively, glancing every now and then at the young scoundrel, who, still feigning an air of imbecility, seemed to be paying no attention whatever to all that went on around him.

'Allow me, your Excellency, to speak to you in private,' the chief of police said at last.

Kirila Petrovitch led him into another room and closed the door after him.

Half an hour later they came out into the hall again, where the young captive was awaiting a decision concerning his fate.

'The master,' the chief of police said to him, 'wanted to

have you locked up in the town jail, flogged, and then sent to a prisoners' settlement, but I interceded on your behalf and asked him to pardon you. Unbind him.'

The boy was unbound.

'Thank the master,' said the chief of police.

The boy went up to Kirila Petrovitch and kissed his hand.

'Go along home then,' Kirila Petrovitch said to him, 'and in future don't steal raspberries from oak-trees.'

The boy went out, jumped merrily down the steps, and then began to run, without looking behind him, across the fields to Kistenevka. On reaching the village, he stopped before a half-ruined cottage at the corner of the road and knocked on the window. The window was opened and an old woman appeared.

'Give me some bread, Grandma,' said the boy. 'I've not eaten since this morning and I'm starving.'

'Ah, it's you, Mitya, and where have you been for so long, you little devil?' the old woman answered.

'I'll tell you afterwards, Grandma, but for God's sake give me some bread.'

'Come inside the hut, then.'

'I haven't got time, Grandma. I've got to run off somewhere else. Bread, for the love of God, bread.'

'What a fidget!' the old woman grumbled. 'Here's a bit of bread then.'

She passed a piece of black bread through the window. The boy bit into it eagerly and was off in a flash, munching. It was beginning to grow dark. He made his way past barns and vegetable gardens into the Kistenevka copse. Reaching two pine-trees, standing like advance guards before the copse, he stopped, looked all around him, gave a short, shrill whistle and then listened. In reply he heard a light and continuous whistle and somebody came out of the copse and drew near to him.

Chapter Eighteen

Kirila Petrovitch paced up and down the hall, whistling his tune louder than usual. The whole house was astir, with the servants running about and the maids bustling to and fro. In the coach-house, coachmen were preparing the carriage, and the courtyard was full of people. In the young lady's boudoir, before the looking-glass, a lady, surrounded by maidservants, was dressing the pale and motionless Marya Kirilovna, whose head bent languidly beneath the weight of diamonds. She started slightly whenever an incautious hand pricked her, but she remained silent, staring absently into the looking-glass.

'Are you nearly ready?' the voice of Kirila Petrovitch was heard through the door.

'In a minute,' the lady replied. 'Marya Kirilovna, stand up and take a look at yourself. Is everything all right?'

Marya Kirilovna stood up but made no reply. The door was opened.

'The bride is ready,' the lady said to Kirila Petrovitch. 'She can take her seat in the carriage.'

'With God,' replied Kirila Petrovitch, taking the icon from the table. 'Come to me, Masha,' he said to her with emotion. 'I give you my blessing . . .'

The poor girl fell at his feet and began to sob.

'Papa . . . Papa . . .' she said, through her tears, and her voice died away.

Kirila Petrovitch hastened to give her his blessing. She was raised to her feet and almost carried into the carriage. Her godmother and one of the maidservants sat with her, and they set out for the church. There the bridegroom awaited them. He came forward to meet his bride and was struck by her pallor and strange expression. Together they entered the cold, empty church, and the door was locked behind them. The priest came out from behind the altar and the ceremony began at once. Marya Kirilovna saw nothing, heard nothing, thought only of one thing – since that morning she had been waiting for Dubrovsky, and her hope had not faded for a single moment. But when the priest turned to her with the customary questions, she shuddered and felt faint; but still she hesitated, still she hoped. The priest, without waiting for her reply, pronounced the irrevocable words.

The ceremony was over. She felt the cold kiss of her unloved husband, heard the joyful congratulations of those who had attended the wedding, and she still could not believe that her life was eternally chained, that Dubrovsky had not flown to her rescue. The Prince turned to her with a few gentle words, but she did not understand them. They went out of the church. Peasants from Pokrovskoye were crowded in the porch. Her eyes ran quickly over them, and then reverted to their former blankness. The newly-weds sat down together in the carriage and set out for Arbatovo, whither Kirila Petrovitch had already gone in order to be able to welcome them. Alone with his young wife, the Prince was not in the least perturbed by her cold manner. He did not bother her with sugary declarations of love or any ridiculous and ecstatic outpourings – his words were simple and demanded no replies. In this way they drove about ten versts. The horses galloped rapidly over the rough country road, and the carriage scarcely swayed at all on its English springs. Suddenly cries of pursuit were heard. The carriage stopped and a crowd of armed men surrounded it. A masked man opened the door on the side on which the young Princess sat.

'You are free, come,' he said.

'What does this mean?' cried the Prince.' Who are you?'

'It is Dubrovsky,' said the Princess.

The Prince, not losing his presence of mind, drew a travelling-pistol from his side-pocket and fired at the masked brigand. The Princess screamed and in terror covered her face with both her hands. Dubrovsky had been wounded in the shoulder and the blood began to seep through his clothes. The Prince, without losing a moment, drew another pistol, but before he had time to fire, the doors were thrust open and powerful hands dragged him out of the carriage and tore the pistol from him. Knives were brandished above his head.

'Don't touch him!' cried Dubrovsky, and his grim accomplices fell back.

'You are free,' repeated Dubrovsky, turning to the pale Princess.

'No,' she replied. 'It's too late. I am already married. I am the wife of Prince Vereisky.'

'What are you saying?' cried Dubrovsky in despair. 'No! You are not his wife. You were forced. You could never have given your consent . . .'

'I consented. I gave my vow,' she replied firmly. 'The Prince is my husband. Order him to be set free and leave me with him. I have not deceived you. I was waiting for you till the last minute. But now, I tell you, it's too late. Leave us.'

But Dubrovsky no longer heard her. The pain of his wound and the powerful agitation of his heart had deprived him of all strength. He fell against the wheel of the carriage, and the brigands surrounded him. He managed to say a few words to them. They lifted him up on to his horse, and two men supported him while a third held the horse by the bridle. They rode off, leaving the carriage in the middle of the road, the servants bound, and the horses unharnessed, but without stealing a single thing, and without causing a single drop of blood to be shed in vengeance for the blood of their leader.

Chapter Nineteen

In the midst of a dense wood, on a narrow grass-plot, there rose a small earthen fortress, consisting of a rampart and a ditch, behind which were grouped several tents and mud huts.

In the yard in front of the buildings, a number of men, immediately recognisable as brigands by the variety of clothes and by the arms they carried, sat bare-headed around a cauldron, eating their dinner. A sentry sat cross-legged on the rampart beside a small cannon. He was sewing a small patch on a part of his clothing, handling the needle with a skill which marked him out as an experienced tailor. He was constantly looking around him.

Although a mug had several times been passed round from hand to hand, a strange silence held sway over the company. The brigands finished their meal. One after another, they stood up and gave thanks to God. Some dispersed to their huts, some into the wood, while others, in Russian fashion, lay down to sleep off their food.

The sentry finished his work, shook his ragged garment, looked admiringly at the patch, stuck the needle into his sleeve, sat astride the cannon and began to sing an old melancholy song in a full-throated voice:

> '*Make no sound, mother forest green,*
> *Do not hinder me, brave lad, from thinking.*'

At that moment the door of one of the huts opened, and an old woman in a white bonnet, neatly and primly dressed, appeared on the threshold.

'That's enough of that noise, Stepka,' she said angrily. 'The master is resting, and yet you start bellowing away. You have neither conscience nor pity.'

'I'm sorry, Yegorovna,' replied Stepka. 'I won't go on. Let our master rest and recover.'

The old woman went back into the hut, and Stepka began to walk up and down the rampart.

In the hut from which the old woman had emerged, the wounded Dubrovsky lay on a camp-bed behind a partition. Beside him, on a small table, lay his pistols, and a sword hung near his head. The floor and walls of the mud hut were covered with rich carpets, and a lady's silver dressing-case and cheval-glass stood in one corner. Dubrovsky held a book open in his hand, but his eyes were closed, and the old woman, looking in at him from behind the partition, was unable to tell whether he was asleep or merely thinking.

Suddenly Dubrovsky started – the alarm had been sounded in the fortress, and Stepka thrust his head through the window.

'Master, Vladimir Andreyevitch,' he cried. 'Our men have given the signal – they're on to us!'

Dubrovsky leaped from his bed, seized his arms, and left the hut. The yard was crowded with noisy brigands. A deep hush fell over them as Dubrovsky made his appearance.

'Is everybody here?' he asked.

'All except the patrols,' came the reply.

'To your positions!' cried Dubrovsky.

Each brigand took up his appointed place. At that moment three men from the patrols came running up to the gate. Dubrovsky went forward to meet them.

'What is it?' he asked.

'There are soldiers in the wood,' they replied. 'They are surrounding us.'

Dubrovsky ordered the gates to be locked, and then went

himself to inspect the small cannon. The sound of several voices, coming nearer, could be heard in the wood. Suddenly three or four soldiers appeared out of the wood, and immediately fell back and fired a signal to their comrades.

'Prepare for battle!' cried Dubrovsky.

A murmur arose among the brigands, and then all was quiet again.

The sound of approaching troops was heard. Their arms glittering among the trees, about one hundred and fifty soldiers burst out of the wood and with loud cries rushed towards the rampart. Dubrovsky lit the fuse of the cannon. The shot was successful – one soldier had his head blown off and two others were wounded. Confusion arose among the soldiers, but the officer in command hurled himself forward, and the soldiers followed him and jumped down into the ditch. The brigands fired at them with their shotguns and pistols and, with axes in their hands, began to defend the rampart, up which the frenzied soldiers climbed, leaving twenty or so wounded comrades in the ditch beneath. Hand-to-hand fighting ensued. The soldiers were already on the rampart, and the brigands were beginning to fall back. But Dubrovsky, walking up to the officer in command, placed his pistol against the other's chest and fired. The officer was blown down on to his back. Several soldiers seized him by the arms and hastened to carry him into the wood. The others, deprived of their leader, stopped fighting. The tattered band of brigands took advantage of this moment of uncertainty, rushed forward and pushed them into the ditch. The attackers took to their heels. The brigands pursued them with loud cries. Victory was won. Dubrovsky, relying upon the total disorder of the enemy, called off his men and locked himself in the fortress, after giving orders for the wounded to be brought in, the sentries to be doubled, and that nobody should leave the enclosure.

These last events drew the attention of the authorities in real earnest to Dubrovsky's daring brigandage. Information as to his whereabouts was obtained. A company of soldiers was dispatched with orders to take him dead or alive. They caught several of the band and from these it was learned that Dubrovsky was no longer among them. A few days after the battle just described, he had called all his followers together and, announcing that he intended to leave them for all time, advised them to change their mode of life.

'You have grown rich under my leadership. Each of you possesses papers which will see you safely to some distant province, where you may spend the rest of your life in comfort and honest labour. But you are all rascals, and you'll probably not want to abandon your present trade.'

After this speech, he left them, taking only one man with him. Nobody knew where he had gone. At first, doubts were felt as to the truth of these assertions: the loyalty of the brigands to their leader was well-known, and it was thought that they were trying to protect him. But subsequent events confirmed their statements. The terrible raids, the fires and robberies all ceased. The roads became safe. According to another report, it was learned that Dubrovsky had gone abroad.

1832 – 1833

(Pushkin never completed this story.)

The Queen of Spades

The Queen of Spades signifies a secret misfortune.

FROM A RECENT BOOK ON
FORTUNE-TELLING

Chapter One

> *And on rainy days*
> *They gathered*
> *Often;*
> *Their stakes – God help them! –*
> *Wavered from fifty*
> *To a hundred,*
> *And they won*
> *And marked up their winnings*
> *With chalk.*
> *Thus on rainy days*
> *Were they*
> *Busy.*

There was a card party one day in the rooms of Narumov, an officer of the Horse Guards. The long winter evening slipped by unnoticed; it was five o'clock in the morning before the assembly sat down to supper. Those who had won ate with a big appetite; the others sat distractedly before their empty plates. But champagne was brought in, the conversation became more lively, and everyone took a part in it.

'And how did you get on, Surin?' asked the host.

'As usual, I lost. I must confess, I have no luck: I never vary my stake, never get heated, never lose my head, and yet I always lose!'

'And weren't you tempted even once to back on a series? Your strength of mind astonishes me.'

'What about Hermann then?' said one of the guests, pointing at the young Engineer. 'He's never held a card in his hand, never doubled a single stake in his life, and yet he sits up until five in the morning watching us play.'

'The game fascinates me,' said Hermann, 'but I am not in the position to sacrifice the essentials of life in the hope of acquiring the luxuries.'

'Hermann's a German: he's cautious – that's all,' Tomsky observed. 'But if there's one person I can't understand, it's my grandmother, the Countess Anna Fedotovna.'

'How? Why?' the guests inquired noisily.

'I cannot understand why it is,' Tomsky continued, 'that my grandmother never gambles.'

'But what's so astonishing about an old lady of eighty not gambling?' asked Narumov.

'Then you don't know . . . ?'

'No, indeed; I know nothing.'

'Oh well, listen then:

'You must know that about sixty years ago my grandmother went to Paris, where she made something of a hit. People used to chase after her to catch a glimpse of *la Vénus moscovite*; Richelieu paid court to her, and my grandmother vouches that he almost shot himself on account of her cruelty. At that time ladies used to play faro. On one occasion at the Court, my grandmother lost a very great deal of money on credit to the Duke of Orleans. Returning home, she removed the patches from her face, took off her hooped petticoat, announced her loss to my grandfather and ordered him to pay back the money. My late grandfather, as far as I can remember, was a sort of lackey to my grandmother. He feared her like fire; on hearing of such a disgraceful loss, however, he completely lost his temper. He produced his accounts, showed her that she had spent half a million francs in six months, pointed out that neither their Moscow nor their Saratov estates were in Paris, and refused point-blank to pay the debt. My grandmother gave him a box on the ear and went off to sleep on her own as an indication of her displeasure. In the hope that this domestic infliction would have had some effect upon him, she sent for her husband the next day; she found him unshake-able. For the first time in her life she approached him with argument and explanation, thinking that she could bring him to reason by pointing out that there are debts and debts, that there is a big difference between a Prince and a coach-maker. But my grandfather remained adamant, and flatly refused to discuss the subject any further. My grandmother did not know what to do. A little while before, she had become acquainted with a very remarkable man. You have heard of Count St-Germain, about whom so many marvellous stories are related. You know that he held himself out to be the Wandering Jew, and the inventor of the elixir of life, the philosopher's stone and so forth. Some ridiculed him as a charlatan and in his memoirs Casanova declares that he was a spy. However, St-Germain, in spite of the mystery which surrounded him, was a person of venerable appearance and much in demand in society. My grandmother remains quite infatuated with him and becomes quite angry if anyone speaks of him with disre-spect. My grandmother knew that he had large sums of money at his disposal. She decided to have recourse to him, and wrote asking him to visit her without delay. The eccentric old man at once called on her and found her in a state of terrible grief. She depicted her husband's barbarity in the blackest light, and ended by saying that she pinned all her hopes on his friend-ship and kindness.

'St-Germain reflected. "I could let you have this sum," he said, "but I know that you would not be at peace while in my debt, and I have no wish to bring fresh troubles upon your head. There is another solution – you can win back the money."

'"But, my dear Count," my grandmother replied, "I tell you – we have no money at all."

'"In this case money is not essential," St-Germain replied. "Be good enough to hear me out."

'And at this point he revealed to her the secret for which any one of us here would give a very great deal . . .'

The young gamblers listened with still greater attention. Tomsky lit his pipe, drew on it and continued:

'That same evening my grandmother went to Versailles, *au jeu de la Reine*. The Duke of Orleans kept the bank. Inventing some small tale, my grandmother lightly excused herself for not having brought her debt, and began to play against him. She chose three cards and played them one after the other: all three won and my grandmother recouped herself completely.'

'Pure luck !' said one of the guests.

'A fairy-tale,' observed Hermann.

'Perhaps the cards were marked!' said a third.

'I don't think so,' Tomsky replied gravely.

'What!' cried Narumov. 'You have a grandmother who can guess three cards in succession, and you haven't yet contrived to learn her secret.'

'No, not much hope of that!' replied Tomsky. 'She had four sons, including my father; all four were desperate gamblers, and yet she did not reveal her secret to a single one of them, although it would have been a good thing if she had told them – told me, even. But this is what I heard from my uncle, Count Ivan Ilyitch, and he gave me his word for its truth. The late Chaplitsky – the same who died a pauper after squandering millions – in his youth once lost nearly 300,000 roubles – to Zoritch, if I remember rightly. He was in despair. My grandmother, who was most strict in her attitude towards the extravagances of young men, for some reason took pity on Chaplitsky. She told him the three cards on condition that he played them in order; and at the same time she exacted his solemn promise that he would never play again as long as he lived. Chaplitsky appeared before his victor; they sat down to play. On the first card Chaplitsky staked 50,000 roubles and won straight off; he doubled his stake, redoubled – and won back more than he had lost ...

'But it's time to go to bed; it's already a quarter to six.'

Indeed, the day was already beginning to break. The young men drained their glasses and dispersed.

Chapter Two

> — *Il paraît que monsieur est décidément pour les suivantes.*
>
> — *Que voulez-vous, madame? Elles sont plus fraîches.*
>
> FASHIONABLE CONVERSATION

The old Countess *** was seated before the looking-glass in her dressing-room. Three lady's maids stood by her. One held a jar of rouge, another a box of hairpins, and the third a tall bonnet with flame-coloured ribbons. The Countess no longer had the slightest pretensions to beauty, which had long since faded from her face, but she still preserved all the habits of her youth, paid strict regard to the fashions of the 'seventies, and devoted to her dress the same time and attention as she had done sixty years before. At an embroidery frame by the window sat a young lady, her ward.

'Good morning, *grand'maman*!' said a young officer as he

entered the room. '*Bonjour, mademoiselle Lise. Grand'maman*, I have a request to make of you.'

'What is it, Paul?'

'I want you to let me introduce one of my friends to you, and to allow me to bring him to the ball on Friday.'

'Bring him straight to the ball and introduce him to me there. Were you at ***'s yesterday?'

'Of course. It was very merry; we danced until five in the morning. How charming Yeletskaya was!'

'But, my dear, what's charming about her? Isn't she like her grandmother, the Princess Darya Petrovna ...? By the way, I dare say she's grown very old now, the Princess Darya Petrovna?'

'What do you mean, "grown old"?' asked Tomsky thoughtlessly. 'She's been dead for seven years.'

The young lady raised her head and made a sign to the young man. He remembered then that the death of any of her contemporaries was kept secret from the old Countess, and he bit his lip. But the Countess heard the news, previously unknown to her, with the greatest indifference.

'Dead!' she said. 'And I didn't know it. We were maids of honour together, and when we were presented, the Empress ...'

And for the hundredth time the Countess related the anecdote to her grandson.

'Come, Paul,' she said when she had finished her story, 'help me to stand up. Lisanka, where's my snuff-box?'

And with her three maids the Countess went behind a screen to complete her dress. Tomsky was left alone with the young lady.

'Whom do you wish to introduce?' Lisaveta Ivanovna asked softly.

'Narumov. Do you know him?'

'No. Is he a soldier or a civilian?'

'A soldier.'

'An Engineer?'

'No, he's in the Cavalry. What made you think he was an Engineer?'

The young lady smiled but made no reply.

'Paul!' cried the Countess from behind the screen. 'Bring along a new novel with you some time, will you, only please not one of those modern ones.'

'What do you mean, *grand'maman*?'

'I mean not the sort of novel in which the hero strangles either of his parents or in which someone is drowned. I have a great horror of drowned people.'

'Such novels don't exist nowadays. Wouldn't you like a Russian one?'

'Are there such things? Send me one, my dear, please send me one.'

'Will you excuse me now, *grand'maman*, I'm in a hurry. Good-bye, Lisaveta Ivanovna. What made you think that Narumov was in the Engineers?'

And Tomsky left the dressing-room.

Lisaveta Ivanovna was left on her own. She put aside her work and began to look out of the window. Presently a young officer appeared from behind the corner house on the other side of the street. A flush spread over her cheeks. She took up her work again and lowered her head over the frame. At this moment, the Countess returned, fully dressed.

'Order the carriage, Lisanka,' she said, 'and we'll go for a drive.'

Lisanka got up from behind her frame and began to put her work away.

'What's the matter with you, my child? Are you deaf?' shouted the Countess. 'Order the carriage this minute.'

'I'll do so at once,' the young lady replied softly and hastened into the ante-room.

A servant entered the room and handed the Countess some books from the Prince Pavel Alexandrovitch.

'Good, thank him,' said the Countess. 'Lisanka, Lisanka, where are you running to?'

'To get dressed.'

'Plenty of time for that, my dear. Sit down. Open the first volume and read to me.'

The young lady took up the book and read a few lines.

'Louder!' said the Countess. 'What's the matter with you, my child? Have you lost your voice, or what . . . ? Wait . . . move that footstool up to me . . . nearer . . . that's right!'

Lisaveta Ivanovna read a further two pages. The Countess yawned.

'Put the book down,' she said. 'What rubbish! Have it returned to Prince Pavel with my thanks . . . But where is the carriage?'

'The carriage is ready,' said Lisaveta Ivanovna, looking out into the street.

'Then why aren't you dressed?' asked the Countess. 'I'm always having to wait for you – it's intolerable, my dear!'

Lisa ran up to her room. Not two minutes elapsed before the Countess began to ring with all her might. The three lady's maids came running in through one door and the valet through another.

'Why don't you come when you're called?' the Countess asked them. 'Tell Lisaveta Ivanovna that I'm waiting for her.'

Lisaveta Ivanovna entered the room wearing her hat and cloak.

'At last, my child!' said the Countess. 'But what clothes you're wearing . . . ! Whom are you hoping to catch? What's the weather like? It seems windy.'

'There's not a breath of wind, your Ladyship,' replied the valet.

'You never know what you're talking about! Open that small window. There, as I thought: windy and bitterly cold. Unharness the horses. Lisaveta, we're not going out – there was no need to dress up like that.'

'And this is my life,' thought Lisaveta Ivanovna.

And indeed Lisaveta Ivanovna was a most unfortunate creature. As Dante says: 'You shall learn the salt taste of another's bread, and the hard path up and down his stairs'; and who better to know the bitterness of dependence than the poor ward of a well-born old lady? The Countess *** was far from being wicked, but she had the capriciousness of a woman who has been spoiled by the world, and the miserliness and cold-hearted egotism of all old people who have done with loving and whose thoughts lie with the past. She took part in all the vanities of the *haut-monde*; she dragged herself to balls, where she sat in a corner, rouged and dressed in old-fashioned style, like some misshapen but essential ornament of the ball-room. On arrival, the guests would approach her with low bows, as if in accordance with an established rite, but after that, they would pay no further attention to her. She received the whole town at her house, and although no longer able to recognise the faces of her guests, she observed the strictest etiquette. Her numerous servants, grown fat and grey in her hall and servants' room, did exactly as they pleased, vying with one another in stealing from the dying old lady. Lisaveta Ivanovna was the household martyr. She poured out the tea, and was reprimanded for putting in too much sugar; she read novels aloud, and was held guilty of all the faults of the authors; she accompanied the Countess on her walks, and was made responsible for the state of the weather and the pavement. There was a salary attached to her position, but it was never paid. Meanwhile, it was demanded of her to be dressed like everybody else – that is, like the very few who could afford to dress well. In society she played the most pitiable role. Everybody knew her, but nobody took any notice of her; at balls she danced only when there was a partner short, and ladies only took her arm when they needed to go to the dressing-room to make some adjustment to their dress. She was proud and felt her position keenly, and looked around her in impatient expectation of a deliverer; but the young men, calculating in their flightiness, did not honour her with their attention, despite the fact that Lisaveta Ivanovna was a hundred times prettier than the cold, arrogant but more eligible young ladies on whom they danced attendance. Many a time did she creep softly away from the bright but wearisome drawing-room to go and cry in her own poor room, where stood a papered screen, a chest of drawers, a small looking-glass and a painted bedstead, and where a tallow candle burned dimly in its copper candlestick.

One day – two days after the evening described at the beginning of this story, and about a week previous to the events just recorded – Lisaveta Ivanovna was sitting at her embroidery frame by the window when, happening to glance out into the street, she saw a young Engineer, standing motionless with his eyes fixed upon her window. She lowered her head and continued with her work; five minutes later she looked out again – the young officer was still standing in the same place. Not being in the habit of flirting with passing officers, she ceased to look out of the window, and sewed for about two hours without raising her head. Dinner was announced. She got up and began to put away her frame, and, glancing casually out into the street, she again saw the officer. She was considerably puzzled by this. After dinner, she approached the window with a feeling of some disquiet, but the officer was no longer outside, and she thought no more of him.

Two days later, while preparing to enter the carriage with the Countess, she saw him again. He was standing just by the front door, his face concealed by a beaver collar; his dark eyes shone from beneath his cap. Without knowing why, Lisaveta Ivanovna felt afraid, and an unaccountable trembling came over her as she sat down in the carriage.

On her return home, she hastened to the window – the officer was standing in the same place as before, his eyes fixed upon her. She drew back, tormented by curiosity and agitated by a feeling that was quite new to her.

Since then, not a day had passed without the young man appearing at the customary hour beneath the windows of their house. A sort of mute acquaintance grew up between them. At work in her seat, she used to feel him approaching, and would raise her head to look at him – for longer and longer each day. The young man seemed to be grateful to her for this: she saw, with the sharp eye of youth, how a sudden flush would spread across his pale cheeks on each occasion that their glances met. After a week she smiled at him . . .

When Tomsky asked leave of the Countess to introduce one of his friends to her, the poor girl's heart beat fast. But on learning that Narumov was in the Horse Guards, and not in the Engineers, she was sorry that, by an indiscreet question, she had betrayed her secret to the light-hearted Tomsky.

Hermann was the son of a Russianised German from whom he had inherited a small amount of money. Being firmly convinced of the necessity of ensuring his independence, Hermann did not draw on the income that this yielded, but lived on his pay, forbidding himself the slightest extravagance. Moreover, he was secretive and ambitious, and his companions rarely had occasion to laugh at his excessive thrift. He had strong passions and a fiery imagination, but his tenacity of spirit saved him from the usual errors of youth. Thus, for example, although at heart a gambler, he never took a card in his hand, for he reckoned that his position did not allow him (as he put it) 'to sacrifice the essentials of life in the hope of acquiring the luxuries' – and, meanwhile, he would sit up at the card table for whole nights at a time, following the different turns of the game with feverish anxiety.

The story of the three cards had made a strong impression on his imagination, and he could think of nothing else all night.

'What if the old Countess should reveal her secret to me?' he thought the following evening as he wandered through the streets of Petersburg. 'What if she should tell me the names of those three winning cards? Why not try my luck ...? Become introduced to her, try to win her favour, perhaps become her lover ...? But all that demands time, and she's eighty-seven; she might die in a week, in two days ...! And the story itself...? Can one really believe it...? No! Economy, moderation and industry: these are my three winning cards, these will treble my capital, increase it sevenfold, and earn for me ease and independence!'

Reasoning thus, he found himself in one of the principal streets of Petersburg, before a house of old-fashioned architecture. The street was crowded with vehicles; one after another, carriages rolled up to the lighted entrance. From them there emerged, now the shapely little foot of some beautiful young woman, now a rattling jack-boot, now the striped stocking and elegant shoe of a diplomat. Furs and capes flitted past the majestic hall-porter. Hermann stopped.

'Whose house is this?' he asked the watchman at the corner.

'The Countess ***'s,' the watchman replied.

Hermann started. His imagination was again fired by the amazing story of the three cards. He began to walk around near the house, thinking of its owner and her mysterious faculty. It was late when he returned to his humble rooms. For a long time he could not sleep, and when at last he did drop off, cards, a green table, heaps of banknotes and piles of golden coins appeared to him in his dreams. He played one card after the other, doubled his stake decisively, won unceasingly, and raked in the golden coins and stuffed his pockets with the banknotes. Waking up late, he sighed at the loss of his imaginary fortune, again went out to wander about the town and again found himself outside the house of the Countess ***. Some unknown power seemed to have attracted him to it. He stopped and began to look at the windows. At one he saw a head with long black hair, probably bent down over a book or a piece of work. The head was raised. Hermann saw a small, fresh face and a pair of dark eyes. That moment decided his fate.

Chapter Three

Vous m'écrivez, mon ange, des lettres de quatre pages plus vite que je ne puis les lire.

CORRESPONDENCE

Scarcely had Lisaveta Ivanovna taken off her hat and cloak when the Countess sent for her and again ordered her to have the horses harnessed. They went out to take their seats in the carriage. At the same moment as the old lady was being helped through the carriage doors by two footmen, Lisaveta Ivanovna saw her Engineer standing close by the wheel. He seized her hand and, before she could recover from her fright the young man had disappeared – leaving a letter in her hand. She hid it in her glove and throughout the whole of the drive neither heard nor saw a thing. As was her custom when riding in her carriage, the Countess kept up a ceaseless flow of questions: 'Who was it who met us just now? What's this bridge called? What's written on that signboard?' This time Lisaveta Ivanovna's answers were so vague and inappropriate that the Countess became angry.

'What's the matter with you, my child? Are you in a trance or something? Don't you hear me or understand what I'm saying? Heaven be thanked that I'm still sane enough to speak clearly.'

Lisaveta Ivanovna did not listen to her. On returning home, she ran up to her room and drew the letter from her glove; it was unsealed. Lisaveta Ivanovna read it through. The letter contained a confession of love; it was tender, respectful and taken word for word from a German novel. But Lisaveta Ivanovna had no knowledge of German and was most pleased by it.

Nevertheless, the letter made her feel extremely uneasy. For the first time in her life she was entering into a secret and confidential relationship with a young man. His audacity shocked her. She reproached herself for her imprudent behaviour, and did not know what to do. Should she stop sitting at the window and by a show of indifference cool off the young man's desire for further acquaintance? Should she send the letter back to him? Or answer it with cold-hearted finality? There was nobody to whom she could turn for advice: she had no friend or preceptress. Lisaveta Ivanovna resolved to answer the letter.

She sat down at her small writing-table, took a pen and some paper, and lost herself in thought. Several times she began her letter – and then tore it up: her manner of expression seemed to her to be either too condescending or too heartless. At last she succeeded in writing a few lines that satisfied her:

> *'I am sure that your intentions are honourable, and that you did not wish to offend me by your rash behaviour, but our acquaintance must not begin in this way. I return your letter to you and hope that in the future I shall have no cause to complain of undeserved disrespect.'*

The next day, as soon as she saw Hermann approach, Lisaveta Ivanovna rose from behind her frame, went into the ante-room, opened a small window and threw her letter into the street, trusting to the agility of the young officer to pick it up. Hermann ran forward, took hold of the letter and went into a confectioner's shop. Breaking the seal of the envelope, he found his own letter and Lisaveta Ivanovna's answer. It was as he had expected, and he returned home, deeply preoccupied with his intrigue.

Three days afterwards, a bright-eyed young girl brought Lisaveta Ivanovna a letter from a milliner's shop. Lisaveta Ivanovna opened it uneasily, envisaging a demand for money, but she suddenly recognised Hermann's handwriting.

'You have made a mistake, my dear,' she said: 'this letter is not for me.'

'Oh, but it is!' the girl answered cheekily and without concealing a sly smile. 'Read it.'

Lisaveta Ivanovna ran her eyes over the note. Hermann demanded a meeting.

'It cannot be,' said Lisaveta Ivanovna, frightened at the haste of his demand and the way in which it was made: 'this is certainly not for me.'

And she tore the letter up into tiny pieces.

'If the letter wasn't for you, why did you tear it up?' asked the girl. 'I would have returned it to the person who sent it.'

'Please, my dear,' Lisaveta Ivanovna said, flushing at the remark, 'don't bring me any more letters in future. And tell the person who sent you that he should be ashamed of . . .'

But Hermann was not put off. By some means or other, he sent a letter to Lisaveta Ivanovna every day. The letters were no longer translated from the German. They were inspired by passion and written in a language, true to Hermann's character, which expressed his obsessive desires and the disorder of an unfettered imagination. Lisaveta Ivanovna no longer thought of returning them to him: she revelled in them, began to answer them, and with each day, her replies became longer and more tender. Finally, she threw out of the window the following letter:

> 'This evening there is a ball at the *** Embassy. The Countess will be there. We will stay until about two o'clock. Here is your chance to see me alone. As soon as the Countess has left the house, the servants will probably go to their quarters – with the exception of the hall-porter, who normally goes out to his closet anyway. Come at half-past eleven. Walk straight upstairs. If you meet anybody in the ante-room, ask whether the Countess is at home. You will be told "No" – and there will be nothing you can do but go away. But it is unlikely that you will meet anybody. The lady's maids sit by themselves, all in the one room. On leaving the hall, turn to the left and walk straight on until you come to the Countess' bedroom. In the bedroom, behind a screen, you will see two small doors: the one on the right leads into the study, which the Countess never goes into; the one on the left leads into a corridor and thence to a

*narrow winding staircase: this staircase leads to my
bedroom.'*

Hermann quivered like a tiger as he awaited the appointed
hour. He was already outside the Countess' house at ten
o'clock. The weather was terrible; the wind howled, and a
wet snow fell in large flakes upon the deserted streets, where
the lamps shone dimly. Occasionally a passing cab-driver
leaned forward over his scrawny nag, on the look-out for a
late passenger. Feeling neither wind nor snow, Hermann
waited, dressed only in his frock-coat. At last the Countess'
carriage was brought round. Hermann saw two footmen carry
out in their arms the bent old lady, wrapped in a sable fur,
and immediately following her, the figure of Lisaveta
Ivanovna, clad in a light cloak and with her head adorned
with fresh flowers. The doors were slammed and the carriage
rolled heavily away along the soft snow. The hall-porter closed
the front door. The windows became dark. Hermann began
to walk about near the deserted house. He went up to a lamp
and looked at his watch; it was twenty minutes past eleven.
He remained beneath the lamp, his eyes fixed upon the hands
of his watch, waiting for the remaining minutes to pass. At
exactly half-past eleven, Hermann ascended the steps of the
Countess' house and reached the brightly-lit porch. The hall-
porter was not there. Hermann ran up the stairs, opened the
door into the ante-room and saw a servant asleep by the lamp
in a soiled antique armchair. With a light, firm tread Hermann
stepped past him. The drawing-room and reception-room
were in darkness, but the lamp in the ante-room sent through
a feeble light. Hermann passed through into the bedroom.
Before an icon-case, filled with old-fashioned images, glowed
a gold sanctuary lamp. Faded brocade armchairs and dull gilt
divans with soft cushions were ranged in sad symmetry around
the room, the walls of which were hung with Chinese silk.

Two portraits, painted in Paris by Madame Lebrun, hung on one of the walls. One of these featured a plump, red-faced man of about forty, in a light-green uniform and with a star pinned to his breast; the other – a beautiful young woman with an aquiline nose and powdered hair, brushed back at the temples and adorned with a rose. In the corners of the room stood porcelain shepherdesses, table clocks from the workshop of the celebrated Leroy, little boxes, roulettes, fans and the various lady's playthings which had been popular at the end of the last century, when the Montgolfiers' balloon and Mesmer's magnetism were invented. Hermann went behind the screen, where stood a small iron bedstead. On the right was the door leading to the study; on the left the one which led to the corridor. Hermann opened the latter, and saw the narrow, winding staircase which led to the poor ward's room . . . But he turned back and stepped into the dark study.

The time passed slowly. Everything was quiet. The clock in the drawing-room struck twelve; one by one the clocks in all the other rooms sounded the same hour, and then all was quiet again. Hermann stood leaning against the cold stove. He was calm; his heart beat evenly, like that of a man who has decided upon some dangerous but necessary action. One o'clock sounded; two o'clock; he heard the distant rattle of the carriage. He was seized by an involuntary agitation. The carriage drew near and stopped. He heard the sound of the carriage-steps being let down. The house suddenly came alive. Servants ran here and there, voices echoed through the house and the rooms were lit. Three old maidservants hastened into the bedroom, followed by the Countess, who, tired to death, lowered herself into a Voltairean armchair. Hermann peeped through a crack. Lisaveta Ivanovna went past him. Hermann heard her hurried steps as she went up the narrow staircase. In his heart there echoed something like the voice of conscience, but it grew silent, and his heart once more turned to stone.

The Countess began to undress before the looking-glass. Her rose-bedecked cap was unfastened; her powdered wig was removed from her grey, closely-cropped hair. Pins fell in showers around her. Her yellow dress, embroidered with silver, fell at her swollen feet. Hermann witnessed all the loathsome mysteries of her toilet. At last the Countess stood in her dressing-gown and night-cap; in this attire, more suitable to her age, she seemed less hideous and revolting.

Like most old people, the Countess suffered from insomnia. Having undressed, she sat down in the Voltairean armchair by the window and dismissed her maidservants. The candles were carried out; once again the room was lit by a single sanctuary lamp. Looking quite yellow, the Countess rocked from side to side in her chair, her flabby lips moving. Her dim eyes reflected a total absence of thought; looking at her, one would have thought that the awful old woman's rocking came not of her own volition, but by the action of some hidden galvanism.

Suddenly, an indescribable change came over her death-like face. Her lips ceased to move, her eyes came to life: before the Countess stood an unknown man.

'Don't be alarmed, for God's sake, don't be alarmed,' he said in a clear, low voice. 'I have no intention of harming you; I have come to beseech a favour of you.'

The old woman looked at him in silence, as if she had not heard him. Hermann imagined that she was deaf, and bending right down over her ear, he repeated what he had said. The old woman kept silent as before.

'You can ensure the happiness of my life,' Hermann continued, 'and it will cost you nothing: I know that you can guess three cards in succession . . .'

Hermann stopped. The Countess appeared to understand what was demanded of her; she seemed to be seeking words for her reply.

'It was a joke,' she said at last. 'I swear to you, it was a joke.'

'There's no joking about it,' Hermann retorted angrily. 'Remember Chaplitsky whom you helped to win.'

The Countess was visibly disconcerted, and her features expressed strong emotion; but she quickly resumed her former impassivity.

'Can you name these three winning cards?' Hermann continued.

The Countess was silent. Hermann went on:

'For whom do you keep your secret? For your grandsons? They are rich and they can do without it; they don't know the value of money. Your three cards will not help a spendthrift. He who cannot keep his paternal inheritance will die in want, even if he has the devil at his side. I am not a spendthrift; I know the value of money. Your three cards will not be lost on me. Come . . . !'

He stopped and awaited her answer with trepidation. The Countess was silent. Hermann fell upon his knees.

'If your heart has ever known the feeling of love,' he said, 'if you remember its ecstasies, if you ever smiled at the wailing of your new-born son, if ever any human feeling has run through your breast, I entreat you by the feelings of a wife, a lover, a mother, by everything that is sacred in life, not to deny my request! Reveal your secret to me! What is it to you . . . ? Perhaps it is bound up with some dreadful sin, with the loss of eternal bliss, with some contract made with the devil . . . Consider: you are old; you have not long to live – I am prepared to take your sins on my own soul. Only reveal to me your secret. Realise that the happiness of a man is in your hands, that not only I, but my children, my grandchildren, my great-grandchildren will bless your memory and will revere it as something sacred . . .'

The old woman answered not a word.

Hermann stood up.

'You old witch!' he said, clenching his teeth. 'I'll force you to answer . . .'

With these words he drew a pistol from his pocket. At the sight of the pistol, the Countess, for the second time, exhibited signs of strong emotion. She shook her head and, raising her hand as though to shield herself from the shot, she rolled over on her back and remained motionless.

'Stop this childish behaviour now,' Hermann said, taking her hand. 'I ask you for the last time: will you name your three cards or won't you?'

The Countess made no reply. Hermann saw that she was dead.

Chapter Four

7 Mai 18**
Homme sans mœurs et sans religion!
CORRESPONDENCE

Still in her ball dress, Lisaveta Ivanovna sat in her room, lost in thought. On her arrival home, she had quickly dismissed the sleepy maid who had reluctantly offered her services, had said that she would undress herself, and with a tremulous heart had gone up to her room, expecting to find Hermann there and yet hoping not to find him. Her first glance assured her of his absence and she thanked her fate for the obstacle that had prevented their meeting. She sat down, without undressing, and began to recall all the circumstances which had lured her so far in so short a time. It was not three weeks since she had first seen the young man from the window – and yet she was already in correspondence with him, and already he had managed to persuade her to grant him a nocturnal meeting! She knew his name only because some of his letters had been signed; she had never spoken to him, nor heard his voice, nor heard anything about him ... until that very evening. Strange thing! That very evening, Tomsky, vexed with the Princess Polina *** for not flirting with him as she usually did, had wished to revenge himself by a show of indifference: he had therefore summoned Lisaveta Ivanovna and together they had danced an endless mazurka. All the time they were dancing, he had teased her about her partiality to officers of the Engineers, had assured her that he knew far more than she would have supposed possible, and, indeed, some of his jests were so successfully aimed that on several occasions Lisaveta Ivanovna had thought that her secret was known to him.

'From whom have you discovered all this?' she asked, laughing.

'From a friend of a person you know well,' Tomsky answered. 'From a most remarkable man!'

'Who is this remarkable man?'

'He is called Hermann.'

Lisaveta made no reply, but her hands and feet turned quite numb.

'This Hermann,' Tomsky continued, 'is a truly romantic figure: he has the profile of a Napoleon, and the soul of a Mephistopheles. I should think he has at least three crimes on his conscience ... How pale you have turned ... !'

'I have a headache ... What did this Hermann – or whatever his name is – tell you?'

'Hermann is most displeased with his friend: he says that he would act quite differently in his place. I even think that

Hermann himself has designs on you; at any rate he listens to the exclamations of his enamoured friend with anything but indifference.'

'But where has he seen me?'

'At church, perhaps; on a walk – God only knows! Perhaps in your room, whilst you were asleep: he's quite capable of it . . .'

Three ladies approaching him with the question: '*Oublie ou regret?*' interrupted the conversation which had become so agonisingly interesting to Lisaveta Ivanovna.

The lady chosen by Tomsky was the Princess Polina *** herself. She succeeded in clearing up the misunderstanding between them during the many turns and movements of the dance, after which he conducted her to her chair. Tomsky returned to his own place. He no longer had any thoughts for Hermann or Lisaveta Ivanovna, who desperately wanted to renew her interrupted conversation; but the mazurka came to an end and shortly afterwards the old Countess left.

Tomsky's words were nothing but ball-room chatter, but they made a deep impression upon the mind of the young dreamer. The portrait, sketched by Tomsky, resembled the image she herself had formed of Hermann, and thanks to the latest romantic novels, Hermann's quite commonplace face took on attributes that both frightened and captivated her imagination. Now she sat, her uncovered arms crossed, her head, still adorned with flowers, bent over her bare shoulders . . . Suddenly the door opened, and Hermann entered. She shuddered.

'Where have you been?' she asked in a frightened whisper.

'In the old Countess' bedroom,' Hermann answered. 'I have just left it. The Countess is dead.'

'Good God! What are you saying?'

'And it seems,' Hermann continued, 'that I am the cause of her death.'

Lisaveta Ivanovna looked at him, and the words of Tomsky echoed in her mind: 'He has at least three crimes on his conscience!' Hermann sat down beside her on the window sill and told her everything.

Lisaveta Ivanovna listened to him with horror. So those passionate letters, those ardent demands, the whole impertinent and obstinate pursuit – all that was not love! Money – that was what his soul craved! It was not she who could satisfy his desire and make him happy! The poor ward had been nothing but the unknowing assistant of a brigand, of the murderer of her aged benefactress! She wept bitterly, in an agony of belated repentance. Hermann looked at her in silence. His heart was also tormented; but neither the tears of the poor girl nor the astounding charm of her grief disturbed his hardened soul. He felt no remorse at the thought of the dead old lady. He felt dismay for only one thing: the irretrievable loss of the secret upon which he had relied for enrichment.

'You are a monster!' Lisaveta Ivanovna said at last.

'I did not wish for her death,' Hermann answered. 'My pistol wasn't loaded.'

They were silent.

The day began to break. Lisaveta Ivanovna extinguished the flickering candle. A pale light lit up her room. She wiped her tear-stained eyes and raised them to Hermann. He sat by the window, his arms folded and with a grim frown on his face. In this position, he bore an astonishing resemblance to a portrait of Napoleon. Even Lisaveta Ivanovna was struck by the likeness.

'How am I going to get you out of the house?' Lisaveta Ivanovna said at last. 'I had thought of leading you down the secret staircase, but that would mean going past the Countess' bedroom, and I am afraid.'

'Tell me how to find this secret staircase. I'll go on my own.'

Lisaveta Ivanovna stood up, took a key from her chest of drawers, handed it to Hermann and gave him detailed instructions. Hermann pressed her cold, unresponsive hand, kissed her bowed head and left.

He descended the winding staircase and once more entered the Countess' bedroom. The dead old lady sat as if turned to stone; her face expressed a deep calm. Hermann stopped in front of her and gazed at her for a long time, as if wishing to assure himself of the dreadful truth. Finally, he went into the study, felt for the door behind the silk wall hangings and, agitated by strange feelings, began to descend the dark staircase.

'Along this very staircase,' he thought, 'perhaps at this same hour sixty years ago, in an embroidered coat, his hair dressed *à l'oiseau royal*, his three-cornered hat pressed to his heart, there may have crept into this very bedroom a young and happy man now long since turned to dust in his grave – and to-day the aged heart of his mistress ceased to beat.'

At the bottom of the staircase Hermann found a door, which he opened with the key Lisaveta Ivanovna had given to him, and he found himself in a corridor which led to the street.

Chapter Five

*That evening there appeared before me
the figure of the late Baroness von V**.
She was all in white and she said to me:
'How are you, Mr Councillor!'*

SWEDENBORG

Three days after the fateful night, at nine o'clock in the morning, Hermann set out for the *** monastery, where a funeral service for the dead Countess was going to be held. Although unrepentant, he could not altogether silence the voice of conscience, which kept repeating: 'You are the murderer of the old woman!' Having little true religious belief, he was extremely superstitious. He believed that the dead Countess could exercise a harmful influence on his life and he had therefore resolved to be present at her funeral, in order to ask for forgiveness.

The church was full. Hermann could scarcely make his way through the crowd of people. The coffin stood on a rich catafalque beneath a velvet canopy. Within it lay the dead woman, her arms folded upon her chest, dressed in a white satin robe and with a lace cap on her head. Around her stood the members of her household: servants in black coats, with armorial ribbons upon their shoulders and candles in their hands; the relatives – children, grandchildren, great-grandchildren – in deep mourning. Nobody cried; tears would have been *une affectation*. The Countess was so old that her death could have surprised nobody, and her relatives had long considered her as having outlived herself. A young bishop pronounced the funeral sermon. In simple, moving words, he described the peaceful end of the righteous woman, who for many years had been in quiet and touching preparation for a Christian end. 'The angel of death found her,' the speaker said, 'waiting for the midnight bridegroom, vigilant in godly meditation.' The service was completed with sad decorum. The relatives were the first to take leave of the body. Then the numerous guests went up to pay final homage to her who had so long participated in their frivolous amusements. They were followed by all the members of the Countess' household, the last of whom was an old housekeeper of the same age as the Countess. She was supported by two young girls who led her up to the coffin. She had not the strength to bow down to the ground – and merely shed a few tears as she kissed the cold hand of her mistress. After her, Hermann decided to approach the coffin. He knelt down and for several minutes lay on the cold floor, which was strewn with fir branches. At last he stood up, as pale as the dead woman herself, ascended the steps of the catafalque and bent his head over the body of the Countess . . . At that very moment, it seemed to him that the dead woman gave him a mocking glance, and winked at him. Hermann, hurriedly stepping back, missed his footing and crashed on to his back against the ground. He was helped to his feet. Simultaneously, Lisaveta Ivanovna was carried out in a faint to the porch of the church. These events disturbed the solemnity of the gloomy ceremony for a few moments. A subdued murmur arose among the congregation, and a tall, thin chamberlain, a near relative of the dead woman, whispered in the ear of an Englishman standing by him that the young officer was the Countess' illegitimate son, to which the Englishman replied coldly: 'Oh?'

For the whole of that day Hermann was exceedingly troubled. He went to a secluded inn for dinner and, contrary to his usual custom and in the hope of silencing his inward agitation, he drank heavily. But the wine fired his imagination still more. Returning home, he threw himself on to his bed without undressing and fell into a heavy sleep.

It was already night when he awoke: the moon lit up his room. He glanced at his watch; it was a quarter to three. He found he could not go back to sleep; he sat on his bed and thought about the funeral of the old Countess.

Just then, someone in the street glanced in at his window and immediately went away. Hermann paid no heed to the incident. A minute or so later, he heard the door into the front room being opened. Hermann imagined that it was his orderly, drunk as usual, returning from some nocturnal outing. But he heard unfamiliar footsteps and the soft shuffling of slippers. The door opened: a woman in a white dress entered. Hermann mistook her for his old wet-nurse and wondered what could have brought her out at this time of the night. But the woman in white glided across the room and suddenly appeared before him – and Hermann recognised the Countess!

'I have come to you against my will,' she said in a firm voice, 'but I have been ordered to fulfil your request. Three, seven, ace, played in that order, will win for you, but only on condition that you play not more than one card in twenty-four hours, and that you never play again for the rest of your life. I'll forgive you my death if you marry my ward, Lisaveta Ivanovna . . .'

With these words, she turned round quietly, walked towards the door and disappeared, her slippers shuffling. Herman heard the door in the hall bang, and again saw somebody look in at him through the window.

For a long time Hermann could not collect his senses. He went into the next room. His orderly was lying asleep on the floor. Hermann could scarcely awaken him. As ususal, the orderly was drunk, and it was impossible to get any sense out of him. The door into the hall was locked. Hermann returned to his room, lit a candle, and recorded the details of his vision.

Chapter Six

> — *Attendez!*
> — *How dare you say to me: 'Attendez!'?*
> — *Your Excellency, I said: 'Attendez, sir'!*

Two fixed ideas can no more exist in one mind than, in the physical sense, two bodies can occupy one and the same place. 'Three, seven, ace' soon eclipsed from Hermann's mind the form of the dead old lady. 'Three, seven, ace' never left his thoughts, were constantly on his lips. At the sight of a young girl, he would say: 'How shapely she is! Just like the three of hearts.' When asked the time, he would reply: 'About seven.' Every potbellied man he saw reminded him of an ace. 'Three, seven, ace,' assuming all possible shapes, persecuted him in his sleep: the three bloomed before him in the shape of some luxuriant flower, the seven took on the appearance of a Gothic gateway, the ace – of an enormous spider. To the exclusion of all others, one thought alone occupied his mind – making use of the secret which had cost him so much. He began to think of retirement and of travel. He wanted to try his luck in the public gaming-houses of Paris. Chance spared him the trouble.

There was in Moscow a society of rich gamblers, presided over by the celebrated Chekalinsky, a man whose whole life had been spent at the card-table, and who had amassed millions long ago, accepting his winnings in the form of promissory notes and paying his losses with ready money. His long experience had earned him the confidence of his companions, and his open house, his famous cook and his friendliness and gaiety had won him great public respect. He arrived in Petersburg. The younger generation flocked to his house, forgetting balls for cards, and preferring the enticements of faro to the fascinations of courtship. Narumov took Hermann to meet him.

They passed through a succession of magnificent rooms, full of polite and attentive waiters. Several generals and privy councillors were playing whist; young men, sprawled out on brocade divans, were eating ices and smoking their pipes. In the drawing-room, seated at the head of a long table, around which were crowded about twenty players, the host kept bank. He was a most respectable-looking man of about sixty; his head was covered with silvery grey hair, and his full, fresh face expressed good nature; his eyes, enlivened by a perpetual smile, shone brightly. Narumov introduced Hermann to him. Chekalinsky shook his hand warmly, requested him not to stand on ceremony and went on dealing.

The game lasted a long time. More than thirty cards lay on the table. Chekalinsky paused after each round, in order to give the players time to arrange their cards, and wrote down their losses. He listened politely to their demands, and more politely still allowed them to retract any stake accidentally left on the table. At last the game finished. Chekalinsky shuffled the cards and prepared to deal again.

'Allow me to place a stake,' Hermann said, stretching out his hand from behind a fat gentleman who was punting there.

Chekalinsky smiled and nodded silently, as a sign of his consent. Narumov laughingly congratulated Hermann on forswearing a longstanding principle and wished him a lucky beginning.

'I've staked,' Hermann said, as he chalked up the amount, which was very considerable, on the back of his card.

'How much is it?' asked the banker, screwing up his eyes. 'Forgive me, but I can't make it out.'

'47,000 roubles,' Hermann replied.

At these words every head in the room turned, and all eyes were fixed on Hermann.

'He's gone out of his mind!' Narumov thought.

'Allow me to observe to you,' Chekalinsky said with his invariable smile, 'that your stake is extremely high: nobody here has ever put more than 275 roubles on a single card.'

'What of it?' retorted Hermann. 'Do you take me or not?'

Chekalinsky, bowing, humbly accepted the stake.

'However, I would like to say,' he said, 'that, being judged worthy of the confidence of my friends, I can only bank against ready money. For my own part, of course, I am sure that your word is enough, but for the sake of the order of the game and of the accounts, I must ask you to place your money on the card.'

Hermann drew a banknote from his pocket and handed it to Chekalinsky who, giving it a cursory glance, put it on Hermann's card.

He began to deal. On the right a nine turned up, on the left a three.

'The three wins,' said Hermann, showing his card.

A murmur arose among the players. Chekalinsky frowned, but instantly the smile returned to his face.

'Do you wish to take the money now?' he asked Hermann.

'If you would be so kind.'

Chekalinsky drew a number of banknotes from his pocket and settled up immediately. Hermann took up his money and left the table. Narumov was too astounded even to think.

Hermann drank a glass of lemonade and went home.

The next evening he again appeared at Chekalinsky's. The host was dealing. Hermann walked up to the table; the players already there immediately gave way to him. Chekalinsky bowed graciously.

Hermann waited for the next deal, took a card and placed on it his 47,000 roubles together with the winnings of the previous evening.

Chekalinsky began to deal. A knave turned up on the right, a seven on the left.

Hermann showed his seven.

There was a general cry of surprise, and Chekalinsky was clearly disconcerted. He counted out 94,000 roubles and handed them to Hermann, who pocketed them coolly and immediately withdrew.

The following evening Hermann again appeared at the table. Everyone was expecting him. The generals and privy councillors abandoned their whist in order to watch such unusual play. The young officers jumped up from their divans; all the waiters gathered in the drawing-room. Hermann was surrounded by a crowd of people. The other players held back their cards, impatient to see how Hermann would get on. Hermann stood at the table and prepared to play alone against the pale but still smiling Chekalinsky. Each unsealed a pack of cards. Chekalinsky shuffled. Hermann drew and placed his card, covering it with a heap of banknotes. It was like a duel. A deep silence reigned all around.

His hands shaking, Chekalinsky began to deal. On the right lay a queen, on the left an ace.

'The ace wins,' said Hermann and showed his card.

'Your queen has lost,' Chekalinsky said kindly.

Hermann started: indeed, instead of an ace, before him lay the queen of spades. He could not believe his eyes, could not understand how he could have slipped up.

At that moment it seemed to him that the queen of spades winked at him and smiled. He was struck by an unusual likeness . . .

'The old woman!' he shouted in terror.

Chekalinsky gathered up his winnings. Hermann stood motionless. When he left the table, people began to converse noisily.

'Famously punted!' the players said.

Chekalinsky shuffled the cards afresh; play went on as usual.

CONCLUSION

Hermann went mad. Now installed in Room 17 at the Obukhov Hospital, he answers no questions, but merely mutters with unusual rapidity: 'Three, seven, ace! Three, seven, queen!'

Lisaveta Ivanovna married a very agreeable young man, the son of the old Countess's former steward and with a good position in the Service somewhere. Lisaveta Ivanovna is bringing up a poor relative.

Tomsky has been promoted to the rank of Captain and is to be married to Princess Polina.

1833

Kirdjali

Kirdjali was a Bulgarian by birth. In Turkish *kirdjali* means 'knight-errant' or 'daring fellow'. I do not know his real name.

By his acts of brigandage Kirdjali brought terror on the whole of Moldavia. To give some idea of him, I will recount one of his exploits. One night, he and the Arnout Mikhailaki together fell upon a Bulgarian village. They set it on fire at both ends and then progressed from hut to hut, Kirdjali doing the killing, Mikhailaki gathering the spoils, and both of them crying: 'Kirdjali! Kirdjali!' The entire village fled.

When Alexander Ypsilanti proclaimed the revolt and began to form his army, Kirdjali presented himself with several of his old comrades. The real object of the Hetairists was not very clear to them, but war was an opportunity to get rich at the expense of the Turks, or perhaps of the Moldavians – and *that* was clear to them.

Alexander Ypsilanti was personally brave, but he did not possess those qualities essential to the role he had assumed with such ardour and imprudence. He had no idea how to control the people whom he was obliged to get on with; and they had neither respect for him nor confidence in him. After the unfortunate battle in which the flower of Greek youth perished, Iordaki Olimbioti advised him to retire and himself took his place. Ypsilanti hastily removed himself to the borders of Austria, from where he sent his curses upon the people, describing them as disobedient, cowardly and villainous. The majority of these cowards and villains perished within the walls of the Seko monastery or on the banks of the River Pruth, desperately defending themselves against an enemy ten times their number.

Kirdjali found himself in the detachment of Georgi Kantakuzin, of whom the same could be said as of Ypsilanti. On the eve of the battle of Skulyani, Kantakuzin asked leave of the Russian authorities to enter our lines. And so his detachment was left without a leader; but Kirdjali, Safyanos, Kantagoni and the others had no need whatever of a leader.

The battle of Skulyani does not seem to have been described, in all its touching reality, by anyone. Imagine seven hundred men – Arnouts, Albanians, Greeks, Bulgarians and rabble of every sort – without the least idea of the arts of war, retreating in the face of fifteen thousand Turkish cavalry. The rebels' detachment kept close to the bank of the River Pruth and set up two small cannons, found in the Governor's courtyard at Jassy, from which salutes were fired on occasions of name-day celebration dinners. The Turks would have been glad to use their grape-shot, but without the permission of the Russian authorities they did not dare to: the shot would have inevitably flown over to our bank. The commander of our lines (now dead) had served in the army for forty years and had never heard the whistle of bullets; God granted him the occasion then. Several bullets whizzed past his ears. The old man flew into a terrible rage and abused the major of the Okhotsky infantry regiment, which was attached to our lines. The major, not knowing what to do, ran towards the river, on the other side of which some of the Turkish officers were prancing around on their horses, and threatened them with his finger. Seeing him, they turned round and galloped off, followed by the entire Turkish detachment. The major who had threatened with his finger was called Khorchevsky. I do not know what became of him.

The next day, however, the Turks attacked the Hetairists. Not daring to use grape- or cannon-shot, they resolved, against their usual custom, to employ cold steel. The battle was cruelly fought and the use of yataghans increased the general slaughter. For the first time lances were seen on the side of the Turks; these were Russian: there were some Nekrassovists in the Turkish ranks. The Hetairists were permitted by our Emperor to cross the Pruth and take shelter within our lines. They began to cross over. Kantagoni and Safyanos were the last to remain on the Turkish bank. Kirdjali, wounded the previous evening, already lay within our encampment. Safyanos was killed. Kantagoni, an extremely fat man, was wounded in the belly by a lance. With one hand he raised his sword, with the other he seized the enemy lance and thrust it further into himself; and in this way he was able to reach his killer with his sword. They fell together.

It was all over. The Turks remained victorious. Moldavia was cleansed. About six hundred Arnouts were scattered throughout Bessarabia. Although they had no means of supporting themselves, they were nevertheless grateful to Russia for her protection. They led lives of idleness, but were not licentious. They could always be seen in the coffee-houses of half-Turkish Bessarabia, long chibouks in their mouths, sipping coffee-grounds from small cups. Their figured jackets and pointed red slippers began to wear out, but they continued to wear their crested skull-caps on the side of their heads, and yataghans and pistols still stuck out from behind their broad sashes. Nobody complained of them. It was impossible to conceive that these poor and peaceful men were the notorious rebels of Moldavia, comrades of the redoubtable Kirdjali who was himself among them.

The Pasha in command at Jassy got to know of this and, in accordance with the peace treaty agreements, demanded that the Russian authorities deliver up the brigand.

The police began a search. They learned that Kirdjali was in Kishinev. They caught him one evening at the house of a fugitive monk, eating his supper in the dark with seven companions.

Kirdjali was placed under arrest. He made no attempt to conceal the truth and admitted to being Kirdjali.

'But,' he added, 'since I crossed the Pruth, I have not touched so much as a hair of another person's property, nor given offence to the lowliest of gypsies. To the Turks, the Moldavians and the Wallachians I am of course a brigand, but to the Russians I am a guest. When Safyanos, having fired the last of his grape-shot, came to collect buttons and nails and watch-chains and yataghan-knobs from the wounded so as to have something to fire, I gave him twenty beshliks and left myself without money. God knows that I, Kirdjali, have since then lived off nothing but charity. Why do the Russians now hand me over to my enemies?'

After that Kirdjali was silent, and he calmly awaited the determination of his fate.

He did not have to wait long. The authorities, not obliged to regard brigands with a romantic eye and convinced of the justice of the demand, ordered that Kirdjali be sent to Jassy.

A man of sympathy and intelligence, at that time a young and unknown official but now occupying an important position, gave me a lively account of Kirdjali's departure.

At the gates of the prison stood a karutsa ... (Perhaps you do not know what a karutsa is. It is a low, wicker carriage to which, not so long ago, were normally harnessed six or eight scrawny-looking nags. Sitting astride one of them, a Moldavian, moustached and with a sheepskin cap, would shout incessantly and crack his whip while the wretched horses ran on at a reasonably smart trot. If one of them began to tire, he would unharness it with frightful oaths and abandon it at the side of the road, without the least concern for its fate. On the return journey he would be sure to find it in the same place, quietly grazing on the green steppe. It was not unusual for a traveller to set out from one station with eight horses and arrive at the next with only a pair. That was about fifteen years ago. Nowadays, in Russianised Bessarabia, they have adopted the Russian harness and the Russian carriage.)

Such a karutsa stood at the gates of the prison in 1821, on one of the last days of September. Jewesses, carelessly dressed and with slippers down at the heel, Arnouts in their tattered but colourful costumes and slender Moldavian women with dark-eyed children in their arms surrounded the karutsa. The men were silent, the women eagerly expectant.

The gates were opened and several police-officials came out into the street; behind them followed two soldiers, leading the shackled Kirdjali.

He seemed to be about thirty. The features of his swarthy face were regular and grim. He was tall, broad-shouldered, and his general appearance seemed to indicate unusual physical strength. A brightly-coloured turban covered the side of his head, and a broad sash encircled his slender waist; a dolman of thick blue cloth, a loose, knee-length shirt and beautiful slippers completed his dress. His expression was proud and calm.

One of the officials, a red-faced old man in a faded uniform with three dangling buttons, and with a pair of tin spectacles pinched on the purple knob that served him as a nose, unfolded a piece of paper and, speaking in a nasal voice, began to read in Moldavian. From time to time he stared haughtily at the shackled Kirdjali, to whom the document apparently referred. Kirdjali listened to him attentively. The official finished reading, refolded the piece of paper and shouted threateningly at the people, ordering them to give way, and for the karutsa to be brought up. Kirdjali then turned to him and spoke a few words in Moldavian. His voice trembled as he spoke, his whole expression changed; he began to cry and threw himself at the feet of the police official, his chains rattling. The police official, alarmed, stepped back;

the soldiers moved forward to pick Kirdjali up, but he stood up on his own, gathered up his shackles, stepped into the karutsa and cried: 'Away!' A gendarme sat himself down beside him, the Moldavian cracked his whip, and the karutsa rolled away.

'What did Kirdjali say to you?' the young official asked the red-faced old man.

'He asked me,' the old man replied with a smile, 'to look after his wife and child, who live not far from Kilia in a Bulgarian village – he's frightened that they might come to harm on his account. The people are so stupid!'

The young official's story moved me deeply. I felt sorry for poor Kirdjali. I knew nothing of his fate for a long time. Several years later, however, I met the young official again. We began to talk of the past.

'And your friend Kirdjali? Do you know what became of him?' I asked.

'Indeed yes, I do,' he replied, and told me the following story:

Kirdjali, having been taken to Jassy, was brought before the Pasha, who sentenced him to be impaled. The execution was put off until some holiday or other. Meanwhile he was imprisoned.

The prisoner was guarded by seven Turks (simple people, and in their hearts as much brigands as Kirdjali); they respected him and, like all Orientals, listened avidly to his strange stories.

A close friendship sprang up between prisoner and guards. One day, Kirdjali said to them:

'Brothers! My hour is near. No one can escape his fate. I'll soon be taking leave of you. I would like to leave you something as a memento.'

The Turks pricked up their ears.

'Three years ago,' continued Kirdjali, 'when I was

plundering with the late Mikhailaki, we buried a kettle full of gold pieces in the steppe not far from Jassy. It has become clear that neither he nor I will be able to recover this treasure. So be it: take it and divide it fairly among yourselves.'

The Turks almost went out of their minds with delight. But how to find the secret spot, they puzzled? They thought for a long time and eventually decided that Kirdjali himself should lead them to the place.

Night fell. The Turks removed the chains from the prisoner's feet, tied his hands with a piece of rope, and went out of the town into the steppe with him.

Kirdjali led them from one mound to another, holding to a single direction. They walked for a long time. Finally Kirdjali stopped by a large stone, measured twelve paces south, stamped his foot and said: 'Here!'

The Turks made their arrangements. Four of them drew out their yataghans and started to dig. The other three remained on guard. Kirdjali sat down on the stone and began to watch them work.

'Well? How much longer will you be? Haven't you found anything yet?' he asked.

'Not yet,' replied the Turks and continued working so hard that the sweat poured off them like hail.

Kirdjali began to show signs of impatience.

'What a people!' he said. 'They don't even know how to dig properly. If I had the job it would be over in two minutes. Come, lads! Untie my hands and give me a yataghan.'

The Turks became thoughtful and began to consult one another.

'All right,' they decided. 'What harm can it do? He is only one and we are seven.'

And the Turks untied his hands and gave him a yataghan.

At last Kirdjali was free and armed. What he must have felt . . . ! He began to dig quickly, the guards helping him . . .

Suddenly he plunged his yataghan into one of them and, leaving the blade in his chest, seized the two pistols which hung from his sash.

Seeing Kirdjali armed with a pair of pistols, the remaining six fled.

Kirdjali is now carrying on his brigandage near Jassy. A short while ago he wrote to the Governor, demanding five thousand levs and threatening, in the event of the sum not being paid, to set fire to Jassy and to get to the Governor himself. The five thousand levs were paid up.

Such is Kirdjali!

1834

Egyptian Nights

Chapter One

Charsky was a native of Petersburg. He was under thirty; he was unmarried; service life did not weigh too heavily upon him. His late uncle, who had been a vice-governor in the good old days, had left him a considerable fortune. His life could have been very pleasant; however, he had the misfortune to write and print verses. In magazines he was described as a poet, and among servants as a story-teller.

Despite the great privileges enjoyed by poets (it must be stated that, apart from the right to use the accusative case in place of the genitive case and other similar so-called poetic licences, we know of no especial privileges accorded to Russian poets), despite every possible privilege, these persons are subjected to great disadvantages and unpleasantnesses. The bitterest evil of all and for the poet the most intolerable is the appellation with which he is branded, and from which he can never break away. The public look upon him as their own property; in their opinion, he was born for their *benefit and pleasure*. Should he return from the country, the first person he meets will ask:

'Haven't you got anything new for us?'

Should he seem pensive on account of the disorder of his

affairs or the illness of some person dear to him, then instantly will a banal smile accompany the banal exclamation:

'Perhaps you're composing something!'

Should he fall in love, the object of his affections will buy herself an album at the English shop, and then await an elegy. Should he call upon a man almost unknown to him to discuss an important matter of business, the latter will call his son and command him to read the verses of so-and-so; and the boy will then treat the poet to a distorted reading of his own compositions. And these are the flowers of his art! What then must be the misfortunes? Charsky confessed that the compliments, the questions, the albums and the small boys irked him to such an extent that he was constantly forced to restrain himself from perpetrating some act of rudeness.

Charsky used every possible effort to rid himself of the intolerable appellation. He avoided the society of his literary brothers, preferring men of the world, even the most simpleminded, to their company. His conversation was extremely commonplace and never touched on literature. In his dress he always observed the very latest fashions, with the diffidence and superstition of a young Muscovite arriving in Petersburg for the first time in his life. In his study, which was furnished like a lady's bedroom, there was nothing to recall the writer: there were no books strewn about and beneath the tables; the sofa was not spattered with ink; there was none of that disorder which marks the presence of the Muse and the absence of broom and brush. Charsky became quite downcast if any of his worldly friends happened to find him with a pen in his hand. It is difficult to believe to what trifles a man, otherwise endowed with talent and soul, can descend. At one time he affected to be a passionate lover of horses, at another, a desperate gambler, and at another, a refined gastronome, even though he had never been able to distinguish between horses of mountain and Arab breed, could never remember what were trumps, and in secret preferred a baked potato to all the possible inventions of a French cuisine. He led a life of great distraction; he was to be seen at all the balls, ate like a glutton at all the diplomatic dinners, and his presence at a soireé was as inevitable as that of ice-creams from Rezanov's.

However, he was a poet, and his passion was insuperable: when he found that his 'silly mood' (so did he term his inspiration) was on him, Charsky would shut himself up in his study and write from morning until late at night. To his genuine friends he confessed that it was only on these occasions that he knew real happiness. The rest of his time was spent in strolling around, standing on ceremony, dissembling and constantly hearing the famous question:

'Haven't you written anything new?'

One morning Charsky felt that happy state of soul when one's imaginings take bodily shape in one's mind, when one finds bright, unexpected words to incarnate the visions, when verses flow easily from one's pen and sonorous rhythms fly to meet harmonious thoughts. Charsky was mentally plunged in sweet oblivion . . . and the world and the opinions of the world and his own personal whims no longer existed for him. He was writing verses.

Suddenly the door of his study creaked and an unfamiliar head showed itself. Charsky gave a start and frowned.

'Who's there?' he asked irritably, inwardly cursing his servants, who were never in the hall when they should be.

The stranger entered.

He was tall, lean and seemed to be about thirty. The features of his swarthy face were expressive: a high, pale forehead, shaded by dark locks of hair, black, sparkling eyes, an aquiline nose, and a thick beard surrounding sunken olive cheeks showed him to be a foreigner. He was wearing a black frock-coat, already whitening at the seams, and summer trousers (although the season of autumn was well-advanced); beneath his ragged black cravat, upon a yellowed shirt-front, glittered an artificial diamond; his shaggy hat seemed to have seen both fine weather and bad. Meeting with such a man in a wood, one would have taken him for a brigand; in society, for a political conspirator; in the hall of someone's house, for a charlatan trading in elixirs and arsenic.

'What do you want?' Charsky asked him in French.

'*Signor,*' replied the foreigner with a low bow. '*Lei voglia perdonarmi se . . .*'

Charsky did not offer him a chair; he himself stood up. The conversation was continued in Italian.

'I am a Neapolitan artist,' the stranger said, 'and circumstances have forced me to leave my fatherland. I have come to Russia on the strength of my talent.'

Charsky imagined that the Neapolitan was intending to give some concerts on the violoncello and was selling his tickets from door to door. He was on the point of handing the man twenty-five roubles in order to get rid of him as quickly as possible when the stranger added:

'I hope, *Signor*, that you will give friendly assistance to your *confrère* and introduce me into those houses to which you have access.'

It would have been impossible to offer a more effective affront to Charsky's vanity. He glanced haughtily at him who called himself his *confrère*.

'Allow me to ask what sort of a person you are and whom you take me for?' he asked, with difficulty restraining his indignation.

The Neapolitan observed his irritation.

'*Signor,*' he answered, stuttering, '*. . . ho creduto . . . ho sentito . . . la vostra Eccelenza mi perdonera . . .*'

'What do you want?' Charsky repeated drily.

'I have heard much of your amazing talent; I am sure that the gentlemen hereabouts account it an honour to accord every possible protection to so excellent a poet,' the Italian replied. 'It is for that reason that I have ventured to appear before you . . .'

'You are mistaken, *Signor*,' Charsky interrupted him. 'Among us there is no such thing as the calling of a poet. Our poets have no need of the protection of gentlemen; our poets are gentlemen themselves, and if our patrons of literature (devil take them!) are not aware of this, so much the worse for them. We have no ragged *abbés* whom musicians take from the street to compose libretti. With us, poets do not go on foot from house to house, beseeching help. Moreover, those who told you that I was a great poet were probably joking. It is true, I once composed a few bad epigrams but, thank God, I have nothing in common with our friends the poets and nor do I wish to.'

The poor Italian was confused. He looked around him. The pictures, the marble statues, the bronzes, the expensive trifles disposed on Gothic book-stands, struck him. He realised that between the supercilious dandy that stood before him in a tufted brocade cap, a gold-embroidered Chinese dressing-gown and a Turkish sash, and himself, a poor, wandering artist, dressed in a tattered cravat and threadbare frock-coat, there was nothing in common. He uttered some incoherent apologies, bowed and made as if to leave. His pathetic appearance touched Charsky who, despite defects in his nature, had a kind and noble heart. He felt ashamed of his peevish vanity.

'Where are you going?' he asked the Italian. 'Wait . . . I felt obliged to disown an undeserved title and confess that I was not a poet. Now let us talk about your affairs. As far as I am able, I am ready to be of service to you. You are a musician?'

'No, *Eccelenza*,' the Italian replied. 'I am a poor *improvisatore*.'

'An *improvisatore*!' exclaimed Charsky, feeling all the cruelty of the reception he had given. 'Why did you not tell me before that you were an *improvisatore*?'

And Charsky grasped his hand with a feeling of sincere regret.

The Italian was encouraged by this sign of friendliness. He spoke naïvely of his plans. His outward appearance was not deceptive; he needed money; somehow in Russia he hoped to set his domestic circumstances to rights. Charsky listened to him attentively.

'I hope,' he said to the poor artist, 'that you will have success. The society hereabouts has never before heard an *improvisatore*. Curiosity will be aroused; it is true that we do not use the Italian language here, and that you will not be understood, but that does not especially matter. The important thing is that you be in fashion.'

'But if no one among you understands the Italian language,' said the *improvisatore* thoughtfully, 'who will come to hear me?'

'They'll come, have no fear: some out of curiosity, others to pass away the evening somehow, others to show that they understand Italian. I repeat, the important thing is that you be in fashion, and you will be, I promise you.'

Charsky politely dismissed the *improvisatore* after having taken down his address, and that same evening he set about trying to help him.

Chapter Two

I am the tsar, I am a slave,
I am a worm, I am God.
DERZHAVIN

The following day, Charsky sought out room number 35 in the dark and dirty corridor of an inn. He stopped at the door and knocked. The Italian of the previous day opened the door.

'Victory!' Charsky said to him. 'Your affairs are settled. The Princess *** offers you her salon. At a large party yesterday I succeeded in recruiting half Petersburg. Have your tickets and announcements printed. I can guarantee you, if not a triumph, at least that you will not be out of pocket . . .'

'And that's the main thing!' cried the Italian, expressing his delight by a spate of lively movements characteristic of his southern origin. 'I knew that you would help me. *Corpo di Bacco!* You are a poet like myself, and it can't be denied that poets are excellent fellows! How can I express my gratitude? Wait . . . would you like to hear an improvisation?'

'An improvisation! But can you do without an audience, without music and without the thunder of applause?'

'Nonsense! Where could I find a better audience? You are a poet, you will understand me better than others, and your quiet encouragement will be dearer to me than whole storms of applause . . . Sit down somewhere and give me a theme.'

Charsky sat down on a trunk (of the two chairs that stood in that narrow, wretched little hovel, one was broken and the other piled up with books and linen). The *improvisatore* took a guitar from the table and stood before Charsky, plucking at the strings with bony fingers and awaiting his orders.

'Here is your theme,' Charsky said to him: 'The poet himself should choose the subjects for his songs; the crowd has no right to direct his inspiration.'

The eyes of the Italian glittered, he struck a few chords, proudly raised his head, and passionate verses – the expression of a spontaneous emotion – flew harmoniously from his lips.

Here they are, freely translated by one of our poet friends from the words as memorised by Charsky:

> 'Eyes open wide, yet seeing nothing,
> The poet goes upon his way,
> And, as he plucks him by the clothing,
> A passing stranger bids him stay.
> "Tell us why aimlessly you wander;
> Your gaze, before you reach the peak,
> Is sinking to the valley yonder,
> And once again the depths you seek.
> Creation's order dimly viewing,
> You walk, oppressed by sterile heat,
> Some trivial object still pursuing
> That moves your mind and lures your feet.
> Genius must soar; the habitation
> Of all true poets is the sky;
> Their singing needs the inspiration
> Which lofty themes alone supply."
> Why does the wind that sets in motion
> The leaves and dust of upland vales
> Forget, upon the breathless ocean,
> The ship that waits with greedy sails?
> Or the grim eagle leave the peak,
> Fly past the towering spire, and seek

Some ruined tree-stump? Ask who knows
Why youthful Desdemona chose
To make a blackamoor her lover,
As moonlight dotes on midnight swart:
But eagle, wind, and maiden's heart
Obey no laws we can discover.
The poet too, like Aquilon,
Stirs what he lists and bears it on;
He flutters, eagle-like, refusing
To stay for leave or heed control,
And clasps the idol of his choosing,
Like Desdemona, to his soul.'

The Italian fell silent. Charsky, astonished and deeply moved, did not speak.

'Well?' asked the *improvisatore*. Charsky seized his hand and pressed it strongly.

'Well?' asked the *improvisatore*. 'What do you think?'

'Astonishing!' the poet replied. 'Why, another man's thoughts have scarcely reached your ear before they have become your own, as if you had fostered, fondled and developed them over a long period. For you, therefore, there exists neither difficulty nor fear of failure, nor that uneasiness which is the prelude to inspiration? Astonishing, astonishing!'

The *improvisatore* replied:

'Every talent is beyond explanation. How does a sculptor see, in a block of Carrara marble, the hidden Jupiter, and how, by chipping off its envelope with hammer and chisel, does he reveal it? Why does the poet's idea emerge from his head already set in rhyming quartets and harmoniously scanned? No one, apart from the *improvisatore* himself, can understand that speed of impression, that narrow link between real inspiration and a strange external will ... In vain would I attempt to explain it myself. However, we must think of my first night. What do you think? What price should I charge for the tickets, so as not to overcharge the public and at the same time to ensure that I don't lose? It is said that *la Signora Catalani* took twenty-five roubles a ticket, isn't it? It's a good price . . .'

It was distasteful to Charsky suddenly to fall from the heights of poesy to the counting-house clerk's desk; but he very well understood the bitter necessity of it, and he discussed the financial side of the arrangements with the Italian. The *improvisatore*, in these dealings, demonstrated such savage greed, such an artless love of gain that he revolted Charsky, who made haste to leave him before losing completely that feeling of rapture aroused within him by the brilliant improvisation. The preoccupied Italian did not observe this change of feeling, and he conducted Charsky along the corridor and down the stairs with low bows and assurances of his eternal gratitude.

Chapter Three

The price of the ticket is ten roubles;
the performance begins at 7.00.

POSTER

The salon of the Princess *** had been placed at the disposal of the *improvisatore*. A platform had been erected and chairs arranged in twelve rows. At seven o'clock on the appointed day, the salon was lit. Selling and collecting tickets at the door behind a small table sat a long-nosed old woman with a grey hat with broken feathers sticking from it, and with rings on all her fingers. Gendarmes stood near the entrance. The public began to assemble. Charsky was among the first to arrive.

He was largely responsible for the staging of the performance, and he wanted to see that the *improvisatore* had everything he needed. He found the Italian in a side-room, impatiently looking at his watch. The Italian was dressed in theatrical attire; he was in black from head to foot; the lace collar of his shirt was thrown back; his bare neck with its strange whiteness formed a strong contrast to his thick, black beard; his hair had been brushed forward and it overshadowed his forehead and eyebrows. All this was not very pleasing to Charsky, who did not like to see a poet in the attire of a wandering juggler. After a short conversation he returned to the salon which was filling up.

Soon all the rows of chairs were occupied by glittering ladies; the gentlemen stood in crowded ranks at either side of the platform, along the walls and behind the last row of chairs. The musicians with their music-stands were positioned on both sides of the platform, in the middle of which stood a table with a porcelain vase upon it. There was a large audience. All impatiently awaited the beginning of the performance; at last, at half past seven, the musicians bestirred themselves, prepared their bows and played the overture from *Tancred*. The people took their seats and fell silent; the last strains of the overture died away ... And the *improvisatore*, met by deafening applause which came from every corner of the room, walked forward to the extreme edge of the platform with a low bow.

Charsky waited uneasily to see what sort of impression the first minute would produce; but he noticed that the theatrical attire, which had seemed to him so unbecoming, did not have the same effect upon the audience. Indeed, Charsky himself saw nothing ludicrous in it when he saw the *improvisatore* on the stage, with his pale face brightly lit up by the numerous lamps and candles. The applause died away; the chatter ceased . . . The Italian, expressing himself in poor French, asked the gentlemen among his audience to name some themes by writing them down on individual pieces of paper. At this unexpected invitation, all looked at each other in silence and made no reply. Pausing awhile, the Italian repeated his request in a shy, humble voice. Charsky, standing immediately beneath the platform, was seized by anxiety; he foresaw that the performance would not be able to continue without his help and that he would have to inscribe a theme himself. Indeed, the heads of several ladies turned towards him, and they began to call out his name, at first in a whisper, and then louder and louder. Hearing Charsky's name, the *improvisatore* sought him out with his eyes and discovered him to be standing at his feet. With a friendly smile he handed Charsky a pencil and a piece of paper. To play a part in this comedy seemed very disagreeable to Charsky, but there was nothing for it: he took the pencil and paper from the Italian's hands and wrote down a few words. The Italian, taking the vase from the table, stepped down from the platform and presented it to Charsky who dropped his theme into it. His example had the required effect: two journalists, each considering it his duty as a literary man to write a subject, did so; the Secretary of the Neapolitan Embassy and a young man recently returned from a trip spent wandering around Florence placed their folded pieces of paper in the urn; finally, with tears in her eyes, a somewhat plain young lady wrote a few lines in Italian at the command of her mother and, blushing to the tips of her ears, handed her piece of paper to the *improvisatore*, while the other ladies looked on at her in silence, with scarcely perceptible smiles. Returning to the platform, the *improvisatore* placed the urn upon the table and began one by one to remove the pieces of paper, reading each out in a loud voice:

> *'La famiglia dei Cenci ...*
> *'L'ultimo giorno di Pompeia ...*
> *'Cleopatra e i suoi amanti ...*
> *'La primavera veduta da una prigione ...*
> *'Il trionfo di Tasso ...'*

'What is the wish of the honourable audience?' the Italian asked in a humble voice. 'Will it as a body indicate to me one of the subjects proposed, or will it have the matter decided by lot?'

'By lot!' said a voice in the crowd.

'By lot, by lot!' the audience repeated.

The *improvisatore* again stepped down from the platform and, holding the urn in his hand, he asked:

'Who will be good enough to select a subject?'

The *improvisatore* cast an imploring glance along the first row of chairs. Not one of the brilliant ladies seated there moved a muscle. The *improvisatore*, unaccustomed to such northern indifference, seemed to be greatly put out. Suddenly, he noticed on one side of the room a small, white-gloved hand held up; he turned quickly and went towards the dignified and beautiful young lady who was seated at the end of the second row. Without the least sign of confusion, she stood up and, with the utmost simplicity, plunged her aristocratic hand into the urn and drew out a roll of paper.

'Would you be good enough to unroll it and read it out?' the *improvisatore* said to her.

The beautiful young lady unrolled the piece of paper and read aloud:

'Cleopatra e i suoi amanti.'

These words were pronounced in a soft voice, but such silence reigned over the salon that they were heard by all. The *improvisatore* bowed low to the young lady and, with a look of profound gratitude, he returned to the platform.

'Gentlemen,' he said, turning to his audience, 'the lot has indicated as a subject for improvisation: Cleopatra and her lovers. I humbly request the person who chose this subject to explain his thought to me: to which lovers does he here refer, *perché la grande regina aveva molto . . .*'

At these words many of the gentlemen laughed loudly. The *improvisatore* became somewhat confused.

'I should like to know,' he continued, 'to which historical event the person who has selected this theme alludes ... I should be most grateful if he would be good enough to explain.'

Nobody hastened to reply. Some of the ladies turned their gaze towards the plain girl who had written a theme at the command of her mother. The poor girl observed this hostile attention and became so confused that tears began to form in her eyes. Charsky could not bear this and, turning to the *improvisatore*, he said to him in Italian:

'The theme was proposed by me. I had in mind that passage of Aurelius Victor's, where he writes that Cleopatra seemed to nominate death as the price of her love. And yet there were found adorers whom such a condition neither frightened nor repelled. It seems to me, however, that the subject is a trifle difficult. Why not choose another?'

But already the *improvisatore* felt the approach of the god . . . He gave a sign to the musicians to play. His face became terribly pale. He began to tremble as if in the throes of a fever; his eyes glittered with a miraculous fire; with his hand he pushed back his dark hair and with a handkerchief he wiped his high forehead, which was covered with beads of sweat. He suddenly stepped forward, crossed his arms on his chest . . . silenced the musicians . . .

The *improvisatore* began:

'The palace shone. The sound of singing
Mingled with notes of lute and fife;
The monarch smiled and chatted, bringing
The sumptuous feast to gayer life.
All hearts went up in adoration
Towards the throne, until she sank
Her wondrous head in meditation
Above the golden cup she drank.

'The banquet paused as if it slumbered,
The mirth was hushed, the music checked,
But now she spoke, no longer cumbered
By thought, her brow once more erect:
"My love, you think, might bring you pleasure?
It is a pleasure you can buy.
Hear me, for now in equal measure
Your longings I will satisfy.
Who'll bid for love in huckster's fashion?
For I will auction mine today:
Who'll buy from me one night of passion,
The price of which his life must pay?

'"I swear that in unheard-of fashion,
Great Mother, I shall play my part,
Serving the bed of lustful passion
With all a common strumpet's art.
Your help, O mighty Cypriot, lend me;
Ye kings who rule the realms of night
And all the gods of hell, befriend me:
I swear, until the morning light,
To tire my masters' lusts, to ply them
With every sweet endearment, till

The secrets of my kisses cloy them,
My harlot's wiles exhaust their will.
But this I also swear: whenever
Undying dawn shall streak again
The purple east, the axe shall sever
The heads of all these happy men."

'She speaks – and all is blank amazement;
Desire springs hot in every heart;
And while they murmur their bedazement,
She plays her cool and daring part.
Then, as she eyes with scornful glances
Her would-be suitors, suddenly
Out of the crowd one man advances,
And two more bring the tale to three.
Their steps are firm, their eyes are shining;
She rises, and the word is said:
Three nights are purchased, each assigning
A lover to the fatal bed.

'The priestly conclave duly blesses,
While all the watchers hold their breath,
The fateful urn from whose recesses
They draw in turn the lot of death.
First gallant Flavus, now grown grey
After long years in Roman pay;
He could not brook a woman's sneers,
But though her proud derision galled him,
Yet Pleasure's deadly threat appalled him
No more than in his warlike years,
When battle's bloody challenge called him.

'The next is Kriton, wise though young,
Who, born in Epicurus' bowers,

Worships and celebrates in song
Cupid's and Aphrodite's powers.
A budding flower of spring he was,
In whom both heart and eye delighted,
This third – but none can tell, because
The record leaves his name uncited.
The first soft down was fresh upon
His cheek; his eyes with rapture shone;
Ardent, undisciplined devotion
Was surging in his youthful breast;
On him the queen, with sad emotion,
Allowed her haughty glance to rest.'

1835

(Pushkin never completed this story.)

The Captain's Daughter

*Look after your honour
when it is young.*

SAYING

Chapter One

A SERGEANT OF THE GUARDS

'*He could enter the Guards as a captain tomorrow.*'
'*But there's no need for that; let him serve in the ranks.*'
'*Well spoken! Let him learn the hard way . . .*'
And who is his father?'

KNYAZHNIN

My father, Andrey Petrovitch Grinev, served under Count
Münnich in his youth and retired from the Service in the year
17** as a lieutenant-colonel. He then went to live on his estate
in the district of Simbirsk, where he married Avdotya
Vassilyevna Yu**, the daughter of a poor local nobleman.
There were nine of us children. Every one of my brothers and
sisters died in their infancy. Thanks to Prince B**, a major
in the Guards and a close relative of the family, I was registered as a sergeant in the Semyonovsky Regiment while my
mother was still carrying me. If, contrary to all expectations,
my mother had given birth to a daughter, my father would
have informed the appropriate quarters of the death of the
sergeant who had failed to come into this world, and there the
matter would have ended. I was considered to be on leave of
absence until the completion of my studies. Children were not
brought up in those days as they are today. At the age of five,
I was entrusted to the care of our senior groom, Savelyitch,
whose sober conduct had rendered him worthy of being my

personal attendant. By the age of twelve, under his supervision, I had learned to read and write Russian and I was a sound judge of the qualities of a greyhound. At this time my father engaged for me a Frenchman, a Monsieur Beaupré, who had been sent for from Moscow together with the yearly supply of wine and olive oil. His arrival greatly displeased Savelyitch.

'Heaven be thanked,' he used to grumble to himself, 'that the child is apparently washed, combed and well-fed. Why waste money getting a "Monsoo"? – as if we hadn't enough of our own people here!'

In his own country, Beaupré had been a hairdresser, then a soldier in Prussia, and he had then come to Russia *pour être 'outchitel'* without a very clear idea of the meaning of the word. He was a good-natured fellow, but flighty and extremely dissolute. His chief weakness was a passion for the fair sex; his tender advances were not infrequently met with slaps, which caused him to groan for whole days at a time. Furthermore, he was (to use his expression) 'no enemy of the bottle', which (in Russian) means that he liked a drop too much. But since, with us, wine was only served at dinner, and then only one glass each, and since the tutor's glass was generally passed over, my Beaupré very soon became accustomed to home-made Russian brews and even began to prefer them to the wines of his own country, claiming that they were far better for the stomach. We made friends immediately, and although the contract obliged him to teach me French, German and all the sciences, he was quick to show that he preferred to learn some scraps of Russian from me – after which we each did as we wished. Our relationship was one of the utmost harmony. I wished for no other mentor. But fate soon parted us, and here is how:

It so happened that one day the laundress, Palashka, a fat, pock-marked wench and the one-eyed dairymaid, Akulka, decided jointly to throw themselves at my mother's feet and, confessing to a criminal weakness, tearfully complained that 'Monsoo' had taken advantage of their inexperience. My mother did not treat such affairs lightly and conferred with my father on the subject. With him, justice was swiftly executed. He instantly sent for that rogue, the Frenchman. He was informed that 'Monsoo' was giving me my lesson. My father went up to my room.

At that moment Beaupré was on the bed, sleeping the sleep of the innocent. I was amusing myself in my own way. I should say that a geographical map had been sent from Moscow for me. It used to hang on the wall, where it was put to no use whatever, and I had long been tempted by the size and quality of its paper. I decided to make a kite of it and, taking advantage of the sleeping Beaupré, I set to work. My father came in at the very moment I was fitting a bast tail to the Cape of Good Hope. Seeing the extent of my geographical exercises, my father boxed me round the ear; then, hastening over to Beaupré, he roused him in extremely brusque fashion and began to heap reproaches upon him. In his confusion, Beaupré attempted to stand up but was unable to do so: the unfortunate Frenchman was dead drunk. As well be hanged for a sheep as for a lamb. My father lifted him off the bed by his collar, pushed him out of the door and banished him from the premises that very same day, to the indescribable joy of Savelyitch. Thus ended my education.

I now lived a life of youthful leisure, chasing pigeons and playing leap-frog with the other boys on the estate. Meanwhile, I had turned sixteen, and at that point my fate underwent a change.

One autumn day, my mother was making some honey-jam in the parlour while I, licking my lips, looked on at the boiling scum. My father was sitting at the window, reading the *Court Calendar* which he received annually. This book always had a powerful effect upon him: he would read it with particular interest, and his reading of it always stirred his bile in the most remarkable fashion. My mother, who had a sure knowledge of all his ways and habits, always endeavoured to shove the wretched book as far out of sight as possible, and in this way the *Court Calendar* would sometimes evade his eyes for whole months at a time. But when my father did happen to find it, he would not let it out of his hands for hours on end. Thus, my father was reading the *Court Calendar*, from time to time shrugging his shoulders and muttering:

'Lieutenant-general . . . ! He was a sergeant in my company . . .! Knight of both Russian orders . . . ! How long ago was it that we . . . ?'

At length my father flung the *Calendar* down on the sofa and sank into a reverie, a habit of his which boded nothing but ill.

Suddenly he turned to my mother.

'Avdotya Vassilyevna, how old is Petrusha?'

'He's nearly seventeen,' replied my mother. 'Petrusha was born the same year that aunt Nastasya Gerassimovna lost her eye, and when . . .'

'Very well,' interrupted my father. 'It's time he entered the Service. He's had enough of running about the maids' workrooms and climbing the dovecotes.'

The thought that she should soon be parted from me had such an effect upon my mother that she dropped the spoon into the saucepan, and the tears poured down her face. My own delight, on the other hand, could scarcely be described. The thought of the Service was connected in my mind with thoughts of freedom and the pleasures of life in Petersburg. I pictured myself as an officer of the Guards – in my opinion, the summit of worldly happiness.

My father liked neither to alter his intentions nor to delay their execution. A day was appointed for my departure. On the evening before, my father announced that he proposed to send a letter by me to my future commanding officer and he demanded pen and paper.

'Don't forget, Andrey Petrovitch,' my mother said, 'to send my best wishes to Prince B**, and say that I hope he'll treat Petrusha kindly.'

'What nonsense is this!' my father replied, frowning. 'Why should I be writing to Prince B**?'

'But you said a moment ago that you were going to write to Petrusha's commanding officer.'

'Well, and so what?'

'But Petrusha's commanding officer is Prince B**. Petrusha's registered with the Semyonovsky Regiment.'

'Registered! What do I care whether he's registered? Petrusha's not going to Petersburg. What would he learn by serving in Petersburg? To squander his money and behave like a rake. No, let him serve in the real army; let him learn to toil and drudge, to smell powder; let him be a soldier and not a mere idler. Registered with the Guards! Where's his passport? Bring it here.'

My mother got out my passport, which she kept in her little box together with my christening robe, and gave it to my father with a trembling hand. My father read it through carefully, put it on the table before him and began his letter.

I was tormented by curiosity. Where was I to be sent, if not to Petersburg? I could not tear my eyes away from my father's pen which moved slowly enough over the paper. At last he finished, sealed the letter in the same packet as my passport, removed his spectacles and, calling me to him, said:

'Here is a letter for Andrey Karlovitch R**, an old friend and comrade of mine. You're going to Orenburg to serve under his command.'

And so all my brilliant hopes were shattered! Instead of a gay life in Petersburg, boredom awaited me in some dreary and distant part of the country. The Service, which, until a moment before, I had thought of with such rapture, now struck me as a grievous misfortune. But it was useless to argue.

On the morning of the following day a travelling-carriage was brought round to the steps; in it were packed my trunk and a hamper containing a tea-service and parcels of buns and pies – final tokens of home indulgence. My parents gave me their blessing. My father said to me:

'Goodbye, Pyotr. Serve faithfully whom you have sworn to serve; obey your superiors, do not seek their favours; don't thrust yourself forward for service, but don't shirk your duty; and remember the proverb: "Look after your clothes when they're new and your honour when it's young."'

My mother tearfully besought me to take care of my health, and Savelyitch to watch over his charge. They helped me on with my hareskin coat and, over that, another one of fox fur. I sat down in the carriage with Savelyitch and set off on my journey, the tears streaming down my face.

That same night I arrived at Simbirsk where I was to spend the whole of the next day so that Savelyitch, who had been entrusted with the task, could buy several articles I needed. I stayed at an inn. In the morning, Savelyitch set off for the shops. Tired of looking out of the window on to a dirty alley-way, I began to wander about the other rooms of the inn. Entering the billiards-room, I saw a tall gentleman of about thirty-five with a long black moustache; he was in his dressing-gown and had a cue in one hand and a pipe between his teeth. He was playing with the marker, who drank down a glass of vodka every time he won, but who, when he lost, was obliged to crawl on all fours under the billiard-table. I stopped to watch them play. The longer the game went on, the more frequently did the marker have to crawl about on all fours, until eventually he remained beneath the table. The gentleman uttered several forceful expressions over him as a sort of funeral oration and invited me to have a game with him. Not knowing how to play, I refused. This seemed to strike him as strange. He looked at me as if with commiseration. However, we got into conversation and I learned that he was called Ivan Ivanovitch Zurin, that he was a captain in the *** Hussar Regiment, that he was in Simbirsk for the reception of some recruits, and that he was staying at the inn.

Zurin invited me to take pot-luck and dine with him in military fashion. I readily accepted his invitation. We sat down at table. Zurin drank a great deal and urged me to do the same, saying that I must become accustomed to the ways of the Service. He related several military anecdotes which nearly made me die of laughter, and we got up from the table firm friends. He then offered to teach me to play billiards.

'It's essential that we soldiers should know how to play. On the march, for instance, you arrive at some small town. How are you going to amuse yourself? One can't always be beating up the Jews. And so, for want of something better, you go to the inn and start to play billiards; and to do that you must know how to play!'

I was completely convinced and set about learning the game with great diligence. Zurin loudly encouraged me, showed surprise at my rapid progress and after a few lessons proposed that we should play for money – only a small stake and not for the sake of gain, but merely so we should not play for nothing, which he held to be a most odious practice. I agreed with him, and Zurin ordered some punch which he persuaded me to try, repeating that I must get used to the life in the Service. What kind of a Service would it be without punch! I obeyed him. In the meantime we continued our game. The more frequently I sipped from my glass, the more daring I became. The balls kept flying across the cushions. I became heated, abused the marker, who was keeping the score heaven only knows how, increased the stake from time to time – in short, behaved like a boy with his first taste of freedom. Meanwhile time slipped imperceptibly by. Zurin glanced at his watch, put down his cue, and announced that I had lost one hundred roubles. I was somewhat confused by this declaration. Savelyitch had my money. I began to apologise. Zurin interrupted me:

'Pray, don't bother yourself worrying. I can wait, and meanwhile let's go to Arinushka's.'

What would you have me do? I finished the day as dissolutely as I had begun it. We had supper at Arinushka's. Zurin kept filling my glass, repeating that I must get used to the ways of the Service. When I rose from the table, I could scarcely stand up straight. At midnight Zurin drove me back to the inn.

Savelyitch met us on the steps. He groaned as he saw the unmistakable signs of my enthusiasm for the Service.

'What's happened to you, master?' he said in a sorrowful voice. 'Wherever did you get so drunk? Oh Lord, never before have you done such a dreadful thing!'

'Silence, you old grumbler!' I replied in an unsteady voice. 'You must be drunk yourself. Go to sleep . . . and put me to bed.'

I woke the next morning with a splitting headache and a hazy recollection of the events of the previous evening. My reflections were interrupted by Savelyitch, who entered my room with a cup of tea.

'You've started early on your pranks, Pyotr Andreitch,' he said, shaking his head. 'And who is it that you take after? Certainly, neither your father nor grandfather were drunkards. It goes without saying that your mother isn't – since the day of her birth she has never touched anything but kvass. Who is to blame for all this? That accursed "Monsoo". He was for ever running round to Antipyevna's with "*Madame, zhe voo pree, vodkyoo.*" Well there's *zhe voo pree* for you! It can't be denied that son of a bitch taught you some pretty habits! And why was the infidel tutor engaged for you in the first place – as if the master hadn't enough of his own people!'

I was ashamed. I turned away from him and said:

'Go away, Savelyitch. I don't want any tea.'

But it was a difficult matter to quieten Savelyitch when he was bent on delivering a sermon.

'Now you can see, Pyotr Andreitch, what it is to get drunk. You've got a bad head and don't want to eat anything. A man who drinks is fit for nothing. Drink up some cucumber pickle with honey or, best of all for the morning after, half a glass of home-made brandy. What do you say?'

At that moment a boy entered the room and handed me a note from Ivan Ivanovitch Zurin. I opened it and read the following:

> '*Dear Pyotr Andreyevitch,*
> '*Be so good as to send me, by the boy, the hundred roubles you lost to me yesterday. I am in urgent need of money.*
> '*Always at your service,*
> '*Ivan Zurin*'

There was nothing for it. I assumed an air of indifference and turning to Savelyitch, who was my treasurer, housekeeper and agent all in one, I ordered him to give the boy one hundred roubles.

'What? Why? What for?' asked the astonished Savelyitch.

'I owe them to him,' I replied as coolly as I could.

'Owe!' exclaimed Savelyitch, becoming more and more astonished. 'And when, master, did you find time to get into his debt? I don't like the sound of this. You may do as you please, master, but I'm not going to give you the money.'

I thought that if, at this decisive moment, I did not gain

the upper hand of the obstinate old man, it would be difficult to free myself from his tutelage later on, and so, looking
at him haughtily, I said:

'I am your master and you are my servant. It is my money.
I lost it gambling because I took it into my head to do so. I
advise you not to philosophise about it and do as you are
told.'

Savelyitch was so struck by my words that he clasped his
hands and stood as if turned to stone.

'What are you standing there like that for?' I shouted
angrily.

Savelyitch began to weep.

'Pyotr Andreitch, my dear,' he said in a trembling voice,
'do not cause me to die of a broken heart. Light of my life,
listen to me, an old man! Write to that brigand and say that
you were joking, that we are not in the habit even of having
that much money. One hundred roubles! God be merciful!
Tell him that your parents expressly forbade you to gamble
with anything but nuts . . .'

'That's enough!' I interrupted him severely. 'Hand over
the money or I'll throw you out by the scruff of your neck.'

Savelyitch looked at me with the deepest grief and went
to fetch my debt. I felt sorry for the poor old man, but I
wanted to assert my independence and show him that I was
no longer a child. The money was delivered to Zurin.
Savelyitch made haste to take me away from the accursed
inn. He came to me with the news that the horses were ready.
With an uneasy conscience and filled with silent remorse, I
left Simbirsk, without saying goodbye to my billiards-teacher
and without thinking that I should ever see him again.

Chapter Two

THE GUIDE

> *O land of mine,*
> *Unfamiliar land!*
> *It is not I who wished to go to you,*
> *It is not my good horse which took me,*
> *But youth and liveliness,*
> *A young man's spirit,*
> *And tavern wine.*

AN OLD SONG

My reflections during the journey were not particularly agreeable. My loss, in terms of the value of money at that time, was of no small importance. In my heart, I could not but confess that my behaviour at the inn in Simbirsk had been foolish, and I felt guilty before Savelyitch. All this distressed me. The old man sat sullenly on the box, his face turned away from me and but for an occasional sigh he was silent. I wanted at all costs to make it up with him but I did not know how to begin. Finally, I said to him:

'Come now, Savelyitch! That's enough, let us be friends. It was all my fault; I can see myself that I was wrong. I behaved extremely foolishly yesterday and offended you for no reason. I promise that I'll conduct myself more sensibly in future and listen to you. Now don't be angry. Let us make our peace.'

'Ah, Pyotr Andreitch, my dear,' he answered with a deep sigh. 'I'm angry with myself; it is I alone who am to blame.

How could I have left you alone in the inn! But what could I do? I was tempted by the devil: I took it into my head to drop in on the clerk's wife who is an old friend of mine. And there it is: I drop in on an old friend, and see what happens. A real calamity! How shall I ever be able to show myself before my master and mistress again? What will they say when they learn that their child is a drunkard and a gambler?'

In order to console poor Savelyitch, I gave him my word that in future I would not spend a single kopeck without his consent. He gradually calmed down, although from time to time, shaking his head, he continued to mutter to himself:

'One hundred roubles! It's no joke!'

I was drawing near to my destination. All around me stretched a desolate wilderness, intersected by hills and ravines. Everything was covered with snow. The sun was setting. The sledge was travelling along the narrow road or, to be more precise, along the track made by the sledges of the peasants. Suddenly, the driver began to look around him and eventually, taking off his cap, he turned to me and said:

'Won't you order me to turn back, sir?'

'Why?'

'The weather doesn't look too hopeful: the wind is beginning to rise. See how it's heaping up the newly-fallen snow.'

'There's no great harm in that.'

'And do you see over there?'

The driver pointed eastwards with his whip.

'I see nothing but white steppe and a clear sky.'

'But there – over there – that small cloud.'

Indeed, on the edge of the horizon, I saw a small white cloud, which at first I had wrongly taken for a distant hill. The driver explained to me that the little cloud presaged a snow-storm.

I had heard about the snow-storms in that part of the country, and knew that whole wagon-trains were sometimes buried by them. Savelyitch agreed with the driver and advised that we should turn back. But the wind did not strike me as being especially strong. I was hoping to be able to reach the next posting-station in good time, and ordered the driver to go on faster.

The driver set the horses at a gallop, but he still continued to look eastwards. The horses ran on harmoniously. The wind, meanwhile, was growing stronger every minute. The little cloud changed into a great white mass, which rose heavily, grew, and gradually began to spread across the whole sky. At first a fine snow – and then, suddenly, big snowflakes – began to fall. The wind howled; the storm burst upon us. In a moment the dark sky merged with the sea of snow; everything vanished.

'Well, sir,' cried the driver. 'We are in for it – a blizzard!'

I looked out of the sledge: all was darkness and whirl-wind. The wind howled with such ferocious violence that it seemed as though it were alive. Savelyitch and I became covered with snow. The horses slowed down to a walking pace and soon stopped altogether.

'Why don't you go on?' I asked the driver impatiently.

'What's the use?' he asked, jumping down from the box. 'God knows where we're going to as it is. There's no road and all around is darkness.'

I began to scold him. Savelyitch took his part.

'Why didn't you want to listen to him?' he said angrily. 'You should have returned to the posting-station, where you could have had some tea and slept undisturbed until morning, when the storm would have abated and we could have gone on. Anyway, what's the hurry? It would be all very well if we were going to a wedding!'

Savelyitch was right. There was nothing we could do. The snow was falling hard. A snowdrift was piling up around the sledge. The horses stood with heads bent, and from time to time a shudder would run through their bodies. Having nothing else to do, the driver kept walking round them, arranging the harness. Savelyitch grumbled. I looked everywhere around me in the hope of catching sight of some sign of a house or a road, but could distinguish nothing save the dense, whirling snow-storm . . . Suddenly I saw something black.

'Hey, driver!' I shouted. 'Look! What's that black thing over there?'

The driver began to peer in the direction I was pointing.

'Heaven knows, sir,' he said, sitting down in his seat again. 'It's certainly not a cart or a tree, and it seems to be moving. It must be a wolf or a man.'

I ordered him to drive towards the unknown object, which immediately started to move towards us. A couple of minutes later we had drawn level with the man.

'Hey, my good man!' the driver shouted to him. 'Do you know where the road is?'

'The road's here; I am standing on a firm strip,' the wayfarer replied, 'but what's the good in that?'

'Listen here, my man,' I said to him, 'do you know this part of the country? Can you take me to a night's lodgings?'

'I know the country well,' the wayfarer replied. 'Heaven be thanked, I have tramped and driven over it in every direction. But you can see what the weather's like: we would be sure to lose the way. You'd do better to stop here and wait – perhaps the storm will abate and the sky clear, and then we can find our way by the stars.'

His composure encouraged me. I had already resolved to commit myself into the hands of God and spend the night in the middle of the steppe, when suddenly the wayfarer climbed nimbly up on to the box and said to the driver:

'Heaven be thanked, there's a house nearby. Turn to the right and then go straight on.'

'But why should I turn to the right?' the driver asked with irritation. 'Where do you see the road? I know, I know, the horses don't belong to you and neither does the harness, so drive on, eh, drive on.'

The driver seemed to me to be right.

'Indeed,' I said, 'what makes you think that we're not far from a house?'

'Because the wind came from that direction,' the traveller replied, 'and I smelt smoke. That shows that there's a village nearby.'

His resourcefulness and keen sense of smell astonished me. I ordered the driver to go on. The horses stepped heavily through the thick snow. The sledge advanced slowly, now mounting a snowdrift, now sinking into a hollow, at one moment rolling to one side, at the next to the other. It was like being aboard a ship in a stormy sea. Savelyitch groaned as he continually jostled against my side. I let down the matting which served as a hood to the sledge, wrapped myself up in my cloak and dozed off, lulled by the song of the storm and by the rocking of our slow journey.

I had a dream which I have never been able to forget, and in which, to this day, I still see something prophetic when I compare it with the strange events of my life. The reader will forgive me for mentioning it since he probably knows from experience that man is naturally given to superstition, however great is his contempt for such prejudices.

I was in that condition of mind and feeling when reality gives way to dreaming and becomes merged into the hazy visions of the first stages of sleep. It seemed to me that the storm was still raging, and that we were still roaming about in the wilderness of snow . . . Suddenly I saw a gateway and drove into the courtyard of our estate. My first thought was one of fear that my father would be angry with me for my involuntary return to the paternal roof, and that he would look upon it as a deliberate act of disobedience. With a feeling of unease I jumped down from the sledge, and saw my mother coming down the steps to meet me, a look of deep grief upon her face.

'Quietly,' she says to me. 'Your father is ill and dying and wishes to take leave of you.'

Struck with fear, I follow her into the bedroom. I see that the room is weakly lit and that a collection of sad-faced people stand by the bed. I approach the bed softly; my mother raises the curtain and says:

'Andrey Petrovitch, Petrusha has arrived; he came back when he heard that you were ill. Give him your blessing.'

I went down on my knees and fixed my eyes on the sick man. But what's happened? . . . I see, in place of my father, a black-bearded peasant gaily looking at me.

Perplexed, I turned to my mother and said:

'What does this mean? This isn't my father. Why must I ask this peasant for his blessing?'

'It's all the same, Petrusha,' my mother answered me. 'This is your father by proxy. Kiss his hand and allow him to give you his blessing.'

I did not consent to this. Then the peasant leapt out of bed, seized an axe from behind his back and began to swing it about in every direction. I wanted to run . . . but I could not. The room was full of dead bodies; I kept stumbling against them and slipping in the pools of blood . . . The terrible peasant called to me gently and said:

'Don't be frightened. Come and receive my blessing.'

Horror and perplexity took hold of me . . . At that moment I awoke. The horses had stopped; Savelyitch was pulling my arm and saying:

'Get out, master, come on. We've arrived.'

'Where have we arrived?' I asked, rubbing my eyes.

'At a country inn. The Lord came to our aid, and we

bumped straight into the fence. Quickly, master, come and warm yourself.'

I got out of the sledge. The storm still continued, although with less violence. It was pitch dark. The innkeeper met us at the gate, holding a lantern under the skirt of his overcoat, and led me into a room which was small but reasonably clean; it was lit by a pine torch. On the wall hung a rifle and a tall Cossack cap.

The innkeeper, a Yaikian Cossack by birth, seemed to be a peasant of about sixty, still quite hale and fresh-faced. Savelyitch followed me in with the hamper and demanded a fire so that he could make some tea, which had never before seemed so necessary to me. The innkeeper went out to see to this.

'Where is the guide?' I asked Savelyitch.

'Here, your Honour,' replied a voice from above.

I looked up at the sleeping shelf above the stove and saw a black beard and two sparkling eyes.

'Well, friend, are you thoroughly frozen?'

'How otherwise in a single thin overcoat! But I'll be frank with you – I did have a sheepskin coat, but I pawned it yesterday with a publican. The frost did not seem to me to be so sharp.'

At that moment the innkeeper came in with a boiling samovar. I offered our guide a cup of tea; the peasant climbed down from the shelf. His appearance struck me as remarkable. He was about forty, of medium height, lean and broad-shouldered. His black beard was beginning to go grey; his large lively eyes were for ever darting about. His face had quite an agreeable but roguish expression to it. His hair had been cropped in a circle round his head; he wore a tattered overcoat and Tartar trousers. I handed him a cup of tea; he tasted it and pulled a face.

'Your Honour, be so good as to tell them to bring me a glass of wine; tea is not the drink for us Cossacks.'

I readily fulfilled his wish. The innkeeper took a square bottle and a glass from the cupboard, went up to him and, looking him in the face, said:

'Oh, so you're back in this area again! Where have you come from?'

My guide winked significantly and replied with this saying:

'I was flying about the kitchen-garden, pecking hempseed. The old woman threw a stone at me, but it missed. And what about your people?'

'Oh, our people!' replied the innkeeper, continuing the allegorical conversation. 'They were about to ring the bells for vespers, but the priest's wife refused to allow it: when the priest is out visiting, the devils play pranks in the graveyard.'

'Silence, uncle,' replied my vagabond. 'If it rains, there'll be mushrooms, and when there are mushrooms, there's a bark basket too. But now' – and here he winked again – 'hide your axe behind your back: the forester's about. Your Honour – your health!'

With these words he took his glass, crossed himself and drank down the contents in a single gulp. He then bowed to me and returned to his shelf.

I could not understand a single word of this thieves' slang at the time; but afterwards I guessed that it referred to the affairs of the Yaikian Army who had only just been brought to order after the revolt of 1772. Savelyitch listened with an air of profound displeasure. He kept looking suspiciously now at the innkeeper, now at the guide. The inn, or 'umyot' as it was called locally, lay on its own in the middle of the steppe, far from any village, and looked very much as though it was a thieves' meeting-place. But there was no help for it. It was impossible to think of continuing our journey. Savelyitch's anxiety gave me great amusement. Meanwhile, I made arrangements for the night and lay down on the bench. Savelyitch decided to make a place for himself on the stove;

the innkeeper lay down on the floor. Soon the whole hut was snoring and I fell into a deep sleep.

Waking rather late the following morning, I saw that the storm had abated. The sun was shining. The snow lay like a dazzling shroud over the boundless steppe. The horses were harnessed. I settled my account with the innkeeper, who charged us such a moderate sum that even Savelyitch made no attempt to quarrel and bargain with him as he usually did, and his suspicions of the previous evening vanished entirely from his head. I called the guide, thanked him for the help he had given us, and ordered Savelyitch to tip him half a rouble. Savelyitch frowned.

'Tip him half a rouble!' he said. 'What for? Because you were pleased to bring him with you to the inn. Do as you wish, master, but we haven't any half-roubles to spare. If we start handing round tips to everyone we meet, we'll soon be starving ourselves.'

I could not argue with Savelyitch. I had promised that he should be completely in charge of the money. I felt vexed, however, at not being able to reward the man who had rescued me, if not from utter disaster, at least from a very unpleasant situation.

'All right,' I said coldly, 'if you don't want to give him half a rouble, then give him something of mine to wear. He is too lightly dressed. Give him my hareskin coat.'

'Mercy on us, dear Pyotr Andreitch!' Savelyitch said. 'Why give him your hareskin coat? The dog will only sell it for a drink at the first pub he gets to.'

'It's none of your business, old man,' my vagabond said, 'whether I sell it or not. His Honour wishes to give me a coat from off his own shoulders: it is the will of your master, and your duty as a serf is not to argue but to obey.'

'Have you no fear of God, you brigand?' Savelyitch answered him in an angry voice. 'You can see that the child is still completely ignorant, and yet you are only too glad to take advantage of his innocence. Why do you want my master's coat? You'll not be able to fit it across your accursed shoulders.'

'Will you please be quiet,' I said, 'and bring the coat here immediately.'

'Good Lord above!' Savelyitch groaned. 'Your hareskin coat is almost brand-new! Give it to someone who deserves it, not to a bare-faced drunkard!'

However, the hareskin coat appeared. The peasant instantly began to try it on. Indeed, the coat, which even I had outgrown, was a little too tight on him. Nevertheless, he managed to struggle into it somehow, bursting the seams as he did so. Savelyitch nearly howled as he heard the stitches give way. The vagabond was extremely pleased with my present. He went with me to the sledge and said with a low bow:

'Thank you, your Honour! May the Lord reward you for your kindness. As long as I live, I shall never forget your goodness.'

He went his own way and I again set out on mine, paying no attention to Savelyitch's vexed condition, and I soon forgot about the snow-storm of the previous day, about my guide and the hareskin coat.

On arriving at Orenburg, I immediately presented myself to the general. I saw a tall man, already somewhat bent with age. His long hair was completely white. His old and faded uniform recalled a soldier of the time of the Empress Anna Ioannovna, and he spoke with a strong German accent. I handed him my father's letter. At his name, he glanced at me quickly.

'*Mein Gott!*' he said. 'It doesn't seem long ago that Andrey Petrovitch was himself your age, and now what a fine young son he's got for himself! *Ach*, how times flies!'

He unsealed the letter and began to read it in a low voice, making his own observations as he did so.

'"Esteemed Sir, Andrey Karlovitch, I hope that your Excellency..." Why so formal? Pshaw, he should be ashamed of himself! Of course, discipline before everything, but is that the way to write to an old comrade? ... "Your Excellency will not have forgotten..." Hm ... "And when with the late Field-Marshal Münnich ... in the campaign ... little Caroline also ..." *Ach, Bruder!* So he still remembers our old pranks? "Now to business ... I'm sending my young rascal to you ..." Hm ... "Handle him with hedgehog gloves ..." What are hedgehog gloves? It must be a Russian saying ... What does "handle him with hedgehog gloves" mean?' he repeated, turning to me.

'It means,' I replied, looking as innocent as I possibly could, 'to treat someone kindly, not to be too severe, to allow as much freedom as possible – that's "to handle with hedgehog gloves".'

'Hm, I understand ... "and do not allow him too much freedom ..." No, it's clear that "to handle with hedgehog gloves" doesn't mean that ... "Enclosed ... his passport ..." Where is it, though? Ah, here we are ... "Strike him off the register of the Semyonovsky Regiment ..." All right, all right: everything shall be done ... "Permit me to embrace you without ceremony and ... as an old friend and comrade ..." Ah, at last he's come to it! ... etc., etc. ... Well, my boy,' he said when he had finished reading the letter and had put my passport to one side, 'everything shall be attended to: you will be transferred as an officer into the *** regiment, and, so as not to lose time, you will leave tomorrow for the Belogorsky fortress, where you will be under the command of Captain Mironov, a good and honourable man. There you will see some real service and be taught the meaning of discipline. There's nothing for you to do here in Orenburg. Dissipation is harmful to a young man. Do me the favour of dining with me this evening.'

'It's getting worse and worse,' I thought to myself. 'What's the use of having been a sergeant in the Guards since the time I was in my mother's womb! Where has it led me? To the *** regiment, and to an out-of-the-way fortress on the borders of the Kirghiz-Kaissak steppes!'

I dined with Andrey Karlovitch, in company with his aged adjutant. A strict German economy governed the table, and I believe that the fear of an additional guest now and then at his bachelor's table was in part the cause of my speedy banishment to the garrison.

The next day I took my leave of the general and set out for my destination.

Chapter Three

THE FORTRESS

> *In this fortress we live,*
> *Bread we eat and water we drink,*
> *But when the fierce enemy*
> *Comes to try out our pies,*
> *A great feast we will prepare for our guests,*
> *And our cannon we will load with grape-shot.*
> SOLDIERS' SONG

> *They are old-fashioned people, dear sir.*
> FONVIZIN

The Belogorsky fortress was situated forty versts from Orenburg. The road ran along the steep bank of the Yaik. The river was not yet frozen and its leaden-coloured waves looked black and melancholy between the monotonous, snow-covered banks. Beyond it stretched the Kirghiz steppes. I was deep in reflection, for the most part of a gloomy nature. Garrison life held little attraction for me. I tried to picture Captain Mironov, my future commanding officer, and the picture that came to my mind was that of a strict, bad-tempered old man, knowing nothing outside the Service, and ready to put me under arrest on bread and water for the merest trifle. Meanwhile, it was beginning to grow dark. We were driving pretty fast.

'Is it far to the fortress?' I asked my driver.

'Not far,' he replied. 'You can see it over there.'

I looked around me in every direction, expecting to see menacing bastions, towers and a rampart; but all I could see was a little village surrounded by a thick wooden fence. On one side of it stood three or four haystacks, half-concealed beneath the snow; on the other, a dilapidated windmill with idly-hanging bark sails.

'But where is the fortress?' I asked in surprise.

'There it is,' replied the driver, indicating the little village, and as he spoke, we drove into it.

At the gates I saw an old cast-iron cannon; the streets were narrow and twisting; the cottages small and for the most part thatched. I ordered the driver to take me to the commandant, and a minute later the sledge stopped before a small wooden house, built on a rise in the ground near the church, which was also made of wood.

Nobody came out to meet me. I went up to the entrance and opened a door into the front hall. An old soldier, seated on a table, was sewing a blue patch on the elbow of a green uniform. I told him to announce me.

'Go in, my good chap,' the old soldier replied. 'Our people are at home.'

I entered a neat, clean room, furnished in the old-fashioned style. In one corner stood a china cupboard; attached to the wall was an officer's diploma, glazed and framed; in bright array around it hung cheap, coloured prints representing 'The Taking of Küstrin', 'The Taking of Ochakov', 'The Choice of a Bride' and 'The Cat's Funeral'. An old woman wearing a warm sleeveless jacket and with a handkerchief over her head was sitting at the window. She was unwinding some thread which a one-eyed old man in officer's uniform was holding outstretched in his hands.

'What can I do for you, good sir?' she asked, continuing with her work.

I replied that I had come to enter the Service and to present myself to the captain in accordance with my duty, and with these words I turned to the one-eyed old man, whom I took to be the commandant. The lady of the house, however, interrupted the speech that I had prepared.

'Ivan Kuzmitch is not at home,' she said. 'He has gone to visit Father Gerassim; but it's all the same, dear sir, for I am his wife. I hope that we shall become friends. Please sit down.'

She summoned the maid and ordered her to call for the sergeant. The old man looked at me curiously with his one eye.

'May I venture to ask,' he said, 'in which regiment you have been serving?'

I satisfied his curiosity.

'And may I ask,' he continued, 'why you have transferred from the Guards to this garrison?'

I replied that such was the wish of the authorities.

'For conduct unbecoming an officer of the Guards, I expect,' continued my tireless interrogator.

'That's enough of your chatter,' the captain's wife said to him. 'You can see that the young man is tired after his journey; he can't be bothered with listening to you . . . Hold your hands straighter now . . . And you, my good sir,' she continued, turning to me, 'you mustn't grieve at being sent to this god-forsaken place. You are not the first, and you won't be the last. You will grow to like it after a time. Shvabrin – Alexey Ivanytch – was transferred to us five years ago for manslaughter. Heaven knows what made him do it. You see, he went out of town with a lieutenant; they both had their swords with them and soon started to prod each other, and Alexey Ivanytch stabbed the lieutenant – before a couple of witnesses at that! Well, there you are – the most learned are liable to err.'

At that moment, the sergeant, a well-built young Cossack, entered the room.

'Maximytch,' the captain's wife addressed him, 'find some quarters for this officer and make sure that they're clean.'

'As you say, Vassilissa Yegorovna,' the sergeant replied. 'Could his Honour not lodge at Ivan Polezhayev's?'

'Don't talk nonsense, Maximytch,' said the captain's wife. 'Polezhayev's is crowded out as it is. Anyway, he's a friend of mine and will remember that we are his superiors. Take the officer ... what is your name, my dear sir?'

'Pyotr Andreitch.'

'Take Pyotr Andreitch to Semyon Kuzov's. It was he, the rascal, who allowed his horse into my kitchen-garden. Well, and is everything in order, Maximytch?'

'Everything's all right, heaven be thanked!' the Cossack replied. 'Only Corporal Prokhorov had a fight in the bath-house with Ustinya Negulina over a tub of hot water.'

'Ivan Ignatyitch,' said the captain's wife to the one-eyed old man, 'find out which of the two, Prokhorov or Ustinya, is to blame and then punish them both. Well, Maximytch, go now and may God be with you. Pyotr Andreitch, Maximytch will accompany you to your quarters.'

I bowed and took my leave. The sergeant led me to a cottage standing on the steep bank of the river at the extreme end of the fortress. One half of the cottage was occupied by the family of Semyon Kuzov, and the other half was given over for my own use. It consisted of one fairly clean room, divided into two by a partition. Savelyitch began to unpack while I stood looking out of the narrow window. The gloomy steppe stretched away before me. On one side stood a few small cottages; several chickens were wandering about in the street. An old woman, standing on the steps with a trough in her hands, was calling to some pigs, who were answering her with good-natured grunts. And this was the spot in which I was fated to spend my youth! I was overcome by dejection. I came away from the window and went to bed without any supper, in spite of the exhortations of Savelyitch, who kept repeating:

'Good Lord above! He won't eat anything! What will the mistress say if the child is taken ill?'

The following morning, I had only just finished dressing when the door opened and a young officer, short and with a swarthy, extremely ugly but most lively face, entered my room.

'Forgive me,' he said in French, 'for coming so informally to make your acquaintance. I learned yesterday of your arrival; and the desire to see at last a new human face so overwhelmed me that I lost patience. You will understand this when you have lived here a little longer.'

I guessed that this was the officer who had been dismissed from the Guards for duelling. We quickly became acquainted. Shvabrin was certainly no fool. His conversation was sharp and entertaining. He gave me a most hilarious description of the commandant's family and friends, and the spot to which fate had brought me. I was laughing fit to burst when the same old soldier who had been mending his uniform in the commandant's front hall came into the room with an invitation from Vassilissa Yegorovna to dine with her and her husband. Shvabrin volunteered to go with me.

Approaching the commandant's house, we saw on the square about twenty old soldiers with long pig-tails and three-cornered hats. They were standing to attention. Before them stood the commandant, a tall, vigorous old man in a night-cap and nankeen dressing-gown. Seeing us, he came up, said a few kind words to me, and then continued to drill his men. We were going to stop and watch, but he asked us to go and join Vassilissa Yegorovna, promising that he would follow us.

'There's nothing for you to see here,' he added.

Vassilissa Ycgorovna received us simply and cordially and treated me as if she had known me all her life. The old soldier and Palashka were laying the table.

'And what's keeping my Ivan Kuzmitch so long at his drill today?' said the commandant's wife. 'Palashka, call your master in to dinner. And where is Masha?'

At that point a girl of about eighteen entered the room; she had a round, rosy face and light-brown hair, combed smoothly away behind her ears, which had gone quite red with embarrassment. I did not take to her very much at first sight. I looked at her with prejudiced eyes: Shvabrin had described Masha, the captain's daughter, as a perfect little fool to me. Marya Ivanovna sat down in a corner and began to sew. In the meantime, the cabbage-soup was brought in. Vassilissa Yegorovna, seeing that her husband was still absent, sent Palashka for a second time to fetch him.

'Tell your master that the guests are waiting and that the soup will get cold. Thank heaven the drill isn't going to run away; he'll have plenty of time to shout himself hoarse later on.'

The captain soon appeared, accompanied by the little one-eyed old man.

'What's been keeping you, my dear?' his wife said to him. 'The food's been ready for an age, yet you wouldn't come in.'

'But I was taken up with my service duties, Vassilissa Yegorovna,' replied Ivan Kuzmitch: 'I was instructing my soldiers.'

'That'll do!' retorted the captain's wife. 'It's all a lot of chatter about your instructing the soldiers; they're not fit for the Service and you don't know the first thing about it either. You would do better to stay at home and pray to God. My dear guests, please take your seats at the table.'

We sat down to dinner. Vassilissa Yegorovna never stopped talking for a single moment and overwhelmed me with questions. Who were my parents? Were they alive? Where did they live, and how much were they worth? On hearing that my father had three hundred serfs, she exclaimed:

'Fancy that now! There really are some rich people in the world! And we, my dear, have only got the one maid, Palashka; but, thank God, we live well enough. Masha is a problem though – she's of marriageable age, but what has she got for a dowry? A fine tooth-comb, a broom and three kopecks (God forgive me!) for a visit to the bath-house. It'll be all right if she can find a good man; if not, however, she'll have to resign herself to being left on the shelf.'

I glanced at Marya Ivanovna; she had blushed all over, and tears were even dropping into her plate. I felt sorry for her, and hastened to change the conversation.

'I have heard,' I said somewhat inconsequentially, 'that the Bashkirs are forming up for an attack on your fortress.'

'Whom did you hear that from, sir?' asked Ivan Kuzmitch.

'I was told so in Orenburg,' I replied.

'It's all rubbish!' said the commandant. 'We've heard nothing of them for a long time. The Bashkirs are a frightened lot now, and the Kirghiz have been taught a lesson, too. Have no fear that they'll attack us; if they tried anything like that, I'd give them such a ticking off as would keep them quiet for the next ten years.'

'And aren't you frightened,' I said, turning to the captain's wife, 'to remain in a fortress which is exposed to such dangers?'

'It's just a question of habit, my dear,' she replied. 'Twenty years ago, when we were transferred here from the regiment – heavens above, how terrified I was of those accursed infidels! If I happened to catch a glimpse of their lynx caps, or if I heard their shrieking – believe me, my heart would freeze!

But now I have got so used to it that I wouldn't move a fraction if someone were to tell me that the villains were prowling round the fortress.'

'Vassilissa Yegorovna is a very brave woman,' Shvabrin observed solemnly. 'Ivan Kuzmitch can bear witness to that.'

'Yes, indeed,' said Ivan Kuzmitch, 'my wife isn't one of the timid sort.'

'And Marya Ivanovna?' I asked. 'Is she also as brave as you?'

'Masha brave?' her mother replied. 'No, Masha is a coward. Even now, she can't bear to hear the report of a gun; it makes her tremble all over like a leaf. And when, two years ago, Ivan Kuzmitch took it into his head to fire our cannon on my name-day, the little darling nearly died of fright. Since that date we've never fired the accursed cannon again.'

We rose from the table. The captain and his wife went off to lie down; I went to Shvabrin's quarters, where we spent the whole evening together.

Chapter Four

THE DUEL

> *Right then, take up your stance,*
> *And you will see how I shall run your*
> *person through!*
>
> KNYAZHNIN

Several weeks passed and my life in the Belogorsky fortress became not only endurable, but even pleasant. I was received as one of the family in the commandant's house. Both husband and wife were most worthy people. Ivan Kuzmitch, who had risen from the ranks, was a simple, uneducated man, but extremely honest and kind. His wife ruled him, which suited his easy-going nature. Vassilissa Yegorovna looked upon the affairs of the Service in the same way as she regarded her own household duties and controlled the fortress as she did her own home. Marya Ivanovna soon ceased to be shy with me. We became friends. I found her a sensible and feeling girl. Imperceptibly, I grew attached to this kind family and even to Ivan Ignatyitch, the one-eyed garrison lieutenant, for whom Shvabrin had invented an illicit relationship with Vassilissa Yegorovna, an accusation devoid of even a vestige of truth; however, Shvabrin did not worry about that.

I received my commission. My service duties were no burden to me. In this God-protected fortress, there were neither parades, nor drill nor guard-duty. The commandant sometimes instructed the soldiers for his own amusement;

but he had not yet been able to teach all of them the difference between their right and left hands, although many, so
as not to make a mistake, crossed themselves at each turn.
Shvabrin owned several French books. I began to read them,
and a taste for literature awakened in me. In the mornings
I read, practised translating, and sometimes wrote verse. I
almost always dined at the commandant's, where I usually
spent the rest of the day and whither, sometimes of an
evening, Father Gerassim repaired with his wife, Akulina
Pamfilovna, the biggest gossip in the entire neighbourhood.
Alexey Ivanytch Shvabrin, needless to say, I saw every day;
his conversation, however, I found increasingly less agreeable. His incessant jokes at the expense of the commandant's
family greatly displeased me, and in particular, his sarcastic
comments about Marya Ivanovna. There was no other society
in the fortress, and I wished for no other.

Despite predictions, the Bashkirs did not rise. Peace reigned
over our fortress. But this peace was suddenly interrupted by
internal dissension.

I have already mentioned that I was occupying myself with
literature. My attempts, for those days, were tolerable, and
Alexandr Petrovitch Sumarokov praised them highly a few
years later. One day I succeeded in writing a song which
greatly satisfied me. It is well-known that authors, under
pretext of seeking advice, sometimes attempt to find a benevolent listener. And so, having written my song, I took it to
Shvabrin, the only person in the whole fortress with any poetical appreciation. After a few introductory words, I drew my
notebook from my pocket and read him the following lines:

> *'I banish thoughts of love and try*
> *My fair one to forget;*
> *And to be free again I fly*
> *From Masha with regret.*

'But wheresoever I may go,
Those eyes I still do see.
My troubled soul no peace may know,
There is no rest for me.

'Oh, when thou dost learn my torment,
Pity, Masha, oh pity me!
My cruel fate is plain to see—
I am prisoner held by thee.'

'What do you think of it?' I asked Shvabrin, expecting the praise I certainly felt entitled to. But to my great irritation, Shvabrin, who was usually pretty indulgent, resolutely announced that my song was bad.

'Why?' I asked him, concealing my annoyance.

'Because,' he replied, 'such verses are of the kind my tutor, Vasily Kirilitch Tredyakovsky, would write, and remind me very much of his love couplets.'

Here he took my notebook from me and mercilessly began to tear every verse and every word to bits, sneering at me in the most sarcastic fashion. I could not stand it and, tearing my book from his hands, I told him I would never again show him my verses. Shvabrin made fun of this threat, too.

'We'll see,' he said, 'if you keep your word. Every poet needs an audience, just as Ivan Kuzmitch needs his quota of vodka before dinner. And who is this Masha, to whom you confess your tender passion and amorous grief? Not Marya Ivanovna by any chance?'

'It's none of your business,' I replied, frowning, 'who this Masha is. I ask neither for your opinion nor your conjectures.'

'Oho, the proud poet and discreet lover!' Shvabrin continued, irritating me more and more. 'But listen to the advice of a friend: if you wish to succeed, don't write songs.'

'What do you mean, sir? Be good enough to explain yourself.'

'With pleasure. I mean that if you wish that Masha Mironov should meet you at dusk, give her, instead of your tender verses, a pair of earrings.'

My blood boiled.

'Why do you have such an opinion of her?' I asked, with difficulty restraining my indignation.

'Because,' he replied with a devilish smile, 'I know her nature and habits from experience.'

'You're lying, you scoundrel!' I exclaimed with rage. 'You're lying in the most shameless fashion.'

Shvabrin's expression changed.

'That will not be overlooked,' he said, gripping my hand. 'You will give me satisfaction.'

'Certainly. Whenever you wish,' I replied, delighted.

At that moment I was ready to tear him to pieces.

I instantly made my way to Ivan Ignatyitch, whom I found with a needle in his hand: the commandant's wife had charged him with the task of threading mushrooms to be dried for use in winter.

'Ah, welcome, Pyotr Andreitch!' he said, seeing me. 'For what purpose has God brought you here, may I ask?'

Briefly I explained that I had had a quarrel with Alexey Ivanytch, and that I had come to ask him, Ivan Ignatyitch, to be my second. Ivan Ignatyitch listened attentively, staring at me with his single eye.

'You mean to say,' he said, 'that you want to kill Alexey Ivanytch, and that you would like me to be a witness to it? Is that so, may I ask?'

'Exactly so.'

'Mercy on us, Pyotr Andreitch! Whatever are you thinking of? You've quarrelled with Alexey Ivanytch – a great misfortune! Words do no injury. He has insulted you, and you have given it to him hot. He lands you a punch on the nose, you give him a box on the ear, another, a third – and then each goes his own way and before long we make the peace between the two of you. Is it right to kill one's fellow man, may I ask? If you were to kill Alexey Ivanytch – all right; I wouldn't care much; I'm not too keen on him myself. But what if he were to run you through? What then? Who would be the loser then, may I ask?'

The logic of the sensible lieutenant had no effect on me. I held to my intention.

'As you wish,' said Ivan Ignatyitch. 'Do as you like. But why should I be a witness to it? To what purpose? People fight, but what's so wonderful about that, may I ask? Heaven be thanked, I've fought against the Swedes and the Turks, and I have seen enough fighting!'

I tried to explain to him as best I could the duties of a second, but Ivan Ignatyitch could not understand me at all.

'Do as you wish,' he said, 'but if I am to be involved in this affair, it will be to go to Ivan Kuzmitch and report to him, as is my duty, that a crime against the interests of the State is being plotted within the fortress, and to ask him to take the necessary measures . . .'

I became alarmed and besought Ivan Ignatyitch not to say anything about it to the commandant. I persuaded him with difficulty; he gave me his word, and I gave up the idea of seeking his active assistance.

As usual, I spent the evening at the commandant's house. I tried to appear gay and indifferent, so as not to arouse suspicion and to avoid a lot of troublesome questions; but I confess that I did not share that coolness which people in my position almost always boast about. That evening I felt disposed to be tender and emotional. I found Marya Ivanovna more than usually attractive. The thought that perhaps I was seeing her for the last time endowed her, in my eyes, with something rather touching. Shvabrin was there too. I took him aside and informed him of my conversation with Ivan Ignatyitch.

'Why should we have seconds?' he said drily. 'We can do without them.'

We agreed to fight behind the haystacks near the fortress, and to be there by seven o'clock the next morning. We appeared to be conversing together in such a friendly fashion that Ivan Ignatyitch nearly let the cat out of the bag in his joy.

'You should have arrived at that long ago,' he said to me with a satisfied expression. 'A bad peace is better than a good quarrel, and an unscarred body more important than honour.'

'What's that, Ivan Ignatyitch?' said the commandant's wife, who was sitting in the corner, telling her fortune by the cards. 'What's that? I did not hear you.'

Ivan Ignatyitch, noting my signs of displeasure and remembering his promise, grew confused and did not know how to reply. Shvabrin came to his rescue.

'Ivan Ignatyitch,' he said, 'approves our reconciliation.'

'And with whom have you been quarrelling, my dear?'

'I had a quite serious row with Pyotr Andreitch.'

'What about?'

'The merest trifle – about a song, Vassilissa Yegorovna.'

'What a thing to quarrel about – a song! How did it happen?'

'In this way: not long ago Pyotr Andreitch composed a song and, while he was singing it to me today, I struck up with my favourite ditty:

> *'Captain's daughter, oh captain's daughter,*
> *Walk not out at the midnight hour.'*

'Discord arose. Pyotr Andreitch became angry, but then considered that everyone is free to sing what he likes, and there the matter ended.'

Shvabrin's brazenness nearly sent me out of my mind with fury; nobody but myself, however, understood his coarse insinuations – at any rate, nobody paid any attention to them. From songs the conversation turned to poets, and the commandant observed that they were all utterly dissolute and terrible drunkards, and advised me, as a friend, to give up writing verse, since such activities did not go with service life and led to nothing but bad.

Shvabrin's presence was intolerable to me. I soon took leave of the commandant and his family. When I got home, I examined my sword, tested its point and went to bed after giving Savelyitch instructions to wake me soon after six o'clock.

At the appointed hour on the following morning, I stood behind the haystacks awaiting my adversary. He soon appeared.

'We may be disturbed,' he said to me, 'so we'll have to be quick.'

We took off our uniforms and, wearing our waistcoats only, we drew our swords. At that moment Ivan Ignatyitch, with about five old soldiers, suddenly appeared from behind a haystack. He summoned us to the commandant. Unwillingly, we obeyed him. The soldiers surrounded us and we set off for the fortress, following after Ivan Ignatyitch who, walking with extreme importance, led us in triumph.

We entered the commandant's house. Ivan Ignatyitch opened the door, and announced triumphantly:

'Here they are!'

Vassilissa Yegorovna met us.

'Ah, my good men! Now what's all this about? How? What? You planned to commit murder in our fortress? Ivan Kuzmitch, place them under arrest immediately! Pyotr

Andreitch, Alexey Ivanytch, surrender your swords this instant! Hand them over now, hand them over! Palashka, take these swords into the lumber-room. Pyotr Andreitch, I did not expect this of you! Aren't you ashamed of yourself? It's all right for Alexey Ivanytch – he was expelled from the Guards for killing a man and he does not believe in God. But you? Do you wish to follow in his footsteps?'

Ivan Kuzmitch agreed fully with everything his wife said, and kept saying:

'Yes, indeed, Vassilissa Yegorovna is speaking the truth. Duels are expressly forbidden by the regulations.'

In the meantime, Palashka took our swords and carried them off to the lumber-room. I could not help bursting into laughter. Shvabrin preserved his solemnity.

'With all due respect to you,' he said to her coldly, 'I cannot but observe that you cause yourself unnecessary trouble in setting yourself up as our judge. Leave it to Ivan Kuzmitch – it is his affair.'

'Ah, my good sir,' retorted the commandant's wife, 'are not husband and wife one in spirit and flesh? Ivan Kuzmitch, what are you gaping at? Have them separated at once and placed under arrest on bread and water until they've regained their proper senses. Then let Father Gerassim impose a penance on them, that they may pray to God for forgiveness and repent before all men.'

Ivan Kuzmitch did not know what to do. Marya Ivanovna was extremely pale. Little by little the storm abated; the commandant's wife calmed down and forced us to embrace one another. Palashka brought us back our swords. We left the commandant's house apparently reconciled. Ivan Ignatyitch accompanied us.

'Aren't you ashamed of yourself?' I asked angrily. 'Reporting us to the commandant after giving your word that you wouldn't?'

'As God is holy, I didn't say a word of it to Ivan Kuzmitch!' he replied. 'Vassilissa Yegorovna wormed it out of me. She arranged everything without the commandant knowing. Anyway, heaven be thanked that it's ended as it has!'

With these words he turned for home, and Shvabrin and I were left alone.

'Our affair cannot end here,' I said to him.

'Of course not,' replied Shvabrin. 'You will have to answer with your blood for your insolence, but they'll probably be keeping an eye on us. We will have to dissemble for a few days. Goodbye.'

And we parted as if nothing had happened.

Returning to the commandant's house, I sat down, as usual, near Marya Ivanovna. Ivan Kuzmitch was not at home. Vassilissa Yegorovna was occupied with household affairs. We conversed in an undertone. Marya Ivanovna reproached me tenderly for the anxiety my quarrel with Shvabrin had caused them all.

'I nearly fainted,' she said, 'when I heard that you intended to fight with swords. How strange men are! For a single word, which they would probably forget in a week, they are ready to murder each other and sacrifice not only their lives but their consciences, and the happiness of those who ... But I am sure that you were not the cause of the quarrel. Alexey Ivanytch was doubtless to blame.'

'And why do you think that, Marya Ivanovna?'

'Because ... because he is so sarcastic. I do not like Alexey Ivanytch. I find him very repulsive, and yet, strangely enough, not for anything would I have him dislike me. It would worry me dreadfully.'

'And what do you think, Marya Ivanovna? Does he like you or not?'

Marya Ivanovna stammered and blushed.

'It seems to me ...' she said, '... I think he does like me.'

'Why do you think that?'

'Because he asked me to marry him.'

'Marry! He asked you to marry him! When?'

'Last year. Two months before you arrived.'

'And you refused?'

'As you can see. Alexey Ivanytch, of course, is an intelligent man, of good family and rich; but when I think that I should have to kiss him beneath the crown before everyone . . . no, not for anything!'

Marya Ivanovna's words opened my eyes and explained many things to me. I now understood the persistent calumny with which Shvabrin pursued her. He had probably noticed our mutual attraction and had tried to turn us against each other. The words which had brought about our quarrel seemed all the more base to me when I recognised that they were not coarse, indecent mockery, but premeditated slander. My desire to chastise the insolent traducer became yet stronger within me, and I impatiently awaited a favourable opportunity to do so.

I did not have to wait long. The next day, as I sat composing an elegy and biting my pen in search of a rhyme, Shvabrin tapped at my window. I put my pen down, took up my sword and went out to him.

'Why delay any further?' Shvabrin said to me. 'Nobody's watching us. Let's go down to the river. We won't be disturbed there.'

We set off in silence. Stepping down a winding path, we stopped at the edge of the river and drew our swords. Shvabrin was more skilful than I, but I was stronger and more daring, and Monsieur Beaupré, who had once been a soldier, had given me several lessons in fencing, which I turned to good account. Shvabrin had not expected to find in me so dangerous an opponent. For a long time neither gave the other the opportunity to do any injury; at length, noticing that Shvabrin was weakening, I began to bear down upon him vigorously and almost forced him into the river itself. Suddenly I heard my name being loudly called. I glanced round and saw Savelyitch running down the steep path towards me ... At that same moment, I felt a sharp jab in my chest, just beneath my right shoulder. I fell and lost consciousness.

Chapter Five

LOVE

Ah, you maiden, pretty maiden!
Do not marry while you are yet so young;
You must ask your father, ask your mother;
Father, mother and all your kin;
Gather, maiden, wisdom and intelligence;
Wisdom and intelligence: these shall be your dowry.

FOLK SONG

If you find one better than me, you'll
forget me,
Worse than me, and you'll remember.

FOLK SONG

On recovering consciousness, I was unable for some time to collect my senses or understand what had happened to me. I was lying in bed in a strange room and felt extremely weak. Savelyitch was standing before me with a candle in his hand. Somebody was carefully unwinding the bandages which had been bound round my chest and shoulders. Gradually my thoughts cleared. I remembered the duel and guessed that I had been wounded. At that moment the door creaked.

'Well, how is he?' whispered a voice which sent a tremor through my body.

'Still in the same condition,' replied Savelyitch with a sigh. 'Still unconscious, and this is the fifth day now.'

I tried to turn my head but could not.

'Where am I? Who's there?' I said with an effort.

Marya Ivanovna came up to the bed and bent over me.

'Well, and how are you feeling?' she said.

'Heaven be thanked!' I replied in a weak voice. 'Is that you, Marya Ivanovna? Tell me . . .'

I had not the strength to continue and fell silent. Savelyitch gave a cry and his face lit up with joy.

'He has come to himself, he has come to himself!' he repeated. 'Thanks be to Thee, good Lord! Well, Pyotr Andreitch, my dear, what a fright you gave me! It was no joke – five whole days!'

Marya Ivanovna interrupted him.

'Don't talk to him too much, Savelyitch,' she said. 'He's still weak.'

She went out and closed the door softly behind her. My thoughts were in a turmoil. So I was in the commandant's house: Marya Ivanovna had been in to see me. I wanted to ask Savelyitch some questions, but the old man shook his head and stopped up his ears. Vexed, I closed my eyes and soon fell asleep.

When I awoke, I called Savelyitch, but, instead of him, I saw Marya Ivanovna standing before me. She greeted me in her angelic voice. I cannot describe the delightful sensation which took hold of me at that moment. I seized her hand and pressed it to me, watering it with tears of emotion. Masha did not withdraw it . . . and suddenly her lips touched my cheek and I felt their hot, fresh kiss. A surge of fire ran through me.

'Dear, good Marya Ivanovna,' I said to her, 'be my wife, consent to make me happy.'

She regained her composure.

'For Heaven's sake, keep calm,' she said, removing her hand from mine. 'You're not out of danger yet: your wound may reopen. Look after yourself, if only for my sake.'

With these words she left, leaving me in an ecstasy of bliss. Happiness revived me. She will be mine! She loves me! This thought filled my entire being.

From that moment I grew hourly better. The regimental barber – there was no other doctor in the fortress – treated my wound and, thank heaven, he did not try to be too clever. Youth and nature accelerated my recovery. I was nursed by the commandant's whole family. Marya Ivanovna never left my side. It goes without saying that, at the first favourable opportunity, I took up my interrupted declaration of love, and Marya Ivanovna listened to me with greater patience. Without any affectation she confessed her attachment to me, and said that her parents would undoubtedly be pleased at her happiness.

'But think it over well,' she added: 'won't there be some opposition on the part of your parents?'

I considered the matter. Of my mother's affection I had no doubts but, knowing my father's nature and way of thinking, I felt that my love would not move him very much and that he would regard it as a young man's fancy. I candidly confessed this to Marya Ivanovna but resolved, all the same, to write to my father as eloquently as I could and implore his paternal blessing. I showed the letter to Marya Ivanovna, who found it so convincing and moving that she had no doubts as to its success and abandoned herself to the feelings of her tender heart with all the confidence of youth and love.

I made peace with Shvabrin in the first days of my recovery. Ivan Kuzmitch, in reprimanding me for the duel, said:

'Well, I should really put you under arrest, Pyotr Andreitch, but you have been punished enough already without that. Alexey Ivanytch, however, I have placed under guard in the granary, and Vassilissa Yegorovna has got his sword under lock and key. It'll give him time to think it over and repent.'

I was too happy to cherish any feelings of hostility in my heart. I began to intercede for Shvabrin, and the good commandant agreed with his wife in deciding to set him free. Shvabrin called on me; he expressed deep regret for what had happened between us, confessed that he was entirely to blame and besought me to forget the past. Not being a resentful person by nature, I sincerely forgave him for the quarrel, and the wound I had received at his hands. I attributed his calumny to the vexation of wounded vanity and slighted love and magnanimously pardoned my unhappy rival.

I was soon well again and able to return to my own quarters. I impatiently awaited an answer to my letter, not daring to hope and trying to suppress my sad forebodings. I had not yet mentioned the matter to Vassilissa Yegorovna and her husband; my proposal, however, would come as no surprise to them. Neither I nor Marya Ivanovna made any attempt to conceal our feelings from them, and we felt certain of their consent beforehand.

At last one morning Savelyitch came into my room with a letter in his hand. I seized it with trembling fingers. The address was written in my father's hand. This prepared me for something important since it was usually my mother who wrote to me, he merely adding a few lines at the end.

For a long time I could not unseal the packet, but kept on reading the solemn superscription:

'To my son, Pyotr Andreyevitch Grinev,
The Belogorsky Fortress,
The Province of Orenburg.'

I attempted to divine from the handwriting the mood in which the letter had been written. At last I resolved to open it and saw from the first few lines that all my hopes were lost. The letter read as follows:

'My son Pyotr,

'Your letter, in which you ask us for our parental blessing and consent to your marriage with Marya Ivanovna, Mironov's daughter, reached us on the 15th of this month, and not only do I not intend to give you either my blessing or consent, but I propose to come and teach you a lesson for your pranks, as I would a small boy, in spite of your officer's rank; for you have shown that you are not yet worthy to carry the sword, entrusted to you for the defence of our native country and not for the purpose of fighting duels with other madcaps like yourself. I shall write instantly to Andrey Karlovitch, asking him to transfer you from the Belogorsky fortress to some place further away, where you will be cured of your folly. Your mother, on hearing the news of your duel and that you have been wounded, fell ill with grief and now lies in bed. What will become of you? I pray God that you will mend your ways, although I do not dare to hope in His great mercy.

'Your father, A.G.'

The reading of this letter aroused various feelings within me. The harsh expressions so unsparingly used by my father wounded me deeply. The disdain with which he referred to Marya Ivanovna seemed to me to be as unbecoming as it was unjust. The thought of my being transferred from the Belogorsky fortress appalled me, but the thing that grieved me most of all was the news of my mother's illness. I felt indignant with Savelyitch and had no doubt that it was he who had told my parents of my duel. After pacing up and down my narrow room, I stopped in front of him and said with a menacing look:

'It seems that you are not content that, thanks to you, I should be wounded and at death's door for a whole month; you wish to kill my mother as well.'

Savelyitch looked thunderstruck.

'In heaven's name, master,' he said, 'what do you mean? My fault that you were wounded? As God is my witness, I was running to shield you with my own chest from Alexey Ivanytch's sword! It was my age – curse it – that prevented me! But what have I done to your mother?'

'What have you done?' I replied. 'Who asked you to write back and inform against me? Have you been placed here to spy on me?'

'I wrote back and informed against you?' Savelyitch replied tearfully. 'Heavenly Father! Be pleased to read what my master has written to me: then you will see how I informed against you.'

He drew a letter from his pocket and I read the following:

'You should be ashamed of yourself, you old dog, for ignoring my strict instructions that you should write to me about my son, Pyotr Andreyevitch, and for leaving it to strangers to tell me of his pranks. Is this how you fulfil your duty and the will of your master? I will send you to tend pigs, you old dog, for concealing the truth and indulging the young man. On receipt of this, I order you to write back to me instantly and inform me of the present state of his health which, I am told, is better;

*also of the exact place of his wound and whether he has
been properly looked after.'*

It was clear that Savelyitch was completely innocent and
that I had been wrong to insult him with my reproaches
and suspicions. I asked his forgiveness, but the old man was
inconsolable.

'That I should have lived to see this!' he kept on repeating.
'These are the thanks I receive from my masters! I am an
old dog, and a swineherd and the cause of your wound as
well! No, my dear Pyotr Andreitch, it is not I, but that
accursed "Monsoo" who is to blame: it was he who taught
you to thrust with those iron spits and to stamp your feet, as
if by thrusting and stamping you could protect yourself from
a wicked man! And we had to take on that "Monsoo" and
throw good money down the drain!'

But who was it then who had taken it upon himself to
inform my father of my behaviour? The general? But he had
shown extremely little interest in me, and Ivan Kuzmitch
had not considered it necessary to report my duel to him. I
was lost in conjectures. My suspicions finally rested on
Shvabrin. He alone would profit by the denunciation, the
consequence of which could be my removal from the fortress
and my separation from the commandant's family. I went off
to tell Marya Ivanovna everything. She met me on the steps.

'What's happened to you?' she said when she saw me.
'How pale you are!'

'It's all over,' I replied, and I handed her my father's letter.

She in turn grew pale. Having read the letter, she returned
it to me with a trembling hand and said in an unsteady
voice:

'It was clearly not for me . . . Your parents do not want
me in your family. In all things may God's will be done!
God knows better than we what is good for us. There's

nothing to be done, Pyotr Andreitch; may you at any rate be happy . . .'

'This is not to be!' I cried, seizing her hand. 'You love me; I am prepared for anything. Let us go and throw ourselves at your parents' feet; they are simple people, not hard-hearted and proud . . . They will give us their blessing; we will be married . . . And then, in time, I'm sure we'll gain my father's approval; my mother will be on our side; he will forgive me . . .'

'No, Pyotr Andreitch,' Masha replied. 'I will not marry you without your parents' blessing. Without it you would never be happy. Let us submit to the will of God. If you find the one destined for you, if you grow to love another – God be with you, Pyotr Andreitch; I will pray for you both . . .'

She burst into tears and left me. I wanted to follow her into her room, but I felt in no condition to control myself and thus returned home.

I was sitting in my room, plunged in deep thought, when Savelyitch suddenly interrupted my reflections.

'Here, master,' he said, handing me a written sheet of paper. 'See whether I am here to inform against my master, or to try to stir up trouble between father and son.'

I took the paper from his hand: it was Savelyitch's answer to the letter he had received. Here it is, word for word:

'Dear Sir, Andrey Petrovitch, our gracious father!

'I have received your gracious letter in which you are pleased to be angry with me, your servant, telling me that I should be ashamed of myself for not fulfilling my master's orders; but I am not an old dog but your faithful servant, and I do obey my master's orders, and I have always served you zealously to my grey hairs. I did not write to you about Pyotr Andreitch's wound,

because I did not wish to alarm you for no reason, and I hear that the mistress, our mother Avdotya Vassilyevna took to her bed with fright and I will pray to God for her recovery. Pyotr Andreitch was wounded under the right shoulder, in the chest, immediately beneath the bone to the depth of one and a half vershoks, and he was put to bed in the commandant's house whither we carried him from the river-bank, and the local barber, Stepan Paramonov, treated him; and now, Pyotr Andreitch, thank God, is well, and I have nothing but good to write about him. I have heard that his superior officers are satisfied with him; and Vassilissa Yegorovna treats him as if he were her own son. And as for the incident that happened to him, the young man should not be reproached: a horse has four legs and yet it stumbles. It also pleased you to write that you will send me to tend pigs; be that your master's will. Herewith I humbly bow before you.

'Your faithful serf, Arkhip Savelyev'

I could not help smiling occasionally as I read the good old man's letter. I was in no condition to write an answer to my father, and Savelyitch's letter seemed sufficient to calm my mother's fears.

From that time my position changed. Marya Ivanovna scarcely ever spoke to me and in every way tried to avoid me. The commandant's house became hateful to me. I gradually grew accustomed to sitting by myself at home. Vassilissa Yegorovna reproached me for this at first but, noticing my obstinacy, she left me in peace. I only saw Ivan Kuzmitch when the Service demanded it. I rarely met Shvabrin, and then unwillingly, the more so since I noticed his veiled antipathy towards me, which confirmed me in my suspicions. My life became intolerable. I fell into a state of gloomy brooding, which was fed by loneliness and inaction. My love grew stronger in solitude and became more and more oppressive to me. I lost the desire for reading and literature. My spirits sank. I feared that I would either go out of my mind or give way to dissipation. Unexpected events, which were to have an important influence on my whole life, suddenly gave my soul a powerful and salutary shock.

Chapter Six

THE PUGACHEV RISING

Listen then, my young lads,
To what we, the old ones, will tell you.
SONG

Before proceeding to a description of the strange events of which I was a witness, I must say a few words concerning the situation in the province of Orenburg at the end of the year 1773.

This vast and rich province was inhabited by a number of half-savage peoples, who had but recently acknowledged the sovereignty of the Russian Tsars. Their continual risings, their unfamiliarity with laws and civic life, their thoughtlessness and cruelty demanded ceaseless vigilance on the part of the Government to keep them in subjection. Fortresses had been erected in suitable places and were garrisoned to a large extent by Cossacks, who had long since held possession of the banks of the Yaik. But these Yaikian Cossacks, whose duty it was to preserve peace and watch over the security of the district, had for some time themselves been a source of anxiety and danger to the Government. In 1772 an insurrection broke out in their principal township. It was caused by the stern measures taken by Major-General Traubenberg to enforce dutiful obedience from the troops. The outcome was the barbarous murder of Traubenberg, self-appointed changes in the administration and, eventually, the suppression of the revolt by cannon-shot and cruel punishments.

This occurred a short while before my arrival at the Belogorsky fortress. All was now quiet, or so it seemed: the authorities had too readily believed in the pretended repentance of the cunning rebels, who bore their malice in secret, and only awaited a suitable opportunity for a renewal of the disorders.

I will now return to my story.

One evening (it was at the beginning of October in the year 1773) I was sitting alone at home, listening to the howling of the autumn wind and staring out of the window at the clouds which raced past the moon. Someone arrived to tell me that I was wanted at the commandant's. I set off immediately for his house. There I found Shvabrin, Ivan Ignatyitch and the Cossack sergeant. Neither Vassilissa Yegorovna nor Marya Ivanovna were in the room. The commandant greeted me with an air of preoccupation. He closed the door, made us all sit down with the exception of the sergeant who was standing by the door and, drawing a paper from his pocket, he said to us:

'Gentlemen, I have important news! Listen to what the general writes.'

He then put on his spectacles and read out the following:

'*To the Commandant of the Belogorsky Fortress,*
Captain Mironov
CONFIDENTIAL
'*I hereby inform you that the fugitive and dissident*
Don Cossack, Yemelyan Pugachev, having committed
the unpardonable insolence of assuming the name of the
deceased Emperor Peter III, has collected a band of
evilly-disposed persons, has excited a revolt in the Yaikian
settlements, and has already taken and destroyed several
fortresses, looting and murdering on every side.
Therefore, on receipt of this, you, Captain, will at once
take the necessary measures to repel the above-mentioned
villain and pretender, and if possible, to annihilate him
totally, should he attack the fortress entrusted to your
care.'

'Take the necessary measures!' said the commandant, removing his spectacles and folding up the paper. 'As you know, it's easy enough to say. This villain is apparently powerful; and we have only got one hundred and thirty men in all, not counting the Cossacks, upon whom we can place little reliance – don't take that as a reproach, Maximytch.' (The sergeant smiled.) 'Still, we must do the best we can, gentlemen. Ensure that we are prepared and establish guard-duty and night patrols. In the event of an attack, close the gates and assemble the soldiers. You, Maximytch, keep a sharp eye on your Cossacks. Have the cannon inspected and thoroughly cleaned. Most important of all, keep all that I have told you to yourselves, so that nobody in the fortress knows about it beforehand.'

Having given these orders, Ivan Kuzmitch dismissed us. I walked away with Shvabrin, reflecting upon what we had heard.

'How do you think it'll end?' I asked him.

'God knows,' he replied. 'We shall see. At this stage I see nothing to be alarmed about. If, however . . .'

He then became thoughtful and began absent-mindedly to whistle a French air.

In spite of all our precautions, news of the appearance of Pugachev soon spread through the fortress. Ivan Kuzmitch, while having the greatest respect for his wife, would not for anything in the world have confided in her a secret entrusted to him in connection with the Service. On receipt of the general's letter, he managed fairly skilfully to get Vassilissa Yegorovna out of the way by telling her that Father Gerassim had received some remarkable news from Orenburg, which he was keeping as a great secret. Vassilissa Yegorovna immediately resolved to call on the priest's wife and, on the advice of Ivan Kuzmitch, took Masha with her, lest she should feel bored on her own.

Ivan Kuzmitch, in sole occupation of the house, had instantly sent for us, after locking Palashka in the lumber-room to prevent her from overhearing us.

Vassilissa Yegorovna returned home, without having succeeded in getting anything out of the priest's wife, and learned that Ivan Kuzmitch had held a council during her absence, and that Palashka had been under lock and key. She guessed that her husband had deceived her and immediately set about interrogating him. But Ivan Kuzmitch had prepared himself for the onslaught. Not in the least confused, he replied decisively to his inquisitive consort:

'You see, my dear, the women hereabouts have taken it into their heads to heat their stoves with straw, and since some misfortune might result from this, I have given strict instructions that from now on the women are not to heat their stoves with straw, but should use dry branches and brushwood instead.'

'But why did you have to lock up Palashka then?' asked

the commandant's wife. 'Why did the poor girl have to sit in the lumber-room until we returned?'

Ivan Kuzmitch was not prepared for such a question; he became confused and muttered something incoherently. Vassilissa Yegorovna perceived her husband's artfulness but, knowing that she would get nothing out of him, she ceased her questioning and changed the conversation to the pickled cucumbers Akulina Pamfilovna had prepared in some very special way. Vassilissa Yegorovna could not sleep a wink all that night, unable to guess what was in her husband's mind that she should not be allowed to know.

Returning from mass the following day, she saw Ivan Ignatyitch pulling from the cannon bits of rag, small stones, wood-chips, knuckle-bones and rubbish of every sort which had been stuffed into it by the children.

'What can these military preparations mean?' thought the commandant's wife. 'Can it be that they're expecting an attack from the Kirghiz? Surely Ivan Kuzmitch would not hide such trifles from me?'

She called Ivan Ignatyitch with the firm intention of discovering from him the secret which tormented her feminine curiosity.

Vassilissa Yegorovna made a few observations concerning her household affairs to him, like a judge who begins an investigation with irrelevant questions so as to put the defendant off his guard from the start. Then, after a pause of a few minutes, she sighed deeply, and said, shaking her head:

'Oh, good Lord, what news ! What will be the end of it?'

'Oh well, ma'am,' answered Ivan Ignatyitch, 'God is merciful: we have soldiers enough, plenty of powder, and I have cleaned out the cannon. Perhaps we'll manage to repulse Pugachev. Whom God helps nobody can harm.'

'And what sort of a man is this Pugachev?' asked the commandant's wife.

At this point Ivan Ignatyitch perceived that he had said too much and bit his tongue. But it was too late. Vassilissa Yegorovna forced him to tell her everything, after giving him her word that she would not say a word of it to anyone.

Vassilissa Yegorovna kept her promise and said not a word of it to anyone except the priest's wife, and that merely because her cow was still grazing in the steppe and might be seized by the villains.

Soon everybody was talking about Pugachev. The rumours about him varied. The commandant sent his sergeant to glean as much as he could from the neighbouring villages and fortresses. The sergeant returned after a couple of days and announced that he had seen a number of fires in the steppe about sixty versts from the fortress, and that he had heard from the Bashkirs that an unknown force was on its way. Beyond that he could say nothing positive since he had been afraid to go further.

Signs of unusual agitation became apparent among the Cossacks in the fortress; they crowded together in little groups in all the streets, conversing quietly among themselves and dispersing at the sight of a dragoon or a garrison soldier. Spies were sent among them. Yulay, a Kalmuck converted to Christianity, reported some important information to the commandant. The sergeant's evidence, according to Yulay, was false; on his return, the treacherous Cossack had announced to his comrades that he had been among the rebels and had presented himself to their leader, who had permitted him to kiss his hand and with whom he had conversed for a long time. The commandant immediately arrested the sergeant and appointed Yulay in his place. This change was received by the Cossacks with manifest displeasure. They murmured loudly and Ivan Ignatyitch, who saw to it that the commandant's instructions were carried out, with his own ears heard them say:

'You'll have it coming to you later, you garrison rat!'

The commandant had intended interrogating his prisoner that same day; but the sergeant had escaped guard, doubtless with the help of his partisans.

A new circumstance served to increase the commandant's anxiety. A Bashkir was caught carrying seditious letters. On this occasion, the commandant again decided to assemble his officers, and for this purpose he again wished to send Vassilissa Yegorovna away under some plausible pretext. But since Ivan Kuzmitch was a most upright and truthful man, he could think of no other method than that which he had employed on the previous occasion.

'Listen, Vassilissa Yegorovna,' he said to her with a slight cough. 'They say that Father Gerassim has received from the town . . .'

'Enough of that, Ivan Kuzmitch!' the commandant's wife interrupted him. 'It's clear that you propose to assemble a council of war to discuss Yemelyan Pugachev without me. You can't fool me!'

Ivan Kuzmitch stared at her.

'Well, my dear,' he said, 'if you know everything already, you may as well stay. We'll talk in front of you.'

'You shouldn't try to be so cunning, my dear,' she replied. 'Call for the officers.'

We assembled again. In the presence of his wife, Ivan Kuzmitch read to us Pugachev's proclamation, which had been written by some illiterate Cossack. The outlaw announced his intention of marching at once against our fortress; he invited the Cossacks and the soldiers to join his band and exhorted the commanders to offer no resistance, threatening execution if they did so. The proclamation was written in coarse but powerful language and must have had a dangerous influence on the minds of simple people.

'What an impostor!' exclaimed the commandant's wife.

'That he should dare to make such a proposal to us! To go out and meet him and lay our flags at his feet! Ah, the son of a dog! Surely he knows that we've been forty years in the Service and that, thanks to God, we've seen a thing or two in that time! Surely no commanders have listened to the brigand?'

'I shouldn't have thought so,' Ivan Kuzmitch replied. 'But I've heard that the villain has already taken many fortresses.'

'It certainly seems that he is powerful, then,' observed Shvabrin.

'We shall soon know his real strength,' said the commandant. 'Vassilissa Yegorovna, give me the key to the storehouse. Ivan Ignatyitch, go and bring the Bashkir here, and tell Yulay to fetch the whip.'

'Wait, Ivan Kuzmitch,' said the commandant's wife, rising from the seat. 'Let me take Masha somewhere out of the house, otherwise she'll hear the screaming and be terrified. And, to tell you the truth, I'm not keen on being a witness to the torturing myself. Good-bye for the present.'

In the old days, torture was so rooted in our judicial system that the beneficent edict ordering its abolition remained for a long time unheeded. It was thought that the criminal's own confession was indispensable for his full conviction – a thought not only illogical, but even totally opposed to sound juridical thinking: for, if the denial of the accused person is not accepted as proof of his innocence, his confession still less should be accepted as proof of his guilt. Even nowadays I sometimes hear old judges regretting the abolition of this barbarous custom. But in those days, nobody, neither the judge nor the accused, doubted the necessity of torture. Thus, the commandant's order caused no alarm or astonishment to any of us. Ivan Ignatyitch went off to fetch the Bashkir, who was under lock and key in the commandant's wife's storehouse, and a few minutes later the prisoner was led into the hall. The commandant ordered him to be brought before him.

The Bashkir stepped across the threshold with difficulty (a block of wood, in the form of stocks, had been attached to his feet) and, removing his tall cap, he stopped by the door. I looked up at him and shuddered. Never will I forget that man. He seemed to be over seventy. He had neither nose nor ears. His head was shaved; instead of a beard, a few grey hairs sprouted from his chin; he was small, thin and bent; however, his narrow little eyes still flashed fire.

'Aha!' said the commandant, recognising by these terrible signs one of the rebels punished in the year 1741. 'It seems you're an old wolf and have fallen into our traps before. With your nut so smoothly planed, it's apparently not the first time you've rebelled. Come nearer; tell me who sent you.'

The old Bashkir was silent and looked at the commandant with an utterly vacant expression.

'Why don't you answer?' continued Ivan Kuzmitch, 'Or don't you understand the Russian language? Yulay, ask him in your own tongue who sent him to our fortress.'

Yulay repeated Ivan Kuzmitch's question in Tartar. But the Bashkir looked at him with the same expression and answered not a word.

'All right, then,' said the commandant. 'I will make you answer my question. Right, lads, take off that ridiculous striped gown of his and stroke his back for him. Yulay, see to it that it's properly done!'

Two old soldiers began to undress the Bashkir. The unfortunate man's face expressed anxiety. He looked all around him like a small wild animal caught by children. When one of the old soldiers seized his hands to twine them round his neck, and lifted the old man on to his shoulders, and when Yulay took up the whip and began to brandish it, the Bashkir uttered a weak, imploring groan and, nodding his head, he opened his mouth, in which, in place of a tongue, moved a short stump.

When I reflect that this happened during my lifetime, and that I now live under the mild reign of Emperor Alexander, I cannot help but feel amazed at the rapid progress of civilisation and the spread of the laws of humanity. Young man, if these lines of mine should ever fall into your hands, remember that those changes which come as a result of moral improvements are better and more durable than any which are the outcome of violent events.

We were all horror-stricken.

'Well,' said the commandant, 'it's evident that we won't get anything out of him. Yulay, take the Bashkir back to the storehouse. And we, gentlemen, have further matters to discuss.'

We were beginning to consider our situation when Vassilissa Yegorovna suddenly burst into the room, out of breath and with an expression of extreme alarm.

'What's happened to you?' asked the astonished commandant.

'Very bad news, my dear!' answered Vassilissa Yegorovna. 'Nizhneozerny was captured this morning. Father Gerassim's servant has just got back from there. He saw it being taken. The commandant and all the officers were hanged. All the soldiers were taken prisoner. The villains will be here at any moment.'

This unexpected news came as a great shock to me. The commandant of the Nizhneozerny fortress, a quiet and modest young man, was known to me; a month or two before, he and his young wife had stayed with Ivan Kuzmitch while on their way from Orenburg. Nizhneozerny was about twenty-five versts away from our fortress. We had therefore to expect an attack from Pugachev at any moment. The fate in store for Marya Ivanovna came vividly to my mind, and my heart sank within me.

'Listen, Ivan Kuzmitch,' I said to the commandant. 'Our duty is to defend the fortress to the last breath; of that no more need be said. But we must consider the safety of the women. Send them to Orenburg, if the road is still free, or to some safer, more distant fortress out of reach of the villains.'

Ivan Kuzmitch turned to his wife and said to her:

'Indeed, my dear, don't you feel that you should go away until we've settled with the rebels?'

'Nonsense!' said the commandant's wife. 'Name a fortress safe from bullets. What's wrong with Belogorsky? Thanks to God, we've lived here for twenty-two years. We've seen off the Bashkirs and the Kirghiz: I dare say we'll manage to hold out against Pugachev!'

'Well, my dear,' replied Ivan Kuzmitch, 'stay if you like, if you have confidence in our fortress. But what shall we do with Masha? It'll be all right if we can successfully resist the enemy or hold out until help comes, but what if the villains capture the fortress?'

'Well, then ...'

And Vassilissa Yegorovna began to stutter and fell silent, with an expression of extreme agitation on her face.

'No, Vassilissa Yegorovna,' continued the commandant, observing that his words had produced an effect upon her, possibly for the first time in his life. 'It won't do for Masha to stay here. Let us send her to Orenburg, to her godmother; there are plenty of soldiers and cannons there and the walls are made of stone. And I would advise you to go there with her; although you're an old woman, consider what would happen to you if the fortress were taken.'

'All right,' said the commandant's wife, 'so be it: we'll send Masha away. But don't dream of asking me: I won't go. Nothing would make me part with you in my old age, to go and seek a lonely grave in a strange corner of the world. We have lived together, we will die together.'

'That's reasonable enough,' said the commandant. 'But we must hurry. Go and get Masha ready for the journey. We'll send her off before dawn to-morrow, and we'll give her an escort, even though we have no men to spare. But where is Masha?'

'At Akulina Pamfilovna's,' replied the commandant's wife. 'She fainted when she heard of the capture of Nizhneozerny; I fear she might fall ill. Heavens above, to have lived for this!'

Vassilissa Yegorovna went off to prepare her daughter's departure. We continued with our discussions. However, I no longer took any part in them, and did not listen to what was said. Marya Ivanovna appeared at supper, pale and tear-stained. We finished our meal in silence and rose from the table earlier than usual; taking leave of the whole family, we returned to our quarters. But I deliberately forgot my sword and went back for it: I had a feeling that I would find Marya Ivanovna alone. Indeed, she met me in the doorway and handed me my sword.

'Good-bye, Pyotr Andreitch,' she said to me with tears in her eyes. 'They are sending me to Orenburg. Keep well and be happy. Perhaps it will please God to let us see each other again; if not . . .'

And she began to sob. I embraced her.

'Good-bye, my angel,' I said. 'Good-bye, my dear one, my heart's desire! Whatever happens to me, trust that my last thought and my last prayer will be for you!'

Masha sobbed and pressed her head against my chest. I kissed her passionately and hastened out of the room.

Chapter Seven

THE ASSAULT

> *Oh my head, my head,*
> *Oh my head, that has served,*
> *Has served my country well*
> *For three and thirty years,*
> *And yet has obtained for itself,*
> *Neither gold nor joy,*
> *Neither words of praise*
> *Nor rank on high.*
> *All that my head has obtained*
> *Is two upright posts,*
> *With a beech-wood cross-beam,*
> *And a silken noose.*
>
> FOLK SONG

That night I neither slept nor undressed. I intended to go at dawn to the fortress gate from which Marya Ivanovna was to leave, and there say good-bye to her for the last time. I felt a great change within myself: my agitation of mind was far less burdensome to me than my recent despondency. Mingled with the grief of separation was vague but sweet hope, an impatient expectation of danger and feelings of noble ambition.

The night slipped by unnoticed. I was on the point of leaving my quarters when the door opened and a corporal came in to announce that our Cossacks had left the fortress during the night, taking Yulay with them by force, and that strange people were riding round the fortress. The thought that Marya Ivanovna would not be able to get away terrified me; I issued a few hasty instructions to the corporal and rushed off at once to the commandant's.

Day had already begun to dawn. I was flying down the street when I heard someone calling me. I stopped.

'Where are you going?' asked Ivan Ignatyitch, overtaking me. 'Ivan Kuzmitch is on the rampart and has sent me to get you. Pugachev has come.'

'Has Marya Ivanovna left?' I asked with a trembling heart.

'No, she was too late,' replied Ivan Ignatyitch. 'The road to Orenburg is cut off; the fortress is surrounded. It looks bad, Pyotr Andreitch!'

We made our way to the rampart, a natural elevation of the ground and fortified by a palisade. All the inhabitants of the fortress were already crowded there. The garrison was under arms. The cannon had been dragged up to the rampart the previous day. The commandant was walking up and down in front of his meagre ranks. The approach of danger had inspired the old warrior with unusual vigour. Riding up and down in the steppe, not far from the fortress, were about twenty horsemen. They seemed to be Cossacks, but among them were also some Bashkirs, easily recognisable by their lynx caps and their quivers.

The commandant made the round of his little army, saying to the soldiers:

'Well, children, let us stand firm to-day for our mother the Empress, and show the whole world that we are brave men, and true to our oaths!'

The soldiers loudly expressed their zeal. Shvabrin stood next to me, looking intently at the enemy. The horsemen riding about the steppe, noticing movement in the fortress, gathered in a little cluster and began to talk among themselves. The commandant ordered Ivan Ignatyitch to point the cannon at the group, and he himself applied the match to it. The cannon-ball whistled over their heads without doing any damage. The horsemen dispersed and immediately galloped out of sight, leaving the steppe deserted.

At that moment Vassilissa Yegorovna appeared on the rampart, accompanied by Masha, who did not wish to be parted from her mother.

'Well?' said the commandant's wife. 'How goes the battle? Where is the enemy?'

'The enemy's not far off,' replied Ivan Kuzmitch. 'God grant that everything will be all right. Well, Masha, are you afraid?'

'No, papa,' replied Marya Ivanovna; 'I should be more afraid alone at home.'

And she looked at me and made an effort to smile. I involuntarily grasped the hilt of my sword, remembering that I had received it from her hands the evening before, as if to defend my beloved. My heart burned. I imagined myself as her knight-protector. I longed to prove that I was worthy of her trust, and waited impatiently for the decisive moment.

At that moment, from behind a rise in the ground about half a verst from the fortress, some fresh groups of horsemen appeared, and soon the steppe was covered by a great number of men, armed with lances and bows and arrows. In the midst of them, on a white horse, rode a man in a red kaftan with a drawn sword in his hand; it was Pugachev himself. He stopped; his followers gathered round him and, on his command as it seemed, four men broke away from the main body of people and galloped at full speed right up to the fortress. We recognised them as our Cossack traitors. One of them held a sheet of paper above his cap; stuck on the lance of another was the head of Yulay, which was shaken off and hurled over the palisade towards us. The head of the unfortunate Kalmuck fell at the commandant's feet. The traitors cried:

'Don't fire. Come out to the Tsar. The Tsar is here!'

'I'll give it to you!' shouted Ivan Kuzmitch. 'Right, lads – fire!'

Our soldiers fired a volley. The Cossack who held the letter reeled and fell from his horse; the others galloped back. I glanced at Marya Ivanovna. Appalled by the sight of Yulay's bloodstained head and deafened by the volley, she seemed to have lost her senses. The commandant summoned a corporal and ordered him to take the sheet of paper from the dead Cossack. The corporal went out into the plain and returned, leading the dead man's horse by the bridle. He handed the letter to the commandant. Ivan Kuzmitch read it through to himself and then tore it up into little pieces. Meanwhile, the rebels seemed to be preparing for action. Soon the bullets began to whistle about our ears and several arrows fell close to us, sticking in the ground and in the palisade.

'Vassilissa Yegorovna,' said the commandant, 'this is no place for women! Take Masha away; you can see that the girl is more dead than alive.'

Vassilissa Yegorovna, quietened by the bullets, glanced at the steppe where much movement could be observed; then she turned to her husband and said to him:

'Ivan Kuzmitch, life and death are in God's hands: give Masha your blessing. Masha, go up to your father.'

Masha, pale and trembling, approached Ivan Kuzmitch, knelt down before him and bowed to the ground. The old commandant made the sign of the cross over her three times; then he raised her and, kissing her, said in a faltering voice:

'Well, Masha, be happy. Pray to God: He will never abandon you. If you find a good man, may God give you his

love and counsel. Live as Vassilissa Yegorovna and I have
lived. Well, good-bye, Masha. Vassilissa Yegorovna, take her
away as quickly as you can.'

Masha threw her arms round her father's neck and burst
into sobs.

'Let us kiss each other also,' said the commandant's wife,
weeping. 'Good-bye, my Ivan Kuzmitch. Forgive me if I have
ever angered you!'

'Good-bye, good-bye, my dear,' said the commandant,
embracing his old wife. 'Now, that's enough! Go home now;
and if you have time, get Masha to put on a smock.'

The commandant's wife and daughter went away. I
followed Marya Ivanovna with my eyes; she glanced back
and nodded to me.

Ivan Kuzmitch then turned back to us and fixed all his
attention upon the enemy. The rebels gathered round their
leader and suddenly began to dismount from their horses.

'Now, stand firm,' said the commandant. 'They're going
to attac . . .'

At that moment frightful yells and cries were heard; the
rebels were running forward towards the fortress. Our cannon
was loaded with grape-shot. The commandant allowed the
enemy to come very close and then suddenly fired again. The
shot fell right in the middle of the crowd. The rebels recoiled
on either side and fell back. Their leader was the only one
to stay out in front . . . He was brandishing his sword, and
he seemed heatedly to be exhorting the others to follow him.
The yells and cries, which had subsided for a moment, were
immediately renewed.

'Well, lads,' said the commandant, 'open the gates now
and sound the drum. Forward, lads, for a sally! Follow me!'

The commandant, Ivan Ignatyitch and I were over the
rampart in a twinkling; but the frightened garrison made no
move.

'Why do you hold back, children?' cried Ivan Kuzmitch. 'If we've got to die, let us die doing our duty!'

At that moment the rebels rushed upon us and burst into the fortress. The drum fell silent; the garrison threw down their arms; I was hurled to the ground, but I got up again and entered the fortress with the rebels. The commandant, wounded in the head, stood in the midst of a group of villains who demanded the keys from him. I was on the point of rushing to his aid when several sturdy Cossacks seized me and bound me with their belts, exclaiming:

'You'll see what'll happen to you, you traitors of the Tsar!'

We were dragged along the streets. The inhabitants came out of their houses, offering bread and salt. The bells began to ring. Suddenly a cry was taken up among the crowd that the Tsar was awaiting the prisoners in the square and receiving oaths of allegiance. The people thronged towards the square; we also were driven thither.

Pugachev sat in an armchair on the steps of the commandant's house. He was wearing a braided, red Cossack kaftan. A tall sable cap with gold tassels was drawn down to his flashing eyes. His face seemed familiar to me. He was surrounded by Cossack elders. Father Gerassim, pale and trembling, stood by the steps with a cross in his hands and seemed silently to be imploring mercy for the forthcoming victims. A gallows was being hastily erected in the square. As we drew near, the Bashkirs drove back the people and presented us to Pugachev. The bells were silent; a deep hush reigned.

'Which is the commandant?' asked the pretender.

Our sergeant stepped out of the crowd and pointed at Ivan Kuzmitch. Pugachev looked menacingly at the old man and said to him:

'How dared you resist me – me, your Tsar?'

The commandant, weakened by his wound, summoned up his remaining strength and answered in a firm voice:

'You are not my Tsar; you are a thief and an impostor, do you hear?'

Pugachev frowned darkly and waved a white handkerchief. Several Cossacks seized the old captain and dragged him to the gallows. Astride the cross-beam sat the mutilated Bashkir whom we had interrogated the previous day. He held a rope in his hand and a minute later I saw poor Ivan Kuzmitch hanging from the gallows. Ivan Ignatyitch was then brought before Pugachev.

'Swear allegiance,' Pugachev said to him, 'to your Tsar, Pyotr Fyodorovitch!'

'You are not our Tsar,' replied Ivan Ignatyitch, repeating the words of his captain. 'You're a thief and an impostor, my dear fellow.'

Pugachev again waved the handkerchief and the good lieutenant was hanged beside his old commanding officer.

It was my turn. I looked boldly at Pugachev, ready to repeat the answer of my courageous comrades. Then, to my indescribable astonishment, I saw Shvabrin, his hair cut in peasant style and wearing a Cossack kaftan, in the midst of the rebel elders. He went up to Pugachev and said a few words in his ear.

'Hang him!' said Pugachev, without even looking at me.

The noose was thrown round my neck. I began to pray to myself, expressing to God a sincere repentance for all my sins and beseeching Him to keep in safety all those who were close to my heart. I was dragged up to the gallows.

'Don't be afraid, don't be afraid,' repeated my executioners, wishing, in all truth perhaps, to give me courage.

Suddenly I heard a cry:

'Stop, you wretches! Hold!'

The hangmen paused. I saw Savelyitch lying at Pugachev's feet.

'Oh, my dear father!' the poor old man was saying. 'What

will you gain by the death of this noble child? Set him free: you'll get a good ransom for him; as an example and for the sake of terrifying the others, hang me if you like – an old man!'

Pugachev made a sign and I was immediately unbound and released.

'Our father pardons you,' the rebels said to me.

I could not say at that moment whether I was glad or sorry at my deliverance. My feelings were too confused. I was again brought before the pretender and compelled to kneel at his feet. Pugachev stretched out his sinewy hand to me.

'Kiss his hand, kiss his hand!' said the people around me.

But I would have preferred the most ferocious punishment to such ignoble degradation.

'Pyotr Andreitch, my dear,' whispered Savelyitch, standing behind me and nudging me forward, 'don't be obstinate. What is it to you? Spit and kiss the villain's . . . pfui! . . . kiss his hand!'

I made no movement. Pugachev let his hand drop and said with a smile:

'His Honour seems bewildered with joy. Lift him up!'

I was raised to my feet and set free. I stood watching the continuation of the terrible comedy.

The inhabitants of the fortress began to swear allegiance. They approached one after the other, kissing the cross and then bowing to the pretender. The garrison soldiers were there, too. The regimental tailor, armed with his blunt scissors, cut off their plaits. Then, shaking themselves, they went forward to kiss the hand of Pugachev, who declared them pardoned and received them into his band.

All this went on for about three hours. At last, Pugachev rose from the armchair and, accompanied by his elders, descended the steps. A white horse, richly harnessed, was led up to him. Two Cossacks took him under the arms and placed him in the saddle. He announced to Father Gerassim that he would have dinner at his house. At that moment a woman's scream was heard. Some of the brigands were dragging Vassilissa Yegorovna, stripped naked, and her hair dishevelled, to the steps. One of them had already managed to attire himself in her jacket. The others were carrying off feather-beds, chests, tea-services, linen and chattels of every sort.

'My fathers,' the poor old woman cried, 'spare my life! Kind fathers, take me to Ivan Kuzmitch!'

Suddenly she caught sight of the gallows and recognised her husband.

'Villains!' she cried in a frenzy of rage. 'What have you done to him? Light of my life, Ivan Kuzmitch, my valiant soldier! You were not harmed by Prussian bayonets or Turkish bullets; not on the field of honour have you laid down your life: you have been killed by a fugitive galley-slave!'

'Quieten the old witch!' said Pugachev.

A young Cossack struck her over the head with his sword and she fell dead at the foot of the steps. Pugachev rode off; the crowd rushed after him.

Chapter Eight

AN UNINVITED GUEST

An uninvited guest is worse than a Tartar.

PROVERB

The square was deserted. I was still standing in the same place, unable to collect my thoughts, confused as I was by so many terrible impressions.

Uncertainty as to the fate of Marya Ivanovna tormented me more than anything else. Where was she? What had happened to her? Had she had time to hide? Was her place of refuge safe? Filled with these alarming thoughts, I entered the commandant's house ... It was completely empty; the chairs, tables and chests had been smashed, the crockery broken and everything else stolen. I ran up the small staircase which led to Marya Ivanovna's bedroom, and for the first time in my life I entered her room. I saw that her bed had been pulled to pieces by the brigands; the wardrobe had been smashed and plundered; the small lamp was still burning before the empty icon-case; the little looking-glass between the windows had survived ... Where was the mistress of this humble, virginal cell? A terrible thought flashed through my mind: I imagined her in the hands of the brigands ... My heart sank ... I wept, bitterly I wept, and loudly called out the name of my beloved ... At that moment I heard a slight noise and Palashka, pale and trembling, came out from behind the wardrobe.

'Ah, Pyotr Andreitch!' she said, clasping her hands. 'What a day! What horror ... !'

'And Marya Ivanovna?' I asked impatiently. 'What has become of Marya Ivanovna?'

'The young lady is alive,' answered Palashka. 'She is hiding at Akulina Pamfilovna's.'

'At the priest's wife's!' I exclaimed in horror. 'My God! Pugachev's there!'

I rushed out of the room, was in the street and tearing headlong to the priest's house in a flash, neither seeing nor feeling a thing. Shouts, bursts of laughter and songs resounded from within . . . Pugachev was feasting with his comrades. Palashka had followed me there. I sent her to go and fetch Akulina Pamfilovna as quietly as she could. A minute later the priest's wife came to me in the entrance, an empty bottle in her hand.

'For God's sake, where's Marya Ivanovna?' I asked with indescribable agitation.

'The dear girl's lying on my bed, there, behind the partition,' the priest's wife replied. 'A misfortune nearly befell us, Pyotr Andreitch, but, thank God, everything went off all right: the villain had only just sat down to dinner when the poor little thing came to and uttered a groan! I nearly died of fright. He heard it and said: "Who's that groaning there, old woman?" I made a very low bow to the thief. "My niece, Tsar; she fell ill about two weeks ago." "And is your niece young?" "She is young, Tsar." "Show me your niece then, old woman." My heart sank within me but there was nothing I could do. "As you wish, Tsar, only the girl's not well enough to get up and come before your Grace." "Never mind, old woman, I'll go and see her myself." And sure enough the wretch went behind the partition, and would you believe it? He actually drew back the curtain and looked at her with his hawklike eyes – but nothing happened . . . God helped us out! But, believe you me, the priest and I were prepared for a martyr's death. Fortunately, the little dear did not know his face. Good Lord above, what things we have lived to see! It can't be denied! Poor Ivan Kuzmitch! Who would have thought it? And Vassilissa Yegorovna ... And Ivan Ignatyitch? Why did they kill him ... ? And how did they come to spare you? And what about Alexey Ivanytch Shvabrin? You know he's had his hair cropped in peasant style, and is now feasting with the rebels at our house! He's a sharp one, and no mistake! When I spoke of my sick niece, would you believe it – he looked daggers at me. However, he didn't give me away, and I can be thankful for that.'

At that moment the drunken shouts of the guests and the voice of Father Gerassim were heard. The guests were demanding wine, and the host was calling for his wife. The priest's wife became flustered.

'Go back home, Pyotr Andreitch,' she said. 'I have no time for you now: the villains are drinking themselves under the table. It would be the worse for you if you fell into their drunken hands. Good-bye, Pyotr Andreitch. What is to be, will be, and maybe God won't desert us.'

The priest's wife went back into the house. Somewhat relieved, I returned to my quarters. As I crossed the square, I saw several Bashkirs assembled around the gallows, dragging the boots off the hanged men's feet; with difficulty I restrained my indignation, feeling that it would be utterly useless to intervene. The brigands were running all over the fortress, looting the officers' quarters. The shouts of the drunken rebels could be heard everywhere. I arrived home. Savelyitch met me on the threshold.

'Thank God!' he cried when he saw me. 'I was beginning to think that the villains had got hold of you again. Well, Pyotr Andreitch my dear, would you believe it – the rogues have robbed us of everything: clothes, linen, our belongings, crockery – there's nothing left. But what of that! Heaven be thanked that you have been spared your life! But did you recognise their leader, master?'

'No, I didn't. Who is he then?'

'What, my dear Pyotr Andreitch? Have you forgotten that drunkard who took your hareskin coat from you at the inn? A brand-new hareskin coat, and the animal burst the seams as he pulled it on!'

I was astonished. Indeed, the resemblance between Pugachev and my guide was striking. I felt sure that Pugachev and he were one and the same person, and now understood why he had spared my life. I could not help but marvel at the strange chain of circumstances: a child's coat given to a tramp had saved me from the hangman's noose, and a drunkard roaming from inn to inn was besieging fortresses and shaking the Government!

'Won't you have something to eat?' asked Savelyitch, his habits unchanged. 'There is nothing in the house, but I'll go out and rummage for something and prepare it for you.'

Left alone, I became lost in thought. What was I to do? To remain in the fortress occupied by the villain, or to join his band, was unworthy of an officer. Duty demanded that I should go where my service could still be of use to my country in its present critical position. But love urged me strongly to stay near Marya Ivanovna and be her defender and protector. Although I foresaw a speedy and inevitable change in the present state of affairs, I trembled at the thought of the danger she was in.

My reflections were interrupted by the arrival of one of the Cossacks, who ran up to inform me that the "great Tsar" wished to see me.

'Where is he?' I asked, preparing to obey.

'In the commandant's house,' the Cossack answered. 'Our master went to the bath-house after dinner and now he's resting. Well, your Honour, he is quite clearly a person of distinction: at dinner he was pleased to eat two roast sucking-pigs, and he had his steam-bath so hot that Taras Kurotchkin could not bear it – he had to give the bath-broom to Fomka Bikbayev and only came to when he was doused with cold water. It cannot be denied: his ways are all so dignified . . . And I was told that he showed his Tsar's signs on his chest in the bath-house: on one breast a two-headed eagle the size of a five-kopeck piece, and on the other his own likeness.'

I did not consider it necessary to contradict the Cossack's opinion and went with him to the commandant's house, picturing to myself in advance my meeting with Pugachev, and trying to guess how it would all end. The reader will easily imagine that I did not feel altogether comfortable.

Dusk had begun to fall when I reached the commandant's house. The gallows and its victims loomed black and terrible before me. The body of the poor commandant's wife still lay at the bottom of the steps, where two Cossacks stood on guard. The Cossack accompanying me went in to announce me and, returning at once, led me into the room where, the evening before, I had taken such a tender farewell of Marya Ivanovna.

I was met by an unusual scene. Behind the table, which was covered by a table-cloth and littered with bottles and glasses, sat Pugachev and about ten Cossack elders, wearing hats and coloured shirts, flushed by wine, with purple faces and flashing eyes. Neither Shvabrin nor our sergeant, newly-recruited traitors, were among them.

'Ah, your Honour!' said Pugachev, seeing me. 'You are welcome; come in and take a seat at our table.'

The company moved closer together. I silently sat down at the end of the table. My neighbour, a handsome, well-built young Cossack, filled my glass with some ordinary wine which I did not touch. I began to examine the company with curiosity. Pugachev occupied the seat of honour, his elbows on the table and his broad fist propped against his black beard. His features, which were regular and pleasant enough, had nothing ferocious about them. He frequently turned to a man of about fifty, addressing him sometimes as Count, sometimes as Timofeitch and sometimes as uncle. All treated each other as comrades, and showed no particular deference to their leader. The conversation turned on the morning's assault, the success of the rising and its future activities. Everyone boasted, advanced his own opinion, and freely contradicted Pugachev. And at this strange council of war it was resolved to march on Orenburg: a bold move and one which was nearly crowned with disastrous success! The march was fixed for the following day.

'Well, lads!' said Pugachev. 'Before we go to bed, let's have my favourite song. Come on, Tchumakov!'

In a high voice, my neighbour started the following doleful bargeman's song and all joined in the chorus:

'Make no sound, mother-forest green,
Do not hinder me, brave lad, from thinking,
For to-morrow I, brave lad, must go before the court,
Before the stern judge, before the great Tsar himself.
And the great Lord Tsar will begin to question me:
"Tell me, young man, tell me, peasant's son,
With whom you have stolen, with whom you have robbed,
And of the companions you had with you?"
"I will tell you, our hope-true Tsar,
I will tell you the truth, always the truth.
My companions were four in number:
My first companion was the dark night,
My second companion was my knife of damask steel,
My third companion was my good horse,
My fourth companion was my taut bow,
And my messengers were red-hot arrows.'

Then up speaks our hope-true Tsar:
"Praise be to thee, young man, thou peasant's son!
You knew how to steal, you knew how to make answer,
And I will therefore make you a present, young man—
Of a tall dwelling-house in the midst of a field,
Of two upright posts and a cross-beam above."'

It is impossible to describe the effect that this peasants' song about the gallows, sung by men themselves already destined for the gallows, produced upon me. Their menacing faces, their tuneful voices, the sad expression they imparted to words already expressive in themselves – all this shook me with some form of poetic terror.

Each of the guests drained a last glass, rose from the table and took leave of Pugachev. I was about to follow them, but Pugachev said to me:

'Sit down; I want to talk to you.'

We remained facing each other.

For some moments the silence continued between us. Pugachev looked intently at me, occasionally screwing up his left eye with an extraordinary expression of foxiness and mockery. At last he burst out laughing with such unaffected merriment that, as I looked at him, I began to laugh myself, without knowing why.

'Well, your Honour?' he said to me. 'Confess that you were scared to death when my lads put the rope round your neck. I expect that you were frightened out of your wits ... And you would have swung from that cross-beam had it not been for your servant. I recognised the old grumbler immediately. Well, your Honour, would you have thought that the man who led you to the "umyot" was the great Tsar himself?' (Here he assumed an expression of mystery and importance.) 'You are guilty of a serious offence against me,' he continued, 'but I pardoned you for your kindness, and because you did me a service when I was forced to hide from my enemies. But you will see greater things! You will see how I shall reward you, when I take possession of my kingdom! Do you promise to serve me zealously?'

The blackguard's question and his insolence struck me as so amusing that I could not help smiling.

'Why do you smile?' he asked me, frowning. 'Do you not believe that I am the great Tsar? Answer me straight.'

I was confused. I could not acknowledge the tramp as Tsar: to do so would have displayed unpardonable faintheartedness. To call him an impostor to his face would be sentencing myself to death, and what I had been ready to do at the gallows before the eyes of all the people, in the first burst of indignation, now seemed to me useless boasting. I hesitated. Pugachev awaited my answer in gloomy silence. Finally (and even now I remember the moment with satisfaction), feelings of duty triumphed over human weakness. I replied to Pugachev:

'Listen, I'll tell you the whole truth. Judge for yourself – how can I acknowledge you as Tsar? You are an intelligent man: you would see that I was merely being artful.'

'Who am I, then, in your opinion?'

'God knows; but whoever you are, you're playing a dangerous game.'

Pugachev looked at me quickly.

'Then you don't believe,' he said, 'that I am Tsar Pyotr Fyodorovitch? All right. But is not success for the bold? Did not Grishka Otrepyev reign in the old days? Think what you like about me, but do not leave me. What is it to you one way or the other? One master's as good as another. Serve me faithfully and truly and I will make you field-marshal and prince. What do you say?'

'No,' I replied firmly. 'I am a nobleman by birth; I have sworn allegiance to my Sovereign Lady, the Empress: I cannot serve you. If you really wish me well, then let me return to Orenburg.'

Pugachev considered.

'And if I let you go,' he said, 'will you at least promise not to serve against me?'

'How can I promise that?' I replied. 'You yourself know that it's not up to me: if I am ordered to march against you, I will – there's nothing for it. You yourself are now a commander; you demand obedience from your men. How would it seem if I refused to serve when my services were needed? My life is in your hands: if you let me go – thank you; if you put me to death – God will be your judge; but I have told you the truth.'

My sincerity struck Pugachev.

'So be it,' he said, slapping me on the shoulder. 'Either put to death or pardon – one or the other. Go where you like and do what you like. Come and say good-bye to me tomorrow, and now go off to bed. I feel quite sleepy myself.'

I left Pugachev and went out into the street. The night was calm and frosty. The moon and the stars were shining brightly, lighting up the square and the gallows. In the fortress all was still and dark. Only in the tavern was there a light, and from it came the cries of late revellers. I glanced at the priest's house. The shutters and gates were closed. It seemed that all was quiet within.

I arrived back at my quarters and found Savelyitch fretting over my absence. The news of my freedom filled him with unspeakable joy.

'Thanks be to Thee, oh Lord!' he said, crossing himself. 'We will leave the fortress before daybreak to-morrow and follow our noses. I have prepared something for you; eat it up, my dear Pyotr Andreitch, and then sleep safely until the morning.'

I followed his advice and, having eaten my supper with a

good appetite, I fell asleep on the bare floor, worn out in mind and body.

Chapter Nine

THE PARTING

Sweet it was to me, my dear,
To learn to know thee;
Sad, sad it is to part;
As though from my soul I am torn.

KHERASKOV

I was awakened by the drum the following morning. I went to the place of assembly. There, Pugachev's men were already drawn up around the gallows, from which the previous day's victims were still hanging. The Cossacks were on horseback, the soldiers under arms. Flags were flying. Several cannons, among which I recognised ours, were mounted on travelling gun-carriages. All the inhabitants of the fortress were also there, awaiting the pretender. At the steps of the commandant's house, a Cossack was holding a magnificent white Kirghiz horse by the bridle. I sought the body of the commandant's wife with my eyes. It had been moved a little to one side and covered with matting. Pugachev finally appeared at the entrance. The people took off their caps. Pugachev paused at the top of the steps and greeted them all. One of his elders gave him a bag filled with copper coins, which he began to scatter among the crowd by the handful.

With cries, the people rushed forward to pick them up, and the affair was not without its casualties. Pugachev was surrounded by his chief accomplices. Shvabrin was among them. Our glances met. In mine he could read contempt, and he turned away with an expression of genuine loathing and affected scorn. Pugachev, catching sight of me in the crowd, nodded and beckoned me to him.

'Listen,' he said to me. 'Set off at once for Orenburg and tell the Governor and all the generals from me that they can expect me within a week. Advise them to receive me with childlike love and obedience; otherwise, they'll not escape a savage death. A pleasant journey, your Honour!'

Then he turned to the crowd and, indicating Shvabrin, he said:

'Here, children, is your new commandant. Obey him in everything; he is answerable to me for you and the fortress.'

I heard these words with horror: with Shvabrin in command of the fortress, Marya Ivanovna would be in his power! Oh God, what would become of her!

Pugachev descended the steps. His horse was brought up to him. He sprang nimbly up into the saddle, without waiting for the Cossacks who were ready to help him mount.

At that moment I saw Savelyitch step out from the crowd; he went up to Pugachev and handed him a sheet of paper. I could not imagine what it was all about.

'What's this?' asked Pugachev importantly.

'Read it and you'll see,' Savelyitch replied.

Pugachev took the paper and examined it significantly for a long time.

'Why do you write so badly?' he said at length. 'My royal eyes cannot distinguish a single word. Where is my chief secretary?'

A young lad in corporal's uniform ran smartly up to Pugachev.

'Read it aloud,' the pretender said, giving him the paper.

I was extremely curious to know what had prompted my servant to write to Pugachev. In a loud voice the chief secretary began to spell out the following:

'Two dressing-gowns, one cotton and one striped silk – six roubles.'

'What does this mean?' said Pugachev, frowning.

'Order him to continue,' Savelyitch replied calmly.

The chief secretary went on:

'One uniform of fine green cloth – seven roubles.

'One pair of white cloth breeches – five roubles.

'Twelve holland linen shirts with cuffs – ten roubles.

'One hamper containing a tea-service – two and a half roubles . . .'

'What is this rubbish?' Pugachev interrupted. 'What have I to do with hampers and breeches with cuffs?'

Savelyitch cleared his throat and began to explain.

'This, sir, you will be pleased to see, is an account of those of my master's articles which were stolen by the villains . . .'

'The villains?' Pugachev asked threateningly.

'I beg your pardon: a slip of the tongue,' replied Savelyitch. 'Even if they're not villains, but your lads, they ransacked the place and stole everything. Don't be angry: a horse has four legs and yet it stumbles. Order him to read on to the end.'

'Read on,' said Pugachev.

The secretary continued:

'One chintz bedspread, another of taffeta quilted with cotton wool – four roubles.

'A fox-fur coat covered in crimson flannel – forty roubles.

'Likewise, a hareskin coat given to your Grace at the inn – fifteen roubles.'

'What's this now!' cried Pugachev, his eyes flashing fire.

I confess that I began to fear for the life of my poor servant.

He was about to enter into further explanations, but Pugachev interrupted him:

'How dare you intrude upon me with such nonsense?' he cried, snatching the paper from the secretary's hands and throwing it in Savelyitch's face. 'You stupid old man! You've been fleeced: what a misfortune! Why, you old grumbler, you should for ever be praying for me and my lads, and thanking God that you and your master didn't swing from the gallows along with the other traitors . . . Hareskin coat! I'll give you hareskin coat! Why, I'll have your bare skin made into a coat!'

'As you please,' replied Savelyitch, 'but I'm not a free man and must answer for my master's goods.'

Pugachev was evidently in a magnanimous frame of mind. He turned away and rode off without another word to Savelyitch. Shvabrin and the elders followed him. The band set forth from the fortress in orderly fashion. The people moved forward to see Pugachev off. I stayed behind in the square alone with Savelyitch. My servant was holding his list of my goods in his hands, looking at it with an expression of profound regret.

Seeing that I was on good terms with Pugachev, he had thought to take advantage of it; but his sage intention had not succeeded. I was about to upbraid him for his misplaced zeal, but could not restrain myself from laughing.

'Laugh, master,' Savelyitch answered, 'go on, laugh; but when we have to equip ourselves completely afresh – then we'll see how funny it is.'

I hurried to the priest's house to see Marya Ivanovna. The priest's wife met me with sad news. Marya Ivanovna had developed a strong fever during the night. She lay unconscious and in a delirium. The priest's wife led me to her room. I softly drew near to the bed. The change in her face shocked me. The sick girl did not recognise me. I stood in front of her for a long time, deaf to Father Gerassim and his good wife who, it seemed, were trying to console me. I was agitated by gloomy thoughts. The condition of the poor, defenceless orphan, left alone among ferocious rebels, terrified me, as did my own powerlessness. Shvabrin, Shvabrin more than anything, tortured my imagination. Invested with power by the pretender, and entrusted with the command of the fortress, where the unhappy girl – the innocent object of his hatred – remained, he was in a position to do anything he wished. What could I do? How could I help her? How could I free her from the villain's hands? There was only one course of action open to me: I decided to leave for Orenburg immediately, in order to speed up the deliverance of the Belogorsky fortress and, if possible, to take a part in that operation. I said good-bye to the priest and Akulina Pamfilovna, warmly entrusting Marya Ivanovna, whom I already considered to be my wife, to their care. I took the poor girl's hand and kissed it, damping it with my tears.

'Good-bye,' the priest's wife said to me, as she accompanied me out of the house. 'Good-bye, Pyotr Andreitch. Perhaps we'll meet again in happier circumstances. Do not forget us and write often. Poor Marya Ivanovna has now no one but you to look to for consolation and protection.'

Going out on to the square, I stopped for a moment, glanced up at the gallows, bowed my head and then left the fortress by the Orenburg road, accompanied by Savelyitch who had never left my side.

I was walking on, occupied with my thoughts, when suddenly I heard the sound of a horse's hooves behind me. I looked round and saw a Cossack galloping out of the fortress, holding a Bashkir horse by the bridle and making signs to me from the distance. I stopped and soon recognised our sergeant. Galloping up to us, he dismounted his own horse and, handing me the bridle of the other, he said:

'Your Honour! Our father wishes you to have this horse and a coat from his own shoulders' (A sheepskin coat was tied to the horse's saddle). 'And he also . . . ,' the sergeant added hesitatingly, '. . . wishes to give you . . . half a rouble . . . but I lost it on the road: be merciful and forgive me.'

Savelyitch looked at him sharply and grumbled:

'Lost it on the road! And what's that clinking under your shirt, you shameless villain?'

'What's that clinking under my shirt?' the sergeant retorted, not in the least put out. 'God be with you, old man! That's the horse's snaffle, and not the half-rouble.'

'All right,' I said, breaking up the argument. 'Give my thanks to him who sent you, and try to find the lost half-rouble on the journey back and keep it for vodka.'

'I'm very grateful, your Honour,' he replied, turning his horse. 'I shall pray for you all my life.'

With these words he galloped back, holding one hand to his shirt and, a minute later, he vanished from sight.

I put on the coat and mounted the horse, Savelyitch taking his seat behind me.

'Well, you can see, master,' said the old man, 'that it was not in vain that I gave that petition to the rogue; the thief's conscience pricked him. Even so, this spindle-shanked nag and the sheepskin coat aren't worth half what the rogues stole from us and what you yourself gave him, but you may be able to find some use for them: from a fierce dog, even a tuft of hair.'

Chapter Ten

THE SIEGE OF THE TOWN

Pitched in hill and meadow,
From the height, like an eagle he
  gazed on the city,
Behind his camp he ordered a rampart
  to be built,
In which to hide his thunderbolts,
  which he brought by night up to the city.

KHERASKOV

As we approached Orenburg, we saw a crowd of convicts with shaven heads and faces disfigured by the hangman's pincers. They were working near the fortifications, under the supervision of the garrison soldiers. Some were carting away the rubbish that had filled the moat; others were digging up the ground with spades; on the rampart masons were carrying bricks and repairing the town wall. Sentries stopped us at the gates and demanded our passports. As soon as the sergeant heard that I was from the Belogorsky fortress, he took me straight to the general's house.

I found the general in the garden. He was inspecting the apple-trees which had been stripped of their leaves by the autumn wind and, with the help of an old gardener, was carefully covering them with warm straw. His face expressed calm, health and good nature. He was delighted to see me and began to question me about the terrible events I had witnessed. I related everything to him. The old man listened to me attentively as he cut off the dry twigs.

'Poor Mironov!' he said when I had finished my sad story. 'I feel very sorry: he was a good officer. And Madame Mironov – she was a fine woman, and what an expert at pickling mushrooms! But what of Masha, the captain's daughter?'

I replied that she had remained at the fortress in the care of the priest and his wife.

'Oh dear, oh dear!' observed the general. 'That's bad, very bad. It's quite impossible to rely on the discipline of these brigands. What will become of the poor girl?'

I replied that the fortress was not far away, and that doubtless his Excellency would not delay in dispatching a force of men to rescue its poor inhabitants. The general nodded his head dubiously.

'We shall see, we shall see,' he said. 'We've got plenty of time to discuss that. Do me the pleasure of having a cup of tea with me; a council of war is to be held at my house today. You can give us some trustworthy information concerning this rogue Pugachev and his army. But now go and rest a while.'

I went to the quarters assigned to me, where Savelyitch had already installed himself, and impatiently began to await the appointed time. The reader will easily imagine that I did not fail to make my appearance at the council, which was to have such an influence on my fate. I arrived at the general's at the appointed hour.

I found with him one of the town officials, the director of the customs-house if I remember rightly, a fat, red-faced old man in a brocade coat. He began to question me about the fate of Ivan Kuzmitch, who had been a friend of his, and frequently interrupted me with additional questions and moral observations which, if not showing him to be a man well-versed in the military art, at least indicated that he possessed sagacity and common sense. Meanwhile, the others invited to the council began to assemble. Apart from the general himself, there was not a military man among them.

When everybody had taken his seat and been handed a cup of tea, the general gave an extremely clear and detailed account of the situation at hand.

'Now, gentlemen,' he continued, 'we must decide in what way to oppose these rebels: offensively or defensively? Each of these means has its advantages and its disadvantages. Offensive action holds out greater hope for the quickest possible destruction of the enemy; defensive action is safer and less dangerous . . . And so, let us begin by putting the issue to the vote in the accepted fashion – that is, beginning with the youngest in rank. Mr Ensign,' he continued, addressing me, 'be good enough to give us your opinion.'

I rose and after giving a brief description of Pugachev and his band, I stated firmly that the pretender had not the means to stand up against a force of professional soldiers.

It was clear that my opinion was received by the officials with disfavour. They saw in it the rashness and temerity of a young man. A murmur arose among them, and I distinctly heard the word 'greenhorn' pronounced in a whisper by someone. The general turned to me and said with a smile:

'Mr Ensign, the first votes in councils of war are usually in favour of offensive action; it is as it ought to be. But now let us get on with the voting. Mr Collegiate Councillor, tell us your opinion.'

The old man in the brocade coat hastily finished his third cup of tea, considerably diluted with rum, and answered the general:

'I think, your Excellency, that we should act neither offensively nor defensively.'

'How so, Mr Collegiate Councillor?' the general replied, surprised. 'What other tactics are there besides offensive and defensive . . . ?'

'Your Excellency, let us proceed by bribery.'

'Ha, ha! Your idea is an extremely sensible one. Military tactics permit bribery, and we will make use of your advice. We could promise for the head of this rogue . . . seventy roubles, or even a hundred . . . from the secret funds . . .'

'And if,' interrupted the director of the customs-house, 'and if that doesn't induce these robbers to give up their leader, bound hand and foot, may I be a Kirghiz ram and not a Collegiate Councillor.'

'We will consider it further and discuss it again,' the general replied. 'We must, however, in any event, take military measures. Gentlemen, give your votes in the customary fashion.'

All the opinions were opposed to mine. All the officials spoke of the unreliability of the troops, the uncertainty of success, the need for caution and so on. All were agreed that it was more sensible to stay behind strong stone walls, protected by cannons, than to try the fortune of arms in the open field. At length, the general, having listened to everyone's opinion, shook the ashes from his pipe and delivered the following speech:

'Gentlemen, I must state that for my own part I am in complete accord with the opinion of the ensign, since his opinion is based on all the rules of sound military tactics, which are almost always in favour of offensive rather than defensive action.'

Here he paused and began to fill his pipe. My self-esteem was triumphant. I cast a proud glance at the officials, who were whispering among themselves with an air of displeasure and anxiety.

'But, gentlemen,' he continued, exhaling, together with a deep sigh, a thick cloud of tobacco smoke, 'I dare not take upon myself so great a responsibility, when the affair involves the safety of the provinces entrusted to me by Her Imperial Majesty, my Most Gracious Sovereign. And so I fall in with the majority vote, which has decided that it would be safer and more sensible to await a siege within the town, and to repel the enemy's attacks with powerful artillery and if possible by sorties.'

The officials in their turn now glanced scornfully at me. The council dispersed. I could not but regret the weakness of this estimable soldier who, contrary to his own convictions, had decided to follow the advice of ignorant and inexperienced people.

Some days after this memorable council, we learned that Pugachev, true to his promise, was approaching Orenburg. I saw the rebel army from the height of the town wall. It seemed to me that their numbers had increased tenfold since the last assault, which I had witnessed. They now had some pieces of artillery, taken from the small fortresses Pugachev had conquered. Recalling the decision of the council, I foresaw a long confinement within the walls of Orenburg, and nearly wept with vexation.

I will not describe the siege of Orenburg, which belongs to history and has no place in a family memoir. I will merely say that this siege, due to carelessness on the part of the local authorities, was disastrous for the inhabitants, who had to endure hunger and every possible privation. It is easy to imagine how quite unbearable life in Orenburg was. Everyone dejectedly awaited the resolution of his fate; everyone groaned about the high prices, which were indeed terrible. The inhabitants grew accustomed to cannon-balls falling in their courtyards; even Pugachev's assaults no longer aroused any excitement. I was dying of boredom. Time wore on. I received no letters from the Belogorsky fortress. All the roads were cut off. My separation from Marya Ivanovna was becoming unendurable to me. Uncertainty as to her fate tortured me. My only diversion consisted in reconnoitring outside the town. Thanks to Pugachev, I had a good horse, with which I shared my meagre ration of food and upon which I daily left the town to exchange fire with Pugachev's horsemen. In these sorties, the advantage was generally with the villains, who were well-fed, had plenty to drink and were well-mounted. The emaciated cavalry from the town was no match for them. On occasions our hungry infantry also went out into the field; but the depth of the snow prevented any successful action against the enemy's scattered horsemen. The artillery thundered fruitlessly from the height of the rampart and, once in the field, got stuck, since our horses were too weak to pull it. Such was the pattern of our military activity! This was what the Orenburg officials called cautious and sensible!

One day, when we had somehow succeeded in dispersing and driving off a fairly large body of the enemy, I caught up with a Cossack who had fallen behind his comrades. I was about to strike him down with my Turkish sword when he suddenly took off his cap and cried:

'Greetings, Pyotr Andreitch! How's God treating you?'

I looked at him and recognised our sergeant. I was delighted beyond words to see him.

'Greetings, Maximytch,' I said to him. 'Is it long since you left Belogorsky?'

'Not long, Pyotr Andreitch, my dear; I went back there only yesterday. I have a letter for you.'

'Where is it?' I cried, crimson with excitement.

'I have it here,' answered Maximytch, putting his hand inside his shirt. 'I promised Palashka that I would get it to you somehow.'

He then gave me a folded piece of paper and immediately galloped off. I opened it and, with a tremor, read the following lines:

'It has pleased God to deprive me suddenly of both father and mother: I have no relatives or protectors on this earth. I turn to you, knowing that you have always wished me well and that you are ready to help any person. I pray to God that this letter may reach you somehow! Maximytch has promised to deliver it to you. Palashka has also heard from Maximytch that he often sees you from a distance in the sorties, and that you take absolutely no care of yourself and do not think of those who pray for you with tears. I was ill for a long time; when I recovered, Alexey Ivanytch, who commands here in place of my late father, forced Father Gerassim to give me up to him, threatening him with Pugachev. I live under guard at our house. Alexey Ivanytch is forcing me to marry him. He says that he saved my life by not exposing Akulina Pamfilovna when she told the villains that I was her niece. But I would rather die than become the wife of such a man as Alexey Ivanytch. He treats me very cruelly and threatens that unless I change my mind and consent, he will take me to the brigands' camp where, he says, the same will happen to me as happened to Lisaveta Kharlova. I have asked Alexey Ivanytch to give me time to think. He has agreed to wait three days; if I do not marry him in three days' time, I can expect no mercy from him whatever. My dear Pyotr Andreitch, you are my only protector: save a poor helpless girl! Beseech the general and all the commanders to send us help as soon as possible, and come yourself if you can.

'I remain your poor, obedient orphan,
   'Marya Mironov'

Having read this letter, I nearly went out of my mind. I started back for the town, spurring on my poor horse without mercy. On the way I devised one plan after another for the rescue of the poor girl, but could settle on nothing. Galloping into the town, I rode straight for the general's house and rushed headlong up to him.

The general was walking up and down the room, smoking his meerschaum pipe. He stopped when he saw me. He was doubtless struck by my appearance; he anxiously asked after the reason for my hasty arrival.

'Your Excellency,' I said to him, 'I come to you as to my own father. For God's sake do not refuse me in my request: the happiness of my whole life is involved.'

'What is it, my dear sir?' asked the astonished old man. 'What can I do for you? Tell me.'

'Your Excellency, allow me to take a company of soldiers and fifty Cossacks, and let me free the Belogorsky fortress.'

The general looked at me intensely, doubtless supposing that I had taken leave of my senses (in which he was not far mistaken).

'How? Free the Belogorsky fortress?' he said at last.

'I guarantee success,' I replied with ardour. 'Only let me go.'

'No, young man,' he said, shaking his head. 'At such a great distance, the enemy could easily cut off your communications with the main strategic point, and gain a complete victory over you. Your communications severed . . .'

I became alarmed when I saw that he was about to enter into a military discourse and I hastened to interrupt him.

'The daughter of Captain Mironov,' I said, 'has written me a letter. She asks for help; Shvabrin is forcing her to marry him.'

'Really? Oh, that Shvabrin is a great rascal, and if he falls into my hands, I'll have him tried within twenty-four hours, and we'll shoot him on the fortress parapet! But meanwhile we must have patience . . .'

'Have patience!' I cried, beside myself. 'But meanwhile he marries Marya Ivanovna . . . !'

'Oh!' retorted the general. 'That won't be such a bad thing. It would be better for her, for the time being, to be Shvabrin's wife: he could show her his protection; and then, when we shoot him, God willing, suitors will be found for her. Pretty widows don't stay single for long; I mean, a young widow will find a husband more quickly than an unmarried girl.'

'I would rather die,' I said in a fury, 'than give her up to Shvabrin!'

'Oho!' said the old man. 'Now I understand: it seems that you're in love with Marya Ivanovna. Oh, that's quite another matter! Poor fellow! But all the same, I cannot give you a company of soldiers and fifty Cossacks. Such an expedition would be mad; I cannot take the responsibility for it.'

I hung my head; despair took possession of me. Suddenly a thought flashed through my mind: what it was, the reader will discover in the following chapter, as the old-fashioned novelists say.

Chapter Eleven

THE REBEL CAMP

At that time the lion was replete, and, although by nature he is ferocious,
He asked kindly: 'What has pleased you to come to my den?'

(SUMAROKOV)

I left the general and hastened to my own quarters. Savelyitch met me with his customary admonitions.

'What satisfaction can you get from fighting these drunken outlaws? Is such the occupation of a nobleman? You never know what may happen: you may lose your life for nothing. It would be all right if you were fighting the Turks or the Swedes, but it would be a sin even to mention the lot you're fighting at the moment!'

I interrupted him with a question: 'How much money have we got altogether?'

'There's enough for you,' he replied with a satisfied expression. 'In spite of the rebels' rummaging about, I managed to hide some.'

And with these words he drew from his pocket a long knitted purse filled with silver.

'Well, Savelyitch,' I said to him, 'give me half of it now, and keep the rest for yourself. I am going to the Belogorsky fortress.'

'Pyotr Andreitch, my dear!' said my good old servant in a trembling voice. 'Have fear of God. How can you travel in times like these, when all the roads are swarming with outlaws! Have pity on your parents, even if you have none for yourself. Where do you want to go? And why? Wait a little while: the troops will soon be here, and they'll catch the rebels, and then you can go wherever you like.'

But I had fully made up my mind.

'It's too late to argue now,' I answered the old man. 'I must go; I cannot not go. Don't grieve, Savelyitch. God is merciful; perhaps we shall see each other again! And don't have any scruples about the money, but spend it as you will. Buy whatever you want, even if it's three times as expensive as usual. This money I give to you. If I am not back after three days . . .'

'What are you saying, master?' Savelyitch interrupted me. 'That I should let you go alone! Don't imagine that. If you have quite decided to go, I will follow you; even if I have to go on foot, I will not leave you. That I should sit behind a stone wall while you are away! Do you suppose that I've taken leave of my senses? Do as you please, master, but I'll not leave you.'

I knew that it was pointless to argue with Savelyitch, and I allowed him to prepare for the journey. Half an hour later, I mounted my good horse and Savelyitch a lean, limping nag, which one of the inhabitants of the town had given to him for nothing, no longer having the means with which to feed it. We reached the gates of the town; the sentries let us through and we left Orenburg.

It was beginning to grow dark. My way led past the village of Berda, one of Pugachev's haunts. The straight road was covered with snow; but the imprint of horses' hooves, daily renewed, could be seen all over the steppe. I rode at a fast trot. Savelyitch could scarcely keep up with me, and kept calling out:

'Slower, master, for God's sake, slower! My accursed nag cannot keep up with your long-legged devil. What's the hurry? It would be all very well if we were going to a feast, but we're more likely going to our deaths. I fear . . . Pyotr

Andreitch ... ! Pyotr Andreitch, my dear ... ! Don't destroy me ... ! Good Lord above, the master's child will surely perish!'

The lights of Berda soon began to sparkle. We approached the ravines which formed the natural fortifications of the village. Savelyitch was still with me, never ceasing his plaintive entreaties. I was hoping to go round the village without being observed when, suddenly, five peasants, armed with clubs, appeared right in front of me in the darkness. It was the advance guard of Pugachev's camp. They challenged us. Not knowing the password, I wanted to ride past them without saying a word; but they immediately surrounded me and one of them seized my horse by the bridle. I took hold of my sword and struck the peasant over the head; his cap saved him, but he stumbled and the bridle fell from his hands. The others became confused and fled; I took advantage of this moment, spurred on my horse and galloped off.

The darkness of the approaching night might have saved me from any further danger but, turning round suddenly, I saw that Savelyitch was no longer with me. The poor old man had not been able to gallop away from the brigands on his lame horse. What was I to do? After waiting for a few moments and assuring myself that he really was caught, I turned my horse about and went back to rescue him.

Approaching the ravine, I heard the noise of cries and my Savelyitch's voice in the distance. I rode faster and soon found myself once more among the peasant sentries who had stopped me a few minutes before. Savelyitch was with them. They had dragged the old man off his nag and were preparing to tie him up. They were delighted at my arrival. They threw themselves upon me with shouts and dragged me off my horse in a twinkling. One of them, apparently the leader, announced that he was going to take us before the Tsar immediately.

'And our father,' he added, 'will be able to decide whether you be hanged now or whether we should wait until dawn.'

I did not resist; Savelyitch followed my example and the sentries led us away in triumph.

We crossed the ravine and entered the village. Lights were burning in all the huts. Noise and shouting resounded everywhere. I met a large number of people in the street; but no-one noticed us in the darkness, and I was not recognised as an officer from Orenburg. We were taken straight to a hut which stood at a corner where two streets met. Several wine-casks and a couple of cannons stood at the gate.

'Here is the palace,' said one of the peasants. 'We'll announce you immediately.'

He went into the hut. I glanced at Savelyitch; the old man was making the sign of the cross and saying a prayer to himself. I waited for a long time. At last the peasant returned and said to me:

'Come inside. Our father has given orders for the officer to be taken before him.'

I went into the hut, or the palace as the peasants called it. It was lit by two tallow candles and the walls were covered with gold paper; otherwise, the benches, the table, the hand-basin on a cord, the towel hanging on a nail, the oven-fork in the corner and the wide hearth piled up with cooking-pots – all were the same as in any other cottage. Pugachev was sitting beneath the icons in a red kaftan and a tall cap, his arms importantly akimbo. Several of his chief confeder-ates were standing near him with expressions of feigned servility on their faces. It was evident that the news of the arrival of an officer from Orenburg had aroused consider-able curiosity among the rebels, and that they had prepared to meet me with pomp. Pugachev recognised me at first glance. His assumed importance immediately vanished.

'Ah, your Honour!' he said to me in a lively way. 'How are you? What's brought you here?'

I replied that I was travelling on personal business and that his people had stopped me.

'And what is your business?' he asked me.

I did not know how to reply. Pugachev, supposing that I was reluctant to explain myself before witnesses, turned to his comrades and ordered them to leave the room. All obeyed with the exception of two, who did not move from their places.

'You can say what you like in front of them,' Pugachev said to me. 'I keep nothing secret from them.'

I glanced out of the corner of my eye at the pretender's confidants. One of them, a puny, bent old man with a grey beard had nothing remarkable about him except for a blue ribbon which he wore across the shoulder of his grey overcoat. But in all my life I shall never forget his companion. He was a tall, corpulent, broad-shouldered man who seemed to me to be about forty-five. A thick red beard, brilliant grey eyes, a nose without nostrils and reddish scars upon his forehead and cheeks gave his broad, pockmarked face an indescribable expression. He wore a red shirt, a Kirghiz robe and Cossack trousers. The first (as I afterwards learned) was a deserter, Corporal Beloborodov, the second, Afanassy Sokolov (nick-named Khlopusha), an exiled convict who had three times escaped from the mines in Siberia. Despite the exceptional feelings of agitation that filled my mind, the company in which I so unexpectedly found myself strongly aroused my imagination. But Pugachev brought me to myself by repeating his question:

'Speak; on what business did you leave Orenburg?'

A strange thought entered my head; it seemed to me that providence, by leading me for a second time to Pugachev, was giving me an opportunity to fulfil my intention. I made up my mind to take advantage of it and, without waiting to consider my decision, I replied to Pugachev's question:

'I was going to the Belogorsky fortress to rescue an orphan who is being persecuted there.'

Pugachev's eyes glittered.

'Which of my people dares to persecute an orphan?' he cried. 'Be he as wise as Solomon, he will not escape my judgement. Speak: who is guilty?'

'Shvabrin is guilty,' I replied. 'He is holding against her will the girl whom you saw ill at the priest's wife's, and wishes to marry her by force.'

'I'll show Shvabrin!' Pugachev said menacingly. 'He'll find out what it means to act on his own and persecute the people when I am master. I'll hang him.'

'Allow me to say a word,' said Khlopusha in a hoarse voice. 'You were in a hurry to appoint Shvabrin as commandant of the fortress, and now you're in a hurry to hang him. You have already offended the Cossacks by putting them under the authority of a nobleman; do not now alarm the noblemen by hanging them at the first accusation.'

'They should neither be pitied nor favoured,' said the old man with the blue ribbon. 'To hang Shvabrin would be no great misfortune; and neither would it be amiss to give this officer a regular questioning: why has he decided to pay us a call? If he does not acknowledge you as Tsar, he cannot appeal to you for justice; if he does acknowledge you as Tsar, why has he been with your enemies in Orenburg until now? Will you not order him to be taken to the prison-office, and there have a fire prepared for him: I reckon that his Grace has been sent here by the Orenburg commanders.'

The old villain's logic seemed pretty convincing to me. My flesh began to creep at the thought of whose hands I was in. Pugachev observed my perplexity.

'Well, your Honour?' he said to me with a wink. 'My field-marshal seems to be talking sense. What do you think?'

Pugachev's mockery gave me back my courage. I replied calmly that I was in his hands, and that he could do with me as he wished.

'Good,' said Pugachev. 'Now tell me, how are things in your town?'

'Thank God,' I replied, 'everything's all right!'

'All right?' repeated Pugachev. 'With the people dying of hunger!'

The pretender spoke the truth; but from duty to my oath of loyalty, I began to assure him that these were idle rumours, and that there was enough of every sort of provision at Orenburg.

'See,' broke in the little old man, 'he's deceiving you to your face. All the fugitives unanimously declare that there is famine and sickness in Orenburg, that they're eating carrion there, and think themselves lucky for that; but his Grace assures us that there is plenty of everything. If you want to hang Shvabrin, then hang this young fellow on the same gallows, and then neither will be jealous of the other.'

The accursed old man's words seemed to cause Pugachev to hesitate. Fortunately, Khlopusha began to contradict his comrade.

'That's enough, Naumitch,' he said to him. 'You would do nothing but strangle and cut throats. What sort of a hero are you? To look at you, it's a mystery what keeps your soul in. You've got one foot in the grave yourself, and yet you want to destroy others. Haven't you enough blood on your conscience?'

'What sort of a saint are you?' retorted Beloborodov. 'Where do you get this compassion from?'

'Of course, I have sinned, too,' replied Khlopusha, 'and this arm' (he clenched his bony fist and, pushing back his sleeve, revealed a hairy arm) '. . . and this arm is guilty of shedding much Christian blood. But I have killed my enemy, not my guest; on the highway at the cross-roads or in a dark wood, not at home, sitting behind the stove; with a club or an axe, not with an old woman's slander.'

The old man turned away and muttered the words:

'Slit nostrils . . . !'

'What are you muttering, you old grumbler?' cried Khlopusha. 'I'll give you "slit nostrils". You wait, your time will come; God willing, you'll smell the hangman's pincers . . . And, meanwhile, watch out that I don't tear your beard off!'

'Generals!' said Pugachev haughtily. 'That's enough of your quarrelling. It wouldn't matter if all the Orenburg dogs were hanging, their legs twitching, from the same cross-beam; but it's a bad thing if our own begin to snap at each other's throats. Now make it up between yourselves.'

Khlopusha and Beloborodov did not utter a word and looked darkly at one another. I saw the necessity of changing a conversation which could end very unpleasantly for me and, turning to Pugachev, I said to him with a jocular expression:

'Oh, I almost forgot to thank you for the horse and the sheepskin coat! If it hadn't been for you, I would never have reached the town, but would have frozen to death on the road.'

My strategy succeeded. Pugachev brightened up.

'One good turn deserves another,' he said, winking and screwing up his eye. 'Tell me now, why are you interested in this girl whom Shvabrin is persecuting? Is she the darling of your young heart, eh?'

'She is betrothed to me,' I answered Pugachev, seeing a favourable change in the weather and no longer finding it necessary to conceal the truth.

'Your betrothed!' cried Pugachev. 'Why didn't you say so before? We'll marry you and have a feast at your wedding!'

Then, turning to Beloborodov:

'Listen, field-marshal! His Honour and I are old friends. Let's sit down and have supper together, and we'll sleep on it: we shall see what we'll do with him to-morrow.'

I would gladly have refused the proposed honour, but there was no escaping it. Two young Cossack girls, daughters of the owners of the cottage, covered the table with a white table-cloth, brought in some bread, fish-soup and several bottles of wine and beer, and for the second time I found myself at the same table as Pugachev and his gruesome associates.

The orgy of which I was an involuntary witness lasted far into the night. Finally, intoxication began to overcome the three companions. Pugachev went to sleep, sitting in his place; his comrades stood up and gave me the sign to leave him. I went out with them. On Khlopusha's orders, a sentry took me to the prison-office, where I found Savelyitch and where we were locked up together. My servant was so stunned by all that had occurred that he did not ask me a single question. He lay down in the dark and sighed and groaned for a long time; at last he began to snore, and I gave myself over to reflections which prevented me from sleeping a wink throughout the entire night.

Pugachev summoned me to him the following morning. I went to him. A sledge, drawn by three Tartar horses, stood by the gate. A crowd had gathered in the street. I met Pugachev at the entrance to the cottage; he was dressed for the road, in a fur coat and a Kirghiz cap. His companions of the previous evening stood round him with an appearance of servility which strongly contrasted with all that I had witnessed the evening before. Pugachev greeted me gaily and ordered me to take my seat beside him in the sledge.

We sat down.

'To the Belogorsky fortress!' said Pugachev to the broad-shouldered Tartar who was driving the troika.

My heart beat violently. The horses began to move, the little bell pealed and the sledge flew off . . .

'Stop! Stop!' cried a voice which was all too familiar to me, and I saw Savelyitch running towards us.

Pugachev ordered the driver to stop.

'Pyotr Andreitch, my dear!' cried my old servant. 'Don't abandon me in my old age among these ras . . .'

'You old grumbler!' Pugachev said to him. 'So God has ordained that we should meet again. Well, get up on the box.'

'Thank you, Tsar, thank you, my dear father!' said Savelyitch as he sat down. 'May God give you a hundred years of good health for protecting and reassuring me, an old man. All my life I will pray for you, and I'll never mention the hareskin coat again.'

The reference to the hareskin coat might have made Pugachev extremely angry. Fortunately, the pretender either did not hear or paid no heed to the inapt remark. The horses galloped off; the crowd in the street stopped and bowed low to the pretender, who nodded his head to both sides. A minute later, we had left the village and were racing over the smooth road.

It is easy to imagine what I felt at that moment. Within a few hours I would be seeing her whom I already thought to be lost to me. I imagined the moment of our reunion . . . I also thought of that man in whose hands my fate lay and who, by a strange chain of circumstances, had become mysteriously connected with me. I recalled the thoughtless cruelty and the bloodthirsty habits of the man who had volunteered to rescue my beloved! Pugachev did not know that she was the daughter of Captain Mironov; the enraged Shvabrin might reveal everything to him; Pugachev might discover the truth in some other way . . . And then what would become of Marya Ivanovna? A cold shudder ran through my whole body and my hair stood on end . . .

Suddenly Pugachev broke into my reflections, turning to me with a question:

'What are you so pensive about, your Honour?'

'How could I be otherwise than pensive?' I answered him. 'I am an officer and a nobleman; yesterday I was fighting against you, and to-day I am riding at your side in the same sledge, with the happiness of my whole life depending upon you.'

'And what of it?' asked Pugachev. 'Are you afraid?'

I replied that, having been spared by him once already, I hoped not only for his mercy but even for his help.

'And you're right, by God, you're right!' the pretender said. 'You saw how my men looked askance at you; and this morning the old man again insisted that you were a spy, and said you should be tortured and then hanged. But I did not agree,' he added, lowering his voice so that Savelyitch and the Tartar should not hear him, 'since I remembered your glass of wine and the hareskin coat. You see, I'm not as bloodthirsty as your brethren say I am.'

I remembered the taking of the Belogorsky fortress, but I did not consider it necessary to dispute the point and made no reply.

'What do they say about me at Orenburg?' asked Pugachev after a pause.

'They say that it'll be difficult to get the better of you. There's no denying, you've made yourself felt.'

The pretender's face expressed satisfied vanity.

'Yes!' he said gaily. 'I don't fight badly. Do you people in Orenburg know of the battle of Yuzeyeva? Forty generals killed, four armies taken into captivity. What do you think: d'you think the King of Prussia could rival me?'

The brigand's boasting amused me.

'What do you think yourself?' I asked him. 'D'you think you could beat Frederick?'

'Fyodor Fyodorovitch? But why not? I've beaten your generals and they've beaten him. Up to now my arms have been successful. Given time, you'll see me march on Moscow.'

'And do you propose to march on Moscow?'

The pretender thought for a while and then said softly;

'God knows. My scope is limited. My men have got their own ideas. They are robbers. I have to keep a sharp look-out: at the first reverse they'll save their own heads at the expense of mine.'

'That's just it,' I said to Pugachev. 'Wouldn't it be better to cut loose from them, in good time, and then throw yourself on the mercy of the Empress?'

Pugachev smiled bitterly.

'No,' he replied. 'It's too late for me to repent. There'll be no mercy for me. I will continue as I have begun. Who knows? Perhaps I'll succeed. Grishka Otrepyev reigned over Moscow, didn't he?'

'But do you know what happened to him in the end? He was thrown from a window, torn to pieces, burned, and his ashes used to fire a cannon!'

'Listen,' said Pugachev with a sort of wild inspiration. 'I'll tell you a story, which was told to me in my childhood by an old Kalmuck woman. The eagle once asked the raven: "Tell me, raven-bird, how is it that you live in this bright world for three hundred years while I only live for thirty-three in all?" "Because, dear eagle", the raven answered, "you drink live blood and I live off carrion". The eagle thought: "I'll give it a try and live off the same food as the raven." Very well. Good. The eagle and the raven flew off. After a time they caught sight of a dead horse and they flew down and alighted upon it. The raven began to peck at it and was well pleased. The eagle tasted it once, once more, shook his beak and said to the raven: "No, brother raven, rather than live off carrion for three hundred years, I would prefer to drink live blood, and then trust to God!' What do you think of the Kalmuck woman's story?'

'Ingenious,' I replied. 'But in my opinion to live off murder and robbery is the same as pecking at carrion.'

Pugachev looked at me with astonishment and made no reply. We both became silent, each of us absorbed in his own thoughts. The Tartar began to sing a sad song; Savelyitch, dozing, swayed on the box. The sledge flew along the smooth winter road ... Suddenly I saw a little village on the steep bank of the Yaik, with its palisade and belfry, and a quarter of an hour later we entered the Belogorsky fortress.

Chapter Twelve

THE ORPHAN

> *As our little young apple-tree*
> *Has neither branches nor a leafy top,*
> *So our young princess*
> *Has neither father nor mother.*
> *No one to prepare her for life,*
> *No one to bless her.*
>
> WEDDING SONG

The sledge drew up in front of the commandant's house. The people had recognised Pugachev's little bell and ran after us in a crowd. Shvabrin met the pretender on the steps. He was dressed as a Cossack and had grown a beard. The traitor helped Pugachev to climb down from the sledge, expressing, in abject terms, his delight and zeal. On seeing me, he became confused; but, quickly recovering himself, he stretched out his hand and said:

'Are you one of us? About time, too!'

I turned away from him and made no reply.

My heart ached when we found ourselves in the long familiar room where the diploma of the late commandant still hung on the wall as a sad epitaph of the past. Pugachev sat down on the same sofa on which Ivan Kuzmitch, lulled by the scolding of his wife, used to doze. Shvabrin himself brought some vodka. Pugachev drained his glass and, pointing at me, he said:

'Pour his Honour a glass, too.'

Shvabrin approached me with his tray; but for the second time I turned away from him. He did not seem to be himself. With his usual intelligence, he had of course guessed that Pugachev was not pleased with him. He cowered before him and glanced at me distrustfully. Pugachev made enquiries about the situation in the fortress, about reports concerning the enemy's troops and so on and then, suddenly and unexpectedly, he said:

'Tell me, brother, who is this young girl you've got locked up here? Show her to me.'

Shvabrin went as pale as death.

'Tsar,' he said in a trembling voice, '. . . she is not locked up . . . she is ill . . . she is in bed.'

'Take me to her,' the pretender said, getting up from his place.

To refuse was impossible. Shvabrin led Pugachev to Marya Ivanovna's bedroom. I followed them.

Shvabrin stopped on the stairway.

'Tsar!' he said. 'You have power to ask of me what you wish; but do not order a stranger to enter my wife's bedroom.'

I shuddered.

'So you're married!' I said to Shvabrin, ready to tear him to pieces.

'Silence!' interrupted Pugachev. 'This is my affair. And you,' he continued, turning to Shvabrin, 'stop trying to be smart and putting on all these airs and graces. Whether she's your wife or not, I take whoever I wish. Your Honour, follow me.'

At the door of the room Shvabrin stopped again and said in a faltering voice:

'Tsar, I should warn you that she is delirious and has been raving incessantly for the last three days.'

'Open the door!' said Pugachev.

Shvabrin began to search through his pockets and said that he had not brought the key up with him. Pugachev kicked the door with his foot; the lock gave way; the door opened and we entered the room.

I looked and was struck dumb with horror. On the floor, in a tattered peasant's dress, sat Marya Ivanovna, pale, thin, her hair dishevelled. Before her stood a pitcher of water covered with a piece of bread. Seeing me, she started and cried out. I do not remember what I felt at that moment.

Pugachev looked at Shvabrin and said with an ironical smile:

'A nice hospital you've got here!' Then, going up to Marya Ivanovna: 'Tell me, my dear, what is your husband punishing you for? In what way have you offended him?'

'My husband!' she repeated. 'He's not my husband. I will never be his wife! I would rather die, and I will die, unless I am delivered.'

Pugachev looked menacingly at Shvabrin.

'And you dared to deceive me!' he said to him. 'Do you know, you scoundrel, what you deserve?'

Shvabrin fell on his knees ... At that moment contempt stifled within me all feelings of hate and anger. The sight of a nobleman at the feet of a fugitive Cossack filled me with disgust. Pugachev softened.

'I'll forgive you this time,' he said to Shvabrin, 'but the next time you commit an offence, I shall take this into account.'

He then turned to Marya Ivanovna and said to her kindly:

'Go, my pretty girl; I give you your freedom. I am the Tsar.'

Marya Ivanovna glanced quickly at him and guessed that the murderer of her parents stood before her. She covered her eyes with both her hands and fell senseless to the ground. I rushed up to her; but at that moment my old friend Palashka very boldly entered the room and began to attend to her young mistress. Pugachev left the room, and the three of us went down into the drawing-room.

'Well, your Honour!' Pugachev said, laughing. 'We have rescued the fair maiden! What do you say to sending for the priest and having him marry you to his niece! If you like, I'll be her father by proxy and Shvabrin can be best man, and then we shall feast and drink without allowing ourselves to be disturbed!'

What I had feared now occurred. Shvabrin, on hearing Pugachev's suggestion, went out of his mind with fury.

'Tsar!' he cried in a frenzy. 'I am guilty; I have lied to you; but Grinev has also deceived you. The girl is not the local priest's niece; she is the daughter of Ivan Mironov, who was hanged at the capture of the fortress.'

Pugachev fixed me with his fiery eyes.

'What does this mean?' he asked, perplexed.

'Shvabrin has told you the truth,' I replied firmly.

'You did not tell me,' remarked Pugachev, whose face became clouded.

'Judge for yourself,' I answered him: 'could I have declared in front of your men that Captain Mironov's daughter was still alive? They would have torn her to pieces. Nothing would have saved her!'

'That's true enough!' said Pugachev, laughing. 'My drunkards would not have spared the poor girl. My good friend, the priest's wife, did well to hoodwink them.'

'Listen,' I continued, seeing that he was in a good mood. 'I don't know what to call you, and I don't wish to know . . . But God is my witness that I would gladly repay you with my life for what you have done for me. Only do not demand of me anything which is against my honour or my Christian conscience. You are my benefactor. End as you have begun: let me go away with that poor orphan wherever God may lead us. And wherever you may be and whatever may happen to you, we will pray every day for the salvation of your sinful soul . . .'

It seemed that Pugachev's harsh soul had been touched.

'All right, as you say!' he said. 'Either punish or pardon – one or the other: that's my custom. Take your beauty with you: take her where you want and may God give you love and advice!'

Then he turned to Shvabrin and ordered him to give me a safe-conduct for all the outposts and fortresses that were subject to his command. Shvabrin, utterly defeated, stood as if turned to stone. Pugachev set off to inspect the fortress. Shvabrin accompanied him; I remained behind under the pretext of wishing to prepare for my departure.

I ran up to Marya Ivanovna's bedroom. The door was locked. I knocked.

'Who's there?' asked Palashka.

I pronounced my name. The gentle voice of Marya Ivanovna was heard from behind the door. 'Wait, Pyotr Andreitch. I am changing my dress. Go to Akulina Pamfilovna's; I'll be there presently.'

I obeyed her and went to the house of Father Gerassim.

He and his wife ran out to meet me. Savelyitch had already warned them of my coming.

'Greetings, Pyotr Andreitch,' said the priest's wife. 'So God has ordained that we should meet again. How are you? There hasn't been a day we haven't talked about you. And Marya Ivanovna, poor soul, what she has had to endure without you . . . ! But tell me, my dear, how you manage to get on so well with Pugachev? Why hasn't he done away with you? That's something to be thankful to the villain for.'

'That's enough chatter, mother,' interrupted Father Gerassim. 'Don't bubble over with everything you know. There's no salvation in too much talking. Pyotr Andreitch, my dear, come in, I beg of you! It's a long, long time since we've seen each other.'

The priest's wife gave me to eat all the food she had in the house. In the meantime she talked incessantly. She related to me how Shvabrin had forced them to hand over Marya Ivanovna to him; how Marya Ivanovna had wept and had not wished to be parted from them; how Marya Ivanovna had kept in constant touch with them through Palashka (a quick-witted girl who had made the sergeant dance to her tune); how she had advised Marya Ivanovna to write a letter to me, and so on. I in my turn briefly related my tale. The priest and his wife crossed themselves when they heard that Pugachev knew of their deception.

'The strength of the Cross is with us!' said Akulina Pamfilovna. 'May God let the cloud pass over. Well done, Alexey Ivanytch! He's a fine fellow and no mistake!'

At the same moment the door opened and Marya Ivanovna entered the room with a smile on her pale face. She had taken off her peasant's dress and was attired, as before, simply and charmingly.

I seized her hand and for a long time could not utter a

single word. We were both silent from fullness of heart. Our hosts felt that they were not wanted and left us. We were alone. Everything else was forgotten. We talked and talked and could not say enough. Marya Ivanovna related to me all that had happened to her since the taking of the fortress; she described to me the full horror of her position, and all the ordeals she had suffered at the hands of the odious Shvabrin. We recalled former happy times ... We were both weeping ... Finally, I began to tell her of my proposals. For her to remain at the fortress that was subject to Pugachev but under the command of Shvabrin, was impossible. So was the idea of going to Orenburg, which was then enduring all the privations of siege. She had not a single relative in the world. I suggested that she should go to my parents in their village. At first she hesitated; she was afraid, knowing of my father's disapproval. I allayed her anxiety. I knew that my father would consider it both a pleasure and a duty to take in the daughter of a distinguished soldier who had been killed in the service of his country.

'Dear Marya Ivanovna!' I said to her finally. 'I look upon you as my wife. Miraculous circumstances have united us for ever: nothing on earth can separate us.'

Marya Ivanovna listened to me simply, with no false modesty or fanciful pretence. She felt that her fate was tied to mine. But she repeated that under no circumstances would she become my wife without the consent of my parents. I did not oppose her. We kissed passionately, sincerely – and in this way everything was decided between us.

An hour later, the sergeant brought me my safe-conduct, signed with Pugachev's scrawl, and told me that Pugachev wished to see me. I found him ready to set off on his journey. I cannot describe what I felt on parting from this terrible man, this outcast, this villain to all but myself alone. Why not speak the truth? At that moment, I felt strongly drawn to him. I fervently wished to take him away from the environment of the criminals he commanded, and to save his head while there was still time. Shvabrin and the people who crowded round us prevented me from expressing all that filled my heart.

We parted friends. Pugachev, seeing Akulina Pamfilovna in the crowd, raised a threatening finger at her and winked significantly; he then took his seat in the sledge, ordered the driver to make for Berda and, as the horse began to move, leaned once more out of the sledge and cried out to me:

'Farewell, your Honour! Perhaps we'll meet again sometime.'

Indeed we did see each other again, but in what circumstances!

Pugachev was gone. For a long time I stood gazing at the white steppe over which his troika glided away. The crowd dispersed. Shvabrin disappeared. I returned to the priest's house. Everything was prepared for our departure; I did not wish to delay any longer. All our belongings had been packed into the commandant's old carriage. The drivers harnessed the horses in a flash. Marya Ivanovna went to say farewell to the graves of her parents, who had been buried behind the church. I wanted to accompany her, but she begged me to let her go alone. She returned a few minutes later, silently weeping. The carriage was drawn up. Father Gerassim and his wife came out on to the steps. The three of us – Marya Ivanovna, Palashka and I – took our seats inside. Savelyitch climbed up on to the box.

'Good-bye, Marya Ivanovna, my little darling! Good-bye, Pyotr Andreitch, my dear!' said the kind priest's wife. 'A good journey, and may God give happiness to you both.'

We set off. I saw Shvabrin standing at the little window of the commandant's house. His face expressed gloom and wickedness. I had no wish to triumph over a defeated enemy and turned my eyes in another direction. At last we passed through the fortress gates and left the Belogorsky fortress for the last time.

Chapter Thirteen

THE ARREST

> *Do not be angry, Sir; according to my duty*
> *I must send you to prison at this very*
> > *moment.*
> *As you please, I am ready; but I hope*
> *That you will allow me to have my say first.*
>
> (KNYAZHNIN)

United so unexpectedly with the dear girl about whom I had been so desperately worried that very morning, I could not trust myself and imagined that everything that had happened to me was an empty dream. Marya Ivanovna gazed pensively, now at me, now at the road, and it seemed that she had not yet fully come to herself. We were silent. Our hearts were too tired. The time slipped by unnoticed, and a couple of hours later we found ourselves at the next fortress, which was also held by Pugachev. Here we changed horses. The speed with which they were harnessed and the servile helpfulness of the bearded Cossack who had been put in command of the fortress by Pugachev, showed that, thanks to our driver's loquacity, I was welcomed as one of their master's more powerful favourites.

We set off again. Dusk was beginning to fall. We drew near to a small town where, according to the bearded commandant, we would find a strong detachment on its way to join the pretender. We were stopped by the sentries. To the challenge: 'Who goes there?' the driver replied in a loud voice: 'A friend of the Tsar with his wife.'

Suddenly a crowd of Hussars surrounded us, uttering the most terrible curses.

'Come out, friend of the devil!' said the moustached sergeant to me. 'We'll make things pretty hot for you and your little wife!'

I stepped down from the sledge and demanded to be taken to their commanding officer. On seeing an officer, the soldiers stopped swearing. The sergeant took me to the major. Savelyitch never left my side, muttering to himself:

'So much for your being a friend of the Tsar! Out of the frying pan into the fire . . . Good heavens above, how will all this end?'

The sledge followed us at walking pace.

Five minutes later, we arrived at a small, brightly-lit house. The sergeant left me under guard and went in to announce me. He returned at once and informed me that his Excellency had no time to see me, but had ordered that I be taken to the prison, and my wife to him.

'What does this mean?' I exclaimed in a rage. 'Has he gone out of his mind?'

'I don't know, your Honour,' replied the sergeant. 'Only his Excellency ordered that your Honour should be taken to prison, and that her Honour be brought to his Excellency, your Honour!'

I dashed up the steps. The guards did not think of holding me back and I ran straight into the room where six Hussar officers were playing cards. The major was dealing. Imagine my astonishment when, glancing up at him, I recognised Ivan

Ivanovitch Zurin, who had once fleeced me at the Simbirsk inn!

'Is it possible?' I cried. 'Ivan Ivanytch! Is it really you?'

'Well, well, well! Pyotr Andreitch! What good wind brings you here? How are you, brother? Would you care to join in the game?'

'Thank you, but I would rather you gave orders for quarters to be found for me.'

'What do you want with quarters? Stay with me.'

'I cannot; I am not alone.'

'Well, bring your comrade along too.'

'I am not with a comrade; I am ... with a lady.'

'With a lady ! Where did you pick her up? Aha, brother!'

With these words Zurin whistled so expressively that everyone burst out laughing, and I became thoroughly confused.

'Well,' continued Zurin, 'so be it. You shall have quarters. But it's a pity ... We might have had a spree as before ... Hey, boy! Why don't they bring along Pugachev's lady friend? Or is she being obstinate? Tell her that there's nothing to be frightened about, that the gentleman's very nice and won't harm her – and then bring her in by the scruff of her neck.'

'What are you saying?' I said to Zurin. 'What lady friend of Pugachev's? It is the daughter of the late Captain Mironov. I rescued her from captivity and am now taking her to my father's village where I shall leave her.'

'What! So it was you who was announced just now? Gracious me, what does this mean?'

'I'll tell you later. But now, for God's sake, set the poor girl at rest. Your Hussars have frightened her out of her wits.'

Zurin immediately made the necessary arrangements. He went out into the street himself to apologise to Marya

Ivanovna for the involuntary misunderstanding, and ordered the sergeant to take her to the best quarters in the town. I stayed to spend the night with him.

We had supper, and when we were alone together, I told him of my adventures. Zurin listened most attentively.

When I had finished, he shook his head and said:

'That's all very well, brother. One thing is not, however: why the devil do you want to get married? As an officer and a man of honour, I have no wish to deceive you, but take it from me that marriage is all rubbish. Why take on all the trouble of a wife and be for ever fussing over children? Have done with the scheme. Listen to me: rid yourself of this captain's daughter. I have cleared the road to Simbirsk and it's now quite safe. Send her off on her own to your parents to-morrow, and you yourself stay in my detachment. There's no reason why you should go back to Orenburg. If you fall into the rebels' hands again, you might not be able to get away from them so easily a second time. In this way your foolish infatuation will die of its own accord and all will be well.'

Although I did not altogether agree with him, I did feel that duty and honour demanded my presence in the Empress's army. I decided to follow Zurin's advice: to send Marya Ivanovna to my father's village, and myself to stay on in his detachment.

Savelyitch came in to help me undress. I told him to be ready the next day to continue the journey with Marya Ivanovna. He began to hedge.

'What, master? Why should I desert you? Who's going to look after you? What will your parents say?'

Knowing how obstinate my servant was, I decided to persuade him by kindness and sincerity.

'My dear friend, Arkhip Savelyitch,' I said to him, 'do not refuse me, but be my benefactor. I shall not need a servant here and I would not feel easy if Marya Ivanovna were to continue her journey without you. By serving her, you will be serving me, since I have firmly resolved to marry her as soon as circumstances allow it.'

At this Savelyitch threw up his arms with a look of indescribable astonishment.

'To marry!' he repeated. 'The child wants to marry. But what will your father say, and what will your mother think?'

'They will give their consent, they will give their consent for sure,' I replied, 'when they know Marya Ivanovna. But I rely upon you. My father and mother have confidence in you. You will put in a good word for us, won't you?'

The old man was touched.

'Oh, Pyotr Andreitch, my dear,' he replied, 'although it's early for you to start thinking of marriage, Marya Ivanovna is such a good young lady that it'd be a sin to miss the opportunity. Let it be as you wish! I will accompany her, the angel, and tell your parents respectfully that such a bride does not need a dowry.'

I thanked Savelyitch and lay down to sleep in the same room as Zurin. My mind was in a state of great turmoil and I began to chatter. Zurin was willing enough to converse with me at first; gradually, however, his words became less frequent and more disconnected; finally, instead of replying to one of my questions, he began to snore and make whistling noises. I stopped talking and soon fell asleep myself.

I went round to Marya Ivanovna the following morning. I informed her of my proposals. She admitted their good sense and at once agreed with me. Zurin's detachment was to leave the town that same day. There was no time to be lost. I said goodbye to Marya Ivanovna there and then, entrusting her to the care of Savelyitch and giving her a letter to my parents. Marya Ivanovna burst into tears.

'Good-bye, Pyotr Andreitch!' she said in a soft voice.

'Whether we shall get the chance to see each other again, God alone knows, but never in my life shall I forget you; till my dying day, you alone shall remain in my heart.'

I could not reply to her. We were surrounded by people. I did not wish to give way before them to the feelings that agitated me. Finally she departed. I returned to Zurin, silent and dejected. He tried to cheer me up, and I was in need of distraction: we spent the rest of the day in noisy and riotous fashion, and set out on our march in the evening.

It was now near the end of February. Winter, which had made military operations difficult, was drawing to its close, and our generals were preparing for concerted action. Pugachev was still besieging Orenburg. Meanwhile, our detachments were joining forces around him and moving in on the villains' nest from all sides. The rebellious villages were restored to obedience at the sight of our troops; brigand bands everywhere fled from us, and everything gave promise of a speedy and successful conclusion of the campaign.

Shortly afterwards, Prince Golitsyn defeated Pugachev beneath the walls of the fortress of Tatishcheva, dispersed his followers, relieved Orenburg and, it seemed, struck the final and decisive blow to the rebellion. Around this time Zurin was sent out against a band of rebellious Bashkirs, who dispersed before we ever reached them. Spring found us in a little Tartar village. Rivers overflowed and roads became impassable. We consoled ourselves in our inaction with the thought that this tedious and trivial war against brigands and savages would soon come to an end.

But Pugachev had not been captured. He showed up in the industrial areas of Siberia, where he collected fresh bands of rebels and again began to perpetrate his acts of villainy. Once more reports of his successes were spread abroad. We heard of the destruction of the Siberian fortresses. Soon, news of the capture of Kazan and the pretender's intention to march on Moscow alarmed the army leaders, who had been slumbering in the carefree hope that the despised rebel was utterly powerless. Zurin received orders to cross the Volga.

I will not describe our campaign and the conclusion of the war. I will only say that the distress became extreme. We passed through villages laid waste by the rebels, and had of necessity to requisition from their poor inhabitants what they had somehow succeeded in saving. Administration everywhere came to a stop. The landowners hid themselves in the forests. Bands of brigands ransacked the countryside; commanders of individual detachments punished and pardoned as the fancy took them; the condition of the whole vast area where the conflagration raged was terrible . . . God forbid that we should ever see a Russian rebellion – so senseless and merciless – again!

Pugachev was in flight and being pursued by Ivan Ivanovitch Mikhelson. We soon heard of his complete defeat. At last Zurin received news of the capture of the pretender and, with it, the order to halt. The war was over. At last I could go to my parents! The thought of embracing them and of seeing Marya Ivanovna, of whom I had received no news at all, filled me with delight. I danced about like a child. Zurin laughed and said with a shrug of the shoulders:

'No, you'll come to a bad end! Once married, you're lost!'

But in the meantime a strange feeling poisoned my joy: the thought of the villain, smeared with the blood of so many innocent victims, and of the execution awaiting him, involuntarily troubled me.

'Yemelya, Yemelya,' I thought with vexation, 'why didn't you throw yourself on a bayonet, or get hit by grape-shot? It would have been the best thing you could have done.'

How could I think otherwise? The thought of him was inseparable from the thought of the mercy he had shown to me at one of the most terrible moments of his life, and of the deliverance of my bride from the hands of the hateful Shvabrin.

Zurin granted me leave of absence. In a few days I would be among my family again, would be seeing Marya Ivanovna once more ... An unexpected storm suddenly burst upon me.

On the day appointed for my departure, at the very moment I was preparing to start on my journey, Zurin came to me in my quarters, holding a paper in his hand and looking exceedingly troubled. Something pricked my heart. I was frightened without knowing why. He sent my orderly away and announced that he had something to tell me.

'What is it?' I asked anxiously.

'A minor unpleasantness,' he replied, handing me the paper. 'Read what I have just received.'

I began to read it: it was a secret order to all detachment commanders to arrest me, wherever I might be, and to send me at once under guard to Kazan, to the committee of inquiry established to investigate the Pugachev Rising.

The paper nearly fell from my hands.

'It can't be helped!' said Zurin. 'My duty is to obey orders. No doubt reports of your friendly journeys with Pugachev have somehow reached the authorities. I hope that the affair will have no serious consequences and that you will be able to clear yourself before the committee. Don't be depressed, and set off at once.'

My conscience was clear; I had no fear of the tribunal, but the thought of deferring, perhaps for several months, the sweet moment of my reunion with Marya Ivanovna daunted me. The cart was ready. Zurin bade me a friendly farewell. I took my seat. Beside me as I drove off along the high road sat two Hussars with drawn swords.

Chapter Fourteen

THE TRIBUNAL

Popular rumour is like a sea-wave.

PROVERB

I was convinced that my unwarranted absence from Orenburg was the only reason for my arrest. I could easily justify myself: sallying out against the enemy had not only never been forbidden, but had even been most forcefully encouraged. I could be accused of excessive rashness, but not of disobedience. My friendly relations with Pugachev, however, could be proved by a number of witnesses and would appear, at the very least, extremely suspicious. Throughout the whole of the journey I thought of the interrogation that was awaiting me and considered the answers that I should make, and resolved to tell the complete truth at the tribunal, believing that this would be the simplest and, at the same time, the surest means of justification.

I arrived in Kazan, which had been devastated and set on fire. Instead of houses, one saw heaps of burnt wood and blackened walls without roofs or windows. Such were the traces left by Pugachev! I was conducted to the fortress, which had remained intact in the midst of the burnt-out town. The Hussars handed me over to the officer of the guard. He ordered a blacksmith to be sent for. Chains were put round my legs and shackled tightly together. I was then taken to the prison and left alone in a narrow, dark cell with blank walls and a small iron-barred window.

Such a beginning did not augur well for me. However, I lost neither courage nor hope. I had recourse to the consolation of all those in affliction, and, after having tasted the sweetness of prayer for the first time, poured out from a pure but tortured heart, I fell into a peaceful sleep, not caring about what might happen to me.

The next morning the gaoler awoke me with the announcement that my presence was required at the committee of inquiry. Two soldiers conducted me through the courtyard to the commandant's house and, stopping in the front hall, sent me into the inner room on my own.

I entered a fairly large room. At a table, which was covered with papers, sat two men: an elderly general, who looked cold and severe, and a young captain of the Guards of about twenty-eight, with a very pleasant appearance and a free and easy manner. At a separate table near a little window sat a secretary with a pen behind his ear, bent over a piece of paper, ready to record my evidence.

The interrogation began. I was asked my name and profession. The general enquired whether I was the son of Andrey Petrovitch Grinev. To my reply, he retorted sternly:

'A pity that such a worthy man should have such an unworthy son!'

I replied calmly that whatever the accusations levelled against me might be, I hoped to refute them by a frank expression of the truth. My assurance did not please him.

'You are sharp, my friend,' he said to me, frowning, 'but we've seen your type before!'

Then the young man asked me under what circumstances and at what time I had entered Pugachev's service, and on what missions I had been employed by him.

I replied indignantly that, as an officer and a nobleman, I could never have entered Pugachev's service, or accepted any missions from him.

'How is it then,' retorted my interrogator, 'that this nobleman and officer was the only one to be spared by the pretender, when all his comrades were villainously murdered? How is it that this same officer and nobleman feasted with the rebels as a friend and received presents – a sheepskin coat, a horse and half a rouble – from the leader of the rebels? How did such a strange friendship come about and on what was it founded, if not on treachery or, at least, on base and criminal cowardice?'

I was deeply offended by the words of the officer of the Guards and heatedly began to justify myself. I related how my acquaintanceship with Pugachev had begun in the steppe, at the time of the storm; how, at the capture of the Belogorsky fortress, he had recognised me and spared me. I admitted that I had no scruples about accepting the sheepskin coat and the horse from the pretender; but I also said that I had defended the Belogorsky fortress against the villain to the last extremity. Finally I referred to my general, who could testify to my zeal at the time of the calamitous siege of Orenburg.

The stern old man took up an opened letter from the table and began to read it aloud:

> 'In answer to your Excellency's inquiry concerning Ensign Grinev, who is accused of being involved in the present disturbance and of entering into communication with the villain, contrary to the regulations of the Service and the oath of allegiance, I have the honour to say that the same Ensign Grinev was in service at Orenburg from the beginning of October of last year, 1773 until 24th February of this present year, on which date he absented himself from the town, and since then has not appeared again under my command. It was heard from some deserters that he was in Pugachev's camp and that he went with him to the Belogorsky

fortress, where he had been garrisoned before. As regards his conduct, I can only . . .'

Here he broke off his reading and said to me severely: 'What do you say for yourself now in justification?'

I was about to continue as I had begun and explain my connection with Marya Ivanovna as openly as the rest of what I had said. Suddenly, however, I felt an overwhelming revulsion. It occurred to me that if I mentioned her by name, the committee would demand her appearance at the inquiry; and the thought of involving her name with the hateful denunciations of the villains and of herself being obliged to confront them – this terrible thought so appalled me that I faltered in my speech and became confused.

My judges, who seemed at first to listen to my answers with a certain good-will, again became prejudiced against me at the sight of my confusion. The officer of the Guards demanded that I be brought face to face with my principal accuser. The general gave orders for 'yesterday's villain' to be brought in. I turned quickly towards the door, awaiting the appearance of my accuser. A few minutes later, to the rattling of chains, the door opened and into the room came – Shvabrin. I was astonished at the change in his appearance. He was terribly thin and pale. His hair, not so long ago as black as soot, was now quite grey; his long beard was tousled. He repeated his accusations in a weak but determined voice. According to him, I had been sent by Pugachev as a spy to Orenburg; every day, I would ride out on sallies with the purpose of transmitting written information about all that had occurred in the town; finally, I had openly gone over to the pretender, had accompanied him from fortress to fortress, trying to bring about the ruin of my fellow-traitors so as to take over their positions and profit by the rewards handed out by the pretender.

I listened to him in silence and was pleased at one thing alone: the name of Marya Ivanovna had not been mentioned by the odious villain, either because his vanity could not bear the thought of one who had spurned him with contempt, or because there lay hidden in his heart a spark of the same feeling which had forced me to keep silent – whichever it was, the name of the daughter of the commandant of the Belogorsky fortress was not uttered in the presence of the committee. I became still more confirmed in my intention to keep her name out of the proceedings, and when the judges asked me what I had to say in refutation of Shvabrin's evidence, I replied that I was sticking to my original statement and had nothing further to say in justification of myself.

The general ordered us to be taken away. We left the room together. I glanced calmly at Shvabrin but did not say a word to him. He smiled maliciously at me and, lifting up his chains, hastened past me. I was taken back to the prison and was not required for a further interrogation.

I was not a witness to all that now remains for me to tell the reader; but I have heard it related so often that the smallest details are engraved upon my memory, and it seems to me as if I had been invisibly present.

Marya Ivanovna was received by my parents with that sincere hospitality which distinguished people of a past age. They regarded it as a divine blessing that they had been afforded the opportunity of sheltering and giving a warm welcome to the poor orphan. They soon became sincerely attached to her, since it was impossible to know her and not love her. My love no longer appeared as mere folly to my father, and my mother wished for only one thing – that her Petrusha should marry the captain's pretty daughter.

The news of my arrest came as a shock to my family. Marya Ivanovna had related the story of my friendship with Pugachev so simply to my parents, that not only had they not worried, but had even often been forced to laugh, about the whole affair. My father would not believe that I had been involved in the infamous rebellion, whose aim it was to overthrow the throne and exterminate the nobles. He questioned Savelyitch closely. My servant did not conceal the fact that I had been a guest of Yemelyan Pugachev and that the villain had shown me favour; but he swore that he had heard no word of any treason. My old parents were reassured and impatiently began to await favourable news. Marya Ivanovna was greatly alarmed, however, but she kept silent, for she was given in the highest degree to modesty and prudence.

Several weeks passed. Then, suddenly, my father received a letter from our relative in Petersburg, Prince B**. The prince wrote to him about me. After the usual compliments, he informed him that the suspicions concerning my participation in the rebels' designs had unhappily proved to be only too well-founded, that capital punishment would have been meted out to me as an example to others had not the Empress, in consideration of my father's faithful services and declining years, decided to spare his criminal son and, commuting the ignominious death sentence, to exile him to a remote part of Siberia for life.

This unexpected blow nearly killed my father. He lost his customary strength of character and his grief (normally silent) poured out in bitter complaints.

'What!' he used to repeat, beside himself. 'My son participated in Pugachev's designs! Blessed Lord, that I should have lived to see this! The Empress spares him from the death penalty! Does that make it any better for me? It's not the death sentence that's so terrible: my great-grandfather's grandfather died upon the scaffold in defence of that which his conscience regarded as sacred; my father suffered together with Volynsky and Khrushchev. But that a nobleman should betray his oath of allegiance, should associate with brigands, with murderers and fugitive serfs ... ! Shame and disgrace upon our name ... !'

Frightened by his despair, my mother did not dare to weep in his presence and tried to cheer him up by speaking of the uncertainty of rumour and the unreliability of other people's opinions. My father was inconsolable.

Marya Ivanovna suffered more than anybody. Being certain that I could have justified myself if only I had wished, she guessed at the truth and held herself responsible for my misfortune. She concealed her tears and suffering from everyone, all the while thinking of means by which to save me.

One evening my father was sitting on the sofa, turning the pages of the *Court Calendar*; but his thoughts were far away, and the reading of the *Calendar* did not produce its usual effect upon him. He was whistling an old march. My mother was silently knitting a woollen vest, and from time to time a tear would drop on to her work. Of a sudden, Marya Ivanovna, who was also in the room, sitting at her work, declared that it was absolutely essential that she should go to Petersburg, and she begged my parents to provide her with the means to do so. My mother was very upset.

'Why do you want to go to Petersburg?' she said. 'Can it be, Marya Ivanovna, that you too wish to forsake us?'

Marya Ivanovna replied that her whole future depended upon this journey and that she was going in search of protection and help from influential people, as the daughter of a man who had suffered for his loyalty.

My father lowered his head: every word that reminded him of the alleged crime of his son was hurtful to him and seemed as a bitter reproach.

'Go, my dear!' he said to her with a sigh. 'We don't want to stand in the way of your happiness. God grant you an honest man for a husband, and not a discredited traitor.'

He stood up and left the room.

Marya Ivanovna, left alone with my mother, in part explained her plan. My mother embraced her with tears and prayed for the successful outcome of her scheme. Marya Ivanovna was fitted out and, a few days later, she set out on her journey with the faithful Palashka and the faithful Savelyitch who, forcibly separated from me, consoled himself with the thought that at least he was serving my betrothed.

Marya Ivanovna arrived safely at Sofia and, learning that the Court was then at Tsarskoye Selo, she resolved to stop there. A small recess behind a partition was assigned to her at the posting-station. The station-master's wife immediately fell into conversation with her and informed her that she was the niece of one of the stove-tenders at the Court, and initiated her into all the mysteries of Court life. She told her at what hour the Empress usually awoke, when she drank her coffee and when she went out for a walk; which great lords were then with her; what she had been pleased to say at table the previous day; whom she had received in the evening – in a word, Anna Vlassyevna's conversation was worth several pages of historical memoirs and would have been a precious contribution to posterity.

Marya Ivanovna listened to her attentively. They went into the grounds of the Palace. Anna Vlassyevna told her the story of every alley and every little bridge and, having strolled about as long as they wished, they returned to the posting-station, very pleased with each other.

Early the next morning, Marya Ivanovna woke, dressed and went quietly into the Palace grounds. It was a beautiful morning; the sun lit up the tops of the linden trees, already turning yellow under the cool breath of autumn. The broad lake glittered motionlessly. The swans, only just awake, came sailing majestically out from under the bushes which overhung the banks. Marya Ivanovna walked towards a beautiful lawn where a monument had just been erected in honour of Count Pyotr Alexandrovitch Rumyantsev's recent victories. Suddenly a little white dog of English breed ran barking up towards her. Alarmed, Marya Ivanovna stopped in her tracks. At the same moment she heard a pleasant female voice saying:

'Don't be frightened; she won't bite.'

And Marya Ivanovna saw a lady sitting on the bench opposite the monument. Marya Ivanovna sat down at the other end of the bench. The lady looked at her intently; Marya Ivanovna, in her turn, by throwing several sidelong glances, managed to examine her from head to foot. She was wearing a white morning-gown, a night-cap and a jacket. She seemed to be about forty. Her full, rosy face expressed dignity and calm, and her blue eyes and slight smile had indescribable charm. The lady was the first to break the silence.

'Doubtless you are a stranger here?' she said.

'Yes, ma'am. I only arrived here yesterday from the country.'

'You came with your parents?'

'No, ma'am, I came alone.'

'Alone! But you are still so young.'

'I have neither father nor mother.'

'I presume you're here on some business or other?'

'Yes, ma'am. I have come to present a petition to the Empress.'

'You are an orphan: I imagine you're complaining of some injustice or injury?'

'No, ma'am. I have come to ask for mercy, and not justice.'

'May I ask who you are?'

'I am the daughter of Captain Mironov.'

'Of Captain Mironov! The same who was commandant of one of the Orenburg fortresses?'

'The same, ma'am.'

The lady was apparently moved.

'Forgive me,' she said in a still kinder voice, 'for interfering in your affairs, but I am often at Court. Tell me the content of your petition and I may be able to help you.'

Marya Ivanovna rose and thanked her respectfully. Everything about the unknown lady involuntarily attracted her and inspired her confidence. Marya Ivanovna drew a folded paper from her pocket and handed it to her anonymous protectress, who began to read it to herself.

At first she read with an attentive and benevolent expression; but suddenly her face changed, and Marya Ivanovna, who was following her every movement with her eyes, was frightened at the severe look on her face, a moment before so pleasant and calm.

'You are pleading for Grinev?' the lady said coldly. 'The Empress cannot pardon him. He sided with the pretender, not out of ignorance and credulity, but as an unprincipled and dangerous scoundrel.'

'Oh, it isn't true!' cried Marya Ivanovna.

'How, not true!' retorted the lady, flushing all over.

'It's not true, in God's name, it's not true! I know all, I'll tell you everything. It was for me alone that he underwent all the misfortunes that have overtaken him. And if he didn't justify himself before the tribunal, it was because he didn't wish to involve me.'

And she related with great ardour all that is already known to my reader.

The lady listened to her attentively.

'Where are you staying?' she asked when Marya Ivanovna had finished speaking. On hearing that she was at Anna Vlassyevna's, she added with a smile: 'Ah, I know! Goodbye, and don't tell anyone of our meeting. I hope that you will not have to wait long for an answer to your petition.'

With these words she rose and walked away down a

covered alley, and Marya Ivanovna returned to Anna Vlassyevna's filled with joyous hope.

Her hostess scolded her for going out so early; the autumn air, so she said, was harmful to a young girl's health. She brought in the samovar and was on the point of launching into an endless series of stories about the Court, when suddenly a Palace carriage drew up at the steps and a lackey entered the room with the announcement that the Empress was pleased to summon the daughter of Captain Mironov to her presence.

Utterly amazed, Anna Vlassyevna began to bustle about.

'Gracious me!' she cried. 'The Empress summons you to the Court. How has she got to know about you? And how, my dear, will you present yourself to the Empress? I don't suppose you know even how to walk in Court fashion . . . Hadn't I better come with you? I could at least put you on your guard against some things. And how can you go in your travelling dress? Shall I send to the midwife's for her yellow Court gown?'

The lackey announced that it was the Empress's wish that Marya Ivanovna should go on her own and in the clothes she was wearing. There was nothing for it: Marya Ivanovna took her seat in the carriage and drove off to the Palace, accompanied by the blessings and advice of Anna Vlassyevna.

Marya Ivanovna felt that our fate was about to be decided; her heart beat violently. A few minutes later the carriage stopped at the Palace. Trembling, Marya Ivanovna went up the steps. The doors were flung open before her. She passed through a long series of deserted, magnificent rooms; the lackey led the way. Finally, arriving at a closed door, he said that he would go in and announce her and left her by herself.

The thought of coming face to face with the Empress so terrified her that she could scarcely stand up straight. A minute later the door opened and she entered the Empress's dressing-room.

The Empress was seated at her dressing-table, surrounded by courtiers who respectfully made way for Marya Ivanovna. The Empress turned towards her with a kind smile, and Marya Ivanovna recognised her as the lady with whom she had recently talked so openly. The Empress summoned her to her side and said with a smile:

'I am glad to be able to keep my word to you and – and to grant your petition. Your business is settled. I am convinced of the innocence of your betrothed. Here is a letter for your future father-in-law.'

Marya Ivanovna took the letter with a trembling hand and, bursting into tears, fell at the Empress's feet. The Empress raised her up and kissed her, then began to talk with her.

'I know you're not rich,' she said, 'but I owe a debt to the daughter of Captain Mironov. Do not worry about the future. I shall take it upon myself to look after you.'

After encouraging the poor orphan, the Empress dismissed her. Marya Ivanovna drove away in the same Palace carriage. Anna Vlassyevna, who had been impatiently awaiting her return, overwhelmed her with questions which Marya Ivanovna somehow answered. Anna Vlassyevna, although disappointed at her poor memory, ascribed it to provincial shyness and magnanimously excused her. That same day Marya Ivanovna, without so much as a glance at Petersburg, returned to the country . . .

The memoirs of Pyotr Andreyevitch Grinev end here. It is known from family tradition that he was released from his imprisonment towards the end of the year 1774 by an edict of the Empress; that he was present at the execution of Pugachev, who recognised him in the crowd and nodded to him with his head which, a minute later, was shown lifeless and bleeding to the people. Soon afterwards Pyotr Andreyevitch married Marya Ivanovna. Their descendants still flourish in the province of Simbirsk. About thirty versts from *** there is a village belonging to ten landowners. In one of the wings of the house there can be seen, framed and glazed, a letter written in the hand of Catherine II. It is addressed to Pyotr Andreyevitch's father and contains the justification of his son and praise to the heart and intelligence of the daughter of Captain Mironov.

Pyotr Andreyevitch Grinev's manuscript was given to me by one of his grandchildren, who had heard that I was engaged upon a work dealing with the times described by his grandfather. With the relatives' permission, I have decided to publish it separately, after finding a suitable epigraph for each chapter and after taking the liberty of changing some of the names.

The Editor,
19th October 1836

ADDITION TO CHAPTER THIRTEEN

(These pages were found among Pushkin's manuscripts after his death. He had included them in his draft version, but excluded them from the final, published version, of The Captain's Daughter. *In the draft, Zurin was called Grinev and Grinev by the name of Bulanin. Pushkin did not alter these original namings in this 'Addition to Chapter Thirteen', and they remain unadjusted in this translation.)*

We were approaching the banks of the Volga; our regiment entered the village of **, and stopped there for the night. The village-elder informed me that all the villages on the other side of the river had risen, that bands of Pugachev's followers were roaming everywhere. I was extremely alarmed by this news. We were to cross over the following morning. I was seized with impatience. On the other side, thirty versts away, was my father's village. I asked if there was anyone to ferry me across. All the peasants were fishermen, so there were plenty of boats. I went to Grinev and informed him of my intention.

'Be careful,' he said to me. 'It is dangerous to go alone. Wait until the morning. We will be the first to cross, and we will pay a visit on your parents with fifty Hussars to cater for any event.'

I insisted in my intention. The boat was ready. I took my seat in it with two boatmen. They pushed off and took up their oars.

The sky was clear. The moon shone. The weather was mild. The Volga flowed smoothly and calmly. Swaying gently, the boat glided swiftly over the dark waves. I was sunk in reverie. About half an hour passed. We had already reached the middle of the river . . . Suddenly the boatmen began to whisper together.

'What is it?' I asked, returning from my reverie.

'God knows, we can't tell,' the boatmen replied, looking to one side.

My eyes followed in the same direction, and I saw in the dark something floating down the Volga. The unknown object was coming closer to us. I ordered the boatmen to stop and await it. The moon went behind a cloud. The floating apparition became yet more indistinct. It was now quite near to me, and yet I still could not make it out.

'What can it be?' the boatmen said. 'The sail is not a sail, the masts are not masts.'

Suddenly the moon came out from behind the cloud and lit up a terrible sight. A gallows, fitted to a raft, was floating towards us, and three bodies hung from the cross-beam. A morbid curiosity took hold of me. I wanted to look at the faces of the hanged men.

At my bidding, the boatmen seized the raft with a boat-hook, and my boat was thrust against the floating gallows. I jumped onto the raft and found myself between the dreadful posts. The bright moon illuminated the disfigured faces of the unfortunate men. One of them was an old Chuvash, the second a Russian peasant, a strong, healthy-looking young man of about twenty. Looking at the third, I was deeply shocked and could not restrain myself from an exclamation of grief: it was Vanka, our poor Vanka, who in his stupidity had joined Pugachev. A black board had been nailed above them, on which was written in bold, white letters: 'Thieves and rebels'. The boatmen looked at all this with indifference and waited for me, holding the raft with the boat-hook. I returned to the boat and sat down again. The raft floated on down the river. For a long time the gallows showed black in the darkness. At last it disappeared, and our boat came to rest against the tall, steep bank . . .

I paid the boatmen generously. One of them led me to the elder of the village, which was situated by the landing-stage. I went with him into a hut. The elder, hearing my demand for horses, was about to receive me somewhat uncivilly, but my guide spoke a few words softly to him, and his dour attitude was immediately replaced by one of prompt obligingness. A troika was ready in a moment, and I sat down in the carriage and ordered to be driven to our village.

I galloped along the high road, past sleeping villages. I feared one thing: being stopped on the road. If my nocturnal encounter on the Volga gave proof of the presence of rebels, it was also proof of strong government counteraction. To be prepared for any event, I had in my pocket the pass given to me by Pugachev as well as Colonel Grinev's order. But I met no one and towards morning I caught sight of the river and the pine grove behind which lay our village. The driver whipped the horses on and after a quarter of an hour I entered **.

The manor-house was at the other end of the village. The horses were tearing along at full pace. Suddenly, in the middle of the street, the driver began to draw them in.

'What is it?' I asked impatiently.

'A barricade, sir,' the driver replied, with difficulty halting his furious horses.

Indeed, I saw a *chevaux-de-frise* and a sentry with a club. The man came up to me and, taking off his hat, asked for my passport.

'What does this mean?' I asked him. 'Why is there a barrier? Who are you watching out for?'

'But, sir, we are rebels,' he replied, scratching himself.

'And where are your masters?' I asked, my heart sinking.

'Where are our masters?' the man repeated. 'Our masters are in the granary.'

'How, in the granary?'

'Well, Andryushka, the clerk, put them in stocks, you see, and wants to take them to the Lord Tsar.'

'My God! Break down the barrier, you idiot! What are you gaping at?'

The sentry dawdled. I leapt out of the carriage, boxed his ears (I regret) and moved the barrier back myself. The peasant stared at me in stupid perplexity. I sat down again in the carriage and ordered to be driven with all speed to the main house. The granary was in the courtyard. Before the locked doors stood two peasants, also carrying clubs. The carriage came to a halt immediately in front of them. I jumped out and rushed right at them.

'Open the doors!' I said to them.

No doubt my expression alarmed them; at any rate, they both ran off, throwing away their clubs. I tried to burst the lock and break open the doors, but the doors were of oak, and the enormous padlock was indestructible. At that moment a well-built young peasant emerged from the servants' hut and, with an arrogant expression, asked me how I dared to make such a row.

'Where's Andryushka the clerk?' I shouted to him. 'Call him to me.'

'I am Andrey Afanassyevitch, not Andryushka,' he answered me, his arms proudly akimbo. 'What do you want?'

Instead of a reply, I seized him by the collar and, dragging him up to the doors of the granary, commanded him to open them. The clerk tried to resist, but *paternal* chastisement had its effect on him. He took out the key and opened the granary. I rushed across the threshold and, in a dark corner weakly lit by a narrow skylight, saw my mother and father. Their hands were bound, their feet in stocks. I ran forward to embrace them and could not utter a word. They both looked at me with astonishment – three years of military life had so changed me that they were unable to recognise me. My mother sighed and burst into tears.

Suddenly I heard a dear familiar voice.

'Pyotr Andreitch! It is you!'

I was stunned . . . I looked round and in another corner saw Marya Ivanovna, also bound.

My father looked at me in silence, not daring to believe what he saw. Joy shone from his face. I hastened to cut with my sword the knots of the ropes that bound them.

'Welcome, welcome, Petrusha!' my father said to me, pressing me to his heart. 'Thank God you have come at last . . .'

'Petrusha, my dear,' my mother said. 'How did the Lord bring you to us! Are you well?'

I made haste to lead them out of their prison . . . but when I went up to the door, I found it locked again.

'Andryushka,' I cried, 'open up!'

'I should say so!' the clerk answered from behind the door. 'You may as well stay where you are. That will teach you to kick up a disturbance and drag officials of the Tsar around by the collar!'

I began to look around the granary, seeking some way, no matter what, to get out.

'Don't bother yourself,' my father said to me. 'I am not the sort of landowner to have my granary full of holes for thieves to get in and out of.'

My mother, a moment before rejoicing at my arrival, fell into despair, seeing that I was to perish with the rest of the family. But I felt more at peace now that I found myself with them and Marya Ivanovna. I had my sword and two pistols; I could still withstand a siege. Grinev should arrive towards evening and in time to free us. I informed my parents of this and succeeded in soothing my mother. They abandoned themselves completely to the joys of reunion.

'Well, Pyotr,' my father said to me, 'you got up to enough mischief, and I was thoroughly angry with you. But let bygones be bygones. I hope that you have sown your wild oats now and have reformed. I know that you have served in a manner suited to an officer of honour. I thank you. You have comforted me in my old age. If I am to be obliged to you for my deliverance, then life will be doubly pleasant.'

With tears in my eyes I kissed his hand and looked at Marya Ivanovna, who was so overjoyed by my presence that she seemed completely contented and at peace.

Around midday we heard an unusual commotion and shouting.

'What does it mean?' my father said. 'Can your Colonel have come to free us?'

'Impossible,' I replied. 'He will not be here before evening.'

The commotion increased. The alarm bell was rung. Mounted men were galloping across the courtyard. At that moment my poor old servant, Savelyitch, thrust his grey head through the narrow skylight and uttered in a sorrowful voice:

'Andrey Petrovitch, Avdotya Vassilyevna, Pyotr Andreitch, my dear, Marya Ivanovna – a terrible misfortune! The villains have entered the village. And do you know, Pyotr Andreitch, who has brought them? Shvabrin, Alexey Ivanytch, devil take him!'

Hearing the hateful name, Marya Ivanovna clasped her hands and remained motionless.

'Listen,' I said to Savelyitch, 'get someone to go on horseback to the ferry at ** to meet the Hussar regiment; and tell him to let the Colonel know of our danger.'

'But who can I send, sir? All the lads have risen, and all

the horses have been seized. Oh! They are already in the courtyard. They are coming towards the granary.'

At this point we heard several voices on the other side of the door. Silently, I gave a sign to my mother and Marya Ivanovna to retire into a corner, unsheathed my sword and leaned against the wall just by the door. My father took the pistols, cocked them both and stood beside me. The lock rattled, the door opened and the head of the clerk showed itself. I struck it with my sword and the man fell, blocking the entrance. At that same moment my father fired one pistol at the doorway. The crowd, which was pressing towards us, ran away with curses. I dragged the wounded man across the threshold and bolted the door from the inside. The court-yard was full of armed men. Among them I recognised Shvabrin.

'Don't be afraid,' I said to the women. 'There is hope yet. And you, father, don't shoot any more. Let us save the last shot.'

My mother prayed silently to God; Marya Ivanovna stood beside her, awaiting the determination of her fate with angelic calm. From the other side of the doors could be heard threats, abuse and curses. I stood at my post, prepared to hack down the first person who dared to show his face. Suddenly the villains fell silent. I heard Shvabrin's voice calling me by name.

'I am here. What do you want?'

'Give up, Bulanin, it is useless to resist. Have pity on your old parents. You will not save yourself by stubbornness. I'll get you!'

'Try, you traitor!'

'I shall not risk my neck to no purpose, or waste my men. I shall order the granary to be set on fire, and then we'll see what you do, Don Quixote of Belogorsky! Now it is time for dinner. In the meantime, sit down and think it over at your leisure. Goodbye, Marya Ivanovna, I shall not apologise to you: I don't suppose you are bored with your knight in the dark.'

Shvabrin withdrew, leaving a sentry by the granary. We were silent. Each of us thought his own thoughts, and did not dare to communicate them. I imagined to myself everything that the infuriated Shvabrin was capable of doing. I scarcely worried about myself. Shall I confess? I was not so horrified by the fate of my parents as by that of Marya Ivanovna. I knew that my mother was worshipped by the peasants and the household servants; my father, in spite of his severity, was also loved, for he was just and knew the true needs of the people subjected to him. Their rebellion was a delusion, a momentary intoxication, and not an expression of their indignation. It was probable that they would be treated with mercy. But Marya Ivanovna? What fate was that corrupt and unscrupulous man preparing for her? I did not dare to dwell on this dreadful thought and prepared myself, God forgive me, to kill her rather than see her for a second time in the hands of a cruel enemy.

About another hour passed. In the village could be heard the songs of drunken men. The sentries guarding us were envious and, turning their ill-feeling on us, swore and sought to frighten us with descriptions of torture and death. We awaited the consequence of Shvabrin's threats. At last there was a great stir in the courtyard, and we heard Shvabrin's voice again.

'Well, have you thought it over? Have you decided to give yourself up to me voluntarily?'

Nobody answered him. Having waited for a short while, Shvabrin ordered some straw to be brought up. In a few minutes a fire burst out and lit up the dark granary; smoke began to force itself through the chinks of the threshold. Then Marya Ivanovna came up to me and, taking me by the hand, said softly:

'Enough, Pyotr Andreitch! Do not allow yourself and your parents to perish on my account. Let me go out. Shvabrin will listen to me.'

'Not for anything,' I cried heatedly. 'Do you know what awaits you?'

'I could not survive dishonour,' she replied quietly, 'but perhaps I could save my deliverer and the family which has so generously protected a poor orphan. Farewell, Andrey Petrovitch. Farewell, Avdotya Vassilyevna. You have been more than benefactors to me. Give me your blessing. Goodbye to you also, Pyotr Andreitch. Be assured that . . .'

At this point she burst into tears and hid her face in her hands. I felt as if I had gone out of my mind. My mother wept.

'Enough of this nonsense, Marya Ivanovna,' my father said. 'Who's going to let you go alone to the brigands? Sit down here and be quiet. If we die, we die together. Listen, what are they saying?'

'Do you surrender?' cried Shvabrin. 'Don't you see, in five minutes you'll be roasted.'

'We will not surrender, villain!' my father answered him in a firm voice.

His face, covered in wrinkles, was animated by astonishing courage, his eyes flashed menacingly from beneath his white eyebrows. Turning to me, he said:

'Now is the time!'

He opened the door. The flames shot up and flew along the beams, which were caulked with dry moss. My father fired the pistol and stepped over the blazing threshold, shouting: 'Everyone, follow me!' I seized my mother and Marya Ivanovna by the hand and quickly led them out into the air. By the threshold lay Shvabrin, shot by the old hand of my father. The crowd of brigands, who had run off at our unexpected sortie, immediately took courage and began to surround us. I succeeded in delivering a few more blows, but a well-aimed brick struck me right in the chest. I fell and lost consciousness for a minute or so. Coming to myself, I saw Shvabrin sitting on the bloodstained grass and all of my family standing in front of him. I was supported under the arms. A crowd of peasants, Cossacks and Bashkirs surrounded us. Shvabrin was dreadfully pale. He had one hand pressed to his wounded side. His face expressed pain and fury. He slowly raised his head, glanced at me and uttered in a weak and indistinct voice:

'Hang him . . . all of them . . . except her . . .'

The crowd of villains immediately closed in on us and with cries dragged us off towards the gates. But suddenly they left us and scattered: Grinev, followed by an entire squadron with drawn swords, was riding though the gates.

The rebels were fleeing in every direction; the Hussars pursued them, hacked at them with their swords and took them captive. Grinev jumped down from his horse, bowed to my father and mother and shook me warmly by the hand.

'Well, I got here in time,' he said to us. 'Ah, and this is your bride!'

Marya Ivanovna blushed to the tips of her ears. My father went up to him and thanked him in a calm manner, although he was clearly moved. My mother embraced him, calling him an angel of deliverance.

'Welcome,' my father said to him and led him to our house.

Walking past Shvabrin, Grinev stopped.

'Who is this?' he asked, looking at the wounded man.

'That is the leader of the band himself,' my father replied with a certain pride, showing up the old soldier in him. 'God helped my senile hand to punish the young villain and to avenge the blood of my son.'

'It is Shvabrin,' I said to Grinev.

'Shvabrin! Delighted! Hussars, take him! Tell our physician to dress his wound and to watch over him like the apple of his eye. Shvabrin must without fail stand before the Kazan Secret Commission. He is one of the main offenders, and his testimony will be important.'

Shvabrin gave us a tired glance. His face expressed nothing but physical pain. The Hussars carried him away on a cloak.

We entered the house. With a tremor I looked around me, remembering my childhood years. Nothing in the house had changed, everything was in its former place. Shvabrin had not permitted it to be plundered, maintaining in his very baseness an instinctive repugnance to the dishonourable practice of cupidity. The servants appeared in the ante-room. They had not taken part in the rising and sincerely rejoiced in our deliverance. Savelyitch was triumphant. It should be known that, in the commotion caused by the brigands' attack, he had run to the stables where Shvabrin's horse was, had saddled and quietly led it out and, thanks to the general confusion, had galloped off unnoticed to the ferry. He had met the regiment taking a rest on this side of the Volga. Grinev, learning of our danger from him, had ordered his men to mount their horses, and had given the command to move forward at the gallop – and, thank God, had arrived in time.

The Hussars returned from their pursuit with several prisoners. These were locked up in the same granary in which we had borne our memorable siege.

Grinev insisted that the village clerk's head be displayed on a pole outside the tavern for several hours. We all went off to our rooms. The old people needed a rest. Not having slept at all the previous night, I threw myself on my bed and was soon fast asleep. Grinev went off to give his orders.

In the evening we came together in the drawing-room,

round the samovar, cheerfully discussing the danger that was now over. Marya Ivanovna poured out the tea; I sat down beside her and occupied myself exclusively with her. My parents seemed to look with favour on the tenderness of our affection for each other. To this day that evening lives in my memory. I was happy, completely happy – and are there many such minutes in this poor, human life?

On the following day my father was informed that the peasants were in the courtyard, requesting forgiveness. My father went out on to the porch to them. When he appeared, the peasants went down on their knees.

'Well, you idiots,' he said, 'what put it into your heads to rebel?'

'We are sorry, master,' they replied in one voice.

'So, you are sorry. You got up to mischief, and you are sorry. I forgive you for the joy that God has brought me of seeing my son, Pyotr Andreitch.'

'We are sorry! Of course we are sorry!'

'All right: he who confesses shall not be scourged. God has given us fine weather; it is time to gather in the hay. But you, you dolts, what have you been doing for three whole days? Village-elder! Put everyone on to haymaking; and see to it, you ginger-haired rogue, that all my hay is in stacks by St. John's Day. Off with you!'

The peasants bowed and went about their work as if nothing had happened.

Shvabrin's wound turned out not to be fatal. He was taken under guard to Kazan. I saw him from a window as he was being put into the carriage. Our eyes met; he lowered his head, and I hastened to move away from the window. I did not want to give the impression of triumphing over an unhappy and humiliated enemy.

Grinev was obliged to proceed further. I decided to go with him, in spite of my wish to spend a few more days among my family. On the eve of my departure, I went to my parents and, according to the custom of the day, went down on my knees before them and asked them for their blessing on my marriage with Marya Ivanovna. The old people lifted me up and with tears of joy gave their consent. I took Marya Ivanovna, pale and trembling, to them. They gave us their blessing . . . I cannot begin to describe what I felt. He who has been in my position will understand me without my having to tell him; for him who has not I can only be sorry, and advise him, while there is still time, to fall in love and receive the blessing of his parents.

The regiment was ready the following day. Grinev took final leave of my family. We all felt certain that military operations would soon cease. I was hoping to be married within a month. As she said good-bye to me, Marya Ivanovna kissed me in front of everyone. I mounted my horse. Savelyitch came with me again – and the regiment moved off.

For a long time, until I could no longer see it, I looked back at the house which I was again leaving. I was disturbed by gloomy forebodings. Someone seemed to be whispering that not all my misfortunes were over. In my heart I sensed a new storm.

I will not describe our campaign and the conclusion of the war with Pugachev. We passed through villages laid waste by him, and were obliged to take from the poor inhabitants what had been left to them by the rebels.

The people did not know whom to obey. Administration everywhere came to a stop. The landowners hid in the forests. Bands of brigands ransacked the countryside. Commanders of individual detachments, sent in pursuit of Pugachev, who was by then fleeing towards Astrakhan, punished and pardoned as the fancy took them . . . The condition of the whole area where the conflagration raged was terrible. God forbid that we should ever see a Russian rebellion – so senseless and merciless – again. Those in our midst who plan impossible revolutions are either young men who do not know our people, or cruel-hearted men who place a low value on their own necks, and an even lower value on the necks of others.

Pugachev was in flight and being pursued by Iv. Iv. Mikhelson. We soon heard of his complete defeat. At last Grinev received news from his general of the capture of the pretender, and with it the order to halt. At last I could return home. I was in raptures, but a strange feeling clouded my happiness.

Notes

THE MOOR OF PETER THE GREAT

EPIGRAPH: from a poem by N. Yazykov (1803–1846).
PETER THE GREAT: Tsar Peter I (1672–1725).

Chapter One

EPIGRAPH: from *The Diary of a Traveller* by the minor poet I. Dmitriev (1760–1837).

THE SPANISH WAR: The War of the Spanish Succession, 1701–1714.

THE DUKE OF ORLEANS: Philippe II (1674–1723), Regent of France from 1715 to just before his death.

LAW: JOHN LAW (1671–1729), Scottish adventurer and financier, became Controller of French finance, established the first French bank, initiated the 'Mississippi Scheme' by which in return for exclusive trading rights with Louisiana he undertook to pay off the French national debt. The failure of this scheme and the ruin of many speculators caused him to flee from France.

DUKE OF RICHELIEU: Louis François Armand du Plessis (1696–1788), Marshal of France, great-nephew of Cardinal Richelieu, famous for his wit and amorous adventures.

Temps fortuné . . . : from Voltaire's *La Pucelle d'Orleans*, Canto 13.

AROUET: François Marie Arouet de Voltaire (1694–1778).

CHAULIEU: Guillaume Amfrye de (1639–1720), poet, wit.

MONTESQUIEU: Charles Louis de Secondat (1689–1755), historian, philosopher, satirist.

FONTENELLE: Bernard le Bovier de (1667–1757), dramatist.

Chapter Two

EPIGRAPH: from the ode *On the Death of Prince Meshchersky* by G. Derzhavin (1743–1816), first outstanding Russian poet.

VERST: 3,500 feet.

KRASNOYE SELO: the summer residence of the Tsar.

NEVA: river flowing into the Baltic at Petersburg.

KATENKA: Empress Catherine (1684–1727), wife of Peter the Great, whom she succeeded at his death in 1725 as Catherine I of Russia.

ORANIENBAUM: summer palace near Petersburg.

POLTAVA: town in Ukraine; Peter the Great defeated the army of Charles XII of Sweden in 1709 at the Battle of Poltava.

PRINCE MENSHIKOV: favourite and adviser of Peter I.

RAGUZINSKY: a merchant (from Ragusa) who acted as diplomatic and trade emissary for Peter I.

Chapter Three

EPIGRAPH: from *Argivyane*, a tragedy by V. Kyukhelbeker (1797–1846), minor poet, Decembrist, Pushkin's schoolmate.

SHEREMETEV: one of Peter I's field-marshals.

GOLOVIN: Admiral.

BUTURLIN: Peter I's orderly and trusted person.

FEOFAN: Archbishop of Novgorod, writer and preacher.

BUZHINSKY: a learned monk.

KOPIEVITCH: a learned priest.

NATALYA KIRILLOVNA: the mother of Peter I.

SARAFAN: traditional Russian dress, a sleeveless smock.

DUSHEGREIKA: a short, warm sleeveless jacket.

Chapter Four

EPIGRAPH: from Pushkin's first long poem written in 1820.

BATTLE OF NARVA: in 1700, Charles XII of Sweden completely overwhelmed the Russian army at Narva; in 1704, Peter I recaptured the city.

EMANCIPATED BY THE EDICTS . . . : before the reign of Peter I, women lived in almost total seclusion; it was to discontinue this custom that the Assemblies were introduced.

BEARDS: eager to introduce the customs of Western Europe, Peter I had ordered that all Russians should shave off their beards.

KVASS: a drink made of rye bread and malt.

PRINCE ALEXANDR DANILOVITCH: Prince Menshikov.

Chapter Five

EPIGRAPH: from *The Miller*, a comic opera by A. Ablesimov written in 1799.

PANCAKEMEN: allusion to Prince Menshikov who was said to have sold pies in the street in his youth.

DOLGORUKY, SHEÏN, TROYEKUROV, MILOSLAVSKY, YELETSKY, LVOV: members of the old Russian nobility.

BOVA KOROLEVITCH AND YERUSLAN LAZAREVITCH: heroes of Russian fairy tales.

A NOVEL IN LETTERS

SASHA: diminutive for Alexandra.

LAMARTINE: Alphonse de (1790–1869), French poet, writer and politician.

KRESTOVSKY ISLAND: one of the islands in the river Neva.

CLARISSA HARLOWE: the eponymous heroine of Samuel Richardson's epistolary novel *Clarissa or The History of a Young Lady* (1747–1749).

ADOLPHE: the eponymous hero of the novel by the French writer Benjamin Constant (1767–1830).

MASHA or MASHENKA: diminutive for Marya.

CHARLOTTE: heroine of Goethe's epistolary novel *The Sorrows of Young Werther* (1774).

VYAZEMSKY: Prince Pyotr (1792–1878), minor poet, friend of Pushkin, translated *Adolphe* into Russian.

HERALD OF EUROPE: an allusion to a criticism of Pushkin's poem, *Count Nulin*, accusing him of indecency and lack of morals.

BOSTON: a popular card game.

FORNARINA: Raphael's model.

CITIZEN MININ AND PRINCE POZHARSKY: Minin, mayor of Nizhny Novgorod, and Prince Pozharsky organised a national levy which freed Moscow, besieged by the Poles, in 1612.

LA BRUYÈRE: Jean de (1645–1696), French moralist.

FONVIZIN: Denis (1745–1792), author of *The Minor* (1782), a comic satire against cruelty, smugness and ignorance.

PROSTAKOVS AND SKOTININS: characters in *The Minor*.

'because they are patriots': a quotation from *Woe from Wit*, a comedy by Alexandr Griboyedov (1795–1829), written in 1822–24, known to Pushkin in manuscript, but first published (with cuts due to censorship) only in 1833.

Un homme sans peur . . . : motto of the Bayard family, French and feudal.

Qui n'est ni roi . . . : motto of the Coucy family, French and feudal.

FAUBLAS: hero of *Les Amours du Chevalier de Faublas*, published 1787–1790, by Jean-Baptiste Louvet de Couvray (1760–1797).

ADAM SMITH: Scottish economist and philosopher (1723–1790), author of *An Inquiry into the Nature and Causes of the Wealth of Nations* (1776).

THE TALES OF
THE LATE IVAN PETROVITCH BELKIN

From the Editor

EPIGRAPH: from *The Minor* by Fonvizin.

CORVÉE: compulsory service paid to a landowner.

The Shot

FIRST EPIGRAPH: from *The Ball*, a poem by E. Baratynsky (1800–1844), a poet greatly respected by Pushkin.

SECOND EPIGRAPH: from *An Evening on Bivouac*, a tale by A. Bestuzhev (1797–1837), a popular short story writer under the pseudonym of 'Marlinsky'.

BURTSOV: A. P. Burtsov, a Hussar officer renowned as a fighter and drinker; fellow officer of Denis Davydov (1784–1839), poet and friend of Pushkin.

HETAIRISTS: members of a Greek secret political organisation opposing Turkish rule.

ALEXANDER YPSILANTI: Prince (1792–1828), leader of the Hetairists, at one time a general in the Russian army; began the insurrection against Turkish domination in 1821.

BATTLE OF SKULYANI: on 29th June 1821, the Hetairists were defeated at Skulyani – in Moldavia, near the River Pruth – by the Turks.

The Blizzard

EPIGRAPH: from the ballad *Svetlana* (1813) by the poet Vasily Zhukovsky (1783–1852), Pushkin's lifelong friend, who translated works by English and German poets – notably Scott, and rendered the Russian language with great mastery and poetic sensitivity.

TULA SEAL: Tula, a town 100 miles south of Moscow famous for its armaments industries and silversmiths.

BATTLE OF BORODINO: 7th September 1812, in which Napoleon defeated the Russian army and opened the way to Moscow.

ARTEMISIA: Queen of Halicarnassus who, in the fourth century BC, erected in memory of her dead husband, Mausolus, a magnificent monument, considered one of the seven wonders of the world.

Vive Henri Quatre: couplets from *Henry IV Goes Hunting*, a French comedy written in 1774.

Joconde: *Joconde ou les Coureurs d'Aventures*, a comic opera by Niccolò Isouard, staged with immense success in 1814 in Paris, at that time occupied by Russian troops as members of the Grand Alliance.

'Hurrah! Hurrah' ... a quotation from Griboyedov's *Woe from Wit*.

BOTH CAPITALS: Moscow and Petersburg.

Se amor non è ...: first half of the opening line of the sonnet by Petrarch (1304–1374), 'Be it not love, then what is it I feel'.

SAINT-PREUX: Julie's lover in Jean-Jacques Rousseau's *Julie ou la Nouvelle Héloïse* (1761).

The Undertaker

EPIGRAPH: from the ode *The Waterfall* by G. Derzhavin.

RAZGULYAY: a district of Moscow near Basmannaya Street, but a considerable distance from Nikitskaya Street.

POGORELSKY'S POSTMAN: reference to a story by Antony Pogorelsky, pseudonym of the writer A. A. Perovsky (1787–1836).

'with axe in hand ...': from a poem by A.E. Izmailov (1779–1831)

The Postmaster

EPIGRAPH: from the poem *The Posting Station* by Vyazemsky.

MUROM: a forested region on the right bank of the river Oka infested by brigands.

AVDOTYA: full name of the diminutive 'Dunya'.

TERENTYITCH: a character in *The Caricature* by I. Dmitriev.

Peasant-Lady

EPIGRAPH: from *Dushenka*, a long poem by the minor poet I. Bogdanovitch (1743–1803).

'But Russian corn ...': quotation from *Satire*, by the minor playwright Prince Alexandr Shakhovskoy (1777–1846).

BOARD OF GUARDIANSHIP: a government council established for the care of widows, orphans, etc.

JEAN-PAUL: Jean-Paul Richter (1778–1825), German romantic writer.

Pamela: the novel by Samuel Richardson, published in 1740.

SBOGAR: name of the mysterious hero, leader of a band of brigands, in the novel *Jean Sbogar* by Charles Nodier (1780–1844).

'sleeves *à l'imbécile* . . .': wide sleeves gathered at the wrist but weighted at the elbow to allow them to hang down.

LANCASTER: Joseph Lancaster (1778–1825), English educationalist, founder of a system of reciprocal teaching.

Natalya, the Boyar's Daughter: sentimental historical tale by Nikolay Karamzin (1766–1826), historian, novelist and poet.

ALYOSHA: diminutive for Alexey.

THE HISTORY OF THE VILLAGE OF GORYUKHINO

HANDBOOK OF SAMPLE LETTERS: an encyclopaedic volume containing elementary information of all kinds, historical and moral tales, anecdotes, poems, folk songs, proverbs and sayings, compiled and published by N. Kurganov in 1769.

THE TWELVE NATIONS: A reference to Napoleon's Grande Armée which comprised batallions from twelve different countries.

NIEBUHR: Berthold Georg (1776–1831), German historian.

BRITCHKA: Lightweight horse-driven carriage for a single passenger.

Hatred and Repentance: play by the prolific German playwright August von Kotzebue (1761–1819), written in 1789.

GOOD INTENTIONS: An occasional publication of principally theatrical reviews.

The Dangerous Neighbour: a comic poem by V. L. Pushkin (1770–1830), Pushkin's uncle.

HISTORY OF OUR NATION: reference to *History of the Russian State,* a twelve-volume work by N. Karamzin published between 1816–1826.

RURIK: Varangian (Norseman) chieftain who died in 879, reputed to be the founder of the Russian state.

Lines on a Moscow Boulevard and *The Presnensky Ponds*: anonymous satirical poems.

ABBÉ MILLOT: Claude François Xavier (1726–1785), French historian.

TATISHCHEV, BOLTIN AND GOLIKOV: eighteenth-century Russian historians, predecessors of Karamzin.

SLAVONIC NUMERALS: numerals were represented by letters of the Slavonic alphabet until the eighteenth century.

A CERTAIN FELLOW-HISTORIAN: the reference is to Gibbon's reflection on completion of *The History of the Decline and Fall of the Roman Empire* (1788).

CENSUS CAPITATION REGISTERS: Lists of persons liable to capitation tax at the next census.

SUMAROKOV: Alexander (1718–1777), minor, though influential, poet, acknowledged as the first Russian dramatist.

ROSLAVLEV

Roslavlev: *Roslavlev or the Russians in 1812*, published in 1831, by M. Zagoskin, a writer whose first book *Yury Miloslavsky* had been enormously successful. *Roslavlev* concerned, as this unfinished story by Pushkin suggests, the liaison between a young Russian girl of good family and a French prisoner-of-war officer captured during Napoleon's march on Moscow in 1812.

A KEY AND A STAR: a key was the insignia of a Court Chamberlain; a star of an Order of the first degree.

CRÉBILLON: (1707–1777), minor French novelist.

LOMONOSOV: Mikhail (1711–1765), one of the first Russian poets.

SIKHLER: fashionable milliner in Moscow.

KOSTROMA: provincial town 200 miles north-east of Moscow.

MADAME DE STAËL: (1766–1817), famous French writer and intellectual of Swiss origin. Banished from France by Napoleon.

Corinne: Madame de Staël's best-known novel, published in 1807.

CHATEAUBRIAND: François-René de (1768–1848), French writer and politician.

KUZNETSKY BRIDGE: Moscow's main and most fashionable street.

RHENISH CONFEDERATION: a union of German principalities (1806–1813), formed under the auspices of Napoleon.

COUNT RASTOPCHIN: Governor of Moscow.

LAFITTE: a famous claret.

CHARLOTTE CORDAY: young woman who knifed Marat in his bath and was executed in July 1793.

MARFA POSADNITSA: widow of the patrician leader of the Republic of Novgorod, she fought unsuccessfully against domination by the State of Muscovy under Ivan III – the Great – (1462–1505) by forming alliances with Lithuania and Poland. After the final subjugation of Novgorod in 1489, she was arrested and imprisoned in a monastery at Nizhny Novgorod.

PRINCESS DASHKOVA: (1743–1810), lady-in-waiting and friend of Catherine the Great, whom she actively helped to carry out the palace revolt of 1762 which secured Catherine's accession to the throne.

Il n'est de bonheur ... : a quotation from Chateaubriand's *René*, published in 1802.

COUNT MAMONOV: Count M. A. Dmitriev-Mamonov (1790–1863), who in 1812 formed a Cossack regiment at his own expense; later a member of one of the first secret political organisations of the Decembrists.

FRENCH *proverbes:* a form of charades.

DUBROVSKY

Part I
Chapter One

VOLODKA: diminutive for Vladimir.

Chapter Two

THE FINDINGS OF THE COURT: this is a literal transcript of a genuine court order (only the names having been changed by Pushkin) dealing with the case of a hamlet called Novopansky.

Chapter Four

EPIGRAPH: from the ode, *On the Death of Prince Meshchersky*, by Derzhavin.

Beat, Drums of Victory!: opening words of a choral song by Derzhavin – music by Kozlovsky – written in 1791 for the festivities arranged by Prince Potemkin – favourite of Catherine the Great – in the palace she had given him.

Chapter Five

ON HIS WAY BACK . . . : Russian superstition that it is a sign of bad luck to meet a priest accidentally.

Chapter Six

THE TURKISH CAMPAIGN: the second Russo-Turkish war (1787–1791).

Chapter Eight

The Complete Cookery Book: probably an allusion to a famous eighteenth-century novel by Tchulikov, *The Comely Cook or the Adventures of a Dissolute Woman*.

SASHA: diminutive of Alexandr.

Part II
Chapter Nine

LAVATER'S SYSTEM: Johann Kaspar Lavater (1741–1801), Swiss poet, theologian and philosopher, whose 'system' consisted in classifying people by the shape of their heads.

KULNYEV: well-known general at the time of the Russo-Swedish war (1808–1809).

MRS RADCLIFFE: (1764–1823), popular English author of tales of mystery and terror.

Chapter Ten

UHLAN: a type of cavalryman or lancer in, especially, the Polish and German armies.

Chapter Eleven

OUTCHITEL: a transliteration of the Russian word for a tutor.

Chapter Thirteen

RINALDO: Rinaldo-Rinaldini, the brigand hero of the extremely popular novel of the same name by the German writer, Vulpius (1762–1827).

AMPHITRYON: host; Greek classical allusion to the husband of Alcmena whom Zeus sought unsuccessfully to seduce.

Chapter Fourteen

KONRAD'S MISTRESS: Konrad Wallenrod, hero of a poem of the same name by Adam Mickiewicz (1798–1855), famous Polish poet and patriot, whose works Pushkin greatly admired.

THE QUEEN OF SPADES

Chapter One

EPIGRAPH: from a letter by Pushkin to Vyazemsky.

FARO: a game of pure chance, at which the players gamble on the order in which certain cards will appear when taken singly from the top of the pack.

THE DUKE OF ORLEANS: Louis Philippe (1725–1785), grandson of the Regent of France.

COUNT ST-GERMAIN: (died c. 1795), reckoned by some as an impostor, by others as endowed with mystical powers.

WANDERING JEW: by insulting Christ on his way to Calvary, the Wandering Jew was condemned to wander the earth until the day of Judgement.

CASANOVA: Casanova de Seingalt (1725–1798), a fashionable adventurer, known for his scandalous memoirs.

Chapter Two

AS DANTE SAYS . . . : reference to Dante's *Paradiso*, xvii. 58.

Chapter Three

MADAME LEBRUN: Elisabeth Vigée-Lebrun (1755–1842), famous French portrait painter for whom the Russian Imperial family sat.

LEROY: a well-known Parisian clock-maker.

THE MONTGOLFIERS: Joseph-Michel (1740–1810) and Jacques-Etienne (1745–1799), inventors of the hydrogen balloon.

MESMER: Franz Anton (1734–1815), Austrian doctor who founded the theory of animal magnetism.

VOLTAIREAN ARMCHAIR: a chair with a high winged back and a low seat.

Chapter Four

Oublie ou regret: the words used by a lady in exercising her right, in certain dances, to present herself to her choice of partner on the floor.

Chapter Five

EPIGRAPH: from the writings of the Swedish mystic Emanuel Swedenborg (1688–1722).

THE ANGEL OF DEATH . . . : reference to the parable of the wise and foolish virgins.

KIRDJALI

ARNOUT: Turkish name for an Albanian.

ALEXANDER YPSILANTI AND THE HETAIRISTS: see notes to 'The Shot'.

THE UNFORTUNATE BATTLE: the battle of Skulyani – see notes to 'The Shot'.

IORDAKI OLIMBIOTI: one of the principal leaders of the Greek revolt who, after the defeat at Skulyani, entrenched himself with the remnants of his army in the monastery of Seko in the Moldavian mountains, where, so as not to surrender to the Turks, they killed themselves by blowing up the powder magazine.

GEORGI KANTAKUZIN: Count Kantakuzin (died 1857), one of the leaders of the Greek revolt whom Pushkin met at Kishinev.

YATAGHANS: long Turkish daggers with curved blades.

NEKRASSOVISTS: Don Cossacks – Old Believers – who revolted under Peter the Great and emigrated, under their leader Ignat Nekrassa, first to Azerbaijan and then to Turkey.

CHIBOUKS: long Turkish pipes.

BESHLIKS: Turkish silver money.

DOLMAN: long, narrow-sleeved garment with buttons on the breast and held together by wide belt.

LEV: principal monetary unit of Bulgaria.

EGYPTIAN NIGHTS

Chapter One

EPIGRAPH: from *The Almanac of Puns*, published in France in 1771.

REZANOV: a fashionable pastry-shop.

Chapter Two

EPIGRAPH: from *God*, an ode by Derzhavin.

La Signora Catalani: Angelica Catalani (1780–1849), a famous Italian singer who sang in Petersburg in 1820.

Chapter Three

Tancred: opera by Rossini (1792–1868), written in 1813.

THE CAPTAIN'S DAUGHTER

Chapter One

EPIGRAPH: from *The Braggart*, a comedy by Yakov Knyazhnin (1742–1791), minor playwright.

COUNT MÜNNICH: (1683–1767), field-marshal and politician who served under Peter the Great and was exiled to Siberia in 1741.

SIMBIRSK (now Ulyanov): town on the Volga some 450 miles east of Moscow.

ORENBURG: town in the southern Urals some 320 miles south-east of Simbirsk.

Chapter Two

YAIKIAN COSSACK: Cossack from the region of the Yaik river, renamed the Ural river after the Pugachev uprisings. The Yaikian Cossacks constituted a separate military organisation, but after their revolt in 1772 their military privileges were annulled.

UMYOT: a military term for shelter or trench.

EMPRESS ANNA IOANNOVNA: niece of Peter the Great, Empress of Russia, 1730–1740.

KIRGHIZ-KAISSAK STEPPES: region east of the River Ural, now territory of Kazakhstan.

Chapter Three

SECOND EPIGRAPH: from *The Minor* by Fonvizin.

KÜSTRIN: a Prussian fortress taken in 1758 by the Russians during the Seven Years War.

OCHAKOV: Turkish fortress taken by the Russians in 1737.

BASHKIRS: Turco-Mongolian tribe inhabiting region north of Orenburg between the River Kama and the Urals.

THE KIRGHIZ: (or Kazakhs), a Turkic nomadic tribe living in the region east of the Ural river.

Chapter Four

EPIGRAPH: from *The Odd Fellows*, a comedy by Knyazhnin.

TREDYAKOVSKY: Vasily (1703–1769), minor poet, translator and scientist, author of *New and Brief Method of Russian Versemaking*.

BENEATH THE CROWN: as part of the marriage ceremony, bride and bridegroom kissed beneath crowns held above their heads.

Chapter Five

VERSHOK: 1¾ in.

Chapter Six

MAJOR-GENERAL TRAUBENBERG: well known for his cruelty and eventually killed by the Cossacks in the Pugachev Uprising.

PETER III: (1728–1762), grandson of Peter the Great and husband of Catherine the Great, reigned for six months to July 1762 when he abdicated. He was later strangled by one of Catherine's many admirers.

BENEFICENT EDICT: instituted by Catherine II.

THE YEAR 1741: violent uprisings took place in the district of Bashkiria in the years 1735–40 and were subdued with incredible cruelty: some 700 villages were burnt down and the noses and ears of the ringleaders cut off.

EMPEROR ALEXANDER: (1777–1825), reigned 1801–1825, grandson of Catherine II, son of Paul I, who was murdered with Alexander's knowledge.

Chapter Seven

OFFERING BREAD AND SALT: the customary welcome to an honoured visitor.

Chapter Eight

TCHUMAKOV: a Yaik Cossack, commander of artillery in Pugachev's army.

GRISHKA OTREPYEV: a monk who claimed to be Dmitri, the son of Ivan the Terrible, who was in fact murdered at the age of nine at Uglitch in 1591. 'False Dmitri' became Tsar in 1605 and reigned for less than a year.

Chapter Nine

EPIGRAPH: from *The Parting*, a poem by the minor poet M. M. Kheraskov (1733–1807).

Chapter Ten

EPIGRAPH: from Kheraskov's *Rossiada*, a very popular epic poem.

LISAVETA KHARLOVA: daughter and wife of fortress commanders in the Orenburg district, both of whom were captured by Pugachev; her father, mother and husband were executed by Pugachev. She became Pugachev's mistress and was later killed by the rebels.

Chapter Eleven

EPIGRAPH: Composed by Pushkin in imitation of Sumarokov's *Parables*.

YUZEYEVA: a village some 20 miles from Orenburg where, on 9th November, 1773, Pugachev inflicted a heavy defeat on Government forces sent to relieve Orenburg.

FREDERICK: Frederick II (the Great) of Prussia (1712–1786).

KALMUCK: Buddhist Mongol race of Central Asia who invaded Russia in the 16th and 17th centuries and settled along the lower Volga.

Chapter Thirteen

EPIGRAPH: Composed by Pushkin in imitation of Knyazhnin's comedies.

PRINCE GOLITSYN . . . : defeated Pugachev on 22nd March 1774.

CAPTURE OF KAZAN: town on the Volga river some 450 miles east of Moscow and 100 miles north of Simbirsk. The capture of the town took place on 12th July 1744.

MIKHELSON: General (1740–1807), responsible for Pugachev's final defeat near Tsaritsyn (now Volgograd, previously Stalingrad) in August 1774.

I WILL NOT DESCRIBE OUR CAMPAIGN AND THE CONCLUSION OF THE WAR: the paragraph preceding this sentence takes the place, in the originally published version of *The Captain's Daughter*, of the 'Addition to Chapter Thirteen' printed in this edition after Chapter Fourteen.

Chapter Fourteen

VOLYNSKY AND KHRUSHCHEV: A. P. Volynsky (1689–1740) and A. F. Khrushchev (1691–1740) – a minister in the government of Anna Ioannovna and his assistant – were convicted of attempting to place Elizabeth, the daughter of Peter the Great, upon the throne and were executed in June 1740.

SOFIA: posting-station and small town near Tsarskoye Selo, summer residence of the Russian Imperial family.

RUMYANTSEV: Count (1725–1795), prominent general at the time of the Empress Catherine II.

Addition to Chapter Thirteen

CHUVASH: a Mongolian tribe which settled in Russia.

VANKA: a character omitted by Pushkin in his final version of *The Captain's Daughter*.

CHEVEAUX-DE-FRISE: iron spikes embedded in timber to check cavalry charges.

ST. JOHN'S DAY: 20th July.

ASTRAKHAN: town on Caspian Sea at the head of the Volga delta.

www.vintage-classics.info